THE CRITICS RAVE ABOUT SHIRL HENKE!

"Sensational Shirl Henke is one of the top ten authors of American romance."

—*Affaire de Coeur*

"A true shining star of the genre."

—*Romantic Times*

"Shirl Henke mesmerizes readers . . . [with] powerful, sensual and memorable historical romances."

—*Romantic Times*

Shirl Henke creates "passionate love scenes, engaging characters and a well-researched, fast-paced plot."

—*Publishers Weekly* on *Bride of Fortune*

"Shirl Henke weaves a spell rich with details . . . mysterious, sensual, heart-wrenching....*Bride of Fortune* has it all!"

—*The Literary Times*

Shirl Henke is "one of the brightest stars in romance . . . . Her engaging characters and talent for storytelling will grip readers from the first page to the last."

—Katherine Sutcliffe

"*White Apache's Woman* is a fascinating book . . . an absolute must for anyone who loves American history."

—Heather Graham

PASSION OR PRETENSE?

This is *Alex,* an insistent voice hammered at her. *This is no dream,* her mind cried out as his long, powerful frame pressed her into the soft mattress. They were sealed together from head to foot. Through the sheer chemise she felt the crisp abrasion of his body hair. Though she could see nothing in the total darkness, she could feel that he was completely naked! She must stop this before it went any further. Why was he acting as if he desired her? Surely he could tell she was not one of his voluptuous and experienced Cyprians.

Her head was spinning as she writhed ineffectually beneath him, pinned helplessly to the bed. Oh, why had she drunk that accursed sherry? She tried to press her hands between them, intending to push him away, but when she touched the sinuous ripple of muscles in his chest, bunching and flexing like satin over steel, her fingers seemed to dig in rather than scratch, to cling rather than repel.

WICKED ANGEL

SHIRL HENKE

LEISURE BOOKS   NEW YORK CITY

A LEISURE BOOK®

April 2001

Published by

Dorchester Publishing Co., Inc.
276 Fifth Avenue
New York, NY 10001

ISBN 0-8439-4854-X

For Vicki DelliQuadri,
the bravest lady I know.

And in memory of
Dr. Carmine V. DelliQuadri, Jr., D.O.
A man for all seasons.

Wicked Angel

Chapter One

"The Lord God Jehovah shall summon down the wrath of heaven upon ye sons and daughters of grievous iniquity!" The resonant voice of a street preacher exhorted the great unwashed in tones crackling with fire and brimstone. Tall and thin as a stork, dressed in crow-black raiment, the cadaverous cleric waved his Bible in the air with a dramatic flourish and pointed at a pockmarked young pimp and his harlot. "Repent and be saved, for the hour of judgment is at hand!"

"Aw, bloody stubble yer cheeseparing piety!" the pimp yelled out, then took a long pull from a gin bottle. A second exceedingly disrespectful sinner lobbed a rotten egg at the preacher's face, missing his mark.

An amused young foreigner, newly debarked on the London docks, stopped to watch. He put down his portmanteau and leaned indolently against the back wall of a warehouse building to observe the show.

"Go preach to old Holy Hannah," a young prostitute yelled defiantly at the preacher.

"Ya speaks like an apothecary. Best tell yer cork-brained banbury tales to the likes of Wilberforce an' 'is saints in Parliament," a burly sailor bellowed. He pulled the elderly preacher from his makeshift pulpit by seizing hold of the frayed lapels of his jacket, then lifted him into the air like a rag doll.

A tall thin female dressed all in gray elbowed her way past the American observer and threw herself at the clergyman's attacker, pounding his mammoth shoulders with a prayer book. "Release him at once, Jem Barker! He's doing the Lord's work!"

"Now, Joss, be easy," the preacher wheezed. His attacker now turned his wrath on the female. In their struggles her thick-lensed spectacles were knocked off her nose and vanished in the melee, which now exploded like the starting gun at a free-for-all Georgia horse race. The shrill whistle of a charley sounded, but for all its piercing intensity, no one paid the slightest heed. Jem Barker grabbed the screeching female and picked her up like a sack of grain.

Angered at the sight of the big brute laying hands on a woman, even if she had instigated the attack, the American stepped past the sputtering preacher and seized the sailor's sweat-stained striped shirt. Barker dropped the flailing female and turned to face his opponent, but before he could do anything, the American's left fist connected solidly with a beefy red nose. The sailor staggered back just as the crowd surged forward, enveloping him and the preacher.

The American looked around for the woman, who also seemed to have vanished. Then he saw the fool female down on the ground, groping myopically for her spectacles. "You'll be trampled, you little idiot," he said with an oath, reaching down and grabbing her around her rail-thin waist.

As he lifted her up against his chest and began hauling her out of the melee, her hat fell off, revealing drab brown hair, center parted and pulled tightly back in an untidy clot of braids at her nape. At first he thought her the preacher's

wife, but now that he held her up close, he could see the
smooth youthfulness of her pink complexion. She was not
as old as he would first have guessed.

"You are the most vile, lecherous man since Nebuchad-
nezzar! Release me this instant, you—you heathen miscre-
ant!" Odd, she had never thought the great fat oaf of a
watchman was so solidly muscled. She let fly her left hand
with her prayer book clutched tightly in it, giving the man
a sharp clap to his left eye before he wrested the awkward
weapon from her and tossed it away.

She writhed and kicked, using her long legs and the solid
wooden heel of her sensible shoes to excellent advantage.
Whack! One heel caught her attacker squarely in the knee-
cap. At his snarled blasphemy, she took a deep breath and
twisted about to claw at his face. With another oath, he set
her firmly on her feet, just in time to save his skin, then
shoved her against the brick wall of a warehouse.

"You dare to call yourself a member of the watch, Harry
Wrexham, assaulting a lady while a man of the cloth is in
danger of his life! Why, I—"

The shrill blast of the watchman's whistle sounded again,
this time from the opposite side of the crowd. She blinked
and squinted harder at the man looming over her. She was
of an uncommon—many said downright ungainly—height,
yet he had a good six inches on her. "You . . . you aren't
Harry Wrexham the watchman, are you?" she croaked in
humiliated shock.

"Not the last I checked," he replied with a grimace. Scarlet stained her pale cheeks as she scrunched up her face,
peering at him while fumbling in the pockets of the gray
sack that passed for her dress. The situation might have
amused him—if not for the wicked throbbing in his right
knee and the fact that the scruffy little missionary lassie
had probably blacked his eye as well!

She pawed frantically through her clothes until she found
the spare pair of spectacles she always carried. Cursing the

13

fair skin and excitable nature that caused her frequent and uncontrollable blushing, she hooked the wire frames around her ears, then blinked and froze.

All the air in her lungs seemed to evaporate, leaving her unable to utter a word for what seemed an eternity. "You . . . you're an American, aren't you? The accent . . . ," she blurted out, then realized how gauche she must appear gawking at him. But she could not seem to help herself. He was not as handsome as an English dandy. No, not at all. He was the most exotic, wildly beautiful mortal she had ever seen. Dark gold hair, far longer and shaggier than was the fashion, framed a swarthy, sun-burnished countenance with deep-set, piercing, chocolate-brown eyes. His prominent, well-proportioned nose and high cheekbones gave an almost oriental cast to his face. The only thing that marred his beauty was the lump beginning to form alongside his left eye. His sculpted lips slashed into an entrancing smile.

"Yes, I'm American. Late of the sovereign state of Georgia and the Muskogee Town of Coweta. Alexander David Blackthorne, at your service."

Her mouth gaped open, revealing surprisingly white, even teeth, no doubt her best feature. Unless she kept out of further street brawls, she was unlikely to keep them much longer, he mused. Her eyes were pale but through the glare of the thick lenses of her spectacles, he could not otherwise discern the color. "Are you injured, miss?" *Better she should be asking* me *the question!*

That smile did it to her again, robbed her both of breath and presence of mind. She stammered, "I'm sorry about your eye. I . . . I'm Joss—Jocelyn Angelica Woodbridge, the Reverend Elijah Woodbridge's daughter—oh! Papa! Those vile ruffians have been threatening to stop his preaching. They may have killed him!" Here she was acting all shallow pated over some wild colonial while her beloved father lay bleeding! "I must find him. Papa!"

14

Alex caught her wrist as she spun about, ready to lunge right back into the fray. "Wait here. I'll find the preacher."

He shoved her against the wall and locked eyes with her, willing her to obey. When she nodded woodenly, he released her and turned to survey the reigning pandemonium. Amid all the ragged denizens of the nearby eastside slums, the black-clad old man would have been difficult to locate were it not for the snowy whiteness of his frayed shirtfront. A rather nasty looking fellow, wearing a red velvet jacket as gaudy as it was filthy, had hold of the skinny old man. He and his equally unsavory companion were dragging their victim into a dark alleyway between two of the warehouse buildings.

Alex maneuvered through the melee, dodging fists, cudgels and even an occasional well-tossed brick. He came upon the alley just as Red Coat raised a knife in his right hand while his cohort held the preacher by the throat. It was apparent they intended cold-blooded murder. With not an instant to spare, Alex freed the knife he kept hidden in his boot and sprinted noiselessly between the buildings. Using the heavy bone handle as a club, he rapped Red Coat on the back of his greasy skull. When his lanky frame collapsed like a house of cards, Alex reversed the knife and pointed it at the startled man still holding the struggling preacher. He was one of the pimps who had been heckling the reverend.

"I'd advise letting him go," Alex said genially to the bulldog-faced villain.

Grinning ear to ear, the pimp revealed a set of greenish rotted teeth. "Don't pay a cove ta stick 'is snout in th' trough. I just might 'ave ta cut it clean off wi' me cold iron." Shoving the coughing preacher to the ground, the man slid an evilly gleaming stiletto from his belt and advanced on Alex.

The two men circled, taking each other's measure. For such a burly fellow, the cutthroat moved with surprising agility, feinting one way, then dancing out of range of Alex's blade. They stepped over the inert body of Red Coat while the preacher stood pinned against the wall, unable to get past the deadly ballet.

The Reverend Elijah Woodbridge looked about the filthy dark alcove. Determining there would be no help save divine intervention, he fell to his knees and commenced to pray.

It was his voice that Joss heard over the ragged breathing and searing hiss of steel scraping on steel. "Papa?" She heard him yet could only see Mr. Blackthorne's back as he faced one of the street toughs who lately had made a sport of disrupting the preaching efforts of her father. Then Alex moved and she could see the gleam of steel in the gloom. They were engaged in a life-and-death struggle—with her poor papa trapped in the thick of it beside the body of another ruffian!

Without considering her actions, Joss seized a piece of broken guttering lying at the entrance to the alley and ran pell-mell to join the fight. Green Teeth saw her coming, brandishing her awkward tin club and shrieking like a berserk banshee. With the cunning born of a lifetime on the streets, he lunged, maneuvering Alex directly into the line of fire as she swung the gutter pipe in a wide arc.

Alex heard a feral screech and sensed someone racing up behind him, yet he dared not take his eyes off his foe's deadly blade. Instead, as he turned to parry an uncharacteristically clumsy thrust, he ducked low to avoid being struck from behind.

It would have worked if the second attacker had been another street tough. The instant the woman tumbled across his shoulder with her weapon clattering against the wall, Alex realized his mistake. With a fierce Muskogee oath, he grabbed a fistful of gray skirt, attempting to yank her out of harm's way while simultaneously parrying his opponent's next thrust.

Red Coat chose that moment to return to consciousness. He sat up groggily with a bleat of pain, trying to focus his eyes. Sparing him not an instant's attention, Alex hauled Joss, kicking and flailing, behind him. "Stay the hell out of the way or you'll get us all killed," he hissed as Green Teeth moved in. The gutter pipe Joss had hurled against the wall bounced off and rolled under his feet, tripping the pimp. Alex seized the opening and plunged his blade to the hilt in his foe's belly, then yanked upward. The man's eyes rolled up in his head and a shocked grimace set his jaw as he died.

"Look out!" Joss shrieked as Red Coat, who had regained his feet, aimed the pistol he had pulled from his sash. As she cried the warning she ran toward the killer, head down, butting him in the side. The shot discharged harmlessly into the air. With a curse he threw the spent weapon aside and reached for the dagger inside his coat. Alex's fist smashed into his jaw with wicked impact, sending him crashing against the wall. His head connected with a loud crunch; then he slid down the bricks, out cold.

The riot had abated now and silence reigned, broken only by the loud petitions of the Reverend Elijah Woodbridge, who had not ceased praying since he first fell to his knees when the altercation began.

"I thought I told you to stay out of the way," Alex gritted out as he helped Joss to her feet.

She rubbed her sore neck and looked up at him. "A civil thank-you for saving your life might be more appropriate, Mr. Blackthorne," she replied crossly. *Beautiful as sin and twice as arrogant*. Then realizing that he had risked his own safety twice to save her and her father, Joss sighed. "I do apologize, Mr. Blackthorne."

Feisty little thing. Well, really not so little. She was nearer his height than any other female of his acquaintance, even the tall women of his father's people. But he was a man who preferred feminine voluptuousness, not waif thin-

17

ness. Still, he could not help admiring her grit. "You have great courage for an Englishwoman."

The backhanded compliment was accompanied by another of those devastating smiles. She could not help but return it. "And you have great charm for a colonial." His laughter was a rich, deep rumble that did peculiar things to her stomach.

They stared at each other for a moment, both bemused by their unfamiliar feelings for a member of the opposite sex. Alex liked her wit as well as her spirit. This was a woman who might, unlikely as it seemed, be a friend. In a man who was used to seeing females as either revered family members or sexual dalliances, it was a remarkable new notion.

Joss, however, had never viewed the male of the species as more than an arrogant annoyance, pompous, condescending and really quite dull. The only exceptions were her beloved father and Mr. Wilberforce, M.P. Yet the longer she looked into Alex Blackthorne's deep, dark eyes, the more she drowned in them. And the more she was smitten.

The reverend chose that moment to conclude his communication with the Deity. He arose on shaky, arthritic knees. Brushing the filth of the alley from his clothes, he peered across the gloom to where his only child stood facing the big fellow who had been sent to answer his prayers.

"We owe you our lives, sir. Pray accept my sincerest thanks for your timely intervention." As Alex took his proffered hand, Joss made introductions. "So, you're a colonial, then."

"I suspect he would prefer to be called American, Papa," Joss interjected with a grin directed at Alex.

"Er, quite so, quite so. What brings you to England—besides the divine providence that led you to rescue us from harm?"

Alex shrugged. "I'm here to learn this end of my father's shipping business and to acquire a bit of polish from my

mother's family—if any will rub off, that is," he added with
a grin.

"I recollect I've heard of a mercantile firm of Blackthorne and Therlow, but who are your English family?"
Joss inquired with more than passing interest.

"The Carutherses."

"Ah, Rushcroft, yes," the reverend said. "I seem to recall
something about the baron . . ."

Remembering the stories of scandal that had rocked London back in the 1780s, Joss interjected, "That was the *late*
baron, not the *present* baron."

"Speaking of whom, we were to meet upon my debar-
kation. I should see if he's about before he sets the watch
out in search of me. I'd hate to be caught with those two
charming fellows. I might be asked some very embarrassing
questions."

"But the one is still alive—injured. Christian charity demands I minister to him," the old cleric said.

"He's only been knocked unconscious. With any luck at
all the authorities will conclude he did in his companion
and haul him off to Newgate."

"Mr. Blackthorne is quite right, Papa," Joss chimed in,
taking his arm. "We really should get out of here while it's
safe to do so."

As Alex ushered the reverend and his daughter from the
alley, he asked, "Any idea why that crew of wharf rats
stirred up a riot, then tried to murder you, Reverend Woodbridge?"

The old man nodded gravely. "I fear so."

"Papa has been preaching in support of my work."

"Your work?" One thick golden eyebrow arched.

If his eyes had not twinkled with amusement at her stiffening demeanor, Joss would have dismissed him as another
condescending, stupid male, but how could she when he
smiled that way? "My mission is among the city's poor and
oppressed. I've organized a society to rescue climbing boys

and a shelter for abused wives and reformed prostitutes."

Alex stroked his jaw, considering the dichotomy between this prim starchy crusader and the fearless hoyden who had launched herself at two dangerous underworld denizens. One moment she was witty and warm, the next leading sinners from the hell of London's slums. A most formidable female indeed!

Drat, she'd done it now. Joss could tell he was quite as put off by her work as all the other men of her acquaintance. Frantically she searched for some way to make him understand. "Life for the lower classes in a city of this size—"

"I say, lad, you are the very image of your father. I could scarce overlook such a tall blond lout, even in this press," a lazy drawling voice interjected as the trio emerged from the alley. "Or should I say, tall blond Indian, eh?" he added, eyeing the still bloody knife Alex held in his left hand.

Alex returned the regard of the whipcord lean Englishman in front of him. He was an aristocrat to his very fingertips, from his graying light brown hair cut in the Brutus mode to the sharply sculpted features and piercing pale blue eyes—eyes the exact same hue as Alex's own mother's. "Uncle Monty, I presume?" he inquired coolly.

Montgomery Caruthers's elegantly shaped mouth sketched the barest hint of a smile. "You may address me as Baron Rushcroft . . . or milord." In a manner duplicating Alex's mannerism, his uncle raised one eyebrow. "Might I inquire the reason for this barbaric display of cutlery?" he asked casually.

"Back in that alley I left one man insensate, a second one quite dead," his nephew replied with relish.

Rushcroft pursed his lips consideringly. "On Albion's soil scarce an hour and already seeking scalps. My, my, I'm certain your sire must be quite delighted with you."

"As a matter of fact, just the contrary. My backwoods escapades led my father to consign me to the bosom of the

Caruthers family . . . for civilizing," Alex replied with his own thinly veiled sarcasm.

"Then I shall have my work cut out for me, shan't I?" Rushcroft purred. "Please display what modicum of manners my sister was able to drum into you and introduce me to your companions."

"Milord," Alex said with a sardonic flash, "may I present the Reverend Elijah Woodbridge and his daughter Miss Jocelyn Woodbridge."

Joss made her curtsy as her father bowed stiffly.

"Woodbridge—you must be Suthington's brother, the nonconformist cleric," Monty replied, eyeing the reverend's tattered collar.

"I am Methodist, milord, much to my brother the earl's displeasure."

"Er, yes, regrettable, most regrettable, that," Monty replied.

Joss was uncertain whether the baron regretted the rift in the Woodbridge family or her father's conversion to Methodism. "We really must get along home, Papa," she said stiffly. "Aunt Regina will fret if she hears of this before we're safely returned." The old woman always heard the latest gossip faster than an East End cutpurse could vanish in the warrens of Whitechapel.

"This rabble-rousing hedge preacher ain't goin' nowhere," a fat, pockmarked watchman said, seizing the Reverend Woodbridge's arm with one sausage-fingered hand.

"What's the charge?" Alex inquired, blocking the charley's view of the bodies in the alley while quickly hiding his knife from sight.

"Eh, hoo er you?"

"Mr. Blackthorne, this is Harry Wrexham. I once made the grave mistake of confusing a member of the watch with a gentleman," Joss said in dulcet tones.

Ignoring her, Wrexham replied to Alex, " 'E's charged wi' startin' this 'ere riot, that's whot. Now come along, revie," he said, yanking on the cleric's arm once more.

"That's absurd! My father was set upon by Jem Barker and his pack of ruffians, who deliberately stirred up the criminal elements," Joss replied hotly. "Just ask anyone respectable who witnessed the event."

"No one respectable would be 'ere, mixin' in where they don't belong," the charley replied.

"I think I shall take umbrage at that remark on behalf of my nephew and myself," Rushcroft interjected, raising his quizzing glass to peer at the watchman haughtily.

Wrexham recognized at once that the man who now stepped forward was Quality. Bowing obsequiously, he stammered, "I'm that sorry, milord, I am. Didn't mean nothin' by it, I didn't."

"Then you would not doubt that the Reverend Woodbridge had nothing to do with inciting the riot."

"Well, Miss Woodbridge is a bit of a rabble-rouser, beggin' yer pardon, milord."

"You doubt the word of a lady?" Monty's voice changed from chilly to icy.

"Wall, no . . . but . . ."

"Certainly you do not doubt my word then, since I witnessed what the lady reported?" Monty's voice was a silky purr now.

"Blimy, no, milord! If 'is lordship vouches for th' reverend and 'is daughter, ole Wrexham, 'e ain't goin' to argue. 'Ave a fine day, yer worship, a fine day indeed," he repeated, bowing. He released his hold on the preacher and scuttled off.

Joss placed her gloved fingers to her lips to suppress a peal of mirth. Perhaps Mr. Blackthorne's arrogant uncle was not so insufferable after all. "I've never seen that fat old poltroon so intimidated. We're greatly in your debt, milord."

Odd, she was almost pretty when she smiled that way, Alex thought, viewing Joss's face in profile. And his uncle had indeed saved the day. Perhaps his banishment to England had some real possibilities after all. He waited as the social amenities of farewells were exchanged between Rushcroft and the Woodbridges, then reached out and took Joss's hand, raising it to his lips for a salute. "Until we meet again, Miss Woodbridge."

"Oh!" she gasped in dismay as she saw the sooty smear staining her white glove, acquired no doubt when she was mucking about on the ground for her lost glasses.

Alex kissed her hand politely, ignoring the gray smudge on the glove. And the even larger one across her mouth.

Chapter Two

"Why on earth anyone should pine away in despair if denied a voucher to this place utterly eludes me," Alex said sotto voce to his uncle as the two men stood near the refreshment table at Almacks.

"You, ungrateful young cur, have no idea what exaggerations and outright prevarications my wife had to invent to secure you a guest's ticket," Monty replied with a grim chuckle. "The patronesses were won over by the fact that you're part red Indian. I suspect they hope you'll stir up some excitement by scalping someone tonight."

Alex's laugh held a hint of genuine amusement. "You only told Lady Jersey of my 'savage' ancestry hoping to get yourself blackballed."

"I should be so fortunate! I fear it quite turned about on me and thus here we are." He sighed as Octavia Caruthers shot him a fulminating glance from across the room. Tiny and birdlike, with unnaturally black hair for a lady at the twilight of her forties, the baroness's apparent fragility was belied by her fierce dark eyes and a mouth pursed so tightly it looked incapable of permitting speech, far less a smile.

"She's bringing Lady Harrington with her. Lud, I bloody hate this."

Having been ensconced at the Caruthers's city house for a scant two days, during which he had scarcely seen either his uncle or aunt, Alex was still uncertain about the peculiar chill in their marriage. His parents, indeed his whole family in America, seemed quite happy with their spouses. He felt not the slightest inclination to give up his freedom for wedded bliss in the foreseeable future, still less could he fathom why a man would become leg-shackled to a woman he detested. "Why did you agree to come here tonight? I assure you, I'd happily forgo stale cakes and buttered bread with warm lemonade," he said with a grimace, looking at the food table.

"I am in attendance here so that your beloved aunt will give me peace, you young lout." At Alex's look of frank disbelief he muttered an addendum. "And so that she will pay my gaming debts and the tailor's bill. Don't look so bloody shocked. Surely you didn't think I married that frigid little bitch for true love."

Masking his colonially gauche shock, Alex asked, "Once she married you, didn't you receive control of her fortune?"

"Would that I had. But her father, damned hag-ridden bastard, saw to it that the bulk of her estate has been tied up in trust. Of course I ran through her marriage portion within the first decade of our connubial bliss. Ever since then I've been begging at her door. He must die, and my darling Octavia as well, if I'm ever to have a sou to call my own. I have resolved to outlive them both, even if it kills me," he drawled through gritted teeth as his wife approached them and made introductions.

Lady Harrington was a blowzy blonde whose voluptuous charms were far enough faded to look downright shopworn under bright light. She deftly trapped Alex into partnering her through an English country dance. As they returned from the floor, she tapped him lightly with her fan, eyes glowing avidly. "La, sir, do any of our young ladies take your fancy? I could arrange an introduction."

"You are most kind, but I don't believe I'm at all a suitable prospect," he said, deciding to see if he could titillate her with his Muskogee blood as his uncle had Lady Jersey.

"You mean because you're American?"

"No, milady. Because I'm Indian."

She blinked and looked at him as if he'd materialized that instant out of a puff of smoke. "Indian," she said consideringly, noting his swarthy skin and deep brown eyes. "The sun often darkens colonials. I would never have guessed but for that exotic slant of cheekbone. My, how positively delicious."

"Lady Jersey thought so. That's why she allowed me admittance," he replied dryly, noting how Lady Harrington quickly deflated when the prospect of spreading such juicy gossip was snatched from her.

"Pray, tell me about life among the savages."

Suddenly the avid gleam in her eyes, the shocked titillation in her voice, was no longer the divertissement he'd hoped it would be. "My father's people are rather tame. They scarcely ever practice human sacrifice anymore. Not like the good old days, I fear. You'd find them quite tedious, milady," he said as he steered her toward his aunt and Lady Jersey.

Sputtering, half in affront, half in excitement, she would have made further remonstrance to draw him out, but Lady Sarah Jersey caught his eye and made her way to them with Octavia following reluctantly. The patroness of Almacks was a young woman in her prime, trim but sturdily built with a plain face guileless of paints or powders. Her heavy dark hair was as simply styled as the green muslin gown she wore.

She inspected him with sharp hazel eyes and said, "So

you're Rushcroft's nephew, the wild Indian. You don't look dangerous."

"Since my father's ship docked two days ago, I have yet to take a scalp," he said as he saluted the white-gloved hand she presented him.

A low chuckle rippled from deep in her throat. "Pray keep it that way, or at least restrict yourself to taking powdered wigs. They come off more easily. Besides, they are so hideously out of fashion." Turning to Lady Harrington, she tilted her head in a regal greeting. "How is Suthington, my dear? He hasn't visited us this season."

"My father sends his regards, Lady Sarah. He shall be in London within the week."

"Your father is the Earl of Suthington?" Alex asked. "I made the acquaintance of your cousin, Miss Jocelyn Woodbridge, when I debarked."

Lady Harrington stiffened, lifting her overlong nose as if scenting something noisome. "I might expect Jocelyn to be walking about the docks," she sniffed.

"She was quite properly chaperoned by your uncle, the Reverend Woodbridge." Alex felt it prudent not to mention the riot or Jocelyn's active participation in it.

"That street preacher. I'm afraid when he deserted the Church of England to join a sect and preach from box tops, the earl quite disowned him," Lady Harrington replied.

"What of his daughter? Surely a child cannot be held accountable for her father's eccentricities," Alex replied.

"The girl's mother was a governess," Octavia interjected scathingly. "She passed on when Jocelyn was quite young. The girl's been allowed, even encouraged to pursue a highly unsuitable education, reading histories and philosophies, espousing social reforms among the lower classes." Octavia shuddered.

"Fancy that," Alex replied solemnly.

"I, for one, regret the gel did not receive a come out," Lady Jersey said, perhaps feeling a glimmer of kinship for another plain young woman lacking her own fortunate social connections. "However is a lady to make a suitable marriage if she does not have a season?"

The question was rhetorical. Everyone among the Quality understood the rules of the ton. Alex was beginning to have a pretty fair idea about them himself. And he did not like them. *No wonder Mother chose not to return to this life.* "I suspect Miss Woodbridge has other matters weighing more heavily on her mind than catching a husband," Alex replied ironically.

"La, sir, whatever is more important to us poor weaker vessels than a proper marriage?" Lady Jersey said, keenly gauging his reaction.

"Miss Woodbridge and the reverend are determined to end the exploitation of climbing boys . . . and prostitutes."

"Prostitutes?" Lady Harrington echoed in a shocked whisper.

Octavia's dark eyes narrowed furiously on her husband, silently accusing him for bringing this graceless colonial clod into their home and social circle.

Lady Jersey smiled thinly but said nothing.

Throughout the exchange, Monty stood back observing with detached amusement. The boy had a deal to learn, but he was young. Lud, had he himself ever been that young? Probably not. Reaching over, he clapped his nephew on the back, saying, "The way you rush to defend Miss Woodbridge, I cannot help but wonder if you'd consider offering for the poor ape-leading bluestocking." The expression of appalled surprise on Alex's face delighted the baron almost as much as the lad's swift recovery.

"I have no plans to wed while I'm in England, neither Miss Woodbridge nor any of the fine young ladies of the ton." Turning from his uncle to Lady Jersey, he added with a devastatingly rakish grin, "Give their mamas my assurance that their progeny are safe from the depredations of this red Indian."

"Come, Mr. Blackthorne. You must tell me about growing up among your father's people," Lady Jersey said, determined to redeem the conversation from its distressingly gauche turn. She took Alex's arm and steered him toward the refreshment table.

"Joss, you've not been attending me. I was saying how my dyspepsia has grown ever so much worse since our last cook ran off with that wretched froggie," Aunt Regina remonstrated. "I think to double my dose of calomel pills for relief."

Lost in reverie, Joss looked up at the old woman. "What? Oh, your dyspepsia, yes," Joss replied vaguely.

"As much of a noddy as you've been the past few days, Jocelyn, I wonder if you received a cosh on the head t'other day at the docks. Or perhaps you've taken to some gentleman," she added, chuckling at the unlikelihood of that.

Joss could feel the heat stealing into her face and fought to control it. "On the shelf as I am, I'd be quite the lackwit to moon over any gentleman," she replied crossly.

"Ha! Why's yer face red as a carbuncle then?" the crusty old woman responded, squinting nearsightedly to assess Joss.

Regina Gower's fleshy nostrils quivered when she was on the scent of fresh gossip. She was not really any kin to Joss, but everyone who lodged at the Fin and Feather called her Aunt Regina. Her slightly askew wig and the tight laces enclosing her thick midsection proclaimed her staunch opposition to the shockingly libertine fashions and mores of the new century.

Joss longed to confide the dreams that had been haunting her to someone, yet could not bring herself to discuss Alex Blackthorne with Aunt Regina, who for all her well-meaning kindness was as incapable of keeping a confidence as a sieve of holding water. No, Alex would remain a cherished secret, deep in her heart. "If you must know, I'm concerned about Papa's insistence on attending that dog-fighting contest tonight," she replied, firmly changing the subject.

"Demned dangerous. That man takes the most sap-skulled notions! Them nobs will be fierce displeased if the reverend stops the show—the owners and their underworld cronies even more. I've heard bets on dogs are devilish high," the old woman said worriedly. "Lord Darter was said to have won ten thousand pounds there last week."

"That's what I'm afraid of. Papa's already made some powerful enemies." She shuddered, recalling the dead fellow lying in the alley, the sour stench of his clothes, his grimy hands seizing her. *So unlike when Alex held me.* Joss mentally shook herself. She was acting like an utter cake over Mr. Blackthorne. *Stop it!*

"Good evening, Joss, Aunt Regina. I've selected the text and prepared my sermon for tonight," Elijah Woodbridge said as he walked into the crowded hearth room of the inn.

Joss arose and walked over to him, taking the papers from his hand and glancing down at his spidery scrawl, which filled them front and back. "Papa, I don't think this is well advised. Aunt Regina said the Quality wager quite heavily at these events. If you deprive the dog owners and their backers of their ill-gotten gains—"

"Tut, m'dear. That is precisely the point. Ill-gotten gains lead men to perdition. It is my Christian duty to stand against gambling and all its attendant ills—drunkenness, oath taking, even fornication."

Joss sighed as the old man's voice began to rise. He was off, primed for tonight. There would be no stopping him. "I expect you are right. Such cesspools of sin must be closed down. Even if the people are beyond redemption, the poor animals they abuse are not."

"My child!" Elijah remonstrated, "you know no man is ever beyond redemption. It only wants that you and I do our best to show them the error of their ways."

"As you wish, Father," she replied with a grin. "I shall accompany you tonight on your mission."

His legs were wobbly and his jaws slack, but the roar of the crowd spurred on his blood lust in spite of his exhaustion. After all, he'd been bred for this. The dirt floor of the rectangular enclosure was slick with blood. Rat carcasses lay scattered around, their necks broken. He had killed a hundred in the past hour. A record in Phineas Goodysale's sporting ring.

"Now the action will really start popping," Lord Haversham said, leaning past Monty to squint at Alex through the stale smoky air. "They'll bring out a badger next. That should put the little rat killer in the suds. A real fight to the death."

"A badger, really? That is a bit overdone, Haversham," Monty replied with a grimace of distaste. "Truth to tell, I've already found the rat fight tiresome in the extreme."

"Getting squeamish, old fellow? Sure your wild colonial Indian here is a true cock of the game. You like your sport good and bloody, don't you, chum? I'd wager you've seen contests to put this one in the shade back among the savages."

"As a matter of fact, I have—but the Muskogee don't abuse animals for their amusement. They break each other's bones quite merrily in chunky matches," Alex replied. He was heartily sickened by the spectacle and wanted nothing but to escape the fetid stench of peat smoke and unwashed bodies.

"Really?" Haversham replied, his bloodshot eyes gleaming avidly. "What sort of contest is this chunky game?"

Before Alex could reply, the master of ceremonies appeared. The dog, a brindle terrier with the most ferocious teeth Alex had seen this side of the Atlantic, stood panting in one corner. Yet it made no move to attack the man when he climbed down into the pit.

31

The crowd comprised all levels and classes of society, mostly male with a smattering of the fairer sex gaudily decked out to display their wares. Silver pocket flasks were upended with regularity as were wine and port bottles. Alex enjoyed a good debauch as much as the next fellow, but the mood of this crowd was ugly. The nature of the gory spectacle they so obviously relished was even uglier. "That dog is too tired to fight anymore. He's earned a good meal and a night's rest," Alex said over the announcer's loud voice.

He stood up, intending to bid his uncle good night, when a loud commotion broke out at the back entrance to the low-ceilinged shanty. "Let me pass, sirrah! For shame on such drunken debauchery! We come on the Lord's work! Gambling is sin and the wages of sin is death!" There was no mistaking the stentorian tones of the Reverend Elijah Woodbridge.

"You mutton-headed marplot, who asked you to put in yer oar?" one of the sporting afficionados yelled belligerently.

The babble of angry voices rose sharply, diverting attention from the pit. In an attempt to remedy the matter, Phineas Goodysale opened the cage containing the badger. Starved and terrified, the creature erupted into the ring when the gate to his cage was raised. With a snarled hiss the forty-pound badger shook his thick shiny coat and waddled straight for his quarry.

The dog stood motionless for a second, sniffing the newcomer uncertainly. City bred, he had never scented such a creature before. When the badger's razor-sharp claws raked across his snout, drawing blood, he jumped back with a loud yip, then circled swiftly, attempting to sink his teeth into his foe's neck. The badger was not only many times larger than a rat, but its skin was draped so loosely on its body that the dog could get no purchase in it with which to snap the neck as he had with the rats. Each time he seized

the badger, it twisted around and raked him wickedly with
its razor-sharp claws.

Joss followed the other members of the Moral Rectitude
Society as they pushed and shoved their way into the
smoky room. What an utterly unsavory crowd! She doubted
there was a redeemable soul in the lot, but she had come
in part out of concern for her father and also to see if the
ghastly reports about cruelty to animals were true.

When she heard the shrill cry of a dog in mortal agony,
the hairs on the back of her neck stood out. What were they
doing to the poor creature? The crowd's attention was di-
vided between the contest in the pit and the arguments
spreading around the perimeter of the room, a few of which
were approaching fisticuffs. Many of the onlookers laughed
and scoffed at the "holy Harrys," comparing the hatchet-
faced Widow Meechen to the badger.

Joss fought her way through the drunken crowd toward
the unearthly sounds emanating from the pit. Then she saw
it. Dear God, the dog, a small, compactly built terrier of
some sort, was pitted against a snarling badger half again
his weight. They rolled across the dirt floor, the dog trying
to escape the death grip his feral foe had on him.

"For the love of God, someone put a stop to this barbaric
cruelty! Save that poor dog!" she cried, searching for something to wield as a club against the badger.

"Gor, Holy Hannah, go back ta yer Bible schools 'n
leave us heathens ta 'ave our fun!" a nasty looking fellow
wearing an eye patch said as his one good eye roamed
insultingly over her body.

Joss ignored him. Seizing a loose board from the top of
the wooden railing of the pit, she pried it free, then started
to climb down. A large hand clamped firmly around her
arms, lifting her away. "Get back, you little fool, or you'll
be torn to bits," Alex said.

Joss looked up at him incredulously, irrationally disap-
pointed to find he was like the rest of the debauched rich

33

and depraved poor. "That dog will be torn to bits if some-one doesn't stop this obscenity!"

With a snarled oath, he shoved her behind him and swung one leg over the fence. "I'll handle it. Just stay the hell out of the pit."

With her heart in her throat, Joss stood transfixed as he jumped to the bloody dirt floor and strode over to where the badger now had the dog backed against the wall, ready to finish it off. In a move so swift she could not follow it, Alex slid that long wicked blade from his boot and threw it squarely into the badger's back. It sank in to the hilt between the animal's shoulder blades.

An outcry of protest had gone up around the pit when his intentions became clear. Now as he reached down to extract his blade from the dead badger and toss the animal onto the pile of rats, the mood of surly drunkenness turned ugly and violent. Epithets were hurled and fists raised, aris-tocratic and criminal elements joining in against the marplot who had ruined their "sport."

Calmly Alex held up the bloody knife in his right hand while sliding a stubby-barreled screw pistol from his waist-coat with his left. The gun was quite accurate and deadly in such close quarters. "*I* kill rats, too," he said, his steely dark gaze raking the assembly.

Somehow the low yet lethal tone of his voice carried over the din. The gamblers and their doxies crowding the ring grew eerily silent. Even the strident arguments between the Moral Rectitude Society members and the patrons of Goodysale's ebbed into confused murmurs, then ceased all together.

Alex motioned to Joss, who clamored over the wall into the ring while he shrugged out of his jacket, juggling gun and knife expertly. "Wrap the dog in this." The girl quickly did as she was bid.

Then Alex walked to the side of the pit with Joss and her burden. He nodded to a short, thin dandy. "Hold the dog while she climbs out." It was an order, not a request. The man hesitated and Blackthorne cocked the hammer of his pistol. The sound was almost deafening in the unnatural silence. The fellow quickly took the dog from Joss and she struggled over the barrier to retrieve her prize.

The dog's blood soaked through the jacket and stained her arms, dripping in crimson spatters across the front of her drab skirts as she walked toward the door. The crowd parted as if Moses' rod had struck it. Several disgruntled sportsmen stepped forward to block her path but one look into Alex's deadly eyes quelled them. They melted back into the press.

"Just a bloody minute 'ere. Ya can't go waltzing off with me best 'ound, not without so much as a by yer leave," Phineas Goodysale cried, puffing as his short fat legs churned to catch up to them.

"This animal's fighting days are over," Alex replied tightly, wanting to get Joss out of the place before one of the idiot do-gooders began another riot. "What's he worth to you?" he asked levelly.

The American's cold expression quelled Phineas's greed. "Er, five shillings would do it, gov," he said hopefully.

Alex tossed the coins to him with a scornful glance, then ushered Joss out the door.

"Thank you," she murmured. She did not break stride until she was well away from the fetid stench of the slaughterhouse. Joss knew her father was following Alex, but when she turned, she was startled to see the baron with them.

"Dem it, lad, you've put me in dun territory now. Deuced if I'd have wagered one hundred pounds on the badger if I'd known you had such an aversion to the beasts," Monty said with amusement as Alex replaced his weapons on his person.

"How can you speak of money when this poor animal is bleeding to death?" Joss cried passionately, not caring that

35

he was Baron Rushcroft and she a street preacher's daughter.

"You'd best have a care, m'dear. That *poor animal* is a killer, born and bred to it. He'd as like take out your throat as a rat's if he were able," Monty cautioned.

"Well, he is not able," she snapped, turning to Alex. "Can't we do something to save him?"

"Perhaps the baron's warning is not amiss, Joss," Elijah said gently. "These unfortunate creatures are taught to kill from birth."

"I can't just let him die, Papa."

"My people know some remedies. I brought my grandmother's medicine bag with me from America." Alex turned to his uncle. "If you'll be so kind as to allow me to bring the dog into the kitchen, I'll treat it."

Monty shrugged and nodded, as he signaled for their coachman to bring round the carriage. "Oh, I wouldn't for the world miss the expression on my dear Octavia's face when you enter her house with this procession in your wake." With a mocking wink he made a leg for Joss as the coachman opened the carriage door for them.

Joss knelt beside Alex as he refolded the intricately beaded buckskin pouch after placing the powders and ointments inside it. The dog lay on the hearth, breathing shallowly. At least he was alive. Alex had succeeded in stopping the bleeding with a yellowish powder; then she'd stitched up some of the deepest gashes. Finally he'd anointed all the dog's wounds with a white salve. The patient had lain very still, watching with liquid brown eyes as the man finished working over him, almost as if he sensed Alex's healing touch.

"You have a remarkable way with animals. Is it . . . ?"

He looked up and met her eyes. "My Indian blood?" He chuckled at her flustered reaction. "I suppose it might be, but my Uncle Quint and his sons have the same gift and not a drop of Muskogee blood in their veins."

Embarrassed at the way he studied her face, trying to read her eyes behind the thick lenses of her glasses, Joss looked down at the medicine pouch. She reached out her fingers and touched the beadwork. "It is ever so lovely. Your grandmother's, you said?"

"Grandma Charity, my father's mother. The whole family calls her that to distinguish her from my elder sister Charity, her namesake. Grandma is half Muskogee. She was educated in mission schools run by the Methodists, so I suppose the Blackthorne clan owes your faith a debt of gratitude, even if we are all Church of England."

"You have a large family?" Joss asked with a wistful smile.

"Too many to count on the American side of the Atlantic. I've yet to meet many of the Carutherses," he added darkly, not at all certain if he cared to do so. Changing the subject, he asked, "And what of you, Miss Woodbridge? Have you siblings, at least cousins by the dozens?"

"Alas, no, although I always longed for a big family. I am my father's only child, you see. My mother died when I was quite small. I remember very little of her. Papa still grieves her loss, I think."

"He's fortunate to have you."

"You're most kind," she replied, feeling suddenly awkward under his scrutiny.

She started to rise but he placed a restraining hand on her arm, gently settling her back to the floor. "You're a very unusual woman, Miss Woodbridge. I've never met your like."

"I'm scarcely what the ton calls a nonpareil," she replied ruefully.

"I'm finding I have little interest in the ton. Almacks was quite frankly a crashing bore."

"Excellent." Joss clapped her hands together. "Then I have missed nothing at all, never receiving a voucher."

"Flat punch and stale buttered bread," he replied gravely. They both laughed at the same time.

"You have a keen sense of humor. Something I always heard was lacking in Americans."

"Many of us can take a jest—or play one. I always prefer to enjoy the lighter side of life. Don't mention it to my Aunt Octavia, but I believe there is much to savor outside the constraints of the drawing room."

"Is that why you visited such a disreputable place as Goodysale's?" In spite of the awfulness of the place, she could not resist the hint of a smile spreading her lips.

"Back in Georgia I always preferred to run wild with my Muskogee cousins—when I could be pried away from the Savannah alehouses. That's why my parents packed me off to London—to transform or reform me into a gentleman. You see before you, I fear, a singularly impenitent sinner, Miss Woodbridge."

The smile of a fallen angel beguiled her. "Not too pernicious a sinner to have risked life and limb for a poor helpless animal." *And for me.* "I really must insist you allow me to repay you for purchasing him from that odious little man."

"Please. Consider him my gift to you. You are the one who operates a charity hospital and shelter for the homeless, are you not? This poor fellow certainly qualifies for some Christian charity and a home after what he's been through."

"Put that way, how can I refuse?"

"Good. Then it's settled."

"Do you so often get your way, Mr. Blackthorne?"

He shrugged. "Mostly . . . at least with the fairer sex." *Wrong thing to say to a religious lady,* Alex chided himself as Jocelyn's expression clouded.

"I may be female, Mr. Blackthorne, but I know I am not fair," she replied, looking him straight in the eye. *A woman would do anything for him. Positively anything.*

"Ah, but—"

"No, do not try to sugar it. I am not fishing for compliments. I never learned to play those games young ladies play," she replied gently.

"A pity. With your wit you would excel at them. I really did mean it when I said I'd never met your like—and I grew up in a household filled with females—a mother, grandmother and four sisters. I honestly believe we could become friends, Miss Woodbridge. That is, if a missionary lady such as you would consider befriending a recalcitrant rogue such as I."

"How could I refuse such an intriguing offer, especially after you've given me the gift of this poor creature's life?" Joss said with a smile as she touched the dog carefully with her fingertips. "So little of his body is uninjured. Do you think he will live?"

"Once as a boy I had a dog that was torn up by a panther. Almost as bad as this. He pulled through. But my uncle's caveat isn't groundless, you know. This dog was raised to kill in the pit. He might not make a pet."

"He made no effort to bite us as we treated him. I think he hates rats, not people."

"Sometimes there's not much difference," Alex replied dryly. "I wish I could see the good in God's creation half so optimistically as you."

"If we are to be friends, Mr. Blackthorne, I shall endeavor to teach you the good," she replied. *And pray God I do not lose my heart in the bargain.*

Chapter Three

London was not such a dreary place after all, Alex decided. He spent a bare minimum of time with Bertie Therlow and his infernal accounts, allowing himself to pursue far more interesting activities under the tutelage of his uncle, a man who had elevated hedonism to an art form, and a man of whom Alex was growing increasingly fond.

In the Georgia backcountry, Alex and his cousin Robert had pursued tavern wenches, consumed prodigious quantities of ale and emerged victorious in some legendary brawls. Such youthful exuberance, indeed, had been the chief reason the family decided to separate him and Rob. Quintin and Madelyne packed their son off to his father's alma mater in Philadelphia while Devon and Barbara decided it best if Alex learn the family business from Thurlow and perhaps acquire a bit of gentlemanly polish from polite society.

But Alex had no more use for polite society than he did for account ledgers. Almacks was run by a rigid set of harridans intent on arbitrating the London marriage mart, a thought to make him shudder in his newly acquired Hessian boots. Even the more exclusive men's clubs to which his uncle introduced him seemed stifling. Brummel and Alvanley were amusing enough—in small doses. But he chafed under the rigid protocols for everything from tying a cravat to inhaling snuff.

Not that he disapproved of the Beau's taste in clothing. The simplicity and elegance of black superfine and snug doeskin breeches was not lost on a tall, slim young man who knew he had the perfect body to display for the fairer sex. Alex spent lavishly at the tailors on Bond Street.

However, after living a life of action in the backcountry, he found the seemingly endless rounds of balls, routs and banquets tame fare indeed. Not so gaming hells, horse races, boxing matches and hunting parties. Of course to gain ingress to such activities, he had to cultivate acquaintances with the young sporting bloods about the ton.

After the incident at Goodysale's, gossip about Caruthers's wild Indian nephew from the colonies spread rapidly. He became an overnight sensation with the more avantgarde members of society. Lady Holland, a divorcée only tolerated on the fringes of the ton, was titillated enough to invite him to her famous salons, where he mingled with painters, actors and writers, many of whom he found genuinely interesting. He created a stir at Tattersalls after bidding fifteen hundred guineas for an Arabian mare to breed with the big stallion he had brought with him from America. When he won twenty thousand pounds in a marathon whist game at Whites, his reputation was made. Every rakish buck in London wanted to be seen with Alex Blackthorne.

His fascination for the women of the Great Wen became equally the rage. Although marriage-minded mamas kept their virginal misses well out of his reach, the more libertine females of the Quality succumbed readily to his dazzling golden looks and the aura of sexual danger that radiated from him. Ladies of the Cyprian class were even more accommodating, going to prodigious lengths to attract his attention.

One performed a perfectly timed swoon and literally tumbled beneath the feet of his horse while he was riding in Hyde Park; another slid down a silken drapery cord at Covent Garden to reach his private box. One Sunday while he was strolling with his current amour in Vauxhall a slighted female admirer accosted them, which resulted in a clawing, shrieking catfight, attracting all sorts of amused and aghast attention until Alex was able to separate the combatants.

Within a few months he settled into a routine of sorts, rising at noon, taking a brisk ride through Hyde Park, then either visiting Gentleman Jackson's to spar with the boxers or perhaps taking a trip to one of the excellent race courses on the outskirts of the city to watch the horses run. The past two weeks he had begun going to Angelo's Haymarket Room, where the master Domenico was teaching him the gentlemanly art of fencing. But his weapon of choice remained the knife he carried in his boot. His evenings were spent dining with friends at various clubs, attending the theater, then on to the gaming hells, where he played faro and whist until the wee hours of the morning.

The only breaks in his sybaritic existence were his occasional visits with Miss Jocelyn Woodbridge, much to the amusement of his uncle, who tweaked him acidly for visiting such a bluestocking. His first visit to Joss's residence had been as much an adventure as their other two encounters. The clean but shabby public rooms of the inn were in stark contrast to the opulence of his uncle's house. The starched respectability of the establishment also contrasted with the seamy underworld of gaming hells and prizefights that he lived in after hours.

A heavyset old woman with sharp gray eyes, wearing a hideously old-fashioned wig, had advanced on him as soon as he had stepped inside the door. "I'm Mrs. Gower, the proprietress. What do ye want?" she asked by way of greeting, quickly judging by the cut of his clothes that he had too much of the ready to desire lodgings. In her experience, rich young dandies were usually bent on mischief.

"Alexander Blackthorne, madam." He sketched a bow with a smile dazzling enough to soften a brass doorknob. "I'm here to call upon Miss Woodbridge and the reverend."

"Cor, are ye now," Aunt Regina said as his charm worked its usual magic. Patting her wig, she graced him with an exceedingly uncharacteristic simper. "Ye'd be the gentl'man Joss first met at the docks. She told me all about ye, she did. Come in my best private dining room and I'll fetch some refreshment. Would ye care for—"

Her effusive hospitality was interrupted by a loud screech and a series of low raspy barks. Then a blur of yellow fur streaked past her feet with a brindle dog in swift pursuit. Feline and canine circled the public room twice. The cat overturned a teapot when it leaped across a table. Barreling after it, the dog knocked aside several chairs in his path, then toppled a small table sending dishes, cups and flatware clattering to the floor.

"Out, out, ye hound of the Apocalypse! Look at the fine mess!" the old woman shrieked, seizing a broom from the corner.

"Oh, no, Poc. Not again! Please don't hurt him, Aunt Regina. Poc, come here, you naughty boy, come," Joss commanded firmly. Abruptly abandoning his chase of the stray cat, Poc obediently trotted up to her and sat while Aunt Regina used the broom to chase his prey out the front door.

"Are you always in the thick of battle, Miss Woodbridge, or does it occur only when I happen in the vicinity?" Alex queried from the sidelines, where he had watched the spectacle.

Joss turned with a startled gasp. "Alex! I mean, Mr.

Blackthorne—I didn't see you—what are you doing here?" *I'm babbling like a schoolroom miss.*

"I came to pay a social call on a friend and to see how her patient is faring," he replied, looking down at the dog. "I see he's mended rather well."

"Thanks to you, Mr. Blackthorne. Your grandmother's herbal remedies are quite remarkable. Poc was up and about in a matter of days."

"Poc?" he asked. The terrier's tail began to thump against the rug excitedly.

"A shortened version of Apocalypse, a name I fear he's earned every day since coming to live with us." Joss cast a placating smile in Aunt Regina's direction. The old woman muttered to herself as she swept up broken crockery. "I must help clean up this mess. Please do have a seat in the back and I shall join you shortly," she said, gesturing to the open door into a private dining area.

Alex shook his head. "Since I am in some measure responsible for unleashing the Apocalypse on this household, please allow me to help you," he replied, walking over to where Mrs. Gower was plying her broom.

With a few economical movements he returned the table and chairs to their proper positions while Joss and Aunt Regina disposed of the broken dishes. If Poc was in any way abashed by his earlier destructive behavior, he did not show it as he followed them into the back room.

"I'll fetch some tea and the plum cake cook baked this morning," the old woman said as she scurried out after providing herself an excuse to return and eavesdrop.

"I assume by the way he obeys you that you've had no trouble with this fellow," Alex said, kneeling down and patting his knee for the dog to approach.

"Not at all. It's just as I said. He loves people and he's the finest ratter Aunt Regina's ever had at the inn. That's why she puts up with his . . . er, playfulness."

Poc trotted up to Alex, his tail wagging with delight.

"You are a fine fellow, aren't you? Do you remember me, eh?"

As Alex made friends with Poc, Joss observed his natural way with animals. She was certain it extended as well to virtually all the humans he met. The crusty old landlady had certainly been won over. While he was occupied with the dog, Joss allowed her eyes to feast on him for a moment, noting his elegant cutaway jacket and faultlessly tied cravat.

He looked a perfect macaroni. She had heard snippets of gossip in the dining room about the scandalous young American who had taken London's elite and the demi-monde by storm. She had hoped he would call, yet feared it, too. Falling under the spell of a man like Alex Blackthorne was sheer folly for a nonpareil, worse for the likes of a tabby such as she.

Laughing, Alex thumped the terrier several times, then stood up as Joss said, "My father is out. He'll be sorry to have missed your visit, Mr. Blackthorne."

"After all the mayhem we've survived together, Miss Woodbridge, don't you think it fitting we dispense with surnames? After all, we did agree to be friends, did we not? Please, call me Alex."

She returned his smile self-consciously. "Then I am Jocelyn—Joss is what Papa and most everyone calls me. That is, those who don't call me bird-witted, bluestocking, long Meg or cow-handed holy Hannah."

He whooped with laughter. "Believe me, I've been called worse names on this side of the Atlantic and the other as well."

"Well, to me you've been a guardian angel."

He continued chuckling and said wryly, "A pretty wicked angel, I fear, Joss."

"I've heard rumors to that effect, sirrah," she replied merrily. "Perhaps it's as well Papa isn't here, else he'd have us all three on our knees in prayer for your immortal soul."

45

"We'd have sore knees in vain, I fear. It's too beautiful a day to waste indoors petitioning the Almighty for a lost cause. Come take a ride in my new chaise instead."

"You tempt me, Alex, but I'm already late for a meeting and then I'm expected at hospital."

"Ye should go, gel. Do ye a world of good to get out. Of course, ye'd need a chaperone . . . ," Aunt Regina added coyly as she waddled into the room, carrying a tray with the plum cake, a pot of tea and three cups.

"Stuff. I'm scarcely a belle on the marriage mart," Joss said to the old woman, all the while stifling a laugh at the look of horror that had flashed across Alex's face when Aunt Regina made her suggestion. "I go unchaperoned to schools and hospitals, the homes of the poor. Why, last week I even entered a flash house by myself."

"A flash house?" Alex's face darkened. "You could've been killed."

"There was not a boy in the awful place above the age of twelve," she retorted.

"That's more than old enough to do you grave injury. What on earth were you doing in such a place?"

"Searching for a five-year-old boy named Billy Jenkins. He'd run away from a brutal monster of a sweepmaster to whom he'd been sold by his mother for a bottle of gin."

"Old Madam Geneva's been the curse of poor folk," Aunt Regina interjected piously.

Alex shook his head in resignation. "I can see there is no hope of stopping your attempts to save the world. Your guardian angel must be run ragged."

"As must yours, for different reasons, I warrant," Joss replied dryly.

"If I cannot induce you to take a pleasure ride, then at least allow me to drive you to your meeting, wherever it may be."

"At the Widow Alsworth's home. The Bible society

meets there every Tuesday at one o'clock. Would you like to join us?" some imp prompted her to ask.

Alex laughed. "I'd as soon spend a week in the stocks, thank you all the same." Turning to Aunt Regina, he smiled and said, "Although I do thank you for your gracious hospitality, dear lady, I must decline the tea and cake. After all, we wouldn't want to have Miss Woodbridge late for her meeting, now, would we?"

"My cook's always got a pot of tea brewing and summat in the oven. Ye just come call another time, Mr. Blackthorne," the old woman replied as Alex took Joss's arm to escort her out. When Poc raised his muzzle to sniff the warm plum cake, Regina snatched it away. "Just try it, ye moldering rat catcher, and I'll have cook spit ye over the hearth for tonight's dinner!"

The room was packed with people, most either hunched over gaming tables or standing behind the players, avidly watching the contests. Hazard, Macao, whist, faro. Whatever manner the patrons chose to be parted from their blunt, they found it in gaming hells such as Wheatie's. The stakes were high, but life was quite cheap in this neighborhood.

Situated in a lower class area noted for prostitution, high crime rates and low numbers of watchmen on duty, Wheatie's drew cold-eyed professional gamblers from all sorts of unsavory backgrounds to rub elbows quite literally with the more reckless and adventurous young bucks of the ton. Alex found the aura of greed and danger stimulating. There were no social niceties to be observed at Wheatie's, but there was sufficient of the ready to be won—if a player was skilled or lucky.

He was both—at least as long as he remained sober, which he usually managed to do. Tonight, however, was an exception. He had imbibed enough champagne at a dinner party to gain a head start on euphoria before setting out with his friend Puck Forrester and cousin, the young Viscount Chitchester.

Sobriety had deserted him, but not luck. Were he in full possession of his faculties, Alex would never have chosen hazard, a game involving little skill. Nor would he have wagered so heavily.

A pert little doxy whose scarlet hair bore no resemblance to any color on nature's palette offered to blow on the dice for him. How could a gentleman refuse, even if she did work for the house? Alex nodded to the croupier seated opposite him across the large green baize expanse of the oval table. The burly man's nose was bent to the left, doubtless a mark of his previous profession—prizefighter. Many of the rougher gambling hells in the district were staffed by such bully boys. Bent Nose grinned, displaying what few yellowed teeth former opponents had left him.

"Well, now, gents, our young American cock o' th' game 'ere would like to try 'is 'and. 'Ere you be, gov. You're the caster."

Alex tossed a twenty-pound note into the betting circle. He knew it was not uncommon for a man to wager his coat, boots, even his breeches in shady places such as this. The redhead blew a kiss in the direction of the dice box for luck before he rolled the dice out onto the green felt.

Wagers on the game escalated all around him as he began a steady winning streak. Among the crowd was a small, dapper-looking young man faultlessly turned out comme Beau. Languidly he extracted a twenty-pound note and bet on Alex. Then he carefully removed an exquisite ivory inlaid snuff box from his jacket and took a precise pinch, placing it upon the back of a snowy white lace-cuffed wrist. As he waited for Alex to roll, he inhaled delicately.

Alex could hear the muttering from the shadows as side bets were placed. This was becoming very interesting. He could feel the dandy's cool green eyes on him, filled with lazy amusement while the doxy once more did her "kiss."

He shook the box and rolled, winning again.

The bent-nosed croupier's expression darkened ominously as the muted voices in the crowd began to rise.

At that point Chitchester stumbled up from the whist tables where he had succeeded in losing his last farthing. Making his way across the crowded room, he tried to elbow a path to view Alex's play, jostling the green-eyed dandy in the midst of another snuff taking. "I say, old chap, can't you make a bit of space for me?" he asked thickly.

Raising his thin blade of a nose, the dandy surveyed the crowded table. "Space would certainly have to be made since none exists," he drawled. A few of the better sort chuckled at the bon mot as the quipster shrugged and stepped over, allowing Chitchester to observe the ongoing contest.

The incredible streak of wins continued for Alex, as did the steady stream of gin the redhead considerably poured for him. The droll little dandy played against Alex for a few more of the escalating bets, then retired from the fray saying, "Dame Fortune, sir, is running high with you this night. I would be beetle-headed indeed to further provoke her."

When Alex nodded and resumed his roll, the dandy began placing wagers on Alex with other onlookers around the table. Inhaling snuff indolently, he observed the scene around him, seeming to enjoy the spectacle of drunken lordlings jostled by profane lightermen while deft-fingered cutpurses lifted what the luck of the gaming tables left the players.

"Dem, if you'll not have cause to be purse-proud by night's end," Chitchester cried with a distinct inebriated burp as his American cousin won another pass. The hour was growing late and Puck Forrester had abandoned them in a funk after losing seven straight hands of whist. The Viscount wove precariously back and forth, fading fast. Before long he took his leave after borrowing enough from Alex for hansom fare.

Alex was nearly as drunk as his cousin, but he'd been seasoned enough by backcountry Georgia whiskey to conceal his state better. Still it was getting devilish tricky reading the dice and the croupier was growing more hostile with every pass the house lost.

"You lose, gov," Bent Nose said triumphantly, quickly reaching out with his stick to snatch up the dice.

Before he could touch them, the dandy's slender hand snaked out and snatched the stick with lightning dexterity, inches from the tabletop. "I believe you've misread the dice, old chap."

Chill green eyes met surly black ones for a pregnant moment. In spite of his slight stature, something in the dandy's manner gave the heavyset croupier pause. "Blimey, yer right. Light's failin' me eyes."

"Mine as well," Alex said, nodding appreciatively to the slender young man. "I'm obliged to you, sir. Alex Blackthorne, late of the sovereign state of Georgia."

"Alvin Frances Edward Drummond, your servant, sir. My friends call me Drum. My enemies have other names for me," he added with a pleasant smile at Broken Nose. "I give you leave to be a friend if you will," he said to Alex.

"Drum," Alex responded with a grin while the redhead pouted prettily, holding the box of dice for him, already blessed.

The game resumed with no further attempts by the croupier to cheat, although he did change dice several times in a vain attempt to stop Alex's winning streak.

Finally, with nearly fifteen hundred pounds in the betting circle, Wheatie himself sidled up to Alex. A short pudgy fellow, Freddie Wheaton was balding with an excess of bushy eyebrows set over small beady eyes that glowed with avarice. His little round mouth curved in an oily, insincere smile as he placed one stubby-fingered hand on Alex's coat sleeve.

"I 'ate ta break up yer string o' luck, gov, but this 'ere's a workin' man's gamin' 'ouse. These stakes is too 'igh by 'alf fer me 'n my reglars ta stand."

The loud babel of voices rose in cacophony, some angry at having the excitement curtailed, others pleased to see the toff put to finish.

Sensing the mood of much of the crowd, Alex shrugged. "It is late and I'm having almost as much difficulty as your croupier reading the dice." Scooping up his winnings, he stuffed twenty- and fifty-pound notes inelegantly into his coat pockets, handing the redhead a generous fistful for her diligence.

"I 'ave a place, duckie, right 'round the corner," she whispered conspiratorially, clinging to him like a limpet.

As his state of inebriation increased, his standards of female comeliness declined. So did his judgment. Alex accepted her offer and they wove their way through the crowd, pausing long enough for the young American to offer his card to Drum, who was languidly lifting his wrist with another pinch of snuff. The dandy accepted it, noting the Caruthers's city house address with a raised eyebrow as Alex vanished out the door.

The chill night air hit him like a nor'easter washing across the deck of one of his father's sailing ships. Alex took a deep breath and looked down at his companion, whose unruly scarlet locks looked ink black in the moonlight.

"Whish way, my lovely?"

She giggled coyly. "Just 'round that corner, luv," she replied, tugging him toward a narrow walkway between two tall buildings.

After spending his boyhood and youth hunting with the Muskogee, Alex had developed a sixth sense for stalking—and knowing when he was being stalked. Had he not con-

sumed all that damnable champagne and gin, that sense
would have been triggered well before he entered the passageway.

There were three of them from Wheatie's establishment.
Alex snapped a quick glance over his shoulder and saw
Bent Nose grinning evilly, slapping a truncheon across one
meaty palm as he advanced on his prey from behind while
his fellows blocked the opening to the next street. The alley
was effectively sealed at both ends. The woman slipped
behind Bent Nose and vanished like a wraith as soon as
Alex turned around. Cursing his own stupidity, Alex inhaled cold air in a vain attempt to clear his head while it
still rested on his shoulders. Pure reflex led him to extract
the blade from his boot. The sight of it gleaming in the
moonlight stopped the croupier's advance.

"Now, gov, alls we want is th' blunt. 'And it over 'n no
one gets 'urt." The malice glittering in his eyes belied the
statement.

Alex cursed silently. He had not carried his pistol this
evening because it created a noticeable bulge in his new
jacket. So much for sartorial splendor. He'd be lucky to get
out of this alley without these pug-uglies creating a bulge
on his skull . . . or worse. He glided closer to the ringleader,
feinting with his blade. "Out of my way and you can keep
your liver."

Swearing, the boxer swung his truncheon, missing Alex's
head by inches but coming down on his shoulder with a
nasty whack that numbed his left arm. Alex barely managed
to hold on to his knife. Quickly he raised his right arm to
block the second blow, smashing his foe's arm against the
brick wall. The truncheon went flying from the croupier's
hand but he yanked a stiletto from his waistband just as
Alex moved in with his knife.

The two men wrestled, blades locked, turning in the narrow confines of the alley. Alex could hear the other two
men coming up behind him and tried in vain to twist

around, placing Bent Nose between himself and them. Suddenly he felt the icy hot slice of steel in his back as one of the men cried, "I 'ave 'im, Jackie!"

Before he went down, Alex swept his foot behind the croupier's knee and shoved hard, then turned, slashing out in the opposite direction with his blade. He sliced the second thief's throat cleanly. As the man gurgled and dropped, Bent Nose recovered his footing and started to lunge in for the kill.

Alex could do nothing to stop him since he was engaged in dealing with the third assailant. Just as he slipped in beneath the thug's blade and drove his own home, he felt the hot breath of death coming up behind him. The wound in his back burned like liquid fire and he could feel the wet stickiness of his own blood rolling down his breeches. *Got to turn around and face him.* Everything began to fade. He knew he was done for as his knees started to buckle.

Chapter Four

Drum heard the sounds of the scuffle coming from the dark alleyway, the yelping cry of a street tough being cut, the breathless hiss of steel on steel. The latter sound was intimately familiar to him. Swiftly and silently he made his way to the fight, withdrawing a gleaming blade from inside his fashionable silver-handled walking stick.

As he approached, Drum saw Alex on his knees, crumpling to the ground. The brute behind him started to lower his knife to deliver the final blow when he felt the prick of cold steel puncture the side of his neck. He started to turn, but the blade only sliced further.

"I wouldn't try it, old fellow. Stand up and move away from Mr. Blackthorne, there's a lad," the dandy offered with mocking encouragement as the huge prizefighter stood.

Deprived of his prey, the assailant snarled an oath when he recognized the little toff. He moved his head to evade the sword, intent on lunging in under it. He had a good eight inches' advantage in reach, not to mention being at least four stone heavier. It should have worked. But Jackie Elem underestimated his slightly built foe's skill with a blade. Alvin Frances Edward Drummond had trained with the finest French fencing masters. Lightning swift and effortlessly Drum ran the sword directly into Elem's heart.

As the East End cutthroat fell, already dead before hitting the ground, Drum withdrew the blade with a moue of distaste. "At least you stood up. I do so hate to dispatch a man on his knees. Isn't sporting."

He withdrew a snowy handkerchief from his jacket and cleaned the blade with a quick practiced stroke, then tossed the linen in the dirt with a sigh. After glancing at the other two men, he replaced the sword inside the cane. "Dead as a ducat," he muttered. The Yankee Doodle had done well, considering all. Now if only he was not done himself.

Kneeling beside Blackthorne, Drummond touched his chest to feel for a heartbeat. The American emitted a low moan and tried to move. "Ah, you're still ticking, I see, but in bad loaf all the same."

The dandy observed the widening puddle of blood trickling from beneath Alex's body. Grimacing with distaste he reached out and tugged at the much larger man's jacket in an attempt to pull him up. "You'll have to help me, my good fellow."

Alex sat up, wincing at the sharp stab of agony in his back. "Damn, those bastards ruined a perfectly tailored jacket. I only picked it up from Schweitzer and Davidson's yesterday."

"Your assailants could not ruin it, my good man. You already succeeded in doing so yourself, stuffing the pockets with blunt. Quite destroys the lines, you know," he sniffed.

"Please forgive my vulgar display," Alex said with a chuckle that ended in a gasp of pain, "and accept my thanks for saving my life. This is twice I'm indebted to you . . . and in only one evening."

"Then think how far into dun territory you'll be after

we've been friends for a fortnight or two," Drum replied genially.

This time Alex stifled the laugh, mindful of his throbbing back. Bent Nose lay spread-eagled in the alley with a red stain blooming across his chest. "How the deuce did you do that?" He saw no place to conceal a weapon in the toff's exquisitely molded jacket or breeches.

"Sword cane," was the succinct reply as he helped the much larger man to his feet. "You really should acquire one. Knives are so frightfully déclassé, even for an American."

"Ah, but I'm not just an American, I'm one of those wild red Indians. We like knives," Alex replied with a grin.

For once Drum had no instantaneous retort. "A blond red Indian. How extraordinarily colorful," he grunted as Alex leaned on him.

"I fear I'm ruining your jacket," Alex said when the little toff placed his arm around Alex's waist to help him walk.

"Not to worry, I've outrun the constable most of my life. Another tailor bill will scarcely matter, considering the prodigious amount I already owe. I'd rather say our concern should be finding you a physician lest you bleed to death." He sacrificed his last clean handkerchief, stuffing it up inside Alex's jacket and pressing it against the wound. "That will have to serve," he murmured at his friend's hiss of agony.

Alex squinted at the sky when they reached the open thoroughfare. "Not quite dawn. Pretty hard to find a physician's office open."

"Or even a hackney," Drum added bleakly. "This certainly isn't Mayfair."

"No, but then being a rude colonial, I'm used to frequenting low places."

"As am I when the lombard fever overtakes me. Boredom, old chap," he added by way of explanation, then cocked his head decisively. "If memory serves me, there is a hospital for the indigent nearby. Considering our present appearance, we should gain easy admittance. Come along."

They made their way down the street and around the corner to a dingy gray stone edifice situated between rows of decaying houses. In spite of the chill late fall air, windows in the residences were without panes, the glass broken. Here and there ragged curtains flapped in the brisk breeze and the sound of a baby crying broke the eerie stillness. The hospital, too, looked grim and forbidding. An unadorned wooden sign unevenly lettered in black hung over the entrance: CHARITY HOSPITAL OF LONDON.

The smell of sickness and unwashed flesh assaulted their nostrils the moment they stepped inside the front door. A long bleak hallway stretched before them. Sounds of groaning emanated from the distant end of it. Drum called out, "Is there a physician present?" There was no response so they began to make their way down the corridor, looking into each door they passed. The small, spartanly furnished cubicles were all empty. "I say, there is a man wounded here—bleeding all over your demned clean floor," he added as Alex's legs suddenly started to give way.

"I think I'd . . . better sit down," Alex rasped, blinking to clear his muzzy head. "Dizzy. So damned dizzy . . ."

Drummond started to guide him into one of the deserted offices, but just then a woman's voice called out from down the hall. "Not in there, across the hall. There is a table to lay him on."

Joss had heard the commotion from the far end of the ward rooms and rushed to see what new emergency had arisen. The best nurse, Peggy Halloran, was home with her sick aunt and Dr. Byington had not yet arrived, leaving only her and one other neophyte volunteer to care for a ward with over twenty people in it. In the dim light she could make out little about the two men. Upon reaching the doorway she could see by the cut of their clothes they were hardly the sort who frequented a charity hospital. A pair of elegant young bucks.

Both were blood smeared, but the small one blocked her view of his compatriot lying on the table. "We need a physician here," Drum announced peremptorily. "Summon one at once."

"Dr. Byington will return in an hour, perhaps two. He's delivering a baby. I'm trained as a nurse. You'd best let me have a look." Her tone matched his, brooking no opposition. She also towered over him by a good four inches. When the little dandy stepped back, she gasped in shock. "Alex!"

"You know my friend?" Drum asked incredulously. Whatever would a flashy cock-of-the walk like Alex Blackthorne do with a long Meg such as this scarecrow?

"Yes, we're friends," she replied, biting her lip as she touched Alex's cheek. There was blood all over him. "Where is he hurt?"

"Summon the physician. Alex has more need of him than—"

"Do not try my patience, sir, nor waste any more time. The doctor is *not* available."

"Then I suppose you'd better look at my back," Alex said, struggling to sit up.

Joss turned to him, ignoring the scowling little toff. "Lie still," she commanded.

"Can't until I get this damned jacket and shirt off," he replied, turning his back to her as he tried to ease his left arm out of the jacket. Drum assisted him.

"What happened?" she asked tersely, taking the blood-soaked coat and tossing it in the corner. When he peeled the ruined shirt off, she gasped. "You've been stabbed!"

"Excellent diagnosis, but I suspect it must be a frequent one in a place such as this," Drum said dryly.

Joss took a deep breath, both to calm herself and for patience. "Yes, we often see victims of taproom altercations," she replied, sniffing the pungent odor of gin and cheap perfume about Alex. The rotter, he'd been slumming in some gin mill about here and gambling, too, from the looks of the wads of banknotes stuffed in his pockets! A square of blood-soaked linen was stuck to the wound. When she removed it he winced. "Serves you right for breaking at least half the Lord's commandments," she said sweetly. The wound was jagged. Thank heaven a lung wasn't punctured. If one was, he would most certainly be spitting up blood and be unable to speak without a rattle in his throat.

"Lie facedown on the table," she instructed. "I'll have to cleanse the wound and perhaps stitch it."

"Now see here, m'dear. The need is not for a laundress and seamstress," Drum said. "We need a surgeon."

Alex swallowed a chuckle as he repositioned himself on the table. Joss and Drum faced each other like a pair of mismatched prizefighters. Although she was half a head taller than he, he remained coolly undaunted. "Forgive me for not making introductions earlier. Miss Jocelyn Woodbridge, may I present Mr. Alvin Frances Edward Drummond, Drum to his friends."

"You may call me Mr. Drummond," he replied without missing a beat. "Your servant, Miss Woodbridge." He clicked his heels and made a sketchy bow.

Ignoring his antics, she said "I'm going to get water and bandages. Hold this on the wound until I return." Joss seized Drum's hand and pressed it over the bloody linen she had replaced on the injury.

"Bossy chit," he sniffed.

"You should see her in a fight. She doesn't even need a knife—or a sword cane."

"A veritable Amazon," Drum said sourly.

Joss returned with medical supplies and began to cleanse the jagged puncture wound. "You must have moved just as he struck the blade into you," she said, biting her lip in concentration.

"I regret I didn't hold still but I had other things on my mind, such as the other fellow who was trying to gut me," he gritted out as she poured some wickedly burning solution into the wound.

"Probably it's as well you did not, else you might have had your lung punctured by a deeper blow. As it is, the cut is jagged and messy but I don't think lethal—unless you take a fever."

As Joss stitched him, her hands touched the bare skin of his back, so dark and sleekly muscled. She occasionally assisted the doctors in surgery. The unclothed male body— at least the upper half of it—was no novelty to her. Yet Alex affected her far more than any other. When she had first recognized him lying caked with blood, her heart had frozen in her chest. How dare he risk his life in a wastrel's lark? She willed herself to anger, hoping it could drive away that other unnamed and terrifying emotion.

He is my friend. Of course I'm concerned for him. One thing Jocelyn Angelica Woodbridge had never done before was deceive herself. She knew the trembling that traveled up from her fingertips to form a knot in the pit of her belly was far, far more than concern over a friend. But she dared not admit it.

"The medicine I brought from the Muskogee will guard against fever," Alex said to keep his thoughts off the pain. "You know, you're almost as good at sewing me up as Grandma Charity."

"I take it she had a good deal of practice working on you," she replied evenly. "I see you have scars aplenty from brawling."

"A few are from chunky, er, a Muskogee athletic contest . . . close enough to brawling by your standards," he murmured, feeling light-headed from the pain in his back.

When she had finished stitching him, Joss enlisted

Drum's aid with the bandaging, beginning by helping Alex to sit up so they could wrap the linen around his torso tightly to prevent more bleeding. She had to admit that for all his fussy ways and superior airs, the dandy was calm and not at all squeamish when it came to doing what needed to be done. Once she had finished with the dressing, she pulled a clean nightshirt from the chest in the corner.

Seeing it, Alex nodded. "Good. I'll need something to wear under my coat. That shirt is beyond repair."

"Surely you don't think you can walk out of here?" she replied incredulously.

"Certainly you don't expect a gentleman to remain in a charity ward?" Drum interjected, equally incredulous.

As Drum picked up his jacket, Alex pulled the shirt over his head. The garment was frayed and much mended but clean at least. "There's no need for me to lie abed, Joss, although I do thank you for stitching me up." The light-weight shirt had been bearable but when he tried to pull the stiff, blood-caked jacket over his shoulder, a blinding wave of dizziness followed the pain. He persevered as Joss stood glaring at him.

Drum assisted him in donning the coat but when he swung his legs off the table and tried to stand up, his knees did the most peculiar thing. Suddenly they weren't there. He felt as if he were floating on his way down to the floor. Drum's oath and Joss's cry as they reached out to break his fall seemed to come from a distance.

Glaring at Alex's companion from behind her thick lenses, Joss said, "Men! Now see what you've done encouraging his folly. If those stitches have broken open I shall take that walking stick of yours to both of you!"

"Not before I withdraw the sword inside of it to defend us, my good madam," Drum retorted as they helped Alex back onto the table.

"I am not a madam. I am a miss."

"And not a good one either. Little surprise no man would

61

wed a long Meg with the disposition of a fishmonger," he muttered sotto voce as Joss stormed from the room, calling for Liddie to prepare another bed.

"You'd best keep your thoughts to yourself. She isn't bluffing about using that cane on you," Alex said groggily.

"Us, old chap, us. She threatened you as well—but 'pon my honor I would defend your life to the bitter end," Drum replied with a dramatic flourish, adding, "and with that forward baggage it would be a bitter struggle indeed."

Within the hour Alex was dozing on a bed set up in one of the cubicles at the far end of the hall and Drum had departed. Joss, who had been working since the previous night, returned to the Fin and Feather for a few hours of sleep after Dr. Byington arrived and pronounced her work on the injured American's wound to be as well done as he could have managed himself. She had an afternoon meeting at the homeless shelter, then a prayer vigil at Mrs. Wallace's home. By evening she was once again hovering over Alex's bed.

"He looks flushed and feverish," she said worriedly, touching his forehead. It was scalding hot to the touch in spite of the chill in the big old building.

"The wound was a nasty 'un, Miss Jocelyn," Nurse Halloran replied. "Fever's ta be expected, but 'e's a strappin' lad, 'e is. Should pull through if any can."

Joss knew many people with injuries far less serious had died of fevers. Remembering his grandmother's Muskogee remedies, she made a decision. "Please inform the doctor that I shall be gone for an hour or so."

Only the thought of Alex lying feverish back at the hospital gave her the courage to approach the baron's elegant brick house and knock, imperiously insisting that the disdainful butler summon the Baron of Rushcroft. Her manner—or Alex's name—must have worked, for she was quickly ushered into an opulently appointed sitting room to wait.

When his lordship entered the room, Joss noted there was little family resemblance between Alex and his uncle. The first time she had seen him, the baron had been at that ghastly riot when she was too bedazzled by Alex's golden spell to take note of anyone else, the second at Goodysale's when Poc was bleeding in her arms. Montgomery Caruthers was certainly not an ill-favored man with his graying sandy brown hair and chiseled features. He was tall and slim yet not quite as tall as his nephew. Nor did his pale patrician face have the bold masculine vigor of Alex's swarthy countenance. His light blue eyes lacked warmth. But the chilly smile was the greatest contrast of all.

Monty inspected the gangly ape leader who was Suthington's niece. Small wonder the old boy never arranged a come-out for her, not that he could do so with that addle-pated nonconformist preacher dragging her about on his crusades. Lud, she looked even worse than she had earlier, if such were possible. Those thick eyeglasses, slightly askew, reflected the candlelight eerily and the faded yellow dress hanging on her was a shapeless horror. He had an uneasy suspicion he would not like what she had to say about Alex. "Good evening, Miss Woodbridge."

"I know it is presumptuous of me to call unannounced this way, milord, but the matter is most pressing." When he raised his eyebrow sardonically she could see the family resemblance to Alex.

"I fear you've come with ill tidings about my scapegrace nephew. Pray, out with it, Miss Woodbridge. I don't doubt but he's in the suds once more. Tell me, has he sent you for a loan to carry him over at the gaming tables?"

Joss knew Alex did not want his family to know about his injury or that he lay in a charity hospital. She had equally selfish reasons for keeping his guilty secret. She wanted him to remain under her care. "No, milord, Alex has not had an unsuccessful time at the tables. Indeed he's been winning quite steadily. That's why he sent me. He brought with him from America some of his Grandmother Blackthorne's Indian remedies and I have need of them at the charity hospital where I work."

"Indian remedies? Well, if they can cure dogs, then perhaps they can cure the indigent. Lud knows nothing else can."

"Education and a fair wage would do wonders for those of them who are in good health," Joss replied before thinking.

Monty was amused at her impertinent response. "You are Elijah's get, no doubt about it. Never saw two brothers less alike than your father and the earl."

She raised her head. "I take that as a compliment, milord."

He chuckled. "You would."

"If I might have the herbals, milord, I shall trouble you no further."

"Why is it, my dear, that I feel you shall trouble this family a very great deal before we're quits, hmm? Very well," he replied, ringing for a footman to fetch from Alex's room the pouch she described.

Alex was able to give her mumbled vague directives about how to make the cherry-bark infusion that she sat spooning down his throat all through the night. She sponged his brow and changed the dressing on his wound, using his grandmother's healing ointment that they had employed so successfully on Poc. As she worked, she was able to study him without those devilish dark eyes to fluster her. He looked so young and vulnerable, almost boyish as he slept.

Thick golden lashes rested against his cheeks and the slashing, expressive eyebrows above them for once were not raised in sardonic amusement. His mouth, so wide and dazzling when he smiled, lay barely closed. She could not resist tracing over his eyebrows, then down his high cheekbones to where the thick gold stubble of his beard abraded the sensitive pads of her fingertips. His lips moved sound-lessly, drawing her irresistibly to touch them and wonder how such a mobile, expressive mouth would feel pressed against her skin.

Joss jerked her hand away, scalded by the very thought, a thought that had never entered her mind about any other man she had ever met. *I'm a silly old tabby,* she scolded herself as she stood up and paced across the room. It was time to check the patients in the ward. The work would keep her foolish hands busy and give her time to get her mind in sensible order once more.

Alex awakened as the first pale rays of sunrise inched over the sill of the narrow window, bathing his face in light. He looked around the bare, unfamiliar room, thoroughly disoriented for a second. Other than one crude wooden chair and a small splintery table, there was no furniture. He lay on a narrow lumpy mattress. When he squirmed, trying to find a more comfortable position, a sharp pain lanced from his upper back straight down his spine. Then he saw Grandma Charity's medicines sitting out on the table and remembered where he was.

Joss stepped into the room at that moment, carrying a tray with fresh water and clean bandages on it. A merry smile, uniquely her own, split her face. "So you're awake. Fever's broken."

"How can you tell from across the room?"

She came in and set the tray down on the table. "After one spends hours nursing feverish patients, one learns to mark the signs—clear eyes, good color, a degree of alert-ness in expression."

"How long have you been working in this place?" he asked.

"I began to work with Dr. Atherton when I was around thirteen. Then Dr. Byington replaced him."

"Thirteen!" he echoed, appalled at the thought of hours,

much less years, in such a hellish environment. "Why, you were only a child."

"That was before I began helping with Papa's missionary work among the climbing boys and prostitutes. After helping to found the shelter, I grew up."

"Why do you do these things—I mean devote your entire life to charity?"

"I want to be useful, to make a difference in this world, Alex. Besides, it's not as if I were offered a carriage load of choices," she added dryly. "Bookish young women with neither beauty nor dowry to recommend them scarce have suitors beating down their doors."

"You have other qualities to recommend you besides a dowry, although your uncle should have seen to that."

"Bother the earl, he disowned his only brother," she said testily. "Besides, I would not want a man who'd wed me for an inheritance."

"What for, then—your mind? You have an agile one. Being bookish is not all so bad a quality if a sense of humor accompanies it."

"Considering your earlier confession about being sent down from university for not attending your studies, that is a remarkably turnabout opinion."

He shrugged, then winced when his stitches pulled. "Believe it or not, I have read a book or two between bouts of debauching."

Her expression was dubious as she began to change his dressing. "So pray tell me about these two books."

One gold eyebrow arched. "You wound me."

"La, your companions of the evening have already done that. At least I gave you the benefit of the doubt and allowed *two* books, not just one."

He squinted in mock concentration. "Let me see if I can recall them. There was Mr. Franklin's remarkable autobiography."

"A pro-French libertine."

"President Jefferson's essays, Tom Paine's pamphlets, Washington Irving's new satire."

"You have read more than I would have credited," she conceded, concentrating on tying off the fresh bandage, "but they're all Americans."

"How about Andrew Marvell?"

She sniffed. " 'To His Coy Mistress' is too risqué to edify the mind or uplift the human spirit. I prefer Wordsworth's 'Intimations of Immortality.' "

Waggling his eyebrows he replied, "Ah, yes, I did experience a bit of 'splendor in the grass' growing up in the Georgia backwoods."

"Somehow I don't believe we experience it in quite the same manner here in England." Bantering like this was truly delightful. She could enjoy matching wits without engaging her heart . . . or so she hoped.

Alex laughed heartily. "Being a lover of all manner of strays, I suppose you enjoyed *The Rime of the Ancient Mariner*."

"As a matter of fact I did, even if Mr. Coleridge is an opium eater."

He shrugged, carefully this time. "No one's perfect."

"My real love, since you mentioned political tracts earlier, is the writing of Olympe de Gouges and Mary Wollstonecraft." She waited to see if he even knew who they were.

He tsked mockingly. "I might have known you'd favor women's rights apologists."

"You don't look at all horrified. Most men—even my father and his friends, are quite appalled that I advocate economic, political and social equality between the sexes."

"I come from a revolutionary country, if you recall," he said, chuckling. "To give your father the benefit of the doubt, perhaps it is not Miss Wollstonecraft's ideas on women's rights he rejects, but those on free love."

She bit her lip consideringly. "Yes, he has mentioned it

a time or two, even though I've assured him I do not share that view with her."

"I'm certain he was much relieved," Alex said dryly. "You are a woman of many parts, Miss Jocelyn Woodbridge."

"And you are an utter charlatan, feigning ignorance of literature and ideas as if you cared more for gaming hells and Cyprians."

He rubbed his chin. "If I had to choose, my dear Joss, I fear you'd be much disillusioned with me. Since discovering all the lusty vices of the Great Wen, I'd be hard pressed to give them up."

"Perhaps some day you shall, Alex." *When you find the right woman.* But Jocelyn Woodbridge knew it would never be she.

Chapter Five

Joss stood by the window gazing out into the warm spring sunshine where the children scampered about Alex. Their squeals of delight had drawn her from her preparation for the afternoon classes. She watched in amazement while Alexander Blackthorne, resplendently dressed in cream doeskin trousers and a deep bottle green jacket, picked up little Verity Blaine, one of the most destitute of the children, and let her grimy little fingers tug on his snowy white cravat, pulling it loose. He seemed unconcerned, laughing and teasing the crowd of urchins surrounding him. They seldom saw a toff in these mean dirty slums. When they did, the "gentlemen" drove recklessly past, cursing, and sometimes running them down as they begged for coins.

But Alex was different. He drew them to him like a golden beam of sunshine. Children had a way of sensing the goodness—or evil—in adults. The moment he'd appeared at the schoolyard gates, they had responded to his warmth and laughter as he asked their names and answered their awestruck questions. Shortly they had gathered from all around the small bare yard to hear stories of his adventures with his Muskogee relatives. He tossed stones with the boys and even joined the girls in a game of hopscotch.

Joss could have stood all day simply basking in the pleasure of watching him. His way with the children did not surprise her. Everything about Alex Blackthorne was magical. She had seen little of him in the months since his awful brush with death. Yet each time when she became certain he had forgotten a boring spinster such as she, he would turn up, enchanting her with charm and laughter. *Perhaps it would be better if he did not come by ever again. I am losing my heart more each time he reappears.* Joss started guiltily, knowing that her heart must have been on her sleeve.

When Mary Breem walked up to her and stared out at Alex and the children, she opined, "A wastrel rogue such as that shouldn't be mixing with young impressionable minds." Mary sniffed primly, her thin, pinched lips compressed in a harsh line.

"Considering that most of their mothers are prostitutes and their fathers—if one could even find them—are probably cutpurses, I doubt Mr. Blackthorne will be much of an additional corruption," she replied crisply.

Mary stiffened indignantly. "The reverend would be shocked to hear you speak of such lascivious matters. 'Tis most indelicate."

" 'Tis the truth, Mary," she answered gently this time, striving for patience. Mrs. Bleem had volunteered long hours helping her organize the school for these children born into hopeless poverty. If Mary was a bit on the priggish and judgmental side, she was a tireless worker and zealous member of her father's congregation.

"I know his type and they prefer the pleasures of the flesh to being about the Lord's work. Why does he come around here?"

"Mr. Blackthorne is a good friend . . . of the reverend's

as well as mine. He saved Papa's life on the docks."

Excusing herself, Joss walked outdoors to greet Alex, fighting the urge to straighten her hair. The knot of braids had come loose earlier when she'd had to break up a fight between two of the boys. Now it hung askew in a most ungraceful clump against her neck. What difference did it make? she chided herself. No matter what she did with her hair, it could add nothing of charm to a squint-eyed, gawky creature such as she.

Alex listened gravely as Tessa Jones explained in a piping lisp how she had lost her two front baby teeth. She looked worshipfully into his face, then giggled at his whispered confidence.

Do I reveal such puppyish adoration? Praying not, Joss cleared her throat as she approached him, calling out for the children to return to the classroom for their noon meal.

"I would not have expected a rakish gamester to have such rapport with children," she said, teasing.

Dusting off his pants, Alex chuckled. "Remember, I grew up in a large family with two little sisters and two elder ones. Believe me, I much preferred the younger ones," he added dryly.

"You mentioned before that you had sisters. Have you any brothers?" she asked, hungry for information about his American family.

"Alas for my poor parents, no. I am my father's sole male heir, a fact my mother loves to tease him about whenever he complains of my roguish proclivities."

"Like father, like son?" she ventured.

"In his day Devon Blackthorne cut quite a swath across the backcountry. His reputation as a brawler and rogue was legendary from the Muskogee towns all the way to Charleston. I am his penance—or so mother would have him believe."

"Mrs. Breem thinks you've come here to corrupt the children," she said with a chuckle.

He shrugged, raising his hands in mock guilt. "Caught out again. I was, in fact, enlisting them to snatch fat purses and gold watches for me in Mayfair."

"Their skills in that area need little sharpening, I fear. Most of them come from families where the law is an enemy and food and coal are scarce as violets in January."

"But you help them."

Joss blushed as he looked at her with frank admiration in his gaze. While his attention lacked the teasing charm and sexual magnetism he reserved for women to whom he was attracted, she knew he liked and admired her. "Yes, I do what I can, as do the others in the charity school movement. Education provides the only hope these children have to escape a life on the streets."

Alex grinned. "And who better to teach them than you?"

She fell in step beside him as they strolled around the schoolyard. "Well, I did learn to read when I was three, mastered Latin at seven and Greek by ten," she replied solemnly.

"Egad! You are a bluestocking indeed!"

"Caught out, too," she said with a sigh, then laughed. "What has brought you here today, Alex? We have a vacant position as schoolmaster for the older boys."

A look of extreme horror crossed his face; then he threw back his head and laughed heartily. "Me, a schoolmaster! As a lad my parents could scarce keep me at my books an hour a day. They'd relish the notion of me as a pedagogue. So would Mellie and Charity."

"Your elder sisters?" she ventured.

"Bookish wenches, both of them."

"So am I. 'Tis not a bad thing for a woman to love books," she said defensively.

"Ah, but you have a sense of humor, which they sadly lack."

"Are they still at home? Did you come to England to escape them?" she asked as she ushered him into the side door of the dilapidated frame building that housed the makeshift school.

"No, both are wed. Mellie's husband, Toby, has become indispensable to my father. He oversees a good portion of the shipping business in Savannah, leaving Papa free to spend more time in the Muskogee towns. He and Mama love to summer in the high country at Grandma Charity's place," he said with fond remembrance of childhood days past.

Joss offered him a seat on one of the small room's two rickety chairs, then set to preparing a pot of tea for them as he talked. Next door the children's voices seeped through the thin walls as they devoured lunch. "It's difficult to imagine an English lady living in the wilderness," she said.

"Equally difficult to imagine one teaching slum children their letters," he replied, accepting a chipped cup of tea, waving away the small scrap of sugar loaf she offered.

Joss was curious about his family. Sitting down, she said, "Lady Barbara must love your father very much."

His expression grew thoughtful. "As a child I never considered what she must have given up for Devon Blackthorne. We were all happy. And as Papa's inland trade and foreign shipping grew, we became prosperous. If Mama ever pined for England, she never indicated it in any way."

"It all sounds very romantic," Joss said with a small sigh that he did not hear.

Alex chuckled. "One never thinks of one's own parents that way, but I suppose it was true. What of your parents, Joss? Were they happy?"

"My parents gave up a great deal to marry. As the second son of an earl, Papa was expected to wed a woman of his class. The family didn't disown him for marrying a governess, although they made their displeasure known and ostracized her shamefully. He was expected to take a vicarage in the established church, which would have provided him and his wife a livable income. It was his conversion to Methodism that led to the final split with his family. But she held fast to him through terrible privations."

"What was she like?" Alex asked, touched by the poverty and hardship of her life.

"I know little. When I was only three she died of child-bed fever after a breech birth. My brother Samuel died too. All I can remember is a soft voice singing hymns and lull-abies."

"I'm sorry. It's difficult for me to imagine not being sur-rounded by family. Although I often complain of them, I do miss not having them about now and then."

"Surely not when you're having a streak of luck at the hazard tables," she teased. Her sad past did not bear dwell-ing upon.

"I confess I've found compensations here in the Great Wen that offset the temporary loss of my family, but I did receive a letter from home this morning. One of the reasons I came to visit you."

She paused with the cup halfway to her lips. "And what was the other reason, since I know you did not intend to volunteer tutorial assistance?"

He placed one hand over his heart theatrically. " 'Pon my honor, Miss Woodbridge, you do me grave injustice. Can't I simply wish the pleasure of your company? You're a refreshing tonic after three days of playing whist at Brooks with Drum and his chums."

"Thank you . . . I think," Joss replied dryly. "You men-tioned a letter from home. Not bad news, I hope?"

"Nothing ill's befallen my immediate family, no. It's the political situation that worries me. If war comes, I'll be forced to return home."

Joss paled. "Surely your president wouldn't declare war against his majesty's government while Britain has her back to the wall fighting that despicable Napoleon?" she said with righteous indignation.

Alex's expression grew uncharacteristically grim as he

considered how to explain the complexities of American politics. "Yes, from what my father writes, it's very possible."

"Over the Royal Navy's search of American ships and impressment of sailors? The French have seized as many American ships as has Britain," she protested.

"True, and war against Napoleon is a possibility as well. But freedom on the seas is only the smallest part of the problem. Most of the war pressure is internal, having more to do with Spain hemming in land-hungry American settlers to the west and south."

"And Spain is Britain's ally." She nodded in understanding. "With a declaration of war, the Americans could sweep down into the Floridas and west into Texas."

Alex grinned in spite of the gravity of the situation. "I should've realized a true bluestocking would understand geography as well as politics."

"Would you join the Americans and fight?" Joss asked, her fear for him written plainly on her face as she reached out and touched his coat sleeve.

"No, I would never do that. It would be a betrayal of my father's people."

"Now I truly don't understand," she replied.

"Since the days of the American war for independence, all the great Indian nations have been sympathetic to the Crown. What little protection they ever received from white squatters on their land came from the British government."

Joss understood European politics, but she knew little about the loose tribal organizations of wild red Indians. "What does your father think will happen now?"

"The situation is like a powder keg sitting next to a hearth. The British have sent ships into the gulf and have men garrisoned at various Spanish forts. They're sending agents to stir up anti-American feeling among the tribes. My father is afraid the Creek nation—of which the Muskogee are a part—may decide to join their old allies the

British once again. Uncle Quint just returned from Washington to inform him that the western congressmen—war hawks they call them—are pushing hard for a fight."

Alex pulled the letter from his pocket to read his father's dire prognostication, but when he looked at Joss's pale, stricken face, he immediately reconsidered. Why worry her with events neither of them could prevent? Instead, he scanned down the pages to his mother's portion of the letter.

"If war breaks out, what will we do?" Joss said desolately.

He looked at her deadpan and pointed his finger as if it were a pistol. "Why, Miss Woodbridge, for the glory of my country I'd have to shoot you."

Joss stared at him for an instant, then started to laugh. He made her so happy. *Please, don't let a war separate us.*

Alex rustled the pages of the letter and said, "Let me read you the latest *on-dits* from Savannah. Mother writes that the French Brutus cut for gentlemen has been greeted with hooting in the public houses. The Georgia courts refuse to admit jurors sporting trousers. They must wear proper attire—knee breeches!"

"Just like Almacks," Joss said merrily, her good humor restored.

"Ah, here it is, the best of motherly advice." He cleared his throat, then read Barbara's bold sweeping script. " 'You must remember, Alexander, that you are your father's sole male heir. You have a duty to contract a suitable marriage, although I would be the last to stand as example for that, having been all but disowned for spurning a viscount for a man of mixed blood. Nevertheless' "—he paused for emphasis, rolling his eyes—" 'you surely will be able to find a young lady who will return your regard. Ask for her hand and bring her home posthaste to meet your family. We miss you . . .' etc., etc., all the usual exhortations from a loving mother to her son. Can you imagine me wanting to settle down, Joss? I've just passed my twenty-second birthday. Papa was twenty-six when he wed."

"And you'd as soon best his record by waiting a few years more," Joss said with a smile. *But some day, Alex, you will find the suitable young lady who returns your regard . . . and how shall I bear it?*

"I certainly will endeavor to break all records in avoiding leg-shackling. Why—"

He stopped midway, replacing the letter in his pocket as a low growl followed the sound of a loud shriek. The door to the small kitchen area where they sat swung open when the business end of a broom smashed against it. The old hag wielding the broom chased a bundle of brindle fur under the scarred pine table, then circled, jabbing wildly at the dog, who held a large ham bone clenched in his sturdy yellow teeth.

"Poc! What have you done?" Joss cried, standing up so abruptly she knocked over her chair and nearly went tumbling down with it.

" 'E's stolen me supper, that's whot th' sneak thievin' worthless rascal done. Bloody wretch—beggin' yer pardon, Miss Woodbridge," the crone added as she and the dog eyed each other warily. Poc showed no sign of letting go of his prize, no matter that his enemy looked fierce as a Sherwood game warden cornering a poacher. Her nose was bulbous, blazing beet-red above a sharkish mouth pulled wide in a grimace that revealed half a dozen rotted teeth.

At least the dog has her beaten if it comes down to a biting match, Alex thought, then reconsidered. Her blackened gums were probably as hard as Toledo steel and her angular lantern jaw could snap a mastiff's neck. He stood up, reaching out to steady Joss when her skirts tangled on her overturned chair leg. Poc tried to make a run for it but the old woman, amazingly agile considering her age and girth, slammed the door shut, cutting off his only means of escape short of leaping through the window glass.

Recovering her balance, Joss stepped between Zelda Grim and her prey just as the cook's helper raised her broom to deliver the coup de grace to Poc, who hunkered against the door, clutching the bone in a death grip. If Alex had not seized the weapon from behind, Joss would have been brained along with the dog.

"Gor! Leave me be, ye bloody jackanapes," Zelda screeched, this time so enraged no apology was forthcoming for her profanity.

"I shall handle this, Zelda," Joss said. "Tell me what happened."

" 'E stole me bone! It were left over 'n I were goin' ta boil it with some greens fer me dinner. Then this 'ere 'eathen come sneakin' in 'n made a mighty leap up on th' stool by the washtub. Afore we knowed it, 'e was off with me bone," Zelda finished on a plaintive whine.

Joss looked down at the dog, who had come out of his hunkering crouch now that Alex had neutralized the threat from the broom. "Bad dog, Poc. You know it's wrong to steal." He looked singularly impenitent with his loot clamped firmly between his jaws.

"The bone's too badly chewed up for anyone to eat it now. Best to let him have it," Alex ventured. He certainly had no intention of trying to get the bone away from thirty pounds of fighting terrier!

Joss sighed. "That would scarcely teach him the error of stealing food. I've tried to break him of sneaking into the kitchen and lying in wait for cook to turn her back. We've little enough to feed the children as it is," she said as she knelt down beside the dog and reached out one hand.

"Joss, be careful. He's a pit dog," Alex said, but the dog released his treasure and backed away after a moment's eye contact with his mistress. Poc laid his chin down on the floor with a piteous whimper as Joss picked up the bone, shaking it like a teacher's rule, scolding him.

"You should be ashamed of yourself and well you know it, Apocalypse."

" 'E's th' very messenger of ole Scratch. Name suits 'im, it does," Zelda said, taking the well-gnawed bone Joss offered her. "Whot am I ta do fer dinner now? I can't be eatin' this," she whined.

"There's not a shred of meat on it. You couldn't have eaten it before the dog seized it," Alex said, taking some coins from his pocket. "Here, buy something at the butcher's for your dinner."

"Gor! Thank 'e, sir, thank 'e," Zelda said, bowing to her benefactor. Her bloodshot eyes almost popped from their sockets as she squeezed the coins in disbelief, then grabbed up her broom and quit the room with a swish of ragged skirts.

"That was kind of you, Alex."

He shrugged. "Did I mention I was very lucky at that marathon whist game? Another of the reasons I came here today—I wanted to give you a gift for the children," he said, handing her a well-laden purse.

"Oh, my," Joss said, startled by the weight of it. When she opened it and saw the amount, she tried to give it back to him. "You've been generous before, Alex, but I can't possibly accept this much—you might need it if your luck deserts you."

A broad smile flashed across his face. "Luck has never deserted me—and even if it did, my father's allowance is most generous. I can spare it, Joss," he replied, placing his hands around hers and gently pushing the purse back to her.

"Are you certain?" she asked dubiously, thinking of all the food, books and medicines the money could buy.

"I'm most certain."

"The children will be so grateful, as am I," she said with a smile.

Poc chose that moment to emit a low, pitiful whimper.

"I think he's saying that everyone has been taken care of but him," Alex said with a laugh, looking pointedly at the chewed ham bone lying on the table beside their tea-cups.

"We're only encouraging him to steal," she replied, re-lenting.

Sensing her capitulation, the dog sat up and began to wag his tail from side to side like a metronome. Poc waited politely as Joss picked up the bone and offered it to him. He took it almost daintily in his mouth, careful not to place his teeth anywhere near her fingers.

"He's amazingly well mannered. I confess I was afraid he might prove dangerous after the way he was raised."

Joss knelt and scratched his head fondly as he gnawed on the bone, cracking it with his powerful jaws. "Poc only kills rats. He's been wonderful at reducing the danger from the nasty things around the school and the hospital. I take him with me everywhere I go now."

Alex raised one eyebrow. "Everywhere?"

She chuckled. "Well, not to church and prayer meetings, but he's fiercely protective of me and of the children. Rat bites are only one of the threats to them. The flash house boys and pimps are afraid of him. Since I brought him here, they don't come around trying to bribe or kidnap my students anymore."

"I'm glad you decided to rescue him then."

"I couldn't have without your help." When the clanging of a heavy brass bell sounded from the next room, Joss said, "I must return to the children. I only have them for another hour."

He helped her to her feet and waited as she dusted off her ugly navy-blue skirt, wondering why she chose such shapeless, unflattering clothes. *Probably they're castoffs since her father's too poor to afford a dressmaker for her.* For some reason, her lack of pretty things bothered him, although he could not for the life of him imagine why since she was so unconcerned. "I must be going, but first I want to tender an invitation."

"An invitation?" She cocked her head, willing her erratically thumping heart to steady its beat. *He'll scarcely ask you to a cotillion,* she scolded herself.

"I'm racing this weekend at a track outside the city. Drum and his chums refuse to go near a racecourse—too smelly and muddy for their delicate sensibilities and elegant tailoring."

"Mr. Drummond would think so," Joss said with a sniff.

Alex chuckled at her sudden pique. "You and Drum don't like each other much, do you?"

"I suspect 'detest' would describe our mutual feelings a bit better. He is an unmannerly misogynist, but what has that odious man to do with me?"

"I don't mean the invitation to sound secondhand, Joss, but since Drum won't be present, would you consider attending the race with me? I've finally been able to convince the track owners to let me run one of the horses I brought with me from America against a field of Britain's best. I need a friend—one brave enough to cheer for the United States."

"And, of course, you thought of me."

"Who else has your courage?"

"I have never been to a horse race. There would be gambling on the race, wouldn't there?" She chewed her lip in vexation, wanting to see Alex on horseback. She knew he would be splendid. What an adventure it would be! *I could spend the day with him!*

"Your father wouldn't approve, I'm afraid," Alex said ruefully. "I'm sorry I tempted you, Joss."

Pray heaven you never realize how *you tempt me.* "No, Papa wouldn't, nor would the ladies of the Missionary Society . . . but I would like to see you race! When is it?" The words burst from her exuberantly before she could stop them. *What have I done?*

81

A dazzlingly white grin split his face. "Saturday next. I'll call for you at ten in the morning!"

Her father would be hurt and frightened for her. Already her friendship with a man of Alex's libertine reputation had caused the reverend much prayerful anguish. She had never before in her life done anything to cause him a moment of worry. Though he would never forbid her to see Alex, Joss knew how concerned he was. If he realized the nature of her feelings for Alex, he'd spend the rest of his life on his knees praying for her deliverance!

She considered how she would explain attending such a sinful event as a horse race. To see if the animals were being mistreated? Or perhaps to investigate what went on at such an event with an eye to organizing a protest march? No, she concluded with a sigh. If she wanted to attend the race, then she must be honest about it and tell her father that she was going to watch Alex race . . . but she would tell him nothing else.

Chapter Six

"Why the deuce do you call him Sumac, old fellow?" one dandified racing enthusiast asked Alex as a group of men crowded around his big roan stallion.

"Sumac because he's red, my dear Puck," his companion responded, nodding to Alex for confirmation.

"Partly. It's also because he's so hard to beat that all the other horse owners avoid him like poison sumac," Alex replied, rubbing the roan's nose affectionately.

"How long is the course?" Puck asked.

Joss stood to the side, a plain brown wren in her shapeless woolen gown. She clutched a shawl around her shoulders to ward off the chill spring wind. Pewter clouds scudded across the sky, hinting at more rain. The racecourse was already soaked from last night's showers. Any further rain would turn the ground into a bog, but Alex seemed unconcerned, even a bit pleased with the weather.

So was Poc, who pranced through the squishy yellow mud in tail-wagging glory, impatient with the restraint of the leash, which Joss kept firmly wrapped around her wrist.

She was grateful she'd had the foresight to confine him, as many of the horse lovers were also dog lovers whose canine friends accompanied them. Poc loved people but was not on overly cordial terms with other dogs. Looking about the elegant assembly of gentlemen in cutaway riding coats and ladies twirling ruffled parasols, she felt it prudent to hold him on a short leash indeed.

"So you believe this uncertain breed from the colonies can win over my Pegasus," Colonel Sir Rupert Chamberlain said smugly, tugging on his immaculate white gloves.

Alex studied the tall, narrow-faced aristocrat, resplendent in his scarlet uniform. A saber cut above his left eyebrow marred what would have been a perfectly molded, if harsh, countenance. His hot yellow eyes looked almost satanic when he returned Alex's level gaze.

"Sumac will take first place," Blackthorne asserted coolly. "He's undefeated in the twenty-six races he's run to date."

"Against American horses?" Chamberlain spoke disdainfully, looking down his long, thin nose at the American, who was dressed in buckskin pants and a loose-fringed shirt of the same material. "Did he perchance triumph over Indian ponies?"

"In America there are a variety of places to find a horse race, in white settlements and Indian."

"My, then it is true! You are part savage?" The small, voluptuous woman standing beside Chamberlain spoke breathlessly, looking at Alex's frontiersman's garb and the soft leather moccasins he wore in lieu of the fashionable riding boots affected by the other men. Cybill Chamberlain's heavily fringed violet eyes had strayed often to the American as he and her husband exchanged words.

"I'm only *part* Muskogee, but I am *all* savage," Alex replied with a cool smile, taking in the stunning black-haired woman's bountiful curves and pouty full lips.

With growing irritation Joss watched the colonel's lady

flirt with Alex. She was clutching one of those tiny Maltese dogs so popular with the ladies of the ton, acting as if she expected Alex to gobble it up in two bites—and herself in three. Poc tugged restively on his leash, sniffing the air as the men resumed their barely civil discussion.

"The gentlemen in Savannah and Charleston paid dearly to see how fast Sumac could run." Alex left the dare hanging pregnant in the chill, damp air, staring at Chamberlain.

The colonel's eyes narrowed, glowing amber like those of a fierce predatory bird. A half smile touched his lips, then fled. "How much would you like to wager that your Sumac takes the field over my Pegasus? Say, one thousand pounds . . . or is that a touch rich for your part-American, part-Indian blood, Mr. Blackthorne?" Chamberlain stroked his chin with a lazy insolence belied by his taut military posture.

It's almost as if he wants to provoke Alex, Joss thought. Then Poc gave a strong tug on his leash, distracting her as Alex replied.

"No, one thousand pounds isn't too rich. In fact, why don't we double it . . . just to make this interesting?"

A murmur spread through the crowd. For a rural race-course far from the city, a two-thousand-pound wager was rich indeed, especially staked upon an unproven horse from abroad. Everyone stared at Chamberlain to see what he would do.

The colonel nodded curtly. "Two thousand it is, Mr. Blackthorne. Who will be riding for you?"

"No one. Sumac isn't civil to strangers. I'll ride him."

Chamberlain's eyebrows rose. "Really? Do you think it advisable? All of the *gentlemen* present employ jockeys."

"My, yes, Mr. Blackthorne, you're so tall. Why, you must surely weigh four or five stone more than those little men." Cybill Chamberlain looked as if she'd enjoy checking his precise weight. Her eyes traveled from his head to his moccasins and back, pausing somewhere in the vicinity below his waist. "It scarcely seems sporting."

"I ride bareback, Mrs. Chamberlain," Alex replied, this time returning her frank sexual perusal with a lascivious smile. If he angered her boorish husband, so much the better. "That always makes a difference—usually in my favor."

"And does fortune always favor you, Mr. Blackthorne?" she asked, moistening her pouty little mouth with the tip of her tongue.

Alex could see the arrogant British colonel watching the exchange but could not read his expression. *What twisted sort of games do these bored blue bloods play?* "They say luck is a lady, Mrs. Chamberlain."

"In that case, you shall certainly win," she replied.

"I have heard that luck is not a lady but rather a female of exceedingly uncertain constancy," Joss interjected. *I am not jealous,* she assured herself, unable to keep silent a moment longer during the licentious display.

Cybill's violet eyes turned almost black as they swept over Joss with contempt. "Only a missionary zealot would see constancy as a virtue," she said dismissively.

"It is, but then perhaps you are not so well acquainted with virtue as to judge it," Joss replied coolly.

Alex could see Cybill's claws coming out as she stepped toward her taller, thinner antagonist, clutching that ridiculous bit of barking fluff to her bosom. Before she could make her furious retort, he extended his hand to the dog, which snapped at him.

"Oh, Bonbon, do behave," she scolded, diverted from Joss. "Did she bite you? She's so high-strung, a result of her impeccable pedigree," Cybill added with a sniff toward Joss's terrier.

"Unlike her owner," Joss murmured sotto voce, knowing the words carried. She simply must stop behaving in such an un-Christian manner. Before she could analyze that problem further, Poc, who had been growing increasingly restive since Cybill approached them, gave a yip of excitement and tried to break free. She tightened her grip on his leash, almost losing her footing in the slippery mud.

By the time she'd calmed the dog, Alex had bid adieu to the hateful colonel's lady and was leading his big roan over to where the other horses and their jockeys stood. Along the way, the American stopped to make additional wagers. Joss could not take her eyes off him. He stood out in the crowd of starched dandies like a powerful golden lion in a litter of mewling house cats.

"My, my, you poor thing, so smitten with that bold American. La, what a pity. With all London at his feet, he must scarcely know you're alive," Cybill purred with vicious sweetness, stroking Bonbon's long white fur.

"We are friends of long-standing, *Mrs.* Chamberlain," Joss replied coldly. "A chaste and honest relationship with which you are no doubt unfamiliar."

A loud hurrah went up at that moment, drowning out Cybill's retort. The race was on. And a rough, no-holds-barred contest it was, as the field of seven horses thundered off, churning through the mud. The jockeys were all significantly smaller than Alex, their whips flailing indiscriminately as each fought to break away from the pack. Alex alone seemed to meld with his horse, become one with the animal as his legs wrapped around its sides and his head lay beside the roan's neck.

Joss cheered unabashedly for Alex and Sumac, forgetting the contemptible Cybill Chamberlain, who shrank away from the splashing water and mud created by the horses as they raced by. The spectators were a rowdy lot. Bets continued to be exchanged as an elegant gray took the lead while the riders disappeared from sight.

The course was four miles long, covering wooded hilly terrain. The length and rugged lay of the land were precisely the reasons Alex had chosen to race Sumac here. Although the finely bred English horses were faster on the level flat courses, the big roan possessed incredible endurance. The rain had been an added bonus, slowing the track. Sumac galloped at a steady, ground-eating pace, churning through the mud with surefooted ease. Alex held him back, letting the jockey on the gray keep the lead. Chamberlain's jockey, too, seemed to be pacing his chestnut for the home stretch.

Several of the riders whipped their steeds—and competitors—mercilessly. More than once Alex was forced to raise an arm to ward off blows. His heavy buckskin clothing absorbed the cutting sting of the whip far better than the wool and linen of the jockeys. When one leaned over to strike at him in an attempt to force Sumac aside, Alex slid effortlessly to the opposite side of Sumac, gripping the horse's flying mane as he clung to his seat by little more than one heel. The jockey lost his balance when his whip cut through empty air. Before he could correct his balance on the flimsy racing saddle, his mount stumbled and he went flying into the mud, narrowly missing being trampled by the other riders.

Alex quickly righted himself on Sumac's back, urging the roan to greater speed. The cool wind stung his cheeks, whipping his hair about his face when it pulled loose from the leather thong at his nape. Sumac pounded the soft earth and he could feel each beat of his mount's hooves as if they were one entity. He murmured low in the stallion's ear, his blood hammering as a wild exhilaration sang in his veins.

He could hear the roar of the crowd when they crested the last hill. By this time two of the other horses had fallen behind on the slow track, the pull of the heavy mud sapping their strength. The finish line was visible at the end of a gradual uphill stretch. It was time to let Sumac have his head. "Let's go, boy," he whispered in Muskogee and the big red horse sprang forward, pulling ahead of the remaining field, except for Pegasus. The two powerful horses now ran neck and neck.

Joss watched the contest narrow to Sumac and Pegasus, yelling with most unladylike exuberance for Alex. How wild and splendid he looked with his golden hair flying behind him as he moved with effortless grace in perfect rhythm with the great stallion. *Two barbarously beautiful males.* Joss felt the heat sting her cheeks as she quashed the thought and returned to cheering while Poc barked excitedly as the red and chestnut horses neared the finish line, still neck and neck.

When Alex urged Sumac ahead of Pegasus, she let out a shrill cry of triumph worthy of a savage red Indian. But her unladylike behavior went unremarked among the other bystanders, who were all caught up in the excitement of the close race. Money still changed hands as the two horses streaked nose to nose toward the finish line. Then in one final burst of speed, the roan lunged ahead by half a length, crossing the finish line ahead of Chamberlain's horse.

Mud flew everywhere as Alex slowed Sumac, then turned him in a wide circle and finally reined him to a stop. Many of the spectators were liberally speckled with the gooey brown substance, Joss included, but she did not mind. Cybill Chamberlain did. When several drops of mud spattered against the slim skirt of her yellow gown, she squealed in dismay, losing her hold on her little lapdog, which jumped to the ground, yipping furiously and scampering through the crowd.

"Bonbon, come back here! Naughty girl!"

Poc caught a fresh whiff of the Maltese, who was in heat—and now on the ground, where she was fair game. Unable to resist this call of nature, he lunged against the restraint of the leash just as Joss was turning to approach the cluster of people surrounding the victorious Alex. The six-foot length of rope quickly slid through her fingers before she realized what was happening. When it drew taut, the end securely looped around her wrist, she was given an unexpected and very hard jolt, unsettling her balance on the slippery ground.

"Poc, no!" Her words were drowned out in the press of the excited crowd, now all bypassing her to rush to the winner's circle, where wagers were being settled. She was being dragged in the opposite direction—until her foot hit a particularly deep puddle and she completely lost her purchase. The leash slipped from her mud-slicked wrist and Poc was free. He flew after Bonbon with single-minded ardor, on a direct collision course with Cybill, who picked her way daintily across the puddle-strewn grounds, holding her yellow muslin skirts up with one hand, her parasol in the other.

"Bonbon, you've gotten your paws muddy, you bad girl," Cybill cried in high dudgeon just before she stepped into the path of the brindle cannonball. As she was knocked flailing into the quagmire, a series of highly inventive and most unladylike oaths tumbled from her pretty, pouty mouth.

Joss scrambled upon the debacle just as Poc and Bonbon dispensed with courtship preliminaries and got down to the serious business at hand. Cybill sat up on all fours in the mud, shaking her fist at the lovers. She peeled off her mud-soaked gloves and threw them down as she regained her footing. Joss had fared little better since her own skirts were sopped with muck up to her knees. Still, the sight of the elegant beauty covered head to toe with slime brought forth a smile, then a chuckle, and finally a full-throated laugh.

Seeing that Bonbon's virtue had already been hopelessly compromised, Cybill turned from the ungrateful little bitch and focused her wrath on the gauche ape-leading bluestocking who had the temerity to laugh at *her*. Violet eyes narrowed, she glared at Joss as she stood up and took a step—only to find her slipper had remained trapped in the ooze.

"I do apologize, Mrs. Chamberlain," Joss managed between hiccuping giggles, trying desperately to regain some small measure of decorum.

A low enraged snarl came from deep in Cybill's throat as she reached out for Joss. "How dare you," she gritted, her long fingers curled, ready to claw out Joss's eyes.

"See here, I did not intend—" Joss's protest was cut short as she was forced to defend herself against the on-slaught by grabbing for Cybill's hands. It was like trying to hold a hurricane. Although nearly a foot shorter, Cybill was compactly built, weighing as much as her lesser endowed enemy. When she barreled into Joss, both women went down into the mud, kicking and pulling each other's hair as they rolled around.

The shrieking catfight quickly drew the attention of the crowd, which circled around them, placing wagers on the outcome. "Five pounds on Mrs. Chamberlain," one cock of the game called out. "Ten pounds says the long Meg beats her," another cried, rubbing his hands.

By the time Alex reached them, Chamberlain was between the two combatants, attempting to end the contest, which had gone decidedly in Joss's favor by virtue of her longer reach. Cybill's black hair hung in clots about her shoulders and the delicate muslin of her gown was torn in several places, revealing even more of her charms. The heavy gray worsted Joss wore remained unscathed but for a liberal coat of mud.

"Hardly Christian charity, Joss," Alex said with a chuckle as he placed one arm about her waist and swung her away from Cybill, who then collapsed in sobs on her husband's chest, smearing his splendid uniform with mud, much to his consternation.

The Chamberlains' angry remonstrances faded as Alex guided Joss away from the crowd. Poc, having had his way with the small fluffy Jezebel, trailed jauntily behind them, dragging his leash. "I realize Cybill is a bit less than civil, but did you have to exact such a harsh penalty?" he asked with amusement.

Joss hiccuped in silent misery, too humiliated to speak. She was covered with mud from head to foot and had behaved like a Billingsgate fishwife. Her father was already greatly upset that she had accompanied a rakehell to a place of iniquity. What would he say when she was forced to explain how she had come to be in this wretched state? Yet clouding her concern for the reverend was the closeness of Alex, whose laughing eyes observed her, waiting for her reply. "It seems every time we meet, calamity ensues," she finally managed glumly. "Perhaps 'tis a sign from heaven that our friendship is doomed."

"More like a sign that you have as great a penchant for attracting trouble as do I," he said with a crooked grin.

When he smiles, celestial choirs must sing, she thought. "I do not believe so. You've just won a horse race and managed to stay clean and dry until you rescued me. I am the one who is always in trouble. I've ruined your clothes and kept you from collecting your winnings."

"These buckskins have seen a lot of red Georgia clay. They'll wash out easily enough. Now as to the colonel's uniform . . ." He looked merrily over at Chamberlain and chuckled.

"He is rather wilted, isn't he?" Joss responded to his good humor in spite of herself. Just then Poc nudged her knee with his head and she looked down. "There you are, you wretched instigator. 'Twas your fault, all of this—you and that shameless little hussy," she said, looking on as Cybill instructed an unhappy footman to pick up the now brown Bonbon.

"Are you referring to the Maltese or her mistress?" Alex asked.

Rupert Chamberlain heard their peals of laughter as he attempted to straighten his ruined uniform. He owed that graceless, insolent colonial two thousand pounds, a bloody fortune! With all Cybill's profligate spending, his officer's pay and the modest income from his estate did not begin to cover their expenses. He was in the utterly untenable position of having to offer his vowel to Blackthorne until he could borrow the money from a ten-in-the-hundred in Exchange Alley.

Cursing his incredible ill luck, he hastily scrawled a marker for two thousand pounds. His footman took it over to Blackthorne, who gave him a curt nod of acknowledgement. At some point he and the American would have a reckoning for this embarrassing loss of face . . . and other matters, Chamberlain thought, glancing back at his wife with slow-burning irritation. He had never minded her dalliances with high-ranking cabinet officials and army officers. Such was an acceptable means of advancing his career. But her fascination for a mixed-blood colonial was quite simply intolerable. He would put a stop to it one way or the other.

"Now queue up, children, and remember, when we go into the garden you must all remain together. Mr. Perkins was most kind to pay our admission, so if we wish to be invited again, we must behave." Joss looked from one small scrubbed face to another as she admonished her charges. How pale and thin they were, their eyes large and shining with excitement. For these children from the East End slums, an afternoon in Vauxhall Gardens was like a journey to paradise.

Andrew Chase Perkins, a member of the Missionary Society and an affluent coal merchant, had offered to do a kindness for the children in her school. Since Alex's money had already provided for books and lunches, she decided a field outing to the fabled park would be an acceptable luxury. Now seeing the autumn sunshine warm on their chalk-white little faces, she knew she had made the right choice.

As she ushered her charges through the gates, Joss was

aware of the hostile disdain of the attendant collecting the money. She had ignored his snide comment about turning loose a pack of flash-house cutpurses on the better sort in the gardens, although she itched to wipe that sour smirk off his face with a good set-down. Why of late was her behavior so impatient and frustrated, her sense of propriety and charity for human foibles so diminished?

Alex would have taken this rude pipsqueak and set him on his ear. The thought came suddenly and she knew the reason for her growing malaise. Alex. Her friendship with the American was both the balm and bane of her life. She enjoyed talking with him, exchanging ideas and sharing laughter. His confidences regarding the quirks of his sisters, nieces and nephews, and his parents' hopes for his own marriage were bittersweet intimations of what it would be like to belong to a large and loving family.

A family from which she would be forever excluded. Alex's friendship was all she could ever aspire to, she continually reminded herself. Yet his way of looking at society, his whole free-thinking philosophy of life, unbound by rules of class and decorum, swept like a clean, rain-washed wind through her staid existence. She chafed under the strictures of society in ways she never had before she met him.

The children's exclamation over the statuary and paintings called her attention back to the matter at hand and she began to instruct them. "That figure is a most famous composer. Can anyone tell me his name?" Several eager hands were raised. "Yes, Charles?"

"Handel, mum. I read the nameplate," the seven-year-old said proudly.

Joss commended him and continued pointing out various things, noting joyously that her small band was enraptured by the nine-hundred-foot-long avenue of elms and the incredibly realistic painting of ancient Near Eastern ruins. These children had never seen any more trees than grew on one of the small city lots of the rich. No green space at all existed in the noisome warrens of stone and wood where they themselves abided. She and her small clutch of chicks made their way down the grand walk, ogling the sights and the occasional elegantly dressed "better sorts" who frequented the garden. Because it was afternoon, the number of strollers was small, for the Quality did not usually deign to turn out until after fashionable five when the evening musical entertainment and fireworks took place. The gardens were open late and revelers often picnicked and held assignations until three A.M.

"Ooh, lookit, Annie, that lady's dress!" little Maggie Warren whispered to her companion. "She ain't got 'ardly a thing over 'er bosoms."

Joss followed her pupil's wide-eyed gaze. The object of the child's attention was obviously one of the demimonde, with brassy yellow hair and heavy face paint. Although cut low to display her ample charms, the round neck of the satin gown was no more scandalous than those worn by women of the upper ten thousand. The children of the slums were quite familiar with prostitutes, albeit not as clean and well turned out as these. Joss quickly guided their attention elsewhere.

The gardens were unfortunately used by Cyprians displaying their wares and rich young toffs who were shopping—or showing off their latest light-skirts. Joss had heard of the regrettable practice, but in the Great Wen, there was nowhere outside of church to escape the pervasive influence of vice. All she could do was to arm the youthful innocents with education and Christian morality.

The children skipped along the wide walk toward the grove where an immense colonnade sheltered a hundred supper boxes. Since one of these meals al fresco cost a whole shilling, Joss planned only to allow the children to see the murals on the back walls. By then it would be time to begin the long journey back to the East End. As they neared the colonnade Joss froze in midstride, and one of the children stepped on her heels, almost tripping her.

"Beg pardon, mum," Billy said, red-faced. "I weren't watchin' my way."

"No, no, it's all right, Billy."

But it was not all right, not all right at all, for there, strolling into one of the supper boxes was Alex and the most stunning redhead Joss had ever seen. Her fiery tresses and milk-white skin were set off by a gown of deep green silk. An emerald the size of a pigeon egg winked from the deep vale of her cleavage, no doubt a gift from the golden-haired man whose swarthy face she was caressing in a wanton public display.

Joss castigated herself for seven kinds of a fool. She knew the sorts of assignations that went on here, and in her heart of hearts she knew, too, that Alex would bring his latest bit-o-muslin here. After all, weren't his exploits among the demimonde touted by every scandal sheet in London? *I'm making a complete cake of myself.*

She tried to hurry the children along before he noticed her gawking like a mooncalf. Yet when he threw back his head and laughed at some bon mot of his companion, then took her hand and pressed the bare palm intimately to his lips, Joss could not seem to look away. What must it feel like, his breath hot against her skin, the pressure of his mouth warm and firm . . . did he touch her palm with his tongue? Joss's face flooded with rosy color at such an indelicate and shockingly lascivious thought. Where had it come from? What had Alexander Blackthorne done to the staid, sensible woman she had been? He had turned her world upside down and he did not even know it, damn the man!

While Joss stood mired in inner turmoil, several of the more adventurous boys, chafing under the strain of behaving for so long, took advantage of the schoolmistress's inattention. Billy Ballum took a small red ball from his pocket and showed it to Pug Wilson.

"Where'd you nick that?" Pug asked, reaching for the well-worn yet coveted toy.

"I didn't nick it. I found it," Billy whispered righteously. "In a wagonload of trash behind some banker's 'ouse, I did."

"Lemme see it," Pug demanded, being the bigger and older of the two.

"It's mine," Billy said, bouncing the ball defiantly under Pug's nose. When he tried to repeat the trick, Pug's hand snaked out and snatched at it, knocking it from Billy's grasp. The ball went bouncing erratically down the smooth surface of the walk. "Cor, see what you done," he cried, dashing to retrieve his lost treasure with Pug right behind him.

Billy ran with his eye fixed on the ball to the exclusion of all else. Just as he bent down and scooped up his toy, Pug overran him and they both went flying headfirst into a couple strolling on a crossing walk. The woman escaped untouched with a squeak of outrage, but the man bore the full force of the collision, stumbling back with a snarled oath. He quickly regained his footing and glared at the two ragged street urchins sprawled in the grass. They looked at his angry face guiltily, then began to scramble away in terror when he pulled a sword from the scabbard at his waist and swung the flat of the blade at them.

"What the deuce are you gutter-scum jackanapes doing here? The park is for your betters, you filthy little wharf rats!"

Pug succeeded in escaping their tormentor with only one stinging blow across his back, but Billy was not so fortunate. The officer seized his frayed coat collar and yanked him back, raising the sword to deliver more punishing blows.

Hearing the boy's frantic cries, Joss looked down the

walk. Pug dashed into her arms, sobbing, "We didn't mean no 'arm, mum, honest! We wuz chasin' the ball—it's all me fault 'e dropped it!"

Joss instructed him to stand perfectly still, then raced toward the ugly scene. Good heavens above, the brute was beating the boy half to death! "Stop this instant, sir!" she cried out, picking up her skirts to run headlong, terrified that the blade might accidentally turn and cut the boy. "In the name of Christian charity, stop!" Joss screamed, reaching up to grab hold of the officer's sword arm when he raised it for another blow. That was when she recognized those cold yellow eyes.

Alex witnessed the commotion from his box on the gently sloping rise. "Chamberlain, you brutal bastard," he muttered as he vaulted over the side of the box and took off down the hill, leaving the redhead staring, her mouth a startled O.

Joss hung like a bulldog on Chamberlain's arm while he tried in vain to shake her off and at the same time keep his hold on the sobbing boy. "Get the bloody hell off of me, you half-blind bitch," Chamberlain yelled as he slammed Billy's squirming body into Joss.

"Thrashing women and little boys hardly seems the thing for a sporting fellow such as you, Colonel," Alex said in a deceptively soft voice. His grip on Chamberlain's arm, however, was as hard as iron.

Chamberlain released Billy, shoving him at Joss, who stumbled back, breathless from her exertions. She knelt and took him in her arms, soothing him as she glared up at the angry bully.

"I should have expected you'd materialize to champion your unlikely damsel in distress again. Tell me, do all colonials have your execrable taste in women?" Sir Rupert asked with an arrogant lift of his chin.

"In America, gentlemen respect women—or pay the consequences," Alex replied levelly, knowing he was being provoked and deliberately returning the insult.

"Really, I doubt there's been a gentleman set foot on that barbarous soil since General Cornwallis sailed in eighty-one," Chamberlain drawled.

"As I recall"—the young American smiled—"he did not really set sail. He set his tail between his legs and slunk back to his kennel. Perhaps you would do well to emulate his example."

Chamberlain's face, already flushed, turned almost purple. "If it were not for the vast chasm that exists between our social stations, I . . ."

"Ah, yes, the famous code duello. I've heard of it," Alex said dryly, then paused. "If you're too cowardly to challenge a savage red Indian . . ." He shrugged insultingly and turned to help Joss to her feet. Chamberlain's slap stung the edge of his cheekbone. "I shall instruct my second to meet with yours this evening—that is, if you have a friend to stand by you in all of London."

Joss gasped. Sir Rupert Chamberlain was one of the most feared duelists in all of England. "No, Alex, please don't do this."

Chapter Seven

Alex stroked his chin, grinning wickedly at Drum, who had agreed to act as his second.

"As the man challenged, you have the choice of weapons. Given that Sir Rupert is reputed to be a dead shot at forty yards and Domenico Angelo's finest fencing student, I doubt pistols or foils would be wise selections," Drum replied dryly. "Of course, you could choose muskets or war clubs . . ." he added, arching one delicately thin eyebrow mockingly, then continued, "but after seeing your back-alley performance the night we met, I rather thought you would fancy my suggestion. Since you were that lethal foxed, I suspect you'll acquit yourself against the colonel well enough sober."

"I'll take care of Chamberlain. The devil of it is I haven't the vaguest idea why he's taken such a personal dislike to me."

"Heigh ho! You've only trounced him at the racecourse, had his wife fair slobbering on your breeches and then publicly accosted him in Vauxhall. Can't think of a reason on earth he should dislike you." Drum's expression was guilelessly somber.

"It's more than that. At our first introduction the fellow was insufferably rude, even by the obnoxious standards of haughtiness among the peerage. He goaded me into offering a wager higher than he thought I could afford."

"Obviously that chamber pot didn't expect to lose. I've heard rumors he's been out at heels ever since he ran through his wife's dowry."

"A rather common practice among the ton, I gather," Alex said sardonically, thinking of the odious relationship between Monty and Octavia. He could not resist a grinning jab at his friend. "You're always in dun territory, Drum. Ever think of leg-shackling yourself to a wealthy heiress?"

Drum clutched his throat with a look of mock horror. Then he carefully laid out a precise pinch of snuff on the back of his wrist and raised it to his nostrils, saying, "I never much fancied the fairer sex. A voluptuous pair of teats never had the same effect on me they most obviously do on you, old chap. But at times I envy your appetites." He met Alex's dark eyes and the two men exchanged a look of understanding.

After inhaling the snuff, Drum sneezed delicately into his handkerchief and went on briskly, "You must be careful of Chamberlain—he is a deadly adversary, battle hardened with ice-cold nerve. But you'll have to disable the bastard without killing him."

Alex looked puzzled. "I'd be better served to kill him and have done. He's not a chap to forgive an enemy."

"Kill a peer of the realm and you'll hang at Newgate," Drum said flatly. "Dueling, even though it's practiced, is quite illegal in this, the center of civility. Sir Rupert has powerful friends in the military, not to mention the foreign office."

"And as a crude colonial interloper, I wouldn't stand a chance of escaping the noose." Alex nodded. "Then I shall have to be doubly wary, else my rather enjoyable life in England will be over."

"In England or anywhere else. Never underestimate the gravity of this situation, or Sir Rupert. Oh, by the by, I have a particular suggestion about how to approach this contest. I shall explain it tomorrow en route. Heigh-ho, I'm off to meet with the colonel's second. The arrangement should be for dawn tomorrow at Chalk Farm."

"Dawn?" Alex echoed balefully.

"It's the done thing, old fellow, the done thing," Drum said placatingly.

A sudden spring storm blew up during the night, soaking the dueling ground, but by the time Alex and Drum rode up, the sky was clearing, with the mauve streaks of dawn giving way to bright pinks and yellows. They waited for Chamberlain, who appeared with his second a few moments later just as a third rider came up on the road. When he dismounted and joined the group, Drum introduced Alex, saying, "This is Sir Reginald Thompson."

Alex nodded and they shook hands gravely. The man had a reputation for impartiality and a rigorous adherence to the code in many such matters of honor.

The small group gathered in the open clearing to review the preliminary rules already agreed upon. *What a surprise stiff old Reggie will have when I open this case,* Drum thought to himself. *Pray God the idea goes off as we planned it.*

The early morning silence was again broken when a hired hackney clattered up the road and lurched to a halt.

"What the devil?" Chamberlain said, his expression suddenly tense. This was his third duel in two years and General Pelton had cautioned him against any further sanguinary pursuits off the battlefield.

A dark-garbed female of uncommon height climbed from the coach before the driver could assist her. She thrust some coins in his hand and made her way swiftly to where the men were standing.

Five pairs of hostile eyes fastened on her as she approached. Alex looked positively thunderous. "Joss," he exclaimed with an oath, "what the hell are you doing here?"

She squared her chin resolutely and swallowed. "Rumor of this duel has spread all over London. You must call it off before the constabulary comes to arrest you."

"Nonsense. I've officiated at numerous such occasions," Sir Reginald replied indignantly. "The authorities will not interfere in an affair of honor."

"I suggest, Mistress Woodbridge, that you attend to those wretched urchins you allow to run wild and leave this matter to be settled by men," Chamberlain said coldly.

Joss ignored the haughty Englishman, keeping her eyes on Alex's hostile face. "I'm not leaving without you. Besides, the hackney is gone."

"You look sturdy enough of limb to walk," Drum ventured with a scathing glance up and down her frame.

"I feel I was to blame for this whole debacle since it was one of my children who precipitated the incident. I have a right to be here, Alex. Besides, I've brought medical supplies—a habit I've acquired since making your acquaintance," she added, stubbornly ignoring Drum just as she had the others.

Alex's furious expression eased. "Your skill with a needle and thread may well be necessary before long." His eyes swept over Chamberlain grimly, then returned to her. A grin spread across his face. "Just stand back and keep quiet, Joss. I know you don't faint at the sight of blood . . . but you might keep an eye on Mr. Drummond."

"I shall deal with you later for that most ill-conceived bon mot," Drum replied dryly as he produced a wooden weapons case of proportions sufficient to contain sabers. When he opened the lid, Chamberlain's second, a hard-faced major named Brighton, muttered a ripe curse and glared at Alex.

"What the hell do you mean by this, sirrah?" he asked.

Thompson, too, seemed taken aback, but he held his peace.

"It would appear he means to carve up your fellow officer, old chap," Drum replied cheerfully.

Nestled inside the velvet-lined case were two wickedly gleaming, long-bladed, ivory-handled . . . chef's knives. Alex gestured for Chamberlain to select one. "I believe it's customary for the challenger to choose first," he said, the soul of courtesy.

Holding up one of the long, razor-sharp blades, Chamberlain said, "This is not a dueling weapon! Why, all it's fit for is to split a capon."

"How observant you are, Sir Rupert," Alex replied, taking the other blade from the case.

Chamberlain's face reddened at the insult. Then he smiled coldly and said, "It's perhaps not all that different from a foil that I cannot use it to serve you up a brochette, you crude colonial mongrel."

Alex raised his blade in a mocking salute and clicked his heels. Both men stood silently as Thompson outlined the rules previously agreed upon by their seconds. "You shall fight until one combatant draws first blood or cries off. Thus shall honor be satisfied."

Honor! Joss fumed silently. Men were such idiots. And whatever on earth were Alex and that odious Mr. Drummond thinking about, using carving knives, for pity's sake!

After a brief conference between Chamberlain and his second, the major turned and said stiffly, "My principal is ready."

Alex watched Drum's mask of indolence slide back into place, as the smaller man turned to announce over his shoulder. "Thank God. You were taking so long my man almost dozed off."

The combatants and their seconds walked toward each other and halted a few feet apart in front of the elderly official. The man intoned, "Seconds, please take your places alongside me. Very good. Gentlemen," he addressed the duelists, "the contest will commence when I give the word. Understood?"

Alex nodded, but Chamberlain fixed the old fellow with a haughty stare. "My good man, I have heard the litany many times before, and I expect I will hear it many times in future—although I suppose it is a good thing for this young savage to hear it this once. I assure you, he shall never hear it again."

In one variation or another, Chamberlain had rattled opponents before with this taunt. He was more than a bit nettled when he turned his gaze on his young antagonist and saw Blackthorne grinning like a wolf . . . a very eager wolf.

The old man stepped back. "All right gentlemen, *en garde!*"

Chamberlain gracefully assumed a fencer's posture—right foot forward, the left a bit behind, both knees slightly bent. His right elbow was almost resting on his right hip as the tip of his blade pointed at his opponent. Alex dropped into a knife-fighter's crouch and began circling to his right.

The Englishman scoffed, "Pray tell, boy, do all of you savages fight humped over like dog-apes?"

Alex did not waste his breath on a reply as he circled, determining his strategy. With an expert's economy of movement, Chamberlain shifted slightly to keep the tip of his blade fixed on the younger man. Then, the young fool committed the mistake that the seasoned duelist knew he would make, sooner or later. Blackthorne moved into range. Chamberlain executed the perfect lunge that could have driven the tip of his blade into the young clod's throat. But as the Englishman's arm fully extended, the "young clod" twisted to his own right and swung the razor-keen chef's knife in an upward slash and then down again in a movement almost too quick for the onlookers to follow. As Chamberlain gasped in agonized surprise, Alex stepped back.

The knife dropped from the Englishman's useless hand—tendons, muscles and artery had been severed to the bone just a few inches above his wrist.

Joss bit her lip to keep from screaming. What if it had been Alex?

As if Thompson were a croupier at a hazard table, he announced in a professionally dispassionate voice, "First blood. The contest is finished."

Chamberlain's voice was shrill. "I'll be demned if it is. I can continue." He was attempting to squeeze off the blood spurting from his wound with his left hand, while trying to pick up the knife with his right.

Both seconds had moved closer and were watching the grotesque fumbling. Drummond's voice broke the silence. He sounded for all the world as if he were discussing a guest's boorish table manners. "I say, Chamberlain old fellow, this really is not the thing. Your fingers are as limp and floppy as uncooked sausages. Please do stop that groping. 'Tis most unsightly."

The wounded man cursed and tried clumsily to pick up the knife with his left hand. Sir Reginald moved forward and placed his foot on the blade. "Give over, sir. You are incapable of continuing. The duel is concluded."

"Humanely done, sir," Drum approved. "Humanely done. It would be beastly if my principal had to disable the chap's other hand. A gentleman with *two* useless hands! How would he ever take his snuff? He'd have to stick his nose in the box and snort, like one of those French pigs rooting up truffles. Would never do."

Joss, who had been standing frozen at the sidelines, at last reacted to the little dandy's flippant remarks. "A man has his lifeblood pumping out onto the ground and you prattle about snuff!" she admonished, brushing past him to where Chamberlain slumped in a sitting position on the turf, his face chalk white, the glaze of shock unmistakable in his eyes. "I am trained as a surgeon's assistant. Let me help," she said to the major, who knelt beside his friend.

"Get away from me, you bitch," Chamberlain snarled, but his voice was thready and his breathing labored.

"He'll bleed to death if I don't tie off those vessels," she said to Major Brighton, ignoring the colonel's venom.

Having spent years on the battlefields of Europe, the man knew she was right. "Rupert, you'll die if we don't stop the bleeding."

Before the argument could proceed further, Chamberlain obligingly passed out. Joss set to work, opening the bag she had brought with her and laying out her equipment on a clean white cloth, all the while issuing instructions to the major about applying a tourniquet.

While Joss and the major administered to Chamberlain, Alex and Drum walked with Reginald Thompson to where the horses were tied some distance away. Alex held the old man's mount as he swung into the saddle with surprising agility. Then Thompson looked down at Blackthorne.

"I have never seen the like of this duel, sir. Demndest thing ever, but your performance was honorable . . . if a trifle unorthodox." With that stiff pronouncement, he rode away.

"Unorthodox," Alex snorted. "Chef's knives are that, I warrant. Why the devil did you pick them?" he asked Drum.

"Had to have a matched set and that marvelous pig sticker of yours will never see its like on this side of the Atlantic. On such short notice, the knives were all I could find. The cutlery was adequately large and sharp and available . . . and you owe me twenty-five pounds, old chap."

Alex threw back his head and laughed. "And most probably my life as well, dear Drum." He sobered then, looking across the clearing to where Joss worked intently over the unconscious Chamberlain. "I still think it's dangerous to leave such an implacable enemy alive. He shall hate you as much as he does me."

"That walking chamber pot has already been my enemy for years."

"But the colonel gave no indication he even knew you," Alex replied, puzzled as well as startled by his friend's cold, cutting words.

"He does not know me. We shared a mutual . . . acquaintance several years ago. We were very close, that fellow and I. Then I was sent off by my family to the Continent. The tour thing, you know. When I returned, I learned that my friend had called Chamberlain out." Drum swallowed and his voice was choked with emotion. "Poor dear Heath, the kindest, gentlest man I've ever known. It was little more than an assassination really. He never stood a chance against the colonel."

Drum paused and when he continued his story, he was once again the flippant dandy. "Now then, Alex, had I been a gallant fool such as my friend, I would have called out Chamberlain myself. You see, I am far better with a foil than you will ever be, but not as good as Chamberlain. Or it could have been pistols. I suspect, my dear wild Indian, that I am also a better pistol shot than you. But still not as good as Chamberlain. I would have died and Heath would not have been avenged.

"So, I waited and watched as the bully swaggered through the best houses in the city. Most men are afraid of him—the few who were not he dispatched with foils or pistols. He relished the formalized butchery far more than he ever did fighting on a battlefield." Drummond's tone had grown increasingly harsh as he told his story to Alex. He seemed exhausted by the venting of so much violent emotion.

Alex stood quietly, then said, "I wish I could have chopped the vicious bastard into fish bait."

"Better this way, my friend," Drum replied in a low, deadly voice. "Now he will learn to chew fear. Legions of men about town will think nothing of taking their walking sticks to him should he dare show his face in any of his old haunts. That hand of his, so feared by so many, will never kill again. Limp and numb it may be now, but in time it will wither and gnarl into a pain-wracked claw, as ugly and twisted as the soul in his filthy body. I hope he lives a long while before a friend of one of his victims kills him, but I fear he has so many enemies he won't last long."

Drummond's eyes glittered in a face that hatred and relived grief had stretched into a satanic mask. Then the expression faded as he turned to Alex with a suddenly stricken look on his face. "I never intended to use you to exact revenge, my friend. I do hope you believe that."

"Considering the circumstances that caused Sir Rupert to challenge me, there is no way you could have had a hand in it—Joss's children were the immediate catalyst. I plead guilty to insulting him into the challenge, but the colonel did go out of his way to provoke me."

"You were an unusual victim, I suspect. He would have enjoyed the sport of toying with you before he dispatched you . . . had you given him the opportunity to use his foil against you."

"So that's why you instructed me to slash that way," Alex replied.

Drum nodded. "Your blade severed muscle, tendons, blood vessels, all. The good Miss Woodbridge can keep the chamber pot alive but no one can repair the hand."

Joss approached them carrying her medical bag. "I've done what I can. He won't bleed to death. The major is going to remain with Sir Rupert, but someone needs to ride posthaste and summon a carriage to convey him to hospital." She looked from Alex to Drum.

The little dandy sighed theatrically. "Very well, I suppose it behooves me to ride pell-mell to summon a hackney, a better alternative than carrying you on my horse, Miss Woodbridge. I should hate to stain my new doeskins," he said, eyeing her skirt, which was smeared with blood and liberally caked with dirt from where she had knelt on the ground.

"Far be it from me to mar your sartorial splendor, Mr. Drummond," Joss replied with overly dulcet civility.

"Your servant, Miss Woodbridge," Drum replied, sketching a bow before he turned to Alex. "You will be all the go at Watiers before midafternoon. I shall expect to see you there for a friendly game of whist." With that he mounted his beautifully turned out little white Arabian and galloped down the road.

Alex observed Joss as she stared after Drum. "You'd best have a care. Your most un-Christian detestation is showing," he said with amusement.

Her cheeks crimsoned. "I know. I can't seem to help it," she replied impenitently.

Alex swung up on his powerful blood roan with such fluid grace that Joss was reminded of a tawny golden lion she had once seen in a traveling circus. Her mouth went dry as dust when he extended his open palm to her. "Give me your satchel; then I'll help you mount," he said.

She stared dumbly for a moment before handing the bag up to him. Her heart hammered painfully in her chest and her breath hitched. *I shall make an utter cake of myself when he touches me,* she thought with a surge of panic as he leaned down, reaching out to her. "Really, Alex, I'm too heavy for you to whisk up in front of you. Let me try climbing up behind you."

He grinned. Skinny as Joss was, her weight would not present a problem. "I think I can manage to lift you. You're naught but skin and bones," he chided.

"N-no," she stuttered, backing away. Only part of her

110

fright came from fear of betraying her feelings once he held her in his arms. "I fear I must make a confession. I am terrified of horses."

He looked at her as if she had just announced she feared white bread. "You can't be serious. You, who calmly stitch up bleeding men and risk life and limb to save a pit dog?"

"Dogs are different," she replied irrationally. "I was almost trampled by a horse when I was a child."

"You never learned to ride at all?" he asked incredulously.

"Not at all. My father could scarcely afford the luxury of owning horses."

He chuckled in amazement. At last his fearless bluestocking revealed a chink in her resolute crusader's armor. "You should have considered how you'd get home before dismissing your coachman so precipitously."

"I was afraid if I did not, you'd send me packing with him."

That small statement of bravado touched him. "Come, Joss, I'll keep you from falling. Sumac doesn't bite, I promise."

Her fear stemmed only in part from an aversion to horses. "Very well," she replied, uncertainly. "My fate shall be in your hands."

A powerful arm encircled her waist as he swung her easily up in front of him and seated her across the saddle. How strong he was. Joss felt dwarfed by the breadth of his shoulders and strength of his arms reaching around her to hold the reins.

As he urged the roan into an easy canter, he murmured against her ear, "A good thing I decided to ride civilized today, not bareback." He sensed her stiffen with what he believed to be fright.

"If you'd ridden without a saddle, I should be walking home," she replied, her fingers clutching at the horse's mane until her knuckles turned white.

"My brave bluestocking. I can scarcely believe Sumac frightens you. He's gentle as a kitten."

Each time he spoke, she could feel a deep rumbling vibration in his chest. His breath was warm and sweet against her cheek. All she wanted on this earth was to turn and press her body tightly against him, to feel his mouth on her skin, his hands—no! She simply must stop thinking this way at once. He must never suspect what she felt.

Finding her voice, she replied, "More like this great red beast is Satan in horseflesh." As if to reward her, Sumac tossed his head and broke stride, nearly unseating her from her precarious perch. She gave a shriek of terror and threw her arms about Alex's neck.

His laughter rang out as he steadied the horse. "Your face is as red as his coat, Joss," he teased when she quickly withdrew her arms. "Don't be frightened of him and he won't be so nervous. All intelligent animals sense our feelings. You know that."

"I do not include horses in my catalogue of intelligent animals," she replied tartly. *Nor are you, my blind darling Alex, thank heavens!* If he had any inkling how his proximity disturbed her, he would have been horrified. She was so grateful for the stallion's diversion that she almost forgave the great beast for frightening her so much.

After all, he allowed you to hold Alex in your arms without betraying yourself, an invidious voice whispered in her ear. She repressed the thought and stared at the road ahead.

Alex also turned his attention to the road, brushing aside a vague thought that had only partially emerged in his consciousness. When Joss had clung to him, she did not feel at all as skinny as she looked in her hideous gown.

Chapter Eight

The juicy scandal over Alex's crippling of the infamous Colonel Chamberlain was displaced by early summer when Sir Rupert mysteriously dropped from sight and the Prince Regent threw his first big ball at Carleton House. The press was so great that waiting coaches backed up for miles, allowing the great unwashed to throng the streets, ogling the Quality who impatiently awaited their turn at the royal trough.

Alex received an invitation but declined to attend, preferring to spend his time in pursuit of carnal gratification. He and a beguiling Cyprian named Solange dined in Vauxhall Gardens and returned to her apartments for a sybaritic evening of delight.

Joss worked diligently at the charity hospital and her school, to which Alex had become a generous patron. The Reverend Elijah Woodbridge was gratified by the support, which he attributed to divine intervention. Joss omitted telling him it was more directly attributable to Alex's luck at the gaming tables. She knew she should approve no more of his vices than her father would—had he known. But she could not condemn him since the money certainly was used for the highest good. In her more honest moments, Joss admitted that any reason that brought Alex to visit her was sufficient to overcome her scruples.

Their friendship—and her one-sided love—grew as summer melted into the fall of 1811. But with the return of chill rain and dreary skies came yet more gloomy news from America. Alex sat before a crackling fire in the Woodbridge's spartan apartment, and disconsolately handed Joss the letter written on black-bordered stationery. His father's bold scrawl contrasted with his mother's flowing script on the pages, but the gist of both messages was the same.

"It would seem I must repair myself to Bertram Therlow's lair posthaste and learn how to keep accounts." He shuddered with loathing as he took another sip from the steaming mug of liquid Joss had brewed for him, uncertain which was worse—the prospect of becoming a man of business or the taste of her fowl nostrum for overindulgence.

Joss quickly scanned the missive. "How tragic for your sister to be widowed at such a young age. It would seem her husband Tobias was much relied upon by your father."

"Toby was a right enough chap, I suppose, even if he didn't approve of me." He sighed and took another swallow, admitting, "Perhaps *because* he didn't approve of me. I grieve more for Mellie than Toby. What a senseless way to die, tripping and striking his head against a hearthstone."

Joss observed his bleak expression and knew he did indeed grieve for his elder sister. He had come to her that morning after a night spent drowning his sorrows in drink. The harsh realities of life were finally catching up with her carefree rake. "Now your father has no one else to rely upon but you. It's time to take responsibility, Alex."

He looked up at her balefully. "I am all too well aware of that fact. Drat, but Toby loved bookkeeping as much as

I abhor it. Drum advised me to break with my family and make my way as a gambler."

"Leave it to Mr. Drummond to suggest such a despicable thing," she sniffed.

"I've been living on my winnings. I could do it . . ."

"But you won't," she replied resolutely.

He smiled ruefully at her. "I have an appointment with old Bertie this afternoon to begin my apprenticeship."

"Your family shall be exceedingly proud of you."

"That remains to be seen. I'm not at all adept at figures—unless they're swathed in muslin and lace."

"You shall do splendidly. I'm certain of it, but spending your nights drinking and gambling must cease."

"Right now I couldn't agree with you more. Lud, I'm always penitent the morning after I've tipped too many. What is in this noisome concoction?" he asked, inspecting the dregs clotted in the bottom of the cup with bloodshot eyes.

"Gingerroot, calomel powders and Saint-John's-wort steeped in black pekoe tea. My father gives it to men he ministers to in the streets who have passed out from drunkenness."

"As a penance for their sins, I don't doubt."

Poc chose that precise moment to burst into the room, his nails clicking across the bare wooden floor as he sprinted up to Alex, tail wagging, barking his welcome.

To forestall any further outbursts, Alex quickly reached down and thumped the terrier affectionately on his sides, then closed his eyes and whispered, "Softly, old boy, softly, lest you shatter my skull with another bark."

As Alex alternately scowled at the dog, then at her, Joss almost smothered her chuckle. "The wages of sin may not always be death, but they are painful."

"At the moment, I am more afraid I shall live than I should be to die and have done," he croaked.

"Here, let me," Joss said. Stepping over Poc, she walked

around the table and stood behind Alex. "Papa often has the headache after he's exerted himself too greatly. I've learned how to ease it a bit."

Her hands with their long slender fingers were cool and clever, soothing away the pounding ache in his skull, which felt as if General Massena's artillery were bombarding it. "Joss, Joss, what would I do without you?"

She closed her eyes, feeling the warmth of his skin and the thick spring of his hair beneath her hands. When he murmured his low rhetorical question, she looked down at the broad expanse of his shoulders and felt such a rightness in the simple act—as if they were long and comfortably married and she performed a wifely task. The fire crackling in the hearth and Poc lying at Alex's feet all presented a warm homey picture. *Pretty daydreams,* she scolded herself, yet she could not break free of the magic of touching him. There were so few opportunities for touching and she craved it so. She only prayed that she would never slip and reveal her true feelings.

"Ah, that is easing. Thank you, Joss," he said at length, taking one of her hands in his and giving it an affectionate pat as he turned on the chair and smiled up at her. Her nails were cut sensibly short and her skin was chapped and red. Scarce the hands of a lady, yet her ancestry was betrayed in their grace and delicacy.

"You work too hard, Joss," he chided.

She gave her best grin and replied teasingly, "And so shall you—starting this very afternoon." Then a thought struck her and the smile vanished. "You—you wouldn't have to return to America because of business, would you? I mean, anytime soon?" She'd always known sooner or later he must go home.

"Not for now. I need to learn the shipping business, but I can do that quite well from this end."

Poc rose from his slumber on the floor and trotted over to the sitting room door, then gave a low growl of warning.

"Who on earth could it be? He only growls at strangers," Joss said, moving toward the door.

Alex's hand stayed her. "Wait. Let me see who it is." He stood up and walked across the wooden floor noiselessly as the slow, clomping footfalls rose higher up the stairs. From below he could hear Aunt Regina calling out, "I never give ye permission to go abovestairs, Lem Smiley!"

Lem, a portly, balding man with the florid face of one who imbibes frequently, ignored her, huffing noisily until he reached the top of the stairs. Then he peered up and down the hall with myopic eyes shaded by drooping lids. "I be lookin' fer Mistress Woodbridge, the reverend's daughter," he called out.

"You know the fellow?"

"He's one of the men my father's aided at his mission." She elbowed her way past Alex as the old man turned toward the sound of her voice.

"Oh, Mistress Woodbridge, I . . ." A great sob wracked his body as he stopped in the hallway with a hat crumpled in two meaty red fists.

An icy premonition washed over her as she strode to Lem and took his arm, guiding him into the apartment. "What is it, Mr. Smiley?" she asked gently.

Assured that the stranger posed no threat, Poc stood quietly at Alex's side while Joss seated the old man at the table. Alex had inquired about the reverend upon arriving and Joss had informed him that her father was not at home. He often spent the night at the mission when there was a need. Now, seeing the look of desolation on Lem Smiley's face, Alex knew his news was dire. He moved to Joss's side as the old fellow gulped out his story.

"When 'e didn't come back to th' mission to preach last night like 'e said 'e would, we all searched. But it were too dark 'n th' charleys made us get off the streets. Ronnie Blevins found 'im, this mornin' mistress, down by th' docks."

117

"Is he injured? I must go to him," Joss said, turning frantically to fetch her cloak, but Alex's hands held her fast.

Looking at the woeful expression on Smiley's face, he asked gently, "The reverend is dead, isn't he, Lem?"

"Aye, sor, 'e is," the old man replied.

Joss saw black and red dots flash behind her eyes. She willed herself not to faint but was grateful for Alex's firm grip as he helped her onto a chair and knelt beside her. Her nails dug into his hand as she held it fiercely while gathering her scattered thoughts. "How did he die?"

Her calmness was belied by the death grip she held on his hand. Alex could feel the agony in her question as he tried to imagine his own feelings if Devon Blackthorne were the one found dead on the London docks. Remembering the two thugs who had tried to assassinate the preacher that day they met, he knew Elijah Woodbridge had not died of natural causes.

Lem verified his hunch. " 'E were coshed on th' 'ead, mistress, real 'ard. 'Is pockets picked clean, even thet fine old timepiece 'e loved so well."

"A gift from his grandmother, the only token he ever kept from his old life," Joss said quietly by way of explanation to Alex. "Papa loved her well. She was the only one who did not disown him."

"You shall have it back, Joss. I know 'tis not much in return for your loss, but all I can offer . . . that and my deepest sympathy. I'll find the men who did this and they shall pay."

Joss felt her eyes sting with tears but she blinked them back. There would be time enough for tears later, an ocean of them. "No, Alex, Papa would not have wanted you to seek revenge for his death."

"Not revenge, Joss, justice. Simple justice."

"You must not stain your hands with blood," she replied firmly.

"Do not distress yourself any further now. I want you to

lie down. I'll go with Lem and fetch your father's body for burial."

She shook her head. "No, no. I can't just sit here and do nothing. I'd go mad. I shall go with you. He would want to be taken to the mission. So many of the people he helped will come there."

"That they will, mistress, that they will," Lem echoed.

"Then it is settled," Joss replied firmly. Taking a deep breath, she stood up and smiled weakly at Alex. "I am so grateful for your help. Oh! But what about Mr. Therlow? Your appointment?"

"Bertie Therlow can wait for a few days more. You need me now, Joss."

You need me now, Joss. Joss sat staring into the dying fire in their rooms—her rooms, she corrected herself. Papa was gone. They had buried him that morning. She had indeed needed Alex to get through the ordeal. Hundreds of people from all across London's teeming slums had come to the mission to pay their last respects to the Reverend Elijah Woodbridge. She had received condolences until her hands ached from being clutched by so many anguished souls.

Throughout it all, Alex had stood by her side, a bulwark of strength and calm. Finally late that evening he had left when he received her promise that she would get some much-needed rest after the long and grueling ordeal of the wake and funeral. But sleep would not come. She huddled beneath the covers, shivering not from cold but from utter desolation. She was alone.

Now that her father was gone she had no one but Alex, and she could not further impose upon his friendship. He had a busy life and new responsibilities that called him. Of course, so did she—the hospital, the shelter, the school. But without the reverend's presence behind her work, she had already learned that much of her support was evaporating.

Yesterday the Society for Moral Rectitude had dolefully

informed her that a lone female could not possibly be placed in charge of the shelter. The same message had come from the mission board this very morning regarding the school. They both explained their decision in terms of utmost Christian charity, being ever so considerate of her frailty and grief. She must have time for a proper mourning. She must fall upon the bosom of her family for refuge and solace.

Her family. The noble Earl of Suthington and his brood of vipers who shared the Woodbridge name with her. Would that she had never heard of them! The earl did not deign to set his ermine-clad foot inside her father's humble mission. Instead he had sent his younger son Ernest to express the family's sympathies. Never was a man so misnamed. The mealymouthed, hypocritical fop had done little to conceal his distaste for the reverend's mission and the people he had served.

Ernest had explained in the most patronizing terms that his father, out of familial duty, would take her in. As if she were a child or an imbecile! Drawing on every ounce of patience she could muster, Joss had declined his offer. But that was before she learned that the various boards and societies who were willing to fund her father's work would not do the same for a lone female. The final blow had come only an hour ago when Aunt Regina, tearful and embarrassed, had informed her that she had a new tenant for the rooms.

Elijah Woodbridge had usually been behind in his rent, often giving away his meager stipend to feed or clothe someone less fortunate. The old landlady had been fairly patient while he lived. But now, hearing of his death, the tinner down the way made an inquiry regarding letting the apartment. He would pay half again as much as the reverend had.

Joss would have to go begging to the earl unless she found new quarters and some means of earning a livelihood. Her educational credentials were as impeccable as her moral character. She could become a governess, but the thought of tutoring the spoiled and horrid offspring of the nobility appalled her while so many bright and eager young minds among the poor starved for knowledge.

She could ask Alex for help and knew he would freely give it, but pride forbade her. She could not live off him like one of his Cyprians. At least he received services from them—services he would not want from a plain, gawky tabby like her.

You need me, Joss. How true it was and how utterly impossible, for the way in which she needed him had nothing to do with food and shelter or even friendship. She needed his love, the one thing her wonderful, wicked angel could never give her.

The flames in the fireplace had long since died to dimly glowing embers. Joss stared into them, trying to divine the future. Useless. Tomorrow she would figure out some way to continue her father's noble work. Perhaps a renewed appeal to the Society of Moral Rectitude would change their position. Failing that, she would simply have to swallow her pride and move to the Suthington city house. At least under the earl's protection, she might be able to persuade the board to renew support for the school. With that thought she drifted into a restless slumber punctuated by dreams of Alex.

Alex walked carefully, every sense alert as he made his way to the small shanty at the far end of the alley. Hidden in shadows, the dilapidated wooden shelter looked like little more than a lean-to or one of the insubstantial brush arbors the Muskogee built as temporary sleeping quarters for warm summer evenings.

"I say, old chap, do you think this John Slocum fellow will be lying about unawares, ripe for the plucking?" Drum asked Alex as they neared their destination.

"According to that charley Harry Wrexham, he's been holed up in there since the day after Reverend Woodbridge's murder."

The little dandy muttered a low oath as one faultlessly shined black Hessian sank into an oily black puddle of water. "Drinking up his pay, what?"

Alex nodded grimly. Acting on information he had wrung from Wrexham, he had already found Jem Barker, the rabble-rousing sailor from whom he had first rescued the Woodbridges last year. Having abandoned the seafaring life, Jem owned a half share in a brothel near the docks. He picked up additional pocket change kidnapping small boys for the sweep masters of the city. The reverend and his daughter had been bad for business.

Jem employed John Slocum, the red coated assassin who had made last year's unsuccessful attempt on the clergyman's life. Or Jem *had* employed Slocum. Since Alex had dealt him justice that morning, Jem would not be employing anyone. Before he died, Barker had given Alex and Drum the name of the man who'd actually done the foul deed.

Motioning for Drum to guard his back, Alex shoved open the door to the dark, smoky interior. The fetid sweetness of opium mingled with the raw, bitter tang of cheap gin and the musky odor of sex. "Celebrating, Mr. Slocum?" Alex inquired in a low, deadly voice as his eyes swept the filthy shanty's meager chairs and table and the bed upon which the killer sprawled with a fat slattern draped over his body.

Still wearing the same filthy red velvet coat he had sported the first time Alex had encountered him, Slocum stared at the intruder with glazed eyes. His slack mouth closed in an ugly sneer as he rolled up from the filthy rags covering the mattress. " 'Oo th' 'ell do ye think ye are, breakin' in on a man's pleasure?" he croaked in a smoke-roughened voice.

"I'd advise you to gather your clothes and get out of here before the trouble begins," Alex said conversationally to the whore, whose pockmarked face paled at the toff's cold eyes. Her body was covered with open sores from syphilis. Consorting with her would kill Red Coat in time, but Alex did not plan to grant John Slocum that time. She scooted hastily past him and out the door as the assassin shook his head to clear it of drink and drugs.

"Whot do ye think ye'r doin'?" Slocum asked with an oath as Alex began pulling open the drawers of a rickety chest and dumping the contents onto the splintery floorboards. Slocum slipped a knife from beneath a pile of rags by the side of his bed and lurched to his feet just as Alex finished perusing the contents of the bottom drawer. Before the tough could strike his back, Alex turned with lightning speed. His hand smashed Slocum's wrist against the wall with a sharp crack and the knife clattered to the floor.

Alex's own blade materialized in his other hand and now pressed uncomfortably against his foe's throat. "I want the timepiece."

"Whot timepiece?" Slocum croaked, stretching up on tiptoe against the wall to avoid the pressure from the gleaming steel.

"The gold one you took off the Reverend Woodbridge's body. 'Tis a family heirloom and his daughter wants it back. With your penchant for finery," Alex said with a disdainful glare at the louse-infested velvet jacket, "I assume you kept the timepiece to complement your sartorial splendor. Pray God you did not sell it . . . did you?" A single drop of bright red blood oozed beneath the blade and dribbled onto Slocum's greasy throat.

"Now, gov, I don't know nothin' 'bout—" His whining voice was cut short by increased pressure from the knife. Now several drops of blood ran free, staining the dingy ruffles of his shirtfront.

"You'd best answer truthfully. If I must, I'll extract the

information with this blade, and let me assure you, I've been taught to wield it with great skill by my family in America—my red Indian family. I know tricks that can keep you alive for days while you pray for death . . . you could ask Jem Barker . . . if he were still alive to answer."

"It's 'ere! I got it, gov. I—I'll give it over, only promise ye won't cut me." Slocum's eyes were totally focused now, all effects of the drugs and gin dissipated by stark terror.

"Very well, I give my word not to cut you," Alex said, releasing him. "Produce the timepiece."

From the doorway, Drum observed the exchange with one eye still on the alleyway outside. Slocum scrambled to the mattress and slipped his arm into a hole concealed in its side. When he pulled it out, the pocket watch gleamed softly in the dim light of the room's lone candle.

"Place it on the table," Alex commanded coldly. As soon as the assassin did so, he reached out with one hand and seized the man by his red coat, yanking him off his feet. When Slocum stumbled forward, Blackthorne's arms wrapped about his neck turning it with one powerful twist until it snapped. As the man dropped lifelessly at his feet, Alex said, "I promised I would not cut you, John, but not that I would spare you."

Drum watched him examine the gold timepiece, murmuring softly, "At least Joss will have this." He stood staring down at the inscription until the dandy cleared his throat and said gently, " 'Tis best we quit this place, Alex. Some of the denizens of this pesthole might try to relieve us of Slocum's ill-gotten gains."

Coming to himself, Alex placed the watch in his waistcoat pocket and turned to Drum. "Thank you, my friend, for assisting me in this ugly enterprise."

The two men walked away from the noisome alley without incident. Drum hailed a hackney and they climbed aboard. Alex remained deep in thought, staring down at the timepiece, which he had extracted from his pocket.

Drum studied his friend in silence for a moment, his keen green eyes riveted on Blackthorne. "Whatever the fascination of that bluestocking, she certainly has you in thrall," he commented, almost to himself.

Alex looked up distractedly, only half hearing Drum's remark. "Were you speaking of Joss?"

"Your very own prim long Meg . . . but considering your own estimable height—from which I would borrow a few inches were it possible—perhaps Miss Woodbridge is not so overtall." He stroked his chin in amusement, a wry smile bowing up his elegant lips. "Yes, you would make up a pair nicely."

"What on earth are you rattling on about?" Alex asked incredulously.

"Why, you and the preacher's daughter, of course," Drum replied innocently.

"As in a *love* relationship!"

Drum only nodded, then said, "My boy, I always *knew* you were an original. Now I have proof. You've fallen in love with a female for her *mind!*"

"Why, that's the most lack-witted, addlepated absurdity I've ever heard!"

Drum tsked chidingly. " 'Methinks the gentleman doth protest too much.' "

"I certainly do not." Alex replied indignantly, unaware that his hand clutched the timepiece tightly.

"If you squeeze that watch much harder, you're apt to melt the thing down to a shapeless lump, old chap," Drum said, pointing to his friend's hand.

Alex unclenched his fingers as if the timepiece had suddenly scalded him, and hastily replaced it in his waistcoat pocket. "Joss is my friend . . . an unconventional one, to be certain. Look, I understand that friendships between men and women are unusual—rare, even, yes, but Joss is just a comrade, someone I enjoy talking to and exchanging quips with. She is not some bloody bit of muslin, for heaven's sake!"

Drum waved one gloved hand in remonstrance. "No, no, my friend, I did not mean to imply such a transient, not to mention immoral, role for the prim Miss Woodbridge."

A look of dawning horror etched Alex's face. "A wife?" He practically choked on the words. Then looking again at Drum with narrowed eyes, he threw back his head and bellowed with laughter. "Lord, you bloody well had me going there for a while, Drum. The very idea that I would consider marriage at all is beyond absurd. If I wouldn't legshackle myself to Helen of Troy, why would I consider Joss, of all females?"

"Perhaps you'd best answer that question for yourself," Drum replied musingly.

Marry? Joss? Alex sat in the library of the Caruthers's city house, staring at the brandy snifter in his hand, deep in thought. He intended to deliver the timepiece to her in the morning, but first he had to muddle through his thoughts and set them in order. The fact that strong drink and clear thinking did not mix well had not occurred to him in this instance. The tall case clock on the far wall struck midnight.

He ruminated about his unusual relationship with Jocelyn Woodbridge. Drum's flippant remarks about his being in love with her were utterly preposterous, of course, typically Drum in one of his infernal hoaxing moods. Yet by the time they had parted company at the end of the hackney ride from Eastcheap, Drum had no longer been affecting droll humor.

Love Joss? Preposterous. Since the day they had met, his paramount urge had most often been to strangle the chit. Of course, he had come to admire her intelligence, her keen wit and gentle sense of humor, her courage, her compassion. In spite of her frequent clumsiness, she possessed a genuine grace for living. Even though she was tall, thin and forced to wear ugly, thick spectacles, he had never heard her complain about what nature had allotted her, except to make jokes at her own expense.

As time passed and their relationship developed, he had ceased to think about her unflattering appearance—unless someone else made a disparaging remark about it, which increasingly annoyed him. It was unfair to value a person only for how he or she looked on the outside. After all, it was one's mind and heart that truly gave one worth. That was a firm teaching of the Muskogee that he had learned at Grandma Charity's knee.

Joss's heart was good. She was brave, honest and caring. The thought that his grandmother would admire her had never occurred to him before. Unbidden, it did so now. But that was the stuff of friendship, not romantic love.

He loved her as he loved his sisters, who also frequently exasperated him. No, that was not quite right, for she was far stronger and more clearheaded than any of that flighty crew, more logical and intelligent—like his mother. But he certainly could not compare their relationship to the one he shared with his mother either. Joss was a friend who just happened to be a woman, that was all.

She was Joss. Dear and disheveled, truly an original . . . but a woman he would fall in love with? He shook his head, positive that was absurd. She would laugh at the idea— laugh at him for even thinking it. Joss had never evinced the slightest interest in playing silly games to catch a husband, any more than he wanted to dance to some female's whims to woo her to wife.

Alex never intended to marry. At least not in the foreseeable future. He had never given any real thought to the matter, save to dismiss the idea of a wife every time his parents brought it up. Now he forced himself to confront his feelings. Outside of his natural bachelor's affinity for unfettered access to the high life, he had no reason to dread matrimony.

Indeed, he had every reason to look forward to it if Devon and Barbara Blackthorne's happiness was an example. His entire family was riddled with felicitous marriages—Uncle Quint and Aunt Madelyne, as well as his sisters. Only his favorite cousin Beth, like him, resisted matrimony because she was determined to pursue an art career. Even her brother Rob had leg-shackled himself to the girl of his dreams.

Of course that was on the other side of the pond. Marriages here were usually arranged for political, social or economic reasons as had been the case in the unhappy union of Octavia and Monty. Yet he was forced to admit that it was not here in England that his aversion to marriage had originated. Deep in his heart he'd always shunned the idea. Why? He swirled the brandy about in his glass and took another sip. It was not the casual, unemotional relationships of the English that put him off, but rather the intense, passionate bonding that characterized the Blackthorne men that frightened him.

Although only whispered about, he knew the secret story of his great uncle Robert Blackthorne, who had been so in love with his wife, the beautiful Lady Anne Caruthers, that he had become insanely—and unjustifiably—jealous of his own brother. The rift had torn the family apart for a whole generation. Alex did not want to love that way. Or even the way his parents did. They were so devoted to each other, so intensely close that he had always felt . . . closed out somehow, a reaction to which his sisters had all been cheerfully immune. He alone, the only son, came to feel that he never wanted to be so wrapped up in a single person that his whole life was entrusted to her hands. What if something happened to her?

"I'm getting maudlin," he muttered to himself. This much introspection was simply not healthy for a man. Should he lay the fault at Drum's feet—or Joss's? He did not desire her, nor did he want her for a wife. He simply

128

loved Joss because she was Joss, and that was that, he concluded, downing the last of the brandy. He would ponder the nature of the relationship no further.

Montgomery Caruthers stood in the doorway, observing his nephew's brown study. He had just come from a winning night at White's card tables and was feeling expansive.

Demned if he had not become fond of the boy, even if he was a wild colonial, with an unorthodox ancestry on his father's side. Still, in a strange way, Alex had become his surrogate son, a fact he had never been able to confess to the lad. A pity he could not invest the Rushcroft title on Alexander Blackthorne. What a royal uproar that would cause about the ton!

Seeing his nephew begin to arise from the chair, he glided into the room. "Mind if I join you in a drink, my boy? You may pour . . . since it would appear you've already had ample practice tonight," he added, eyeing the nearly empty decanter of his best brandy.

Alex ignored the remark and rationed out the last of the amber liquid between two cut-crystal snifters. "You're out late."

"You're in early," Monty countered. "I must say you've exceeded even my wildest expectations as successor to my rather dubious claim to fame as a cock of the game. But then, I have tutored you well." He raised his glass in salute.

Alex chuckled, returning the toast. "I served quite an apprenticeship in Georgia with my cousin Rob. Even though he's the eldest, my Uncle Quint used to say—"

"Quintin Blackthorne is *not* your uncle. I am your uncle," Monty interrupted sharply, then caught himself as Alex stared at him, startled. "That is to say," he continued more urbanely, "he is merely your father's cousin, hence your own, two degrees removed."

"He and my father were raised as brothers," Alex replied, amazed at this most uncharacteristic outburst of jealousy. He could see Monty was embarrassed by the revelation and hastened on to add with an affectionate grin, "I've always called him uncle, milord."

"You've no need of shirttail backwoods kin," the baron replied with a nod of appreciation for Alex's wit. "You now reside in the Great Wen. By the by, where the deuce have you been keeping yourself the past few days? I ran into Chitchester and Forrester, who were lamenting at Whites this evening that they haven't seen a whisker of you in nearly a week."

"Well, they wouldn't have found me at Whites in any case."

"I'm aware of your penchant for the . . . shall we say, more gamey side of London," Monty replied with amused disdain. "I'm only surprised that you have deserted your sad bluestocking's side so soon."

"My absence was on Miss Woodbridge's behalf, but why should you be interested?" Alex replied with an edge in his voice. Damnation! He was heartily sick of everyone speculating about his relationship with Joss.

"No particular reason, other than the gossip that's begun over what Suthington will do with her."

"Suthington? What the hell does that old goat care? He never before evinced a grain of concern for her or his only brother. He could not even be bothered to attend Elijah Woodbridge's funeral."

"Yet he has taken her in. Speculation is rampant about how the two of them shall deal together, old Everett the tight-arsed Tory and Miss Woodbridge, the crusading Whig."

Alex set down his glass and looked at Monty. "What do you mean, he has taken her in?"

"You didn't know? You must have been far underground in your delicious dens of iniquity. It seems Miss Woodbridge was to be put out on the streets. Something about her landlady receiving a more lucrative offer to let her apartment. And the Methodist mission officials declined to leave a female without proper male guidance in charge of the charity school. Without some sort of family backing, her sources of largesse for the poor were cut off."

"So she went to her dear uncle Everett for help," Alex said, stung that she had indicated nothing of her plight to him. Or had she? He had been off searching for Elijah's killers since the day after the funeral, not bothering to read his mail, which lay piled up in his sitting room.

"I daresay Everett is at wit's end over what to do with the chit," Monty said, chuckling.

"Joss will never come to an accord with that arrogant old goat. If you'll excuse me, milord, I must catch up with my week's mail."

Monty nodded regally at Alex's mocking farewell, then drained his glass and stood staring thoughtfully at the open door. "Now what is all this about, my boy, hmm?" he murmured to himself.

Alex returned to his private apartments and sifted through the mail after dismissing his valet. He extracted one missive written in Joss's distinctive hand and tore it open to read the terse lines indicating that regrettable circumstances had forced her to decide upon living with her uncle in Mayfair. Leave it to Joss to describe such dire straights as eviction and penury with the words "regrettable circumstances." And to indicate that moving under that old curmudgeon Suthington's roof was her "decision."

"Why didn't you come to me, Joss?" he asked the empty room.

But he knew her too well. Pride. Independence. That fierce free spirit of hers would never have allowed her to be a burden to someone upon whom she had no claim but friendship. At least Suthington was her beloved father's brother, even if the earl was sour, manipulative and full of himself.

In spite of his hurt feelings, he grinned. "Ah, Joss, you'll make that old bastard rue the day he first met you."

Tomorrow he would call on Miss Jocelyn Woodbridge, the earl's niece, and return her father's timepiece. They would sort out the rest later . . . and the "rest" did not include her living under Suthington's roof. Alex intended to make damned certain of that.

Chapter Nine

"That dog is an agent of the devil! He shall be dispensed with immediately," Sir Everett announced the moment Joss set foot into his study in response to his summons.

"I will not give up Poc! He's all I have left of my old life—"

"That speaks volumes for the quality of that life, does it not, you silly chit? Haven't a dem whit more sense than my maggoty-brained brother," he muttered half to himself.

Joss bit back a furious retort as he fixed her with his icy blue eyes, eyes the color of her father's but completely devoid of the warmth and kindness of the gentle reverend.

"That beastie has terrified your maid. She refuses to set foot in your rooms. The gel costs a pretty penny and I shan't lay out my blunt for services not rendered."

"I did not request, nor do I require, a ladies' maid. I'm used to dressing myself."

Suthington looked over her ratty knot of braids and shapeless gray gown, then sniffed, "Nothing could be more apparent. I fancy 'tis a waste of effort attempting to turn mutton into lamb. I shall simply dismiss the gel."

"Oh, but I didn't intend to cost Bluesette her position," Joss interjected, horrified at the prospect of anyone facing eviction without a job, even the disagreeable French maid her cousin Lady Harrington had bequeathed to her. Poc had taken a singular aversion to the volatile Frenchwoman.

"Either the dog goes or the maid goes," the earl pronounced with an imperious tilt of his leonine head. He was a well-favored man, blessed with a talented tailor who knew how to conceal his thickening middle. Only the puffy lines around his eyes and mouth gave away his overindulgence in rich food and aged port.

"I will keep both," Joss stated calmly. In the scant week she had spent beneath Sir Everett's roof, she'd learned how dangerous conciliation was. Before he could pounce, she continued, "Bluesette can enter my quarters by the sitting room door. I shall confine Poc in my bedroom whenever she is about."

"If I receive another complaint from the upstairs maid about chewed-up bed linens, that shall be the end of the creature."

"It shan't happen. We were—er—playing and things got a bit out of hand. He's not used to being confined indoors. I shall take him with me on duty today. That should give him exercise enough."

"Duty?" the earl echoed, squinting at her through his quizzing glass. His raised eyebrows nearly touched the curved edge of the old-fashioned but meticulously coifed wig he wore to conceal his thinning hair.

"My hospital duty. After a week of mourning, I feel it best to resume my nursing schedule at the charity hospital."

"No one living beneath my roof shall be seen anywhere near the rabble that finds itself cast abed in charity hospitals! And you, a female, exposed to men's unclothed limbs . . . Why, it is utterly intolerable. My brother was mad raising a gel in such a manner. Small wonder you've become an ape leader. You shall never even mention that hospital again. Is that clear?"

"Quite crystalline, my lord. I shall go about my duties without breathing so much as a syllable about them to you again," Joss replied dulcetly. "Nor shall I discuss the school where I teach—or at least I shall continue to teach until the Methodist mission board can locate a man to oversee the program."

The earl's ruddy face became apoplectic with outrage. "You are a saucy, ungrateful, ill-mannered chit whose impertinence knows no bounds. I shall have you locked in your rooms until you come to your senses. No one under this roof defies me."

"Then I shall be forced to follow my sire's noble example and quit your roof, my lord," Joss stated as calmly as she could. *Dear Lord, where will I go?*

Before she reached the door to the library, the earl had rung for a footman, who stood filling the door frame, awaiting instruction. "You will go nowhere, you ninny. Much as we may both regret the circumstance, you are a female relative without a protector. The sorry task of your care has fallen to me now and I cannot allow you to walk out onto the streets. The ton would not approve, no matter your ingratitude."

Joss could see the servant's implacable expression and knew he would not let her pass until she had settled matters with Sir Everett. She abhorred duplicity, but her uncle left her little choice. "I understand your unenviable position, my lord. Indeed, as you have pointed out, I have nowhere to go. If I may not continue useful work with the poor, what would you have me do?"

"Do?" He looked at her incredulously. "Since when do ladies need to *do* anything? Go embroider a sampler, play the pianoforte, paint a watercolor—do frivolous female things. Better yet, I'll have my daughter take you to the

135

mantua maker for some clothes that do not look as if they came from a rag picker's wagon!"

"Whatever you wish, my lord. I do not want to embarrass you," Joss replied with barely veiled sarcasm.

Suthington studied her for a moment, his lips thinned in aggravation. "Only remember, mistress, much as neither of us desires it, you live by my charity. You will behave appropriately."

Joss cast down her lashes to conceal the flash of fire she knew was in her eyes. *Patience. How often had dear Papa counseled patience!* She must bide her time and put into action the plans she had made the past week. The earl had demanded she engage in some properly ladylike activities. She could arrange for him to believe she had acquiesced to his wishes . . . if she was very clever. And Jocelyn Woodbridge could be exceedingly clever when circumstances required it.

"Mr. Alexander Blackthorne is here to see you, Miss Woodbridge. Are you at home?" the punctilious footman inquired, handing Joss an elegant calling card while eyeing Poc guardedly as he sat by his mistress's side.

"Of course, Kennett, I shall be down directly. Please show Mr. Blackthorne into the green sitting room," Joss replied. "Alex is here, Poc!" she told the dog, whose tail now wagged excitedly. Joss had begun to worry about her friend. He had been such a comfort through the funeral, then mysteriously vanished.

"Come, Poc, let us attend our guest." As she made her way across the small sitting room off of her bedroom, Joss glanced in the large girandole looking glass hanging on the wall. Merciful heavens, she looked a fright. As usual, her glasses were askew and that hateful maid Bluesette had been so distracted watching for Poc, who sat growling behind the bedroom door, that she had hopelessly snarled Joss's heavy hair, trying to brush it out. The result was an even rattier, more frizzed knot of braids twisted haphaz-ardly atop her head.

Looking down at her best pale yellow dimity dress, she saw a dark blue smear across the skirt. She must have brushed against the inkwell again. The elegant little spinet desk was simply too small for her books and papers. Her whole apartment was cluttered with bric-a-brac left behind by her cousin Priscilla when she had wed Lord Harrington. Joss missed the spartan useful life she had once led.

"No use bemoaning my fate, any more than trying to improve my appearance," she said to the terrier. "Alex is used to me this way." The duo rushed downstairs to the green sitting room to meet their friend.

"Alex, I've been worried about you," Joss said, unable to keep a hint of censure from her voice. Poc simply barked an exuberant welcome as Alex squatted down and thumped his sides. "Wherever have you been?" she scolded.

"How have *you* been might be a more pertinent ques-tion," he replied, standing up and looking around the room. "Lud, this place is a brocade-lined prison, Joss." He took her cold hands in his, chafing them as he studied the haunted expression on her face.

She smiled too brightly. "Yes, it is a bit . . . er, ostenta-tious for my taste."

Alex's dark eyes studied her. "And what of dear Uncle Everett?"

"I fear the earl and I are not dealing very well together," she replied primly.

He chuckled in spite of himself. "Why do I suspect that is a masterpiece of understatement?"

She walked over to the window and took a seat on a small ugly chair, motioning for him to take the one across from her. "I shall have to learn patience at last, something Papa always found deficient in me. His lordship has for-bidden me to nurse at hospital or teach the children."

"Not the done thing, I fear, for a lady to be useful in this world."

"Ladies are to be ornaments, I know, but seeing how hopeless that function is for me, I will continue to be useful . . . even if I must employ some little craft and subterfuge to do so," she added, lowering her voice conspiratorially.

Alex cocked his head and a faint trace of a smile pulled at his lips. "What are you planning, Joss?"

"I shall announce to the earl that I am undertaking instruction in the art of becoming a lady, skills in which my education left me sadly lacking. I shall schedule appointments with Monsieur LeBeau for painting in the mornings—the light is better then, you know," she said in mock seriousness. "And in the afternoons I shall attend Signore Valpolla for pianoforte lessons."

Alex grinned openly now, catching her drift. "The earl will be paying quite handsomely for such an education."

"Quite so. And to such worthy causes the contributions will go—school and hospital! While he believes I am pursuing the arts, I shall have my days free to do my work."

"Won't the earl become suspicious?"

She shrugged dismissively. "Not if I come home with a smudge of paint on my frock occasionally and practice my chords in the evenings now and then. I already know how to play," she added devilishly.

"Ah, that's my old Joss. It's so good to see you smile," he said fondly, reaching out to clasp her hand in brotherly affection. "I was distressed when I found out you'd been forced to leave your old home at the Fin and Feather."

Joss shrugged. "It wasn't Aunt Regina's fault really. She knew I had no means to pay her anything."

"Couldn't any of those societies for the betterment of everything pay you a stipend to teach school or to run the shelter for climbing boys?"

Her cheerfulness crumbled for a moment, giving way to

bitterness at the injustice she had suffered. "I was a female without a protector. They were quite certain that my circumstance made it impossible for me to continue teaching or running the shelter without my father's guidance."

"The hell with what those noddys think is proper! You can do anything you set your mind to do, Joss."

She smiled at his vehemence. "Thank you for believing in me, Alex."

"Why didn't you come to me, Joss? I would have helped. I have plenty of money. Why, I—"

"I could not live off your largesse Alex. There is no price on friendship."

"Precisely, there is not. That is why you should come to me for help, not play games to survive under Suthington's roof."

"What would the ton say if I lived under your roof, Alex? Would they not assume *we* were playing games, too? Oh, I know it's absurd—me an unattractive old tabby, but there would be talk. It would not be right," she finished stubbornly.

Alex sighed. "Do we give a damn about the ton?" Then he added firmly, "You must promise me, if the earl becomes impossible, if you are ever in trouble again, you must confide in me. We'll find some way to work it out together. Promise?"

Grudgingly she replied, "I promise, but never fear, I have the old devil in hand. You see, he does cloak my activities with respectability, even if he remains unaware of what I'm doing."

"Because he is your uncle and therefore providing you guidance?"

She nodded with a sprightly smile. "Now, you rascal, tell me what you have been about. Breaking all the Cyprian hearts or winning at the whist tables?"

His mood grew somber as he shook his head, then reached into his waistcoat pocket and extracted the timepiece.

Joss saw the glint of gold, then gasped when he laid the family heirloom in her palm. She felt the familiar weight and her fingers closed over it before she opened the case and lovingly traced the inscription engraved inside. "Where did you find it, Alex? How?"

"That's where I've been these past days, Joss—searching out the lair of the assassins who took this from your father," he said gently, as her eyes filled with tears.

She blinked them back and met his gaze head-on. "You found out who murdered Papa?"

He nodded. "Jem Barker. He hired an assassin whose name was John Slocum."

"Past tense, Alex? You . . . you killed these men?"

"Let's simply say I dispensed justice," he replied evenly.

It was her turn to nod. "I see. My faith teaches me to forgive, not exact vengeance, yet because they would have preyed on so many more innocent victims, I cannot regret their deaths. But you've risked your life once again for me. You could've been killed on such a dangerous quest."

Alex grinned now, reassured at her scolding mien. "As Grandma Charity always says, I'm too much of a rascal to die young. Besides, I wasn't alone. Drum helped me."

"Then I am in his debt as well. I shall have to thank him." Her lips thinned imperceptibly at the prospect.

Alex chuckled. "You look as if you've just swallowed a persimmon, Joss."

The long winter months melted into the spring of 1812 and talk of impending war with the upstart Americans was eclipsed by the assassination of Prime Minister Spencer Percival on May 11. By month's end the government fell. While the lower classes rioted in the streets of London, the salons of the literati were abuzz over the remarkable new poet who had written *Childe Harold's Pilgrimage*.

Alex attended a few soirees where the new literary lion was present, but the scandalous excesses of Lord Byron held little interest for Joss. She continued to slip away from her uncle's city house, using the pretext of lessons, teas and other suitable social gatherings. At first she had feared he would insist upon her accompanying him to the country when he went on one of his frequent visits, but he granted her wish to remain near her "tutors," doubtless relieved to be free of a troublesome burden.

Her work at the hospital took most of her afternoons. The mission board allowed her to teach in the mornings since they were able to find another clergyman to oversee the school.

Things had continued smoothly while the irascible earl spent most of the winter months at his ancestral estate. But when he returned to London in April, matters became quite sticky. Joss detested lying, but there was simply no help for it if she wished to do the work that gave her life meaning.

To further complicate the situation, his lordship took an intense dislike to Alex, whom he considered one of the ungrateful colonial rabble who dared to threaten the British government. After Alex's last visit ended in a fierce argument in which he and the earl almost came to blows, Joss decided it might be prudent for her and Alex to meet away from the city house whenever her uncle was at home.

Alex's reputation as the wicked angel of sex and sin was equaled only by that of Lord Byron himself. Although he would regale her with humorous accounts of his wins and losses at the gaming tables and racecourses, he never mentioned the beauteous Cyprians with whom she knew he kept company. Marriage-minded young misses pined over him and set their caps for him. That he did discuss with amusement, for he had no intention of leg-shackling himself to any of the puff-brained debutantes. Joss secreted her dreams deep in her heart and prayed that her eyes never revealed the ache of longing that tore at her soul.

Their lives might have gone on indefinitely in this manner if not for Poc. One summer afternoon while Joss was at the hospital, he came walking proudly up the street with the largest rat ever seen on the wharf clamped firmly in his jaws. By nightfall word of the prodigious feat spread far and wide. Unfortunately, word also spread that the remarkable Staffordshire terrier was owned by the dead preacher's daughter.

When Joss arrived home that evening, the earl was waiting for her in his "lair," as she had come to think of the imposing study with its trophy boar's head glaring down from the wall with beady red eyes. The boar's malevolence was as nothing compared to the icy blue glare of the eighth Earl of Suthington.

"I have had a most distressing report, Jocelyn. One that I devoutly wish to be untrue," he began without preamble as soon as she took a seat in front of his Chippendale desk.

Joss had prayed the gossip would not reach Mayfair, but knowing the ways of servants and tradesmen, she supposed it was inevitable that her ruse would be discovered. "What report is that, milord?" she inquired innocently as her mind raced.

He smiled thinly, a harsh, nasty, scowling smile. "What report, indeed! A Staffordshire terrier has set a record of sorts, it would seem, for rat killing. And he brought his prize to his owner, a nonconformist cleric's daughter, at the East End charity hospital. Is this so? The truth, gel!"

Joss moistened her lips, then inquired, "That Poc killed a huge rat that everyone made a fuss over or that I was at hospital?"

"Blast the rat and the dog to perdition! Were you at that wretched hospital, performing heaven knows what shockingly unnatural tasks?"

She held up her head and stubbornly set her chin as she replied, "I was volunteering at hospital, yes, but I do not consider nursing the sick as either shocking or unnatural. My faith enjoins me to perform acts of kindness."

"Does this Methody humbug also enjoin you to lie and steal?" His tone shifted from furious to scathing now.

Joss stiffened. "The Methodist religion is not a humbug, milord. I have acceded to your wishes and worshiped with you in the established church, but I still consider myself a follower of Mr. Wesley. As to my telling you I was otherwise occupied when I was at hospital, I am guilty. I took the money for the music and art tutors and bought medical supplies with it. They were badly needed. I would hope that you could—"

"What—excuse your impossible behavior? Condone your taking my funds under false pretenses? Forgive you making me the laughingstock of the ton after I took you in from the very streets?"

"I am sorry that I was forced to deceive you, Uncle Everett." Not exactly a handsome apology as those things went, but there it was. She simply did not regret her work at the hospital or using a pittance from the earl's stockpile of wealth for a good cause. She waited as his voice rose in pitch and volume along with the heightening purple stain on his cheeks. "You are an ingrate and an unnatural female. I can do nothing about the former, but I shall take steps to remedy the latter."

A prickle of alarm brushed her neck. "What do you mean, milord?"

"I need not answer you, nor shall I," he said, dismissing her.

By week's end word of her shameful escapades would be on everyone's tongues. What cork-brained impulse had led him to offer her the protection of his august name and rank? Of course if he had left his only brother's orphaned daughter destitute, that would have reflected poorly on him as well. Neither alternative was acceptable. There was only one solution. He would marry her off. Even an ungainly long Meg who championed the great unwashed could be wed—if the price were right. It would be money well spent in his books.

Alex sat staring morosely down at his mother's latest letter as Constanzia massaged his neck with practiced hands. He sat in the overfurnished parlor of her apartment, for which he was currently paying the rent.

He flexed his bare shoulders and leaned back in the chair. Lud, his head ached abominably from an excess of Chitchester's excellent brandy. It was a good life . . . if he did not weaken. As Constanzia ministered to him, she tried to read surreptitiously over his shoulder. "What does your mama say, *querido,* she asked in a throaty, purring voice laced with a thick Spanish accent.

Responding to her query, he said offhandedly, "Just the usual, pet, exhortations to work hard, to take care of my health." *To get married.*

He shuddered.

"Are you cold, *querido.* I will have Bram lay a fire."

The room was already stifling from her heavy perfume and their recent bout of lusty sex. "No, I'm not cold, although I must get dressed. I have to be at the warehouse at half past the hour."

Her carmined lips puffed out in a moue of disappointment. "That wretched bookkeeping again . . . do not go, my stallion . . . I know ways of spending the afternoon . . . which are much finer than adding dull columns of numbers." She punctuated her words with nibbling kisses on his neck and shoulders, bending over him until her full breasts pressed against his back and the thick fall of her loose raven hair spilled over his arm.

Alex sighed in resignation, then stood up. "Sorry, 'Stanzia, but I've already missed a day this week for the running at Newmarket. Old Bertie was quite put out." He folded the letter, which his footman had just delivered, and slipped it into his jacket, then began dressing.

He had not been much in residence at the Caruthers's city house since acquiring Constanzia, who was constant neither in temperament nor in loyalties. For the moment, the reigning queen of the Cyprians was taken with the whispers about his exotic lineage and the aura of danger that clung to him. He planned to enjoy her inventiveness in bed until one or the other of them grew bored, then move on. There were so many fascinating challenges in the world of the demimonde. Alex intended to sample every female who took his fancy.

Unless his parents had their way. The thought did not bear considering. As he slipped on his jacket and inspected himself in the cheval glass in Constanzia's bedroom, he tried to forget his mother's impassioned plea. Damn Toby for having the unmitigated bad grace to pass on last year. Charity's and Susan's husbands wanted nothing to do with the shipping trade. His youngest sister Polyanne had just announced her engagement to a highly successful portrait painter from Williamsburg, and to put a cap on it, his widowed sister Mellie was courting with a farmer from Carolina!

That left the responsibility for the family business resting heavily on his shoulders. But if that were all he was asked, Alex would have been willing to make the sacrifice. In the past year he'd actually come to find the complexities of running a large export and import house to be an intellectual challenge. He had a flair for selecting oriental artwork and African ivory, which wealthy British and American customers bought eagerly. Even Bertie Therlow was pleased with his work. Well, most of the time . . .

But running the business was not paramount in his parents' minds. Marrying him off was. With the last of her daughters soon to be wed, Barbara had focused her full attention on her only son. She worried about him. And were those scandalous stories about gambling and loose women true?

Lady Barbara Caruthers had been reckless and high living after her come-out. Since she knew firsthand about all the vices to which the Quality fell prey, he could not hope to fool her. His parents had decided it was time for him to settle down, to find one special young lady with whom to spend the rest of his life, a wife who would make him truly happy.

An oxymoron if ever he'd heard one, he thought morosely as he made his way to the warehouse. Since Constanzia's quarters were not far from the docks, he often walked, preferring the brisk exercise to sitting closed up in a stuffy hackney. So deep was he in thought, brooding over his troubles, that he was nearly run over by a dray. He ignored the drayman's curses and shaking fist as he crossed the cobblestones.

"If only there were some way to placate my mother," he murmured to himself, garnering some odd looks from the working people on the street. Of course, it was not just his mother, but his father as well, who was determined to see Alex wed. Devon had gone so far as to indicate he might disinherit Alex if he did not grow up and assume his responsibilities, the primary one being providing the next generation of little Blackthornes to carry on the family name. No matter that his cousin Rob was already doing that. Devon and Barbara wanted *their* son to provide them with Blackthorne grandchildren.

Most unreasonable. He could have made his own way without his father's allowance, but Alex loved his parents a great deal and did not wish to hurt them by spurning what they had worked so hard all their lives to create. This last letter from his mother was wistfully sad and fretfully worried. He had to do something. But what?

He affirmed that it would not, most assuredly, be to saddle himself with a wife and children. That resolution made, Alex entered the dark, musty interior of the warehouse, where the exotic aromas of Chinese teas blended with the musky tang of Spanish oranges. As he wended his way through the narrow aisles between crates and bales, he pondered exactly what he could do to pacify his family and maintain his present lifestyle. No immediate solutions came to mind. When he reached the door to the business office, he expected to find crotchety old Bertie ready to scold him for ordering too large a shipment of teak furniture. He was taken aback to see Joss pacing back and forth across the bare wooden floor.

The moment she heard him enter the room, Joss turned and flew into his arms with a hiccuping sob. "Oh, Alex, you must book passage for me on one of your ships. I have to leave England at once!"

Chapter Ten

"Leave England? Joss . . ." He tipped her face up and removed the eyeglasses from her red-rimmed eyes. Tears leaked down her cheeks and her complexion was ashen. As long as he had known her, Alex had never seen Jocelyn Woodbridge so distraught—almost hysterical. Even when word of her beloved father's death came, she had been incredibly self-possessed. "What is wrong?" he asked gently, guiding her through the crowded office and into another smaller room where Bertram Therlow worked.

"Would you mind if I spoke privately with Miss Woodbridge, Bertie?" he asked the corpulent, elderly man who sat hunched over an account ledger.

"Eh? What, what?" Therlow asked, holding an ear trumpet up to an ear covered by the curls of a hideously outdated and frazzled wig. When Alex repeated his request, the old man muttered some disparagement regarding the younger generation as he scooped up his books and scuttled out into the front office.

Alex led Joss over to where a pair of lolling chairs sat

neglected in one corner, gathering dust. When she began to sit, he stopped her, retrieving a stack of yellowed papers from the seat, then dusting it off with a snowy white handkerchief. "Now, sit down and explain what's happened," he instructed as he handed her back her spectacles and pulled up the adjoining chair.

Joss squeezed her puffy eyes to blink away the last of the tears, then replaced her eyeglasses so she could see Alex's dear face. "I feel like an utter cake, barging in this way. I'm certain Mr. Therlow thought I was an escaped bedlamite when I arrived, desperate to speak with you. I could think of no place else I might hope to find you when I was told by the butler that you were not currently in residence at the Caruthers's town house." She took a deep breath in an attempt to calm herself.

"Why on earth would you wish to leave England?" he asked in bewilderment, steering her back to the topic at hand.

"Heaven forbid, I don't *wish* to leave England, Alex. I must. That or Uncle Everett"—she stressed his name with taut anger—"will force me into the most heinous misalliance ever contrived."

Alex watched her shiver in revulsion. "Misalliance? You mean he's trying to marry you off?" Joss would not have any reasonable prospects, which meant the old earl had offered some impoverished peer a bribe to rid himself of the girl. "To whom?"

"Sir Cecil Yardley," she replied indignantly.

"Yardley?" Alex echoed incredulously. The old rake was sixty if he was a day, toothless, fat and if rumor were to be believed, quite poxed, not to mention vicious-tempered and a profligate spender who had always lived well beyond the modest means of his estate.

"None other than that foul-smelling, mean-spirited old viscount who, according to the earl, is desperate to wed again and produce an heir before he dies. He's already outlived two wives who failed to give him a healthy child."

"That's because he has the syphilis, Joss. It's probably what killed his wives, too." When she paled even more, he hastened to assure her, "Don't fear. I shall never allow you to be bartered off to any man against your will."

She felt her nails digging into the wooden arms of the chair to keep from throwing herself at him again and embarrassing them both. His steadfast reassurance was balm for her soul, yet the problem admitted no ready solution. "Alas, you will have little to say in the matter, my friend, for the earl is my legal guardian and a powerful man. He made it quite clear to me that I had no recourse whatsoever to avoid this odious union. When I refused to wed the viscount and announced that I would find other lodgings, he laughed at me and said my father had raised an utter lackwit. He placed me under lock and key until the arrangements with Yardley are finalized."

"How did you get here then?" he asked.

"I climbed out the second-story window of my bedroom and walked over a ledge to the arbor trellises, then climbed down and slipped out the back gate," she confessed.

Knowing how deuced clumsy Joss could be, Alex paled. "You took a dangerous chance."

"I had no choice, Alex. The law is on his side. My only means of permanent escape is to flee my homeland forever—or at least until the earl is dead."

The thought of Joss landing in some strange port all alone was horrifying. He rubbed the bridge of his nose and tried to think of what they might do. "I could send you to my parents in Savannah. They'd be pleased to have another daughter now that Poly is leaving the nest . . ."

"I could not impose. Besides, if I go anywhere that could be easily traced, he will find me. He knows of our friendship. This will be the first place they look once I'm discovered missing. No, I shall go somewhere utterly untraceable—I was thinking India . . ."

"India?" he thundered, aghast. "Do you have any idea what you're saying? Have you ever *been* to India?"

"Have you?" she countered, desperately grasping at straws to keep her hopes alive.

"Yes, when I stowed away aboard one of our trading vessels as a lad. It's an alien and dangerous place for a well-armed man—no place at all for a lone white woman. You'd be sold to some slaver before you could walk off the Calcutta wharf."

"Then perhaps somewhere in America without ties to the Blackthornes—Boston or New York. Rumors of war between our countries are rife. Heaven forbid it should come to that, but if diplomatic ties were broken . . ."

As he leaned back in his chair, resting his chin on his fists, Alex studied Joss. An idea began to take shape in the back of his mind . . . an utterly insane idea . . . or was it? He turned it over as Joss rattled on about all the unlikely ports of call where she could hide. She was so thoroughly English that he had a difficult time imagining her living anywhere else, certainly not in some godforsaken hellhole such as New South Wales or Malacca, not even in Greece or Italy.

But she was right about the earl. The haughty old bastard resented being crossed by anyone, especially an impoverished female, and legally he could marry her off to anyone he chose . . . unless she were already wed. Even considering the idea that had popped into his mind caused a fine sheen of perspiration to dampen his upper lip. Damn Drum for his incessant drivel about his friendship with Joss, he thought crossly. Still, the idea had merit.

Have you gone stark raving lunatic? He chided himself. But the thought would not leave his head once formulated.

Joss, seeing Alex stare off into space as if in a trance, ceased her frantic discourse and sighed, reaching out gingerly to touch his arm. "Alex, are you all right? I did not mean to overburden you with my troubles. Perhaps it would be best if I simply resigned myself to the odious marriage and tried to reach some accord with Yardley. Failing all else, I could slip laudanum into his tea on our wedding night or cosh him on the head with a fireplace poker."

Alex leaned forward, shaking his head as he reached for her hand. "No, Joss, you won't ever have to deal with Yardley. I have an idea that might solve your problem as well as my own. . . ."

Joss looked into his liquid brown eyes and felt herself drowning in their depths. Whatever did he mean? His touch sent a tingling premonition dancing up her arm straight to her heart. Her breathing hitched. "Your problem, Alex?" she queried, suddenly breathless with anticipation.

Well, it's now or never, some inner voice urged him. "You know my family has been putting increasing pressure on me to marry over this past year."

Her heart gave a painful lurch. "You mean they've selected a young lady for you?" Visions of some wildly beautiful colonial lass filled her imagination. How could she bear it?

"No, Joss. My parents know better than to try that."

"B-but then, what is your problem if they are not forcing you into marriage—and how does it relate to my present difficulty?" Now she was the one bewildered.

Alex released her hand for a moment and combed his fingers through his hair with a grin. "It's sort of complicated—my problem, that is. I . . . oh, hell, Joss, I suppose I'm utterly incorrigible in spite of all your prayers. I like the life I lead, the freedom I have to drink and gamble and . . . er, pursue other pleasures not appropriate to mention in a lady's presence."

Joss nodded, biting her lip, half in vexation, half in amusement at her Alex, her angelic rake. "Working on the docks, I'm acquainted with that profession. Bit o' muslin' is the euphemism, I believe?" she asked dryly.

Alex felt a sudden need to stand up and pace. "Er, well,

yes, that is one. But getting back to my family," he continued doggedly, "I feel guilty about worrying them. Since Poly's gone and found herself a husband, they've turned their full attention on me. What I mean to say, is, well . . . I need to find a wife—not a real wife," he hastened to add, then faltered once more. "I just need to be married so that my parents will cease hounding me and fretting about the way I choose to live my life."

A horrible suspicion was beginning to form in Joss's mind, but it was so presumptuous, so wildly preposterous that she dared not voice it aloud. Instead she moistened her dry lips and said, "Pray continue."

She was not making this any easier, he thought pettishly, trying to read her expression. Those damnable thick glasses always seemed to catch the candle's light in such a way as to obscure her eyes. "Well, Joss, I know this sounds ridiculous, but I could marry you—a marriage in name only, of course," he hastened to add. "You need protection from your uncle. What better way to foil him than to turn up with a husband before he can force Yardley on you?"

The earth would open up and swallow her now. Surely it would. It must! Her worst suspicions were realized. *I know this sounds ridiculous, but I could marry you.* She sat frozen, not daring to breathe as Alex, her beautiful golden Alex, resumed pacing nervously across the crowded office. She clenched her hands into painful fists, and concealed them in the folds of her skirt as he warmed to his scheme, continuing to lay it out.

"My uncle could procure a special license. He has some very influential friends. Once the matter had been legalized and presented to the earl as a fait accompli, there would be nothing he could do about it but give over, Joss. And when I informed my parents that I had married, they'd rejoice and cease hounding me. It would serve us both handily." When she made no further response, Alex went on. "You would be free to continue your work at the hospital and school, do anything you wished." He stopped and looked directly at her for the first time in several moments.

Joss sat perfectly still, flummoxed over how to respond. "How would we live, Alex? Surely the Carutherses would not desire us to share their city house." *Why am I even considering this!* she railed at herself.

"Since I began working here I've been drawing commissions on the profits. Oddly enough, my income from honest toil nearly equals my ill-gotten gains at the tables and the track," he said with a rueful laugh. "That has led me to consider finding my own lodgings. I can afford nice quarters, perhaps a place on Chapel Street that I inspected just last week. There are rooms upstairs that could be converted into your own private apartment. Where we live would be your choice, Joss."

"And you would keep the downstairs." It was not quite a question. She knew he would continue to live as he had, bringing Cyprians to share his bed while she languished in loneliness upstairs.

Alex grinned in that rakish, bone-melting way that made her heart stop. " 'Pon my honor, you would never be exposed to my wicked, wicked ways, Joss," he replied, holding up one bronzed hand in mock pledge.

And you would never have any idea that I love you. How could she do it?

How could you give up your one opportunity to be with him for the rest of your life? an inner voice tormented her. This was her one golden opportunity—if she had the courage to seize it. "I do not know, Alex . . . ," she replied gravely.

Alex could hear the uncertainty in her voice. "Damnation, Joss, can't you see—"

His frustrated protest was cut short by shouts echoing through the warehouse. "Search everywhere. Leave not a bale or cask standing until you locate her!"

"The earl!" Joss gasped, looking frantically around their cramped quarters for a means of escape.

Alex bolted across the room and rushed through the door to the outer office. "Bertie—you must keep the earl from searching here. Tell him you've not seen Miss Woodbridge or me. It's of the utmost urgency!" he said in the old man's ear trumpet.

When Therlow nodded with a somewhat befuddled expression on his face, Alex left him, turning the lock on the inside door. "Quickly, follow me," he whispered, siezing her by the hand.

A second small door in the little room was partially hidden by a tall case cabinet stacked with records. He shoved it open, then dragged her through it, closing and locking it behind them. They were once more out in the warehouse. Before she could catch her breath, he took off in a swift dash, nearly yanking her arm from its socket.

They raced past kegs of molasses and crates of oriental pottery, zigzagging through the maze of narrow aisles, headed to one corner of the immense building where a rickety flight of stairs led up to a loft.

"Where are we going?" she managed to gulp out as they approached the steps.

"There's a window and a gutter pipe beside it, if memory serves me," he replied, starting to climb.

"Memory had best serve you or you'll be serving a sentence at Newgate," she replied, then stumbled on the second step before breaking free of his protective hold to gather up her skirts. Thanking heaven for her sensible flat-soled shoes, she scrambled up the narrow wooden risers.

"There—up there, yer lordship," one of the earl's servants yelled, and the chase was on.

Misjudging the depth of the last step, Joss pitched face forward into the cobweb-strewn loft. Alex scooped her up and resumed dragging her toward a small sooty window in the far corner. It was high and narrow. As he forced open

155

the glass, he asked her, "Can you climb through after me and catch hold of the drainpipe?"

"Do I have a choice?" she hissed, pulling the back of her skirt between her legs and fastening it into her waistband, forming makeshift britches as she'd seen the washerwomen do down at the docks.

"Good girl," Alex said with a chuckle as he climbed through the window and seized hold of the heavy pipe, shinnying down far enough to allow her room. "If you lose your grip I can catch you—or break your fall," he said by way of encouragement.

Trying not to look at the ground, Joss ignored that dubious bit of reassurance and swung out of the window, clinging like a leech to the rusty pipe. As she half slipped, half scooted down, she felt Alex's hand indelicately but helpfully supporting her derriere.

Then without more warning than a sharp expletive, his one-handed purchase abruptly slipped and he was forced to release Joss in order to keep from falling. As soon as he let go of her surprisingly well rounded buttocks—a fact that did not register in the distress of the moment—she gave a startled "murph" and slid rapidly down. Her legs scissored frantically until they came in contact with the first obstruction, which happened to be his head and shoulders. Involuntarily, using muscles she did not even know she possessed, Joss clamped his neck with her thighs and squeezed.

Alex was the one who now gave a loud grunt of surprise and dismay as her weight landed solidly on his shoulders, nearly causing him to drop the remaining twenty feet to the cobblestones below. When her legs imprisoned his head, he stiffened in surprise. Then the hem of her skirt worked loose from her waistband and flopped over his face. Now completely blinded, not to mention suffocated by layers of cloth, Alex coughed and tried to take a deep breath, which proved to be a grave error since all he succeeded in doing was to suck in a sheer linen petticoat.

He scrambled down faster, certain that if he did not break his neck in a fall or have it wrenched from his shoulders by Joss, he would asphyxiate before they reached the ground.

"They're making for the alley," a voice called out from above.

With a strangled curse, Alex picked up speed in his desperate descent. "How far are we from the ground?" he hissed, spitting out muslin with every word.

"I'm too afraid of heights to look," she replied, squeezing her eyes closed, completely unaware that her lower extremities reacted similarly, tightening around her victim's neck. Alex gurgled something unintelligible in reply.

Feeling one of the pursuers on the pipe above them, he took a chance and jumped clear. They landed, Joss on top of him, on the hard, cold cobblestones. Luckily the fall was only eight or ten feet. Unluckily, one of her heels landed in an exceedingly vulnerable part of his anatomy.

"Alex, are you all right?" Joss asked fearfully, squinting as she pulled her skirt away from his slightly greenish face.

"Couldn't . . . be . . . better," he replied, rolling up as stars spun crazily in front of his eyes.

The noise of the two men climbing down the pipe drew their attention. Joss untangled herself from Alex's semi-prone body and seized hold of the shaking pipe in an attempt to dislodge it. It was loose but she needed something for leverage. The bottom section of the pipe worked free when she yanked on it. Joss swung it with all her strength against the pipe still attached to the wall, then jammed it between the bricks and the rusty metal and pulled back. She was rewarded with a sharp screech, followed by a loud snap.

Their two pursuers fell one on top of the other, much as she and Alex had, but from more than twice the height. As they lay dazed and groaning, Joss tugged frantically on Alex's arm. "We have to go!"

Shaking his head to clear it and ignoring the ache in his nether regions, he lurched up and started off, keeping a tight grip on her hand. They rounded the end of the alley and came out on a busy thoroughfare, where he quickly hailed a hackney.

Collapsing on the shabby velvet cushions, he groaned and looked over at Joss, saying, "It's a bloody good thing this is to be a marriage in name only, for I fear you've damaged my ability to perform husbandly duties for some time."

A startled expression swept over her as she recalled landing, with him cushioning the fall. Then her face crimsoned in acute embarrassment. "Oh," she squeaked, raising one rust-stained glove to her warm face, only to bring it away with cobwebs clinging to it. Her own horrid dishabille was forgotten as an image of that disastrous climb flashed into her mind.

"I had my l—limbs around your . . . your head! Oh, Alex, I shall simply die of mortification!"

He managed a rueful chuckle. "Frankly, my dear Joss, it wasn't your limbs' proximity to my head that distressed me most."

"Will you give me no peace, Alex? Think of my sensibilities," she chided, deciding there was no hope of redeeming her dignity under such circumstances.

"My prim bluestocking, you have far more sense than sensibility, thank God." He looked at her dirt-smeared face and cobweb-coated hair with a lopsided grin. Somewhere in their escape she had lost her bonnet and her braids hung askew on the nape of her neck. They had landed in a puddle of rainwater in the alley and her clothes were damp, giving off a distinct scent of eau de rust. Joss never changed.

I do really love her, he thought suddenly. He certainly did not desire her, he hastened to assure himself with an inward chuckle, but she was more fun than any of his sisters and by far the brightest person he knew. There was no one, not even Drum, in whom he could confide with more confidence. "I think we shall rub on quite splendidly together, Joss."

"I haven't agreed to your bizarre proposal," she reminded him. "Think, Alex, about what you are doing. What if you change your mind one day? What if you fall in love with a woman you wish to truly make your wife?" she asked, playing devil's advocate. "Then you shall be stuck with me."

"Never fear. I have no plans to fall in love with one single female. I love the infinite variety of them all far too much," he replied with a devilish wink.

Of course the idea never crossed his mind that she would find a man who might wish to wed her, Joss thought with a pang. *I was content when I met you, Alex, having forsaken those painful girlish dreams of husband and children. Now you make me want to dream again.* And dreaming, Jocelyn Woodbridge knew, was a bittersweet torment indeed.

"See here, Joss," he said, breaking into her preoccupation, "if you are concerned that I might wish to cry off one day—which I assure you I will not—well, we could always apply for an annulment. I would provide for you so that you would never again be at anyone's mercy. And I promise never to subject you to . . . well, to impose upon you."

Joss digested this. Could she bear to grant him an annulment after they had been together for years? *Every golden moment you can spend with him is worth any cost,* that inner voice urged.

"Well, Joss?" he cajoled as they climbed down from the hackney. "What's it to be?"

"Very well, Alex. I shall marry you," she replied in a small voice, uncertain whether she had just opened the gate to paradise or Pandora's box.

Alex gave her a brotherly hug of delight. "I knew you'd

159

see the logic in my plan! Come, let us break the news to Drum," he replied, taking her arm.

She balked. "Drum?" she echoed, squinting up at the elegant flat where the hackney had let them off. She'd heard Alex give an address to the driver but in the confusion of their harrowing escape, had not thought to ask precisely where they were going.

"We could not return to Uncle Monty's house and I did not think you would favor meeting my latest 'bit o' muslin' any more than she would you . . . so that rather left Drum."

In spite of her melancholy thoughts about mistresses and annulments, she could see the humor in their situation. "He shall be positively flummoxed. I cannot wait to see the look on his face when you announce our impending nuptials."

"Then what are we waiting for?" he dared. She took his proffered arm and they walked up the steps.

Drum idly stirred a tot of brandy into his afternoon tea while he studied Miss Jocelyn Woodbridge, soon to be Mrs. Alexander Blackthorne, as she sat primly on the Grecian couch in his parlor. In spite of her attempts to freshen her appearance, she looked like one of the rats her dog dragged in. Limp frizzy hair was clumped on top of her head in a great wad. Her pale face was smudged and her thick glasses were askew on the bridge of her nose. The frumpy tan dress she wore was wrinkled and stained, hanging on her body like a sail that had lost the wind.

Whoever would have believed Alex would marry her? Drum had stood in gauche amazement while Alex laid out their insane scheme, but then as they had discussed the rash plan, he had observed the interchange between the "bridal couple" and it troubled him, troubled him very much indeed. The way she looked at Blackthorne when she thought no one was watching . . .

For almost two years he'd been more than passing curious about the nature of Alex's friendship with the preacher's daughter. Though he had teased the American about desiring this female for her mind, he never dreamed Alex would be so precipitous as to actually leg-shackle himself to her.

She'd always been snappish and cool around him. Although he'd come to a grudging admiration of her wit, he knew she tried to conceal her genuine detestation of him because he was Alex's friend. Alex looked on her as a friend, just as he did Drum. But marriage certainly placed extreme stress upon friendship. If he was still uncertain about Alex's finer feelings for Jocelyn Woodbridge, he had become increasingly more certain about hers for Alex. After observing the two of them that afternoon before Alex went in search of his uncle and a special license for marriage, Drum was positive that she was quite in love with his friend.

"You keep staring at me as if you expect I'll grow fangs and pounce on you as Poc would fall upon a juicy rat," Joss said at length. They had endured an uneasy silence since Alex departed. She took another sip of her tea and waited the odious little man out.

"An interesting idea, but I rather fancy the female of the species as a spider industriously spinning her web to entrap her hapless victim," he drawled.

"And that is how you see Alex—as my hapless victim?" He shrugged. "Perhaps."

" 'Twas *he* who proposed this most unconventional arrangement, not I. It suits him as much as it does me . . . perhaps more," she added softly, thinking of the succession of Cyprians who would sleep in his bed while his wife lay alone abovestairs.

"Aha, but 'tis he who shall be the husband—or did you not know, Miss Woodbridge, that it is the poor male spider who is devoured by his mate?"

"You have my assurance, Mr. Drummond, that I shall

refrain from devouring Alex in the foreseeable future," she replied, striving for a light tone.

"I wonder . . . hmmm," he mused, cool green eyes fixed steadily on her.

Joss resisted the urge to fidget under his basilisk gaze. "Why do you dislike me so, Mr. Drummond?"

"Odd, I was about to ask you the same question. Do you always strike out so boldly? Perhaps it's part of why Alex has been so taken with you. Colonials are a cheeky lot themselves."

"You have not answered my question," Joss persisted. Two could play at the game of intimidation, she decided.

Drum sighed and the brittle mask slipped from his face for an instant. "I find, much to my surprise and chagrin, Miss Woodbridge, that I no longer dislike you. It might amaze you to know that I suspect we may have something in common—but that is of no moment," he added quickly, shifting back to his familiar, drawling amusement. "Let us resolve to be civil to each other from this day onward. Perhaps in time, who knows?" he added expansively as he raised a carefully positioned pinch of snuff on his wrist. "We might even come to be friends."

Joss considered his rather startling suggestion, then nodded. "I have never thanked you for saving Alex's life."

Drum chuckled. "He was in bad loaf that night. Started out a veritable mushroom after a few hours at the hazard tables, all puffed up with his winnings. Quite foxed, too, else I doubt that slattern could have lured him down the alley."

"What makes men do such foolish things?"

"Wine, women and cards?" Drum shrugged. " 'Tis the nature of the beast, m'dear. The way he lives . . . it upsets you, does it not?"

"His life is desperately dangerous. I see every reason to be concerned."

"Most especially about the women, I warrant," he replied, studying her reaction.

Joss stiffened. "Strong drink and gambling are equally damning."

He chuckled but it was a gentle laughter. "Spoken like a good little Methodist, but you feel more than religious zeal for our rakehell comrade."

"He is my friend as he is yours."

Drum nodded. "Too true, m'dear, altogether too true. . . ."

By dusk Alex returned with Montgomery Caruthers and a stern-faced Anglican priest. After viewing the disheveled bride and groom in their filthy, torn clothing, he wished nothing so much as to perform the ceremony and be gone. Joss and Alex stood before the cleric, speaking their vows with nervous solemnity while Monty and Drum acted as witnesses.

Drum's usual veneer of foppish indolence was discernibly absent. He studied the bridal couple with keen interest, seemingly quite preoccupied. Although the baron announced that the unlikely match was a marvelous joke on the priggish old earl, his amusement was also tempered with a certain watchfulness.

When the simple exchange was over and the final benediction given, the priest beat a hasty exit. Monty raised Joss's hand in a proper salute, welcoming her into the family. After slapping Alex on the back in congratulation, he suggested an evening at Whites to Drum, who opined that the whist tables beckoned him like a siren. Alex and Joss were left alone after what seemed a startling blur of events.

Feeling suddenly awkward, Alex said, "While Uncle Monty was securing the license, I made arrangements for that place on Chapel Street I spoke of earlier. If you don't like it, we shall secure other lodgings as soon as possible."

"I'm certain it will be quite adequate, Alex." Did her

voice squeak? Good Lord, she hoped not, but her tongue seemed to cleave to the roof of her mouth. She forced herself to meet his eyes and continued, "Remember, I was raised in humble circumstances. The Fin and Feather was quite the nicest place in which Papa and I ever lived. I trust your good taste implicitly."

"Well, in that case, shall we go, Mrs. Blackthorne?"

When he offered her his arm, she felt positively lightheaded. *What have I done?* She could have drowned in his liquid brown eyes. They were warm, caring . . . *Get a hold of yourself, Joss,* she scolded, taking his arm. He loved her platonically, as a friend.

But this is your wedding night, a voice cried out from the depths of her soul as they left Drum's flat and walked out into the soft spring air.

Chapter Eleven

Joss sat before a crackling fire in her upstairs parlor. Logs snapped and popped, giving off a cheery glow to dispel the chill of the spring rain that had begun falling sometime after midnight. After Alex left, she could not sleep, in spite of the late hour. Joss sat alone, pondering the day's incredible events. *Mrs. Alexander Blackthorne.* Repeating the words aloud did not make them sound any more believable.

Yet here she sat in his elegant town house, only a few doors down from the Beau's famous address. Her upper-story quarters were commodious in the extreme, the sitting room furnished with delicate French furniture and Tabriz carpets, all done in shades of muted blue and gold. There was a master bedroom and a smaller one adjoining it, as well as a library of sorts with ample room on the shelves for her books, the only material possessions she had ever owned.

Her surroundings were luxurious, her finances secure and she was free to resume her life's work. Why then did she sit staring into the flames feeling more desolate than she ever had in her life, worse even than the day her father was buried? The answer, of course, was Alexander Blackthorne. Her husband.

He had been so quiet, so constrained by courtesy on the carriage ride to their new home. Alex, her laughing, teasing comrade in whose company she had always felt more supremely at ease than with any other person alive. That dear Alex seemed to be gone. The man who was now her husband acted unsure of what to say or do around her, awkward and uncomfortable.

Not that Joss herself felt any more at ease. What did one say to a husband under such contrived circumstances? She recalled his awkward pause when they reached the downstairs entrance to their new residence. She was certain that he was wondering whether it was appropriate to sweep her up into his arms and carry her across the threshold as was traditional. But the moment fled as he debated. She imagined that he decided she would think such behavior inappropriate.

Instead, he had simply unlocked the door and ushered her into the foyer with its highly polished marble floor, then given her a cursory tour of the first-floor library, dining room and sitting room. After hastily mentioning that his sleeping quarters and the kitchen were down the interior hallway, he had escorted her upstairs to her domain, taking care to point out the private entrance at the side of the house that he would use for his late-night activities.

They had chatted about inconsequential matters, any redecorating that she might choose to do, arrangements for moving their belongings to the new accommodations, hiring servants. He had arranged a cold collation to be set out by the cook who came with the place. While they dined downstairs, they considered how to deal with the earl. At least that was one matter of substance they could discuss.

Hovering in the background were the unspoken fears of both bride and groom that they had made a precipitous mistake. They no longer felt at ease in each other's company. All Alex's earlier charming insistence and enthusiasm for his impetuous proposal seemed to have fled with the harsh finality of the priest's words: "I now pronounce you man and wife."

Joss had tried desperately to conceal her true feelings about the marriage. Had she somehow, by a look or a touch, some word or action, betrayed her absurd longing? She had gone over and over every hour since she had come to his office in the warehouse, reviewing each moment until the mysterious messenger had arrived just as they were concluding their evening repast. She could think of nothing she had done that could have alarmed Alex, which left only the obvious—he was appalled at being leg-shackled to a tall, homely female with a willful temperament and an unconventional reputation.

Small wonder he had fled without revealing the nature of his summons, saying only that he did not know when he would return. She should not wait up for him. Implicit in his words was the suggestion that they would begin their arrangement immediately. He had departed to pursue his old life on the town and she was left to ascend the stairs to her quarters. Alone.

Being deserted on her wedding night should not have hurt so much. After all, she had known this would be no true marriage. She had certainly not expected to share his bed. But neither had she thought he would bolt from their house the way he had. What was in the missive sent by his uncle's servant? Probably nothing more serious than an invitation from one of his Cyprians, in whose arms he now reposed.

"Try not to think of that, Joss. You've made your solitary bed and now you must lie in it," she chided herself. There was no point in being morose or in dwelling on his liaisons with beautiful women. There would doubtless be a procession of them discreetly filing into his quarters after tonight.

All she could do was resolve to win back his friendship. After all, she had been given a splendid opportunity to share a much larger portion of Alex's life than she had known before. They could grow closer as confidants, living in such proximity. This arrangement would work. She would make certain that it did.

But what the devil *was* written in that accursed note . . . ?

As he climbed down from the hackney, Alex was surprised at the modest façade of the residence, considering the importance of the person living there. When he knocked on the heavy oak door, it swung open immediately and a somber servant ushered him down the hallway into a small, crowded library. A birdlike man with stooped shoulders and sharp gray eyes crossed the room, extending a veined hand slightly smudged with ink.

"Welcome, Mr. Blackthorne. I greatly appreciate your coming."

"Your message indicated considerable urgency, Mr. Russell," Alex replied, returning the surprisingly firm handshake. "How may I be of service to you, sir?" Alex was at a loss as to why he had been summoned to this meeting with the American chargé d'affaires.

"Before we continue, Mr. Blackthorne, I must have your word of honor not to divulge anything discussed here with anyone, whether you decide to help us or not."

Alex considered. "I must confess your clandestine summons has piqued my curiosity. Very well, you have my word."

"Please be seated. I'll be as brief as possible. My agents inform me that you are acquainted with Colonel Sir Rupert Chamberlain and his wife Lady Cybill."

A sardonic smile fleetingly touched Alex's lips. "If your intelligence is half as good as I suspect, you know the colonel and I dueled. He was severely injured, and he and his wife have both dropped from sight," Alex replied.

"We have just learned Colonel Chamberlain has been dispatched on a secret mission with several ships under his command."

"With all due respect, sir, I find that difficult to believe. His sword hand was rendered useless—surely his military career has ended."

The diplomat shrugged. "Apparently Sir Rupert is a more resourceful man than you imagined. We need to know where he is taking those ships and what their mission is. If he has sailed to join Wellington, it is of little consequence. However, if he sailed for Mobile Bay . . . With the tense situation between Britain and the United States over American land claims in Spanish Florida, a man like Chamberlain could be highly dangerous."

Thoroughly confused, Alex replied, "Sir, I am no spy. I fail to see how I might procure this information."

With a wry chuckle, the elderly statesman continued. "Only the past week Lady Cybill has returned to London and resumed her social schedule. She did at one point exhibit a certain tendresse for you, did she not? You possess a remarkable reputation with the ladies and you have entrée to the highest circles of British society through your mother's family."

"I will not use my uncle or any member of my family to gain information—not even for the United States," Alex replied stiffly.

"I am not asking you to do so, my boy. Surely you feel no such loyalty to Mrs. Chamberlain? The information we seek is vital to the safety of your country . . . not to mention your people in the Creek Confederation."

For the past year his father's letters had been full of concern that the British had agents stirring up the Red Sticks, a faction of the Muskogee who wanted to drive out all whites from their tribal lands. Alex knew his people would be mere pawns if they allied with the British. Running his hands through his hair, he considered a moment longer, then capitulated. "You do your research quite thoroughly, Mr. Russell."

"Then you shall do it?" Jonathan Russell's keen gray eyes glowed with triumph.

Alex nodded with an ironic smile. "If you think Lady Cybill will be so foolish as to whisper British Foreign Office strategy in my ear, I'll try to learn what I can from her."

"Splendid, Mr. Blackthorne, splendid."

"There is one more thing, however. If I learn anything that materially affects my father's people, I will warn him about it." He watched as the ambassador considered.

"I suppose that is only fair," Russell said at length.

"Then we have an agreement," Alex replied, rising from his seat.

"I knew your country could rely on you."

Alex shook the chargé d'affaires's hand saying, "Now I'll just have to see if I can rely on Lady Cybill."

"From what I have heard regarding your prowess with women, I should think she will fall in line quite handily. There is a ball at Lord Aston's Tuesday next. Mrs. Chamberlain will attend. If you would like—"

"No, I prefer to reacquaint myself with the lady in my own way," Alex said as they walked to the door. He considered informing Russell about his recent marriage, then decided against doing so. It would require too many explanations regarding his personal life and Joss's. He felt suddenly protective of her and did not want their arrangement to be the subject of gossip or speculation.

Little chance of avoiding that, he supposed, once it became obvious that the marriage was one that fettered neither spouse. Joss's crusade among the indigent would continue to horrify Suthington while her husband would acquire yet another in his succession of mistresses.

As he climbed into a hackney, he thought with a twinge

of amusement that there would be one unexpected benefit of this peculiar assignment. Constanzia had grown annoyingly possessive of late. He was pleased to have an excuse for pensioning off the beauteous Spaniard.

In keeping with her wedding night vow, Joss confronted Alex the following day and made clear her determination that they should resume their old friendship as if the marriage had never taken place. Alex seemed relieved at her declaration and pledged that he would treat her just as he had before the wedding. He even apologized for his absence the preceding night, although he did not give any reason for his abrupt departure.

Together they called upon the earl to announce their nuptials, which were written up in all the newspapers the following day. The interview with Suthington was ugly in the extreme and ended with the apoplectic old man calling down the wrath of heaven on them for such perfidy. Afterward Alex and Joss shared a good laugh over the unliklihood of anyone in the firmament heeding an invocation from Everett Woodbridge. Joss suspected that the earl was secretly relieved to be rid of his unmanageable niece and her hound from hell.

In the weeks that followed, they each went their separate ways, attempting to rebuild their previous lives as if the marriage did not exist, which in fact it did not. They saw each other little more than they had before. Joss rose with the dawn to begin her tasks at hospital and school while Alex slept late, spending afternoons at the shipping office and his nights in clubs and gaming hells. They did from time to time share a brief luncheon or afternoon chat. On the surface, their friendship had been renewed, but it remained irrevocably altered.

The spring of 1812 was cool and tranquil, although the political situation was not. When American forces moved into the Gulf Coast region surrounding the Bay of Mobile, the British government sent a harshly worded protest and the two nations slid another step closer to war. Heartened by favorable reports from Wellington on the peninsula, Britain was in no mood to brook insolence from her brash, land-hungry former colonists.

Closer to home, the ton was utterly titillated by gossip about the smoldering relationship between the wicked American and Colonel Chamberlain's beautiful wife. They were seen together dancing at balls and riding on Rotten Row. The fact that both were married only added spice to the forbidden stew. After all, wasn't it Alex Blackthorne who had crippled Lady Chamberlain's husband in that infamous duel? And wasn't Jocelyn Blackthorne the reforming zealot who shocked London by running away from the Earl of Suthington's household to elope with the American? How utterly delicious it all was!

Alex's pursuit of Cybill Chamberlain proceeded according to plan. The lascivious lady eagerly responded to his advances, fairly gloating with satisfaction when she encountered her in public. The problem was, Alex found that he did not enjoy the chase as he always had in the past. He ascribed this disconcerting fact to his ulterior motives and her marital state, not his own.

His life was on course, he assured himself. Work at the shipping office was going smoothly and his luck at the gaming tables had been especially good of late. *Lucky at cards, unlucky in love,* he mused.

"A penny for your thoughts, darling," Cybill purred, pressing her breasts against his shoulder as she leaned around to nuzzle his throat and brush his lips.

They were standing by a huge bow window overlooking the rose gardens at the Marquess of Brownlea's country estate, where they had been invited for a weekend of hunting and parties. Alex turned into her eager arms, expertly moving her behind the cover of the draperies as he returned her kiss.

172

Cybill Chamberlain was a beauty, no doubt about it. Her raven hair gleamed with a blue-black luster and lush, milk-white breasts spilled from the top of her low-cut gown. He looked down into brilliant violet eyes framed by thick black lashes. "The marchioness will send us packing if you persist in such public displays, pet."

"Bother the old biddy, everyone in London knows we're having an affair," she replied as one busy hand insinuated itself inside his waistcoat and slid beneath his shirt, while the other one rubbed the bulge in his trousers with practiced, deft fingers.

He lifted one eyebrow sardonically. "We haven't *had* an affair . . . yet."

"And whose fault is that? You seduce and promise paradise . . . and then something always intervenes," she said, pouting. "I'm tired of excuses."

"Half the thrill is in the chase, rather like foxhunting. Which reminds me, we're supposed to ride in a quarter hour and you're not dressed."

Cybill licked her lips with a small pink tongue and whispered, "We could ride right now . . . and I need not dress at all."

"Tempting," Alex replied, extracting her hand from his clothes and pressing a kiss on the soft palm. "But we'd be missed, I fear. The old marquess is a stickler for having everyone participate in the hunt."

Her violet eyes glowed with pure lust. "Very well. I shall leave you to eat my dust . . . until tonight when you may feast on something else . . . I shall slip into your rooms. The marchioness always gives the largest beds to her gentlemen guests."

He chuckled, giving her well-padded rump a swat as she turned to walk away. Once she vanished up the circular staircase to the second floor, his expression turned sour. Tonight he would have to bed her. She was beautiful, experienced and lusty, precisely the sort of female he preferred. Why then did the thought of tonight's assignation hold so little appeal?

Cybill was right. He had invented continuous excuses for not consummating their relationship. To date he had learned only bits and pieces of information to pass along to the chargé d'affaires. Chamberlain was indeed somewhere out of the country, although she did not specify where, and he found no subtle way to press her for more details. He had learned the reason Chamberlain's injury had not cost him his commission. The colonel had taught himself to use his left hand with as great a proficiency as he had previously used his right. Cybill could not resist taunting him with the threat of another challenge from her still deadly husband.

Alex was not certain what her motives really were. Did she desire him because he was the only man ever to best Chamberlain? Was it simple lust because her husband was absent? Or did she play a deeper game? No matter what her reasons, tonight she would get her wish. He would bed her. Silently damning life in general and Jonathan Russell in particular, Alex headed toward the sound of baying hounds and laughing houseguests.

Everything around her was a fuzzy blur, as if she were underwater, trying to see shifting distorted shapes through the murky haze. Drat, where were those accursed spectacles? She always felt so helpless without them. In early childhood she had been plagued with this disorientation, feeling utterly at the mercy of her surroundings, until her father had had her fitted with her first pair of eyeglasses. Even now the terrifying memories still frightened her.

Joss rummaged through the pockets of her dress searching for her spare pair, which she was never without—until now. How had she become so forgetful of late?

Poc gave a startled yelp when she accidentally stepped on his tail. "Sorry, fellow, but I can't see a thing unless I get down on my hands and knees and crawl about like a charwoman cleaning floors."

Sighing, she knew there was no help for it. She would have to do just that. Her spectacles had fallen from her face to the carpet while she was roughhousing with the dog. Somehow they must have bounced, because they were nowhere nearby. She lowered herself to the floor, groping very carefully so as not to step on them and break the lenses inadvertently.

Poc followed her every move now, brushing against her shoulder and planting a series of cold, wet kisses on her face to cheer her on. "Pray, don't *you* step on them," she scolded, trying to shove him back as she made a circuit around her bed.

Just as she reached the edge of the Tabriz rug, her hand came in contact with a wire earpiece. "Thank heaven," she cried, reaching out her hand to seize them while starting to get to her feet. When she stood up, Joss forgot the end table situated at the foot of the bed. Her shoulder struck it and she flinched, feeling the delicate narrow top teeter on its high spindly legs, setting off a fearful clatter of china vases, brass statuary and candlesticks.

Candlesticks! The lighted branch of candles tumbled off the table directly onto the thick cushion of the bed, setting fire to the sheer bed curtains. Joss clamped her glasses on her nose and glanced frantically around for something with which to smother the flames.

A blanket lay folded at the opposite end of the bed. In her haste to reach it, she forgot about Poc, who stood beside her sniffing at the smoke. When she turned she tripped over him and sprawled headlong across the carpet, landing in an ignominious heap across the floor while the fire blazed on.

By now thick, black smoke was beginning to fill the room. Joss's coughs were punctuated by the dog's alarmed barking. She scrambled to her feet, calling loudly for help as she fought her way to where the blanket lay, miraculously still untouched by the flames. Seizing it she rushed over to dunk it in the basin of water on the dry sink, then threw it over the curtains, which had burned free of the brass frame suspending them around the bed. As the flaming material fluttered onto the satin spread, the heavy wet blanket followed it down, snuffing out the conflagration.

Unfortunately by this time the fire had already jumped to the lace doilies on the bedstand and the linen scarf on the table across from it. Shrieking "Fire, fire!" at the top of her scorched lungs, Joss grabbed up the blanket and attacked the spreading blaze.

By this time her cries and the dog's frantic barking had brought two footmen, the cook and her helper all scrambling to help put out the fire. Within a few moments, which seemed like hours to Joss, they had the flames subdued to a smoldering mess of foul-smelling bed linens and charred wood.

Joss surveyed the once beautiful room's soot-stained walls and paint-bubbled furniture. "What will Alex say?" she wailed. "How could I have been so clumsy?"

"It weren't yer fault, mistress," Bonnie the cook replied, patting Joss's arm with a beefy red hand. "That silly chit of a maid set that brace of candles where they wasn't supposed to be."

"Yes, they belong on the pier table against the wall," Archie the footman said. The servants rallied around their sobbing mistress, whom they all loved dearly for her kindness, attempting to cheer her.

"Don't fret. The master is a good 'un. He'll not have a care about refitting the room. No real damage done that a coat of paint, some refinishing and a few new linens won't fix," Bonnie said, ushering Joss from the wreckage of her bedroom. "I'll have Mary fix up the bed in the next room for you to sleep on tonight."

*　　*　　*

Sleep eluded her. Her nose was stuffy and her throat raw in spite of the posset the cook had insisted she drink at bedtime. She coughed, then sneezed. Utterly wretched, Joss sat up and blinked owlishly in the darkness. As usual, she could see nothing but fuzzy outlines blurring into the inky blackness.

The pungent odor of smoke still hung heavy on the night air in spite of the window she had flung wide open before retiring. Unfortunately, the window was in the fire-damaged bedroom. The small one in this room had been so thoroughly painted shut that she could not budge it.

"A—a—achoo!" There was no help for it, she thought crossly. She had been deathly allergic to smoke ever since she was a small child. Her father had been forced to keep her away from the common room at the Fin and Feather because the men's pipes had caused her nose to stuff up and run.

She would get no rest until she got away from the smoky air. Vowing to get Archie to pry open the window in this room first thing in the morning, she sat up in bed and groped for her glasses. Once she had them safely settled on her nose, she swung her legs over the side of the bed and reached for her robe, shivering because she had been forced to sleep in her thin cotton chemise. The long flannel night rails she usually wore were casualties of the fire.

"Thank goodness Alex is out of town for the weekend," she murmured to herself as she made her way down the back stairs, holding a lone candle in one hand to guide her way. Although she had never been in his private quarters, she knew there was a second small bedroom similar to the one in her apartment. She would just have to sleep in it for tonight.

No need to trouble any of the servants, who were all asleep above the carriage house. Joss walked slowly down the long dark hall, peering through the first doorway. The room was large, filled with heavy masculine furniture.

Alex's room. Something drew her to step inside. A huge four-poster bed sat uncurtained in the center of the room, dominating it.

How would it feel to sleep in Alex's bed?

"No!" Joss whispered aloud, appalled at the very thought of invading his privacy.

But he's not home, the insidious voice wheedled.

She took another step closer. Her palms felt damp and her heart raced. She took a deep breath, relieved to find her head had cleared up in the fresh air. But it was not really clear, else she would not be contemplating such a wicked thing.

Where is the harm in it? He'll never know.

"But *I* will," she agonized. How bittersweet to lie there and imagine that her husband was coming to lie beside her. Or, worse yet, to imagine all the other women he would make love to in that bed. Visions of Cybill Chamberlain's plump, pale body entwined with Alex's made her squeeze her eyes closed in misery.

"No! I won't think of that," she whispered resolutely in the silent room, then backed out and walked farther down the hall to the second door. The small cubicle had been refitted into a dressing room with a large brass bathtub in one corner, a valet's pressing board and various irons in another. The rest of the space was taken up by a huge armoire and clothes chests. There was no bed.

She had two choices—return to the smoky upstairs and snuffle away the night or sleep in Alex's bed. Well, he was not using it. . . . To bolster her courage Joss retraced her steps into Alex's sitting room, where she knew he kept spirits. Over the weeks of their marriage he'd attempted unsuccessfully to convince her of the restorative benefits of sherry for a lady. Well, tonight she needed all the restorative benefits she could get.

Pouring a snifter full of the sweet, tangy liquid, she swallowed it down like medicine. Perhaps one more for good measure. Downing a second snifter as quickly as she had the first, Joss felt a languid euphoria settling over her as she made her way to the big bed. "Now I shall get a good night's sleep."

Alex lay staring at the ceiling where shadows danced, reflected from the lone candle flickering on the candlestand. What a bloody tangle his life had become. A month ago he was the happiest, most carefree man in London. Now . . . No, best to concentrate on the task at hand. Odd that bedding a beautiful woman had somehow become a matter of duty rather than pleasure. It left a sour taste in his mouth.

His troubling reverie was interrupted by the soft hiss of the bedroom door swinging open as Lady Cybill glided in. She was dressed in a sheer, voluminous robe of pale raspberry silk that did less to conceal the lush full curves of her milky flesh than did her long ebony hair, artfully arranged to fall in a shiny curtain over her breasts. She carried a candle in one hand, which she set on a table by the door, deliberately silhouetting her body in its light as she made her way slowly across the room to where he lay on the bed.

She's performing for me, he thought with grim amusement as he watched her slowly shed the whispery silk robe to reveal a low-cut sleeping gown in a deeper shade of magenta. The rich satin molded itself to her heavy breasts and rounded hips.

"Do you always stalk your men, Cybill?" he asked, swinging his long legs over the side of the bed and sitting up.

"Do you always wait for your lovers still clad?" she replied. Although barefooted and shirtless, he still wore his doeskin breeches.

"I'm scarcely dressed." He was not aroused either, in spite of her display of feminine pulchritude.

"What is it, Alex . . . hmmm? Are you afraid of Rupert?

You bested him once. Surely his having regained his skill left-handed should not worry you . . . or does it?"

An opening . . . of sorts. He strolled over to the piecrust table and filled two cut-crystal glasses with some of Brownlea's fine aged port, handing her one, then raising his in a mocking salute. "Let us just say this situation is different from our last contretemps. I don't relish having an irate husband charge in here to challenge me for bedding his wife."

"You, worried about scandal?" she scoffed, sipping the port as an amused smile bowed her pouty mouth.

"I did not relish maiming a man, no matter what you believe, Cybill. The next time I'd have to kill him . . . and then the British peerage would raise a hue and cry to hang me. I do relish my neck."

She polished off the port and set the glass aside, then pressed her hands into the curly hair of his chest, kneading the muscles like a contented cat. As she wound her arms around his neck and rubbed her lush breasts against his chest, she purred, "No reason to worry about my husband for now."

Alex reached between them to tweak her swollen nipples through the smooth satin gown. "How can you be so sure of that?" he asked, moving his mouth closer to hers.

Blind hunger glazed her eyes as she tried to pull his head down for a kiss. "Because Rupert is half a world away, in the American gulf at some godforsaken outpost in Spanish Florida."

As he nibbled her earlobe he said, "I thought Wellington had all the experienced English military officers in Spain."

Cybill shivered, nuzzling a flat male nipple with her raspy tongue. "All this lovely bronze skin. Perhaps I should have sailed with Rupert so I could have sampled others of your kind," she said with a husky air of excitement thickening her voice.

"My kind?" he echoed ominously.

Lust turned her eyes as black as ink in her white face. "Mixed bloods, red Indians. The ones they call by that name—red . . . somethings."

"Red Sticks?" *Renegades!*

"Yes, Red Sticks. Rupert is to meet with two of their leaders, Weatherford and McQueen."

"Weatherford and McQueen?" he echoed as nonchalantly as he could.

"Do you know them? Are they as wicked as you, my darling Alex, black-eyed with skin bronzed even where the sun does not touch it?" She panted as her fingers slid beneath the waistband of his trousers. "I want to see if all of you is so deliciously dark."

He knew those men! Peter McQueen was a renegade who lived on hatred, but William Weatherford was an educated man of peace. If a wealthy planter such as Weatherford would meet with Chamberlain, the situation on the frontier must be far more volatile than even his father had imagined. How appropriate that the British war office would send a snake like Rupert Chamberlain to offer the Creek Confederacy a devil's bargain.

While his mind turned over the information Cybill had just given him, she worked on satisfying her lascivious curiosity, unbuttoning his breeches and shoving the tight doeskin lower. "You are dark all over," she squealed excitedly. "Savage, primitive beauty!"

His face was harsh with disgust as he reached down and seized her wrists, pulling her hands off his buttocks, shoving her away from him. "So that's the fascination I hold for you. You want to say you've bedded a savage—a red Indian. A far superior trophy compared to an ordinary English rake." The loathing was plain on his face as he glared down at her and refastened his breeches.

"You needn't act so petulant, darling," she snapped. "Never mind all your lovely money, your savage blood is the real reason the ton has feted you. Surely, you know that."

"Rather like Mr. Johnson's dog who walks on his hind legs, eh?" he said furiously as he yanked on his shirt and boots. " 'Tis not that my social skills are as refined as a gentleman's but merely that a red savage can tie his cravat and eat with a fork that elicits English amazement."

He seized his jacket and stormed toward the door.

"Alex! Wait," she commanded, her voice rising in anger. "Where are you going?"

"Back to London. I find I've had quite enough of the Quality for one weekend!" As he slammed the door, Alex heard her stomp a bare foot with surprising force. The sound of one of Lady Brownlea's Meissen figurines crashing against the wall followed him down the hallway.

Fortunately Alex had ridden Sumac to the Brownleas'. He saddled the big roan and rode hard for the city, making good time in spite of a chill spring drizzle. In two hours he was pounding on the American chargé d'affaires's door. Exceedingly disgruntled and sleepy, Russell received his report, which quickly awakened the old man. "Damn and blast, the British aren't letting any grass grow beneath their feet, are they?"

"If the Red Sticks take to the warpath with British arms, there'll be no grass—or anything else—growing from Georgia to the Mississippi River," Alex replied. He went on to detail the positions of influence McQueen and Weatherford held with the Muskogee and the history of broken treaties that the Creek Confederacy had suffered at the hands of the American government. The old diplomat was far more interested in British operations on the gulf, questioning Alex about where Chamberlain would set up his headquarters with the Spanish, concluding Fort Charlotte on Mobile Bay was most likely.

By the time his disquieting interview was over, Alex was wet, cold and utterly out of sorts. For all the good it would do his Muskogee people, he might as well never have been involved with a viper like Cybill. The thought of bedding her sickened him. But to tell the truth, he was hardly shocked at the reason for Cybill's lust. Hell, half the women he bedded were fascinated with him because of his Indian blood. That had never bothered him before. But for some reason, Cybill's open admission threw him into a rage tonight, even though he had been without a woman for weeks, an unheard-of duration of celibacy for Alex Blackthorne.

Disgruntled and weary, he repaired to Chapel Street, unwilling to seek out his usual pleasure haunts. "All I really want tonight," he convinced himself, "is to tie on a roaring drunk and get a good night's sleep."

Chapter Twelve

Mmm, what a delicious dream. If a glass of sherry before retiring brought on these wonderful sensations, Joss dreamily concluded, she should indulge more often. Utterly sensual, startlingly unfamiliar sensations rippled over her body. As a large, long-fingered hand cleverly caressed her breast, she rolled over onto her back, allowing a second hand access to the other breast. The nipples tightened into hard little buds that burned; yet it was a most agreeable sort of fire.

The hands glided away from her breasts, one moving downward to the flat of her belly, tracing around her navel through the sheer softness of her well-worn old chemise while the other stroked the curve of her hip, gliding beneath the bunched-up cotton.

"What have we here, hmmm?" Alex whispered in brandy-soaked bemusement. Sweet, soft feminine flesh warming his bed. A most pleasant surprise, but how had she come here? Was she sent by Puck or perhaps Chitchester? He would puzzle that out later, his drink-befuddled brain decided. Right now his body demanded he partake of this unexpected gift.

A fleeting thought of Joss sleeping innocently upstairs crossed his mind, but quickly evaporated in brandy fumes. The silky wraith moaned. He leaned over her and brushed her partially open lips. The faint aroma of sherry blended with the more potent smell of the liquor on his breath. Thus enticed, he slanted his mouth over hers for a long, exploratory kiss.

Joss felt the first magical sweep of his lips across hers, light as butterfly wings. This was an exceedingly wondrous dream, the very best she'd ever had. With Alex. She knew his voice, low and rich as velvet, wickedly seductive. The whole weight of his body settled intimately over her, one long leg insinuated between hers, his hard chest pressed against her aching breasts while his mouth, no longer quite so gentle, took hers. His tongue teased along the seam of her lips, demanding entry. In panic—or was it instinct?— she opened them.

This is *Alex,* an insistent voice hammered at her. *This is no dream,* her mind cried out as his long powerful frame pressed her into the soft mattress. They were sealed together from head to foot. Through the sheer chemise she felt the crisp abrasion of his body hair. Though she could see nothing in the total darkness, she could feel that he was completely naked! She must stop this before it went any further. Why was he acting as if he desired her? Surely he could tell she was not one of his voluptuous and experienced Cyprians.

Her head was spinning as she writhed ineffectually beneath him, pinned helplessly to the bed. Oh, why had she drunk that accursed sherry? She tried to press her hands between them, intending to push him away, but when she touched the sinuous ripple of muscles in his chest, bunching and flexing like satin over steel, her fingers seemed to dig in rather than scratch, to cling rather than repel.

Joss whimpered as his mouth relinquished her lips, only to trail fierce, hungry kisses across her face and into her hair, which she had neglected to braid after brushing last night. Taking great fistfuls of her heavy long mane, he held her head immobilized, kissing her temples, her fluttering eyelids, the strong line of her jaw, then her throat, where a pulse thrummed in fear and excitement.

Perhaps if she had not drunk the sherry, she would have screamed and kicked until he withdrew, not acquiesced so swiftly. Perhaps if he had not drunk the brandy, he would have sensed her frightened response and known she was no courtesan.

"Ah, my lovely, you taste delicious," he whispered as his beard rasped against the delicate skin of her throat. He could feel her slender body writhe beneath him, inflaming his lust. He returned his attention to her mouth, feeling her hot, breathless little pants against his lips. Irresistible! He plunged his tongue into the sherry-sweet cavity.

Joss had never imagined such physical intimacy. Through her work in the East End slums she had learned the most basic facts of life. In a vague, shadowy way she knew that men bedded women, but beyond that she had never allowed her mind to consider exactly how they did so. Now, with his tongue thrusting in her mouth and his hips pumping a rhythmic counterpoint below, she was beginning to get a pretty good idea. His male member pressed into her belly. This was not a shapeless flaccid appendage hanging beside his leg like those she had occasionally glimpsed on the men at hospital. No, this was hard as iron, long and thick, standing upright, prodding against her as if . . . as if . . .

She should be repelled by this animalistic roughness . . . but it was Alex, her husband. He had a right to her body. Her nails dug into his shoulders as he continued to kiss and caress her. A low, insistent ache was spreading like smoldering tinder from her tender breasts to deep inside her abdomen where his hardness touched her. Something urged her to rub against it, like a cat twining as it is petted.

"So, you want more, hmm?" he murmured as he reached up and ripped open the neckline of the filmy garment she wore, exposing those pert, lovely breasts to the cool night air. The tips were pebble hard, ready for his mouth.

Joss almost rose off the mattress when he drew a sensitive nipple between his lips, pressing them together and teasing the tip with his tongue, then drawing the whole deep into his mouth to suckle. Her whole body went rigid with sharp pleasure and she dug her fingers into his thick golden hair, urging him to continue. Strange, wonderful sensations seemed to travel from her breasts down to her belly, centering on her most secret place, which mysteriously throbbed. What was happening to her?

"So eager, little one?" he said raggedly, switching from one breast to the other as he felt her nails dig into his scalp, urging him on. He raised his knee and pressed it hard against her mound and was rewarded with another startled panting whimper. His staff ached fair to bursting. How could he endure an instant more of waiting? She must be ready. He sat back on his heels, slightly disoriented in the darkness, and reached for the hem of her night rail, which was rucked up about her hips.

His hands glided over the satiny curves of her hips as he grasped the soft cotton and pulled it up. Joss knew he was stripping away the last infinitesimal layer of protection she had against him. She should protest. She should move away.

She helped him. Raising her arms and lifting her heavy hair, she shrugged out of the already ruined chemise. He tossed it aside, then pressed his body against hers once more. She gloried in his heat. It scorched her, hottest of all that hard, throbbing member that prodded insistently in her belly.

Should she touch it? Part of her wanted to, yet she was

187

afraid. As she hesitated, his hand slipped between her thighs as his knees spread them wide. When his fingers stroked her intimately a sudden raw jolt of the most excruciating pleasure she had ever felt, ever imagined, radiated through her body.

He could feel her wetness, soft, creamy, welcoming, yet his own rampant lust, dulled by drink, kept him from feeling the tiny flinch of apprehension that she gave. "Now," he breathed raggedly, guiding his engorged staff to the gateway of paradise. Just as its scalding heat touched her, she bucked her hips involuntarily. "Yes," he cried out, plunging deep inside in one triumphant thrust, which buried him to the hilt in her silky sheath. She was so incredibly tight, felt so gloriously good that he could not stop himself from thrusting, long, hard strokes, each building to a greater glory.

When he first touched her, the sensation was lovely beyond compare. She felt his male part press against her, and its hard heat intensified her craving. But when her body arched into his, the brief moment of bliss was all too quickly finished. Where there had been sweet aching anticipation and exquisite pleasure, now there was a sudden slicing pain, followed by the feeling that she was being stretched, filled, torn apart.

So this is how it is, a tiny kernel of calm deep inside her said as his great hard instrument began a steady rhythm of strokes, withdrawing, then plunging back into her slick flesh. Now she understood what the fierce savage kisses meant . . . a weak imitation of this primitive mating.

The pain quickly subsided once her fright at the way he had stretched her body came under control. She would not tear or break, only endure. In a few moments it became almost pleasant. That earlier low, anticipatory ache of excitement renewed itself once more.

Joss could feel her whole body sliding against his, damp with perspiration from his exertions, his muscles sleek and hard as they bunched and flexed over her. His breath came in harsh gasps as if he were in far more desperate pain than she had been earlier. His need seemed to intensify with each powerful thrust of his hips.

She raised her thighs, cradling him, drawing him instinctively into her as her arms wrapped around his broad shoulders. Her face burrowed against the corded column of his throat and something made her flick out her tongue to taste of him. *Alex is in my arms, making me his wife.* He tasted salty and male and she loved it.

He tried to hold off, to make the unbelievable pleasure last. God, if a few weeks of abstinence would make each sexual liaison as incredible as this, he might actually be persuaded to moderation! Then he felt the rasp of her small tongue against his throat, the tip darting out, flicking against his hammering pulse. And he was undone.

Joss became frightened when he suddenly stiffened and cried out, his whole body shaking like an ague patient as his male member seemed to swell even more, deep inside her. Then he quieted just as suddenly and she was left with a nagging ache at the place of their joining, something unfulfilled, despite the way his body filled her. She craved more, but it was not to be, whatever the elusive "more" might be.

Alex was in her arms. She was truly his wife now. The marriage had been consummated. Glorying in that, she held him tightly, not caring that his far greater weight pressed her deep into the mattress. Placing a soft kiss on his cheek, she closed her eyes and felt the beating of his heart in sync with her own.

His release had come in such great shuddering waves, it seemed never to end. When it was finally over, he collapsed on top of the woman, exhausted and replete. His hands tangled in her long mass of hair. So thick and luxurious. He wanted to see what color it was, to see her glorious body, her face. He could imagine her lying naked on the bed with her hair spread across the pillows like a mantle. And then he fell sound asleep.

Joss awakened to a faint whistling noise. She was being crushed by a great leaden weight. The low rhythmic noise registered as male snoring. Alex! She was asleep in Alex's bed. His body lay half covering her, one thigh thrown possessively across her hip, his arm curving protectively around her ribs, resting just beneath her bare breasts. She was lying against him as if they'd been made to fit as perfectly as two spoons in a drawer.

Thinking of what else they'd fitted together in the night brought a scalding flush to her face. Joss turned ever so carefully in his arms, trying to pull free of his grasp. Her hair was caught under his shoulder, but when she pushed gently, he rolled slowly onto his back, freeing her. She sat up, only to feel the loss of his body heat replaced by the chill of spring air.

There was not a stitch on her body. Instinctively she groped over to the bedside table and seized her eyeglasses, clamping them on her nose so that she could see. Her eyes flew to the remains of her torn chemise, tossed carelessly onto the floor. She clasped her arms around her breasts, shivering in fright. Her mouth tasted as if she'd chewed on one of Poc's dead rats and her head swam woozily.

What have I done? Looking down at her sleeping husband's face, its bronzed planes gilded in the first narrow shaft of dawn peeking in from between the closed draperies, Joss felt her heart stop beating. He was so splendid while she . . . she perched beside him with her tangled hair and gawky body, like a mud lark next to a nightingale. She remembered the overpowering aroma of brandy. He must have been quite drunk. How appalled he would be to awaken and discover to whom he had made love in the darkness!

I've broken our agreement. Shame coursed through her

in punishing waves as she imagined the expression of incredulity, then dawning horror on his face. Joss could not bear to see that. Moving very slowly, she carefully slid from the bed without disturbing the covers, then slipped on her robe and scooped up her torn chemise.

Frantically her eyes scanned the big, boldly masculine room for any further incriminating evidence. A pair of her old scruffy slippers peeped from beneath the bed. She stuffed her feet into them. Squinting at the bedcovers and pillows, she saw a long brown hair lying accusingly on the snowy linen. With trembling fingers she plucked it up. The only other evidence of her stay was the sherry glass sitting on the opposite side of the big bed. Did she dare retrieve it?

Alex chose that instant to roll toward her, the even sound of his soft snoring broken as he resettled himself in the covers. No, she might do something clumsy and awaken him. The glass could do no harm. After all, the piece of Waterford was from the table in his own sitting room.

Quickly she walked to the door, but something made her hesitate on the threshold and turn back for one last glance at his sleeping figure. *Please don't let this ruin our friendship, Alex.* With that she fled upstairs.

Alex heard his valet Foxworthy tidying up his dressing room. Blinking, he focused his eyes and peered at the brilliant spring sunlight pouring like warm butterscotch across the bed. It must be close to noon. He sat up, cradling his aching head in his hands. His mouth tasted like the bottom of the spittoon in Polly Bloor's old tavern in the Georgia backwoods.

Then the whole incredible night's events replayed in his mind. The fight with Cybill, the ride to the chargé d'affaires's house, the incredible interlude with the woman in his bed . . . this bed! He looked around him. There was no trace of her except for a glass sitting on the table, one of his heavy Waterford wineglasses. He reached over for it, sniffing the rim, and smiled. He thought she'd tasted of sherry, probably the sweet Portuguese.

Was she still about, sitting in the dining room at breakfast? What a lush, passionate piece she had been. If only he could remember the night more clearly. All that remained with him was the impression that making love to her had been the most singular experience of his life. Surely she had not left. Then came a flash of panic. Pray God, she had not collided with an early-rising Joss! He threw aside the covers and swung his legs over the side of the bed. Then he froze. Faint smears of blood stained the snowy white bed sheets. Damn, even his thighs were bloody.

"She must have been a virgin," he whispered to himself, aghast at the lusty tumble he'd given her. Now faint memories of her writhing body niggled. In his drunken hunger to ease himself, had he mistaken struggling for ardor? No wonder she had fled!

How the devil had she come to him, a virgin, sleeping in his bed? He'd heard rumors of some of the more expensive and perverse bordellos that procured innocents for the jaded tastes of wealthy clientele. Had one of his friends purchased her as a gift for him?

The other possibility was so remote, so inconceivable that it only belatedly occurred to him. Joss. She was his wife. But as soon as the absurd notion entered his mind, he dismissed it. Joss had never indicated anything but aversion to marriage and physical intimacy. He'd had to practically drag her before the priest even after pledging that they would both retain their freedom and that he would make no demands on her.

They had an agreement. Joss was a woman of high moral principles who would never break her word. The idea of her slipping into this bed, well fortified with drink, to seduce him was well beyond the improbable. Dismissing that disquieting thought from his mind, he called out for Fox-worthy to draw him a bath.

When he entered the dining room, he was startled to see Joss sitting at the table, toying with a plate of kippered salmon and eggs. "What are you doing home at this scandalously late hour?" he inquired more sharply than he intended. Normally she rose at dawn and was off to the hospital or the school well before he came in to break his fast.

"Oh, good morning, Alex." She took a deep breath, clutching the fork in her hand so tightly she must surely have bent the soft sterling. "Lady Wyckham sent round a note canceling the Mission Society meeting this morning. I decided to wait until Archie brings Poc home before I walk to the hospital. Mr. Vincent asked if he could take him to the school yesterday evening. The children had been frightened by another big rat." Her voice was steadier than she'd hoped but she could not meet his eyes.

"Ah, I wager he's made short work of it by now," he replied. "I wondered where he was when I came in last night." Why would she not look at him? *Dear God, don't let it be!*

"I might ask you why you're home from the country so soon. Weren't you to remain for hunting until Monday?"

He shrugged, studying her nervous fidgeting with increasing foreboding. "I became bored with Brownlea's crowd. . . . Is there something you wish to say to me, Joss?" he asked at length, standing rigidly by the sideboard, staring at the congealing eggs on the platter.

"Well . . ." She moistened her lips and took a deep breath. "There was a fire while you were gone."

His head jerked up and their eyes collided. "A fire?" he echoed dumbly.

"I started it. I'm sorry I'm so clumsy. I was playing with Poc and overturned a branch of candles in my quarters. Bonnie says the damage can be fixed with a bit of fresh paint but some furniture must be refinished, too."

She looked so wretchedly contrite and he felt so utterly relieved that he almost picked her up and kissed her. "Was no one injured?" he asked, chuckling aloud when she brightened and shook her head.

"I'm ever so glad you aren't cross, Alex. I couldn't bear it if you were out of sorts with me. Bonnie and Archie both said you wouldn't be."

"They were right, Joss. What kind of ogre do you think I am? Now you can at last spend some of my ill-gotten gains on yourself. Refurbish the upstairs to your taste," he said expansively as he filled a plate with kippers, eggs and a generous portion of kidney pie.

It was uncommonly reassuring to know that his drunken lust had not destroyed his camaraderie with Joss. Now if only he could track down his "gift." He would begin first thing this afternoon.

"Haven't the foggiest, old chap," Drum said, lifting his wrist to his nose as he flicked his emerald-encrusted snuff box closed with his other hand. "You have my word, I did not procure that chit for you, nor have I heard rumors regarding who did." He inhaled and sneezed precisely in a snowy linen handkerchief. "Sounds like Forrester to me."

Alex paced in frustration. "I've already asked Puck. And Chitchester and Alvanley, everyone I could think of."

Drum's cool green eyes looked amused. "I was last on your list, I assume," he observed dryly.

Alex scowled at his friend's good humor. "I have observed . . . shall we say, your rather surprising sense of protectiveness toward Joss since we were married."

Drum laughed. "Your lady is in as much need of protection as General Massena is from the Austrian army." He studied Alex's agitated pacing. "That chit must've been quite a sybaritic delight for you to search her out this way."

Alex had not mentioned his midnight lady's virginity . . .

but his fascination with her went beyond even that. He wished he knew precisely what compelled him. Drum's next comment brought him from his brown study.

"Have you considered Rushcroft as your benefactor?"

"He would certainly know where such an expensive delicacy could be procured," Alex replied. "Yet I doubt he was the one. I had planned to visit him last." Frankly he dreaded facing Monty's mocking amusement when he was forced to enlist his aid. Alex had always made it clear that the decadent diversions of the peerage held no charms for him, refusing his uncle's invitations to visit "viewing rooms" to watch other men perform on women, even boys. An appalling variety of perversions, active and passive, were available if one possessed sufficient blunt . . . and the ennui required for one to wish this sort of entertainment.

His uncle professed to know nothing of Alex's gift. "A virgin, you say? Are you certain? There are ways to fake it involving surgical skills acquired in the Orient."

"She was most certainly a virgin. I've had enough women of both kinds to tell the difference," Alex replied stiffly, looking about the deserted alcove in Whites where he and Monty sat sharing a drink.

"You were foxed, were you not?" Monty asked, lifting one brow.

The old devil's enjoying this. "Not nearly that drunk. Can you help me find her? How many places deal in genuine innocents?"

The cynicism in the baron's eyes glowed. "I told you marrying that Methody wench was a mistake. She may be twice as smart as Octavia but she's equally cold."

"Leave Joss out of this. She's a good and loyal friend. We were speaking of bedmates."

"You'd have been better served to defy your father and remain single. Lud, it's not as if you needed the blunt."

"You're an odd one to preach against a marriage of convenience. And I did not accuse you of wedding just for money. You did it as a duty to your family, don't deny it."

Monty shrugged. "I do admit to a once and faded hope for an heir to claim the title . . . but after my wife suffered two miscarriages, her physicians assured me she would be barren. Your arrangement neatly precludes even the possibility of legitimate Blackthornes."

"My parents are already provided with ample heirs," he replied, uncomfortable now for an entirely different reason.

"But your sister's children won't be Blackthornes, will they? You could bed the bluestocking," Monty said, shifting the subject back to Joss.

A faint hint of color heated Alex's dark countenance. "Why must everyone persist in throwing Joss at me?" he replied with an oath.

"Perhaps because you married her," the baron suggested dryly. A rich, mocking chuckle came from him as he signaled a waiter to refill their drinks. Then seeing the mutinous set of his nephew's jaw, a characteristic that reminded him fondly of his younger sister, he said, "I shall make inquiries with several of the more discreet and pricey establishments that most likely were the source of your mysterious gift. Are you quite certain you can't describe her with any greater clarity?"

Alex raked his fingers through his hair, newly cut in the latest Brutus fashion. Frustration was etched on every plane of his face. "I told you 'twas black as a moonless night in the Apalachicola swamplands. I could *feel*, not see. She had long, long hair, lots of it, thick and soft, a slender body, high breasts—rounded but not large, flared hips and sleek curved calves."

Monty chuckled. "At least 'tis obvious it could not have been your wife come to claim her marital rights of you." At Alex's look of guilty horror, the baron laughed again, then said, "I shall see what I can do to locate your vanishing virgin, my boy."

* * *

In the following weeks, warmer weather finally arrived along with some distressing news from America. Barbara Blackthorne was coming to meet her new daughter-in-law. But there was still no word regarding the identity of Alex's mysterious bedmate. To further add to the turmoil in his already complicated life, his relationship with Joss, which had subtly shifted from the hour they'd spoken their marriage vows, had now deteriorated still more.

At first he had thought she would get over her maidenly discomfort at sharing a house with a man who lived in his style. He gave her time to adjust. They shared occasional meals and discussed matters of mutual concern—politics, social reform and her work. But the easy camaraderie, the teasing laughter seemed less spontaneous than it had before they shared a name and a roof.

Since the silly accident with the fire, the situation had grown decidedly worse. Joss seemed to avoid him at every opportunity. When they did meet accidentally, she always seemed to have a ready excuse for not sharing a meal or spending the evening together. Over the course of the past year and a half he had come to expect her to welcome him whenever he felt in need of her cheer. He relied on her companionship far more than he'd realized. Now the shoe seemed to be on the other foot. It was he who waited and she who came and went as she wished.

At times he wondered if she had somehow found out about the virgin he'd taken in their home. The thought of asking her directly left him frankly terrified. What would her reaction be? He assured himself that the chance she knew anything of the event was so remote as to be nearly impossible, unless the chit had ventured upstairs to confront his wife. But that was an equally remote possibility inasmuch as the mystery woman, virgin or no, was a professional who had doubtless been well paid.

Whatever the baffling reasons for this estrangement, Alex was coming to realize that his original misgivings when he'd proposed this arrangement to Joss might have been well founded. Marriage had become the ruination of a rare friendship.

It helped not a whit that he was as sexually frustrated as a fourteen-year-old at Eton. For some utterly perverse reason, since the virgin, none of the women who had crossed his path appealed to him. Lady Cybill pouted a while, then cast her lure once more, but he was heartily sick of her and all her sisters under the skin from drawing rooms to bordellos.

Truth be told, he was finding many of his earlier wastrel pleasures to be a source of boredom. He found himself working longer hours at the warehouse and brooding about the virgin who seemed to have vanished from the face of the earth. If only he could find his bedmate, he was certain at least one of his problems would be solved. But Monty had not been able to turn up a trace of her in spite of his formidable connections.

For the moment a more pressing difficulty loomed, however. The imminent arrival of his mother. He must at all costs keep her from learning the true nature of his arrangement with his wife. But how could he make her believe that a woman like Joss had ever attracted him in the first place? Barbara Blackthorne was no fool and she knew her only son's taste in females quite well. The situation was almost enough for him to wish for war between Britain and the United States, thus keeping her safely at home across the Atlantic.

But war had not arrived and his mother's ship had. The *Savannah Star* would be docking that very afternoon. Somehow he and Joss must join forces to convince Barbara of their domestic felicity. Nervously he waited for his wife to join him for luncheon. With no appetite whatsoever, he stared at the cold collation of fruit, cheeses and thinly sliced beef that Bonnie had set out.

"My, you look as if you planned to slaughter that cow

all over again," Joss said to her scowling husband as she entered the dining room. Her forced gaiety ill concealed her unease regarding her mother-in-law. What would a beautiful woman such as Barbara Blackthorne think of her son being wed to a clumsy, half-blind bluestocking such as Jocelyn Woodbridge?

Alex looked up and smiled. "I hope your morning was productive. No trouble at the school?"

"No. Poc's freed the building of rats and sweep catchers."

At the mention of his name, the dog gave a cheerful bark and sat expectantly at the end of the sideboard, his keen nose twitching at the smell of food.

"Just be certain you never walk about that neighborhood or anywhere near the hospital without him along to protect you."

"I've always been quite safe, Alex." Unspoken between them lay the memory of her father's untimely death. Like Elijah, his daughter had made many enemies. She studied her husband's face as he filled their plates, mindful that she disliked Stilton cheese and preferred her beef well done. "This isn't about my safety, is it, Alex?" she said after they sat facing each other at the table.

He sighed and leaned back in his chair, shoving the small pot of freshly grated horseradish in circles on the pristine white linen tablecloth. "No, it isn't. We have to come to some sort of understanding about my mother."

"She won't like me, will she?" Joss asked, clutching her napkin tightly in her lap.

"Of course she'll like you. You're bright and witty and charming," he soothed.

"But not at all what she'll expect your wife to be."

Alex swore and shoved back his chair, started to get up, then leaned forward and met her gaze. "Not exactly," he equivocated, then rushed on, "but we can convince her we're suited."

"Frankly, since none of your friends or mine believe it, I fail to understand how we shall pull it off."

"She's already indicated that she'll be staying with Monty and Octavia, so that should make matters less complicated. We won't be forced to share a bed." As he blurted out the bald facts, his face heated almost as much as Joss's did.

"We shall be much in her company, Alex, in spite of that," she reminded him.

He reached up and rubbed his eyes, searching for a way to say what he meant to say. Bloody hell, when had it become so difficult to talk with Joss? "While we're in her company, we shall have to . . . that is . . . well, act as if we were . . . friends," he finished weakly.

"As we did before we were married?" she asked quietly.

He cleared his throat nervously. "Er . . . perhaps friends isn't quite right either." He wondered if he looked as utterly wretched as he felt. Finally managing a crooked grin, he said, "There is no way to ice this smoothly, Joss. We shall have to pretend to be lovers—only pretend," he hastened to add when she emitted a small gasp.

The pain startled her, squeezing her throat dry for a moment so that she could not speak. *Pretend to be lovers.* As if the idea were so utterly ludicrous as to be unimaginable! But they *had* been lovers, at least for one night. One glorious blissful night when she had slept in his arms. Joss blinked back the burn of tears and nodded. "I understand, Alex, but I've no practice at such arts. I shall follow your lead." *And pray Barbara Blackthorne's visit is a brief one.*

Chapter Thirteen

Barbara stood on the deck of the *Savannah Star*, flagship of her husband's mercantile fleet, as it glided along the London quay. Her heart thrummed with excitement as she scanned the crowded pier, hoping to catch sight of Alex's golden head. She missed her only son quite desperately and had already decided to pay him a visit when the letter announcing his marriage reached them.

She chewed her lip in vexation, praying she and her new daughter-in-law would like each other. The marriage had been sudden and unexpected. *Perhaps she's already rounding out with my next grandchild,* she thought with an arch grin. Impending fatherhood and family responsibility would serve to tame the young hellion . . . as much as any Blackthorne male could be tamed.

On the dock, Joss stood beside her husband, myopically scanning the large ship's deck for her mother-in-law. Alex had never described Barbara Blackthorne except to say she was considered a beauty. What would she think of her handsome son's unlikely choice of a bride? Alex's gloved hand pressed against her own, which rested possessively in the crook of his arm. She could feel his steely biceps flex as he moved, and her mouth went dry.

Joss had donned her best gown, a light gray poplin with lace collar and cuffs. Her hair was smoothed back into a neat coil, for once centered on her head, but the weight of it pulled miserably at her scalp. She felt a headache coming on, but knew it was as much from nervousness as from her braids. *I look as good as I can,* she repeated silently to reassure herself. It did not work.

Then Alex began waving and Joss saw Barbara Blackthorne. Observing the statuesque woman with pale gold hair and exquisitely chiseled features gliding down the gangplank, Joss would have sworn she was Alex's sister, not his mother. Her son's offhand comment that she was considered a beauty was a gross understatement. She was a vision in soft pink muslin.

Only as the woman drew closer could Joss see the glint of silver at her temples, blending in with curling masses of hair several shades paler than her son's. Her whole face beamed when she smiled, revealing straight white teeth and a few tiny wrinkles at the corners of her eyes.

"Alex, my darling, it's been so long!" she cried as he swept her up into his arms and swung her around like a child. When he set her back on the ground, Joss stared at mother and son. She was tall for a female, almost as tall as Joss, although Alex's massive body dwarfed hers. His bronze skin and chocolate eyes were obviously inherited from his mixed-blood father, but there was a bit of something about the mouth and the jaunty tilt of his head that spoke of Barbara.

They turned from each other and Alex performed the introductions, carefully taking Joss's hand like an attentive bridegroom as she made her curtsy to her new mother-in-law.

"Welcome to London. I am very pleased to make your

acquaintance," Joss said, trying to be natural, yet knowing how stilted the words sounded. She could sense Barbara's bright turquoise blue eyes sweeping over her, but there was nothing scornful or hostile in the gaze.

Barbara moved forward and embraced Joss warmly, saying, "It is long past time this wild rogue was brought to heel. I am delighted to meet the woman formidable enough to accomplish the trick! Welcome, Jocelyn, to the Blackthorne family."

She smelled faintly of violets and her embrace felt so sincere that a bit of the stiffness left Joss's body. "Thank you, milady. You are most kind."

"Stuff. I haven't considered myself a *lady* since I left England thirty-two years ago. You must call me Barbara. I fear I'm a thoroughly reconstituted American, Jocelyn."

"More so than my father, who was born in Georgia," Alex said with a grin, delighted that his mother accepted Joss.

"Speaking of that rascal, he sends greetings to you both and welcomes you, Jocelyn, as the newest Blackthorne. So do Mellie, Charity, Susan and Polyanne and all their husbands."

"All?" Alex asked. "I take that to mean Mellie has gone and married her farmer."

"His name is Aaron and he dotes on her."

"It must be wonderful to have such a large, happy family," Joss said wistfully. "Alex has spoken often about his sisters."

"No doubt to tell you how they tormented him," Barbara replied with a chuckle, then took Joss's hand and squeezed it. "Now you, too, are a part of our large, happy family."

"Tell me about Alex as a little boy," some imp made Joss ask as they traversed the busy wharf to where Alex's coach awaited them.

While the coachman loaded up Barbara's trunks, Alex

protested as his mother related anecdotes of a lone boy growing up surrounded by sisters.

As they prepared to climb into the carriage, Alex felt constrained to ask, "Are you certain you don't wish to stay with us, Mama? We have enough room."

"Nonsense, you are still newlyweds, who deserve privacy in your quarters. Monty and Octavia are rattling about in that huge city house with several wings to spare—and a good thing, too, for I shall keep at least one between my sister-in-law and me at all times," she added with a merry peal of laughter.

"Uncle Monty wanted to be here to meet you, but his manager arrived this morning from the estate with some sort of difficulty the baron must deal with immediately," Alex explained, greatly relieved his mother would not be observing their sleeping accommodations firsthand. He gave the coachman the Caruthers's city house address and they were off.

"What do you think of your son's bluestocking bride, Babs?" Monty Caruthers asked his sister as he handed her a late-night libation.

Barbara accepted the brandy, then sat down in an oversize leather easy chair in his book-lined study. "Do I detect a hint of mockery in your voice?" she asked sharply.

The baron shrugged. "You must confess she's hardly the sort of female one would expect Alex to marry," he replied dryly. They, along with his now retired wife, had just spent the evening entertaining the newlyweds at dinner and the theater.

"She's in love with him," Barbara announced. "Quite desperately so and he has not the faintest notion of it."

Monty studied her over the rim of the crystal. "I wonder if he does . . . oh, not consciously, no," he hastily amended when she raised one eyebrow quizzically. "But you should have been here the evening he came barging in to ask my help in securing the special license. A man don't leg-shackle himself without a demn strong reason. Mine was money. Alex has plenty of the blunt and the gel's penniless. I concluded his reason must be something not at all apparent, even to him. Always was curious about why he kept sniffing about that one. Met her the day he arrived in London. I tried to talk him out of it, you know."

"Whatever for? She's quite perfect for him," Barbara said heatedly.

He threw back his head and laughed. "Is it to be matchmaking then, puss? You ever were the romantic."

"Well, something must be done to wake him up. Men are such fools. His father was quite determined that we should not suit until I took matters into my own hands."

A brief hint of pain flickered in his eyes, then was gone as the cynical mask of bored peer slipped back into place. "And so you drove me away at gunpoint and remained behind in that barbaric colonial wilderness. Tell me, Babs, is that how you convinced Devon to wed you—at gunpoint? I don't believe that will work with Joss and Alex's marital arrangement."

Although they had parted bitterly on that fateful day in Savannah, Barbara had long since forgiven her beloved elder brother for his attempt to force her to return to England. Smiling, she said, "I was able to convince my red Indian by somewhat more subtle means, although if all else had failed, I would have had no qualms about dragging him before the priest at gunpoint. As to making Alex see that he desires Jocelyn, I have an ace or two to play before I resort to firearms."

Early the next morning Barbara arrived at the newlyweds' home on Chapel Street just as they'd agreed upon the preceding evening. Alex had escaped to an unusually early business meeting, leaving Joss to await his mother's arrival. The bride was nervously pacing in their sitting room as

Archie opened the front door to usher the elder Mrs. Blackthorne inside. Dinner and the play had been pleasant enough, considering that they were forced to endure Octavia's hateful company. But now Joss and her mother-in-law would be alone together. Much as she liked the beautiful Barbara, Joss was terrified of her.

How can I continue this charade for a whole month? She asked herself as her mother-in-law whisked into the room and gave her a cheery buss on the cheek.

"Alex tells me you are an early riser. I confess that I never was until the children came. There is no way to remain dozing away the morning with two little girls shrieking and giggling and a small boy yelling at the top of his lungs that they've stolen his rock collection."

"You explained how he avenged himself on them," Joss replied with a chuckle. "How horrid it must have been for Mellie and Charity to find that garter snake in their jewelry box."

They chatted of inconsequential things as Joss showed Barbara around their home, deliberately leaving Alex's bedroom off the tour. All the personal items in her own quarters upstairs had been carefully concealed so the room would look unoccupied. Poc, however, refused to budge from the foot of her bed where he was taking a nap. She hoped Barbara did not attach any significance to that.

They entered the sitting room, where Bonnie had placed the silver tea service between two shield-back chairs facing the bay window. After the two women were seated, Joss began to pour. She almost scalded herself when Barbara said, "You are in love with Alex, aren't you, Jocelyn." Her gentle tone indicated it was not a question.

Joss tried to smile brightly. "Of course I love him. He is my husband." She willed her hand not to tremble as she set the pot aside and inquired, "Lemon or milk?"

"We've chatted around the matter since I arrived, my dear. Let the tea cool," she urged, reaching out and placing her hand over Joss's. Her clear aqua eyes were kind yet shrewd as she studied her daughter-in-law. "This is no ordinary marriage, is it?"

"I told Alex we wouldn't be able to fool you about our arrangement."

"Perhaps you should explain this 'arrangement,' " Barbara prompted.

Joss's mind raced. Alex would be terribly upset if she confessed that he had set out to deceive his family . . . yet his mother could already see that it was so. Perhaps if she shouldered the blame, it might not be as bad. She moistened her lips and plunged in, starting with their first disastrous meeting on the docks and the ensuing friendship that developed from the encounter. "He really is quite remarkable, this son of yours, rescuing pit dogs and preacher's daughters, supporting charity hospitals and playing with slum children at a mission school."

Barbara's smile was tinged with sardonic amusement. "From this paean of praise, I can certainly see why you fell in love with him, but I know there is another side to Alexander David Blackthorne. He was not sent to London as a reward for his sterling nobility," she said dryly. "His reputation for brawling, drinking, gambling and . . . baldly put, wenching, was legendary across the Georgia backcountry all the way to the Muskogee towns. Indeed it was his Grandmother Charity's suggestion that we pack him off to his English family to mend his ways."

"I'm afraid Alex did not find London to be a penance," Joss said in monumental understatement.

Barbara's expression was droll as she chuckled at the irony. "Knowing my brother as he did, Devon was dubious about the plan. Truth be told, so was I, but we had visited Monty and Octavia when Alex was a small boy, and his uncle was quite taken with the lad. Monty had settled down and seemed to be meeting his responsibilities. Quite frankly, I could come up with no other solution which would not have caused Alex to walk away from us."

" 'Tis true, he's developed a bit of a reputation as a rake about the ton, but he's also been working quite successfully at the warehouse," Joss hastened to add. "Mr. Therlow has praised his diligence and industry." A bit of an exaggeration about sour old Bertie, but Joss figured she was already deep in the suds with Alex as things stood.

"So, you and Alex became fast—if unlikely—friends. But you must explain this 'arrangement,' " Barbara said, directing the conversation back to their relationship once more.

Joss bit her lip, trying to gather her thoughts. Strange, but her uncle's threats had never unnerved her the way Barbara's shrewd, gentle questioning did. "It all began when my father was killed . . ." She outlined the events leading up to her desperate appeal to Alex in the warehouse office. "So, you see, I was in need of protection and we could contrive no other way to prevent the earl from forcing me to wed Yardley."

"And Alex nobly offered to sacrifice his freedom to save you?" Barbara asked with one slim eyebrow raised dubiously. At that moment the resemblance between mother and son was quite unmistakable.

"Well, he did agree to marry me," Joss equivocated.

Barbara had a pretty fair idea of what had transpired. "A marriage of convenience in which he was free to continue his libertine life while you returned to your work among the poor. You are not sleeping together, are you, Jocelyn?"

One time, one glorious time, was on the tip of her tongue, but the shameful way it had occurred made her unwilling to speak of it. "No, we are not. My quarters are abovestairs, his in the master suite down the hall," she said in a subdued voice.

"I see." Barbara's fingertips tapped on the arm of the shield-back chair.

"Please do not blame Alex . . . or hate me too much. I

know I will never be able to give him heirs—but . . . the marriage can be annulled when he finds a suitable wife." God forgive her, she would lie to set him free. Alex, having no inkling that the marriage had indeed been consummated, would not perjure himself. *But how can I give him up?*

Barbara moved to Joss's side and startled her with a swift embrace. Hugging her protectively, she said, "Jocelyn, my daughter, of course I do not hate you, although I do blame Alex for being so blind that he cannot see he already has a most suitable wife. The problem is not you—it is his aversion to being well and truly married."

To her utter mortification, Joss felt the tears trickling down her cheeks and blinked them back, struggling to speak. "But . . . but I am *not* suitable, not suitable at all. I am tall and plain and clumsy. I—"

"Twaddle. You *are* tall, but considering Alex's size, that's an asset. As to the rest, we can easily enough remedy your appearance. Hmm . . . let me see."

She stood up and walked around Joss's chair, then removed her glasses and studied the girl's face from several angles. "You have excellent features, strong and cleanly molded. Don't squint your eyes. They're quite a lovely shade of clear light blue with good thick lashes."

"But I can't see a thing without my glasses."

"We shall decide what to do about that later. For now . . ." She began to unpin Joss's hair, exclaiming over its thickness and length. "Why ever have you concealed so much hair in such an unflattering braided bun?"

"As you say, there is so much of it. I just wanted to get it out of my way," Joss said practically.

Barbara held one long strand out to the morning light streaming in the window. "The color is a bit dull. I have just the thing, an aloe wash to make it shine, and we shall rinse it in lemon juice to lighten it and bring out more bronze and gold. "Stand up," she commanded, pulling Joss from the chair.

"What are you—" Joss's protest was cut short when Barbara began to tug at her oversize, heavy brown dress.

"I warrant this is large enough to make blankets for every bed in your hospital—about the right weight and color too," she added. "A trip to the dressmaker shall be first on our list."

"Barbara, you are acting as if you can make me over into someone else," Joss said sadly. This was all quite hopeless.

"No, my dear. You already are a bright, witty, good-hearted and firm-willed young woman. I would not change your personality one whit. That is why you and Alex suit so well—he needs a strong and intelligent wife to stand up to him. All I am going to do is tinker a bit with the outer wrapping."

"One cannot make mutton into lamb," Joss said as she once more attached her spectacles to her face.

"Ah, but one can help a duckling become a swan. Leave it all to me."

Alex scarcely saw his wife or mother in the following week. The two had become quite inseparable friends, laughing and talking as if they had known each other for years. They embarked upon a perpetual round of shopping excursions and spent hours mysteriously closeted in Joss's upstairs "sitting room" as they had dubbed her quarters for his mother's benefit, doing heaven knew what. Although he was happy that his mother was so taken with Joss and that she seemed unaware of the true nature of the marriage, he remained distinctly uneasy. Something was afoot. He could sense it in his bones.

But what the devil were they up to?

While Alex fretted, Barbara spent what Joss considered a ghastly sum of money on the complete new wardrobe Alex had told her to buy when they first were wed. She had not done it then, because she had not the faintest idea about what to buy or whom to buy it from, even if she had been inclined to spend anything on herself.

After Joss had been pinned, poked, draped and shod, Barbara began experimenting secretly with hair and skin treatments, various new hairstyles and a few subtle cosmetics, the latter being scandalously wicked indulgences to Joss.

Since Barbara's arrival they had dined out every evening either at the Caruthers's city house or elsewhere, but during that time Alex noticed no change in his wife's appearance. Indeed, there was little. The only thing discernable was a slight lightening of her hair, still well concealed in its usual tightly braided bun. Barbara was as eager to unveil her makeover as Joss was to forestall it. They decided to wait until her wardrobe arrived from the dressmaker before dazzling Alex with the "new" Joss. She and Alex had no time to talk privately, which suited Joss just as well, for she was growing increasingly nervous about Barbara's plan.

Finally the big night arrived.

"There is no reason to be so tense, Jocelyn. 'Tis only a small dinner party in your own home. The four of us and Alex's friend. Octavia won't even be here."

"But Alex's *friend* Drum will," Joss said tartly.

"I take it the two of you do not get on?"

Joss sighed. "He and Alex are fast friends and he has saved Alex's very life. I do owe him much. I am learning to feel . . . charitable toward him."

Barbara chuckled as she finished arranging Joss's hair in a soft poof of curls piled high atop her head. "There. You look all the crack if I do say so myself." Barbara stood back to admire her handiwork as Joss stood up uncertainly in new slippers with fashionable pointy heels.

The gown was so sheer and low cut she felt nearly naked. She inspected the tall, slender figure in the mirror with awe. Her dress molded tightly around her breasts and clung provocatively to her hips. Could those curves possibly belong to her—tall, gawky, shapeless Joss?

Seeing the way Joss's hands plucked at the delicate sky-blue mull, Barbara said, "See, Madam Fabre told you your figure was extraordinary. I especially like the shade your hair turned out—not too light at first. Perhaps we shall lighten it a bit more later, gradually."

As if to speak his piece, Poc looked at his newly tricked out mistress and gave a tail-wagging bark of approval.

Glancing down at him Joss said, "I want no shrieking cooks and stolen meat courses tonight, not to mention any more remonstrances from Fitch, that overbearing butler Uncle Monty has foisted upon us. You, rascal, shall be confined upstairs for the rest of the night."

But what would happen when the party was over? Would Alex ask her to spend the night in his bed? A deep shiver of excitement snaked down her spine at the thought. Her palms grew damp and her heart thrummed frantically when she heard his voice downstairs calling up, "Joss, Mama, our guests have arrived."

"I shall greet them and usher everyone into the sitting room for a libation before dinner. Then you shall make your entrance. But you must forgo these," she said, removing Joss's spectacles. "They quite spoil the effect. Thursday next we have an appointment with Doctor Torres to see about correcting your vision a bit. Remember, do not at any cost squint. Just hold on to things as we practiced earlier."

Just hold on to things. Hah! Easy for someone with normal vision to say, Joss thought, focusing on the issue of her eyeglasses to keep from considering what she would say to Alex—and how he would react to her. "Don't squint," she repeated like a mantra as she crossed the room slowly and made her way to the stairs. As a talisman, she placed her glasses in the tiny reticule she carried on her wrist. Very carefully she began to descend the long flight of steps, hearing the jovial banter between Alex, Monty and

Drum. Then she heard Alex inquire about her absence.

"I do believe you shall consider her tardiness well worth the wait," Barbara replied as she stood in the sitting room doorway looking into the foyer as Joss approached the bottom of the stairs. "Come, Alex. Greet your wife."

Joss's depth perception had never been good even with her eyeglasses. Without them it was nonexistent. When she glanced down to take the last step, her high-heeled slipper caught in the hem at the back of her gown. In reflex, her foot kicked out, further unsettling her balance. She jerked backward and both her feet slipped on the carpeted stairs, flying out in front of her. Before she could do more than utter a horrified yelp, she went clumsily down in a bone-jarring thunk while her sheer muslin gown ballooned gracefully up in a soft swish. She landed on the edge of the bottom step, with sufficient force to loose the pins from her elaborate hairdo. Her legs were splayed straight out on the floor and the perverse skirts settled high on her thighs, revealing an exceedingly unladylike amount of ankles and undergarments.

Desperate to pull herself up, Joss floundered, grasping for something to hold on to, clawing frantically for the railing. In her blind groping she missed the rail and clutched a large Meissen vase filled with fresh peonies, bringing it crashing down against the polished walnut newel post. Peonies, shards of porcelain and a cloudburst of water rained directly over her head.

The magnificent cluster of curls Barbara had labored to create was the first casualty. The sodden mass of hair fell across her face and tangled around her shoulders. She bit back a welling sob of humiliation as she heard Alex's voice from across the foyer, exclaiming, "My God, Joss!"

Alex could not for the life of him imagine what had happened. Joss lay sprawled out across the stairs, soaking wet, decorated with bright red and gold pieces of porcelain, foliage and flowers. One pale pink peony jutted garishly from the bodice of her dress. Another was tangled in her hair. "Are you hurt?" he asked, striding across the foyer as she sat up, clawing at the long strands of sopping hair plastered to her face.

"Nooo," she wailed, blinking her eyes and scrunching up her face.

Something sooty—he would have thought kohl, but in Joss's case surely it could not have been—was running in dark streaks down her cheeks as he extended his hand, saying, "Here, let me help you up."

Poc, having heard his mistress's cries of distress, came cannonballing down the stairs to the rescue. As he reached the bottom, his momentum would have slammed him directly into Joss's back—if he had not leaped agilely over her head and landed with a solid whack against Alex's chest.

The force of thirty pounds of flying terrier toppled Alex flat on his back on the highly polished marble floor. His body went sliding at an alarming speed across the foyer. A startled Poc sat up on top of his chest, only jumping clear at the last second before Alex crashed into a delicate console table on the opposite wall. Another Meissen vase of flowers sitting atop it teetered for a heart-stopping moment, then toppled onto his head in a cascade of water and blossoms as the fine porcelain shattered on his skull.

The dog raced frantically between his soaked and battered mistress and master as both struggled to sit up. He barked in alarm over the voices of the men who directed their attention to Alex while Barbara helped Joss to her feet.

"Demned dog rode 'em like a sled across the room," Monty said in awe.

"I say, Alex, peonies don't suit you. The pink clashes dreadfully with your waistcoat," Drum added scoldingly.

Sitting up, Alex's dazed eyes traveled to Joss across the room. She had somehow replaced her glasses and stared with numb horror at her soaked, flower-covered husband.

They matched like a pair of bookends. As if to make amends for his unintentional landing, Poc began licking Alex's face.

Fitch, the new butler, chose that moment to appear in the doorway, announcing solemnly, "Dinner is served, sir."

Chapter Fourteen

"I won't ever part with my spectacles again, Barbara. You saw what happened when I did," Joss said stubbornly as their carriage pulled up in front of the modest offices just off Exchange Alley, next door to Jonathon's, a popular lodging house. A small sign on the door said BENJAMIN TORRES, PHYSICIAN in neat gold lettering.

"This Doctor Torres has a splendid reputation treating eye problems, Joss. It won't hurt to have him examine you."

"It won't help either. I shall never go without glasses again. Poc might have killed poor Alex and it would all have been my fault!" She bit her lip, remembering the ghastly debacle.

"My son's skull is sufficiently thick to withstand a good deal more than bumping into a flimsy table," Barbara replied dryly.

"Don't forget the vase that broke over that same skull," Joss said, wincing as she climbed from the hackney. Every muscle and bone in her body was still bruised.

Barbara chuckled. " 'Twas no bigger than the one that coshed you. Of course," she added consideringly, "you do have much more hair to cushion the blow."

"I made an utter cake of myself, trying to be the belle."

"Do consider the humor in it, Joss. Alex did . . . once he revived."

"Your brother and Drum found it exceedingly amusing."

"Their laughter was at Alex's expense, Joss, not yours," Barbara reminded her gently.

Joss sighed in resignation as they entered the small, well-appointed office, whispering, "I still think this is a foolish waste of time."

An earnest young man greeted them, ushering them into a book-lined room with a large window at one end. Brilliant sunlight streamed in, revealing the excellent quality of the Bidjar carpet and Windsor furniture. Dr. Torres appeared to possess a most lucrative practice indeed.

"If I had not already agreed to the appointment, I should not have wasted your time coming, Barbara," she said as they waited for the physician. "It was vain and feckless to trick myself out and pretend to be something I'm not."

Barbara looked at Joss's hair, the lovely highlights obscured by the way it was pulled straight back into a tight bun of braids at her nape. She again wore a shapeless navy blue gown and clumpy, square-toed shoes. Barbara forbore mentioning Joss's reversion to her old ways this morning. After raising five children, she knew when to hold her peace. Joss had been humiliated last week and Barbara blamed herself in large measure. She had not realized how utterly helpless her daughter-in-law was without those eyeglasses. If only Dr. Torres could help, it would do wonders for the girl's self-confidence.

As if on cue, the physician entered the room, smiling his greeting. Of Sephardic Jewish ancestry, Doctor Benjamin Torres was tall and blond haired, astonishingly handsome with a quiet, winsome smile. After brief pleasantries he

217

went directly to business, examining first Joss's spectacles, then her eyes.

While his wife and mother were with the doctor, Alex spent the morning working on the docks where a large tobacco shipment had just arrived from America. It should have been a perfectly ordinary day, spent inventorying and unloading cargo until the captain mentioned escaping from a British man-o'-war off the cay at Bermuda.

"What's unusual about a British warship near Bermuda?" Captain Heath asked when Alex questioned him about it. " 'Tis a crown colony, after all. Perhaps I shouldn't have cut so close, but the winds were favorable." He shrugged. "We outran them. None of my men were impressed."

"You're certain it was HMS *Walsingham*?" Alex reiterated.

"Aye. When the fog cleared I could see the name clear as day."

Dismissing Heath, Alex returned to his office to consider what he should do. Notify Jonathan Russell, without doubt. Within the hour he was seated in the chargé d'affaires's office.

"I had all but given up on you as an agent, Mr. Blackthorne. I feared your wife must have put a damper on any further liaisons with Mrs. Chamberlain." Russell paused briefly, but when Alex volunteered nothing, he cleared his throat and said, "Your message indicated the matter was of utmost urgency."

"One of my captains encountered Chamberlain's ship off the coast of Bermuda. A bit off course for a man assigned to Mobile."

Russell grunted. "Not surprising. It confirms several reports I've received from my agents in Whitehall."

Alex's eyes narrowed. "What is Sir Rupert up to?"

"Deuced if I know." He studied Alex with keen gray eyes. "None of the people working for me have access to the upper echelons, only what they can snitch from waste bins and eavesdropping at keyholes. You can wager it was something of import since it is bringing him all the way home on the eve of war."

"Is it that close then?" Alex asked. What would he do about Joss? The idea of leaving her behind disturbed him even more than did the end of his libertine existence in London.

"The admiralty will not stand down from its impressment policy and the government is becoming increasingly distressed by American expansion along the southern frontier. Given the corresponding anti-British sentiments in Congress, I do believe a declaration of war will pass before summer."

"I'd wager Chamberlain's return has something to do with the Anglo-Indian alliance he was sent to create," Alex mused aloud.

"You would be in a unique position to learn more, Mr. Blackthorne," Russell said suggestively, then paused a beat. ". . . If your English wife does not object."

Alex flashed him an angry look, then stared out the window. The shadows of evening grew long. What should he do? "Leave my wife out of this, sir."

"I only wondered if she had . . . er influenced your loyalties."

"I gave you my word I would never discuss what was said in this room with anyone except my father. I have not done so. As to my loyalty, I want only to protect the Muskogee. If those hotheaded fools in Congress are land hungry enough to war against the British Empire, may God rot both sides."

"In the meanwhile, will you see what Lady Cybill can tell you?"

"I shall consider it," Alex said brusquely, rising. The idea of renewing the amorous game with Cybill Chamberlain left him feeling dirty.

"I must be becoming a bloody eunuch," he muttered savagely to himself after he took his leave and strode to the front gate of the embassy. Even the thought of finding his missing virgin had lost its allure. What was wrong with him?

All he seemed to think about was Joss. Would she be upset if a war separated them? Not seeing her smiling face, matching wits with her, even sharing in her penchant for misadventures left him feeling decidedly upset. Then, of course, there was the matter of his mother and her mysterious agenda. Whatever she was up to, closeted away with Joss for hours on end, it boded ill for him, he'd wager on that. And if word reached her that he was having a fling with Mrs. Chamberlain, well, it did not bear thinking about.

Over the next week, Alex warred with his conscience, utterly at sea concerning what he should do about Cybill. To further add to his uncertainties, both his wife and his mother continued to act most peculiarly. Ever since the debacle at their dinner party, Joss had been even more skittish around him in spite of his attempts to elicit her formerly excellent sense of humor. The whole evening had the makeup of a comedy by Sheridan, but for some reason Joss did not see it that way. She had lost the ability to laugh at herself. Alex had no idea why, other than the certainty that his mother was responsible.

If only she would return home next week as she had originally indicated. Alas, yesterday she'd announced her intention to remain for "a few more weeks or so," however long that meant. All he knew for sure was that her presence was having an exceedingly insalubrious effect on Joss.

"What am I holding in my hand?" Barbara repeated, then admonished, "Now don't squint. It quite ruins your lovely eyes."

"Blast my eyes," Joss said. Instantly horrified at her outburst, she put her fingers to her mouth. "Oh, dear! I never used to curse. I'm cross all the time and so on edge. Please forgive me. I don't know what is happening to me."

Barbara had a pretty fair idea but did not venture an opinion on the matter. Instead she repeated her earlier question, holding up a piece of ceramic fruit from the bowl in her hand.

" 'Tis an apple," Joss replied in a subdued voice.

"The belladonna extract is working even better than Dr. Torres expected. Now, let's try from a greater distance," she said, moving all the way to the end of the hall before extracting a pear from the bowl. When Joss identified it correctly, Barbara set the bowl on the table and clapped her hands excitedly. "You can see distances perfectly normally as long as you use the drops. Now, on the next matter. We have an appointment with Monsieur Baudelier on the half hour."

Joss sighed. "Barbara, all I have succeeded in doing is tromping the poor man's feet to blisters."

"What is a hop merchant for? He's taught far less adept pupils. You love music."

"I love to *listen* to music, Barbara, not dance to it," Joss replied, knowing her protest would not be heeded, any more than Barbara had listened about the outlandishly expensive ball gown. Barbara's great aunt, the Dowager Duchess of Chitchester, had invited them to a gala and Barbara was determined that Joss, with her newly corrected vision, would be the belle of the ball.

"La, you shall be swept off your feet by every male between the ages of sixteen and seventy."

"Off my feet and onto my derriere, without a doubt."

"Joss, do have a bit more confidence in yourself. You will be beautiful enough to attract any man at the ball. Alex will be green with jealousy by the end of the evening."

"As I recall, he was quite green enough a fortnight ago, covered with all that foliage, peonies and porcelain, not to mention the color of his skin as Monty and Drum were trying to revive him," Joss replied, trying for a witty tone, but ending on a forlorn one.

"That unfortunate incident occurred because you could not see where you were going. This time you shall do just splendidly. How many things could possibly go wrong?" Barbara asked breezily.

"How many stars are there in the night sky?" Joss returned glumly.

"Alex sent a note by messenger. He will be detained for an hour or so. We are to meet him at the Chitchester's city house. Monty and Octavia shall call for us with their carriage." At Joss's look of dismay, Barbara hastened to add, "It will be better this way. He'll see you dancing from a distance, possibly not even recognize you. I shall offer to make introductions. He shall be positively flummoxed when he sees how you've blossomed."

"If I can contrive not to trip and fall headlong into the punch bowl before he arrives," Joss replied, inspecting herself in the mirror. "At least this time I can see myself without my spectacles."

"And you're not even squinting." Barbara surveyed her handiwork over Joss's shoulder. The gown was a masterpiece of sheer French silk, the color a deep vivid crimson shot with gold thread. The rounded neckline plunged to reveal the soft swell of Joss's breasts and shimmered over the curve of her slim hips. A single bloodred ruby hung from a gold filigreed chain around her throat.

Joss eyed her red satin slippers with considerable trepidation. In spite of the hours Barbara had drilled her walking in them and holding her skirt above the high heels, she was still nervous. She tilted her head and the ruby teardrops in her ears danced through the tawny tendrils of hair that fell around her cheeks.

"I especially like the way your dress emphasizes the gold and bronze tones in your hair."

"I'm not certain you should have lightened it so much more," Joss said dubiously. "You must have used a whole shipload of lemons."

Barbara laughed. " 'Tis quite perfect. Hair that long and thick is a dream to work with," she said, adjusting one of the heavy gold combs that held the curling mass high on Joss's head.

"Come, my dear, I hear Monty's carriage pulling up. I simply cannot wait to see the expression on Alex's face when I introduce him to his own wife!"

"You indicated something urgent, sir?" Alex said as he was ushered into Jonathan Russell's office.

Eyeing Alex's black superfine coat and trousers and richly brocaded charcoal waistcoat, he said dryly, "I hate to tear you away from your busy social life, Mr. Blackthorne. Do you know a man named Wilbur Kent, a fellow American, I believe?"

Alex's eyes narrowed. "I met him briefly a number of years ago. He's distantly related by marriage to my family through my grandfather's first wife. Why do you ask?"

"I have reports from Virginia"—he shuffled several papers on his crowded desk—"which indicate that he is in the pay of the British."

"A spy? Hmm. The Kents always were an unsavory lot from what I gather. But why does he concern you?"

"Because he, too, has come to surface here in London."

"And you suspect a connection between that and Sir Rupert's return?"

"It is more than coincidence, wouldn't you imagine?"

Alex nodded. "And I would also imagine you wish me to find out precisely what the colonel and the spy are planning."

"If it would not inconvenience you, your country would be greatly appreciative," Russell said dryly.

Alex merely grunted in reply.

On the brief carriage ride to the ball, he turned over the pieces of the puzzle in his mind. He had written to his father about Chamberlain's mission in the gulf with Weatherford and McQueen. Devon had indicated considerable concern about the situation. The whole frontier was sitting on a powder keg and John Bull was holding flint and tinder over it.

His driver pulled to a halt and jumped down to open the door, but Alex had already anticipated him and quickly jumped to the pavement. As he climbed the wide marble stairs to the massive front door, the soft strains of a waltz came lilting out. He was in bad loaf now. The dancing had already begun. Rather than being announced at the front entry, he decided to slip quietly in the side and seek out his womenfolk so his tardiness would not be remarked upon.

His mother would be in a taking and Joss . . . for the life of him he found it difficult to imagine how Barbara had even gotten her to attend the soiree. Probably by saying her Great Aunt Lucretia would be terribly hurt if Joss refused. He snorted. Her grace, Lucretia, Dowager Duchess of Chitchester, wouldn't be hurt if a six in hand ran over her at a full gallop!

Joss would be ill at ease, though. He needed to be with her so she would not sit alone, a self-conscious wallflower who did not know how to dance even if any of the young gallants had the courtesy to ask a plain, overly tall female such as she. Why on earth had his mother dragged poor Joss here in the first place?

He stood at the edge of the crowd, surveying the glittering assembly in the ballroom. His carousing companion the young duke hovered near the punch bowl, raising his glass in salute to Alex. Chitchester's expression was rather pe-

culiar, almost gloating. Alex dismissed it as an excess of
port and returned his attention to the silk- and satin-swathed
females clustered around the perimeter of the dance floor.

That was when he saw her.

Alex stood transfixed by the tall, regal woman in crimson
who whirled by in the arms of a vacuous young viscount.
She was slim but curvaceous with a striking profile. Great
heavy masses of tawny hair were piled high on her head
with a few delicate curls falling down her slender back. She
was a diamond of the first water—no, a ruby.

Ruby! He squinted incredulously at the antique ruby pen-
dant and earrings she wore. The Caruthers rubies. His
mother's rubies! As if on cue, the fascinating female turned
as the music ceased, looking directly at him over her part-
ner's shoulder. Their eyes met from across the room and
held. Joss looked startled and shy. Alex was simply poleaxed.

Before he could gather his scattered wits, a bevy of men
surrounded her, some actually tall enough to obscure his
view of her. Then a familiar voice, low and throaty, purred
in his ear.

"Whoever would have imagined your wilted wallflower
would bloom?" He turned to Cybill, eager to rid himself of
her cloying coyness and go to his wife, but her fingers dug
into his arm, demanding attention. "I've missed you, darling."

"My lady, when last we parted, it was not, as I recall,
on fond terms." He was about to turn away when a man
materialized from the shadows. Although he had not seen
the bounder in ten years, it was Wilbur Kent, he was almost
certain of it.

Cybill pouted prettily. "I was cross with you, darling.
You did run off and leave . . . unfinished business. . . ." Her
beringed fingers climbed up his arm to rest possessively on
his shoulder. Damn! The music had started up again. He
prayed Joss was occupied, not watching this.

"Are you ready to leave, m'dear? We've paid our respects to the duchess. I find the company's become quite tedious," Kent said in a lisping Virginia drawl, while his cold, pale eyes swept up and down Alex insolently.

Cybill set her jaw mulishly, refusing to relinquish Alex's shoulder in spite of Kent's arm sliding around her waist. "Don't be tiresome, Willie. Can't you see I am already engaged?"

"We have an important meeting on the half hour, need I remind you?" he said, gritting out each word.

As Kent and Cybill clashed, Alex did some swift calculation. A meeting—with Sir Rupert? Someone from the war office? Whatever, it was a valuable source of information. Smiling, he took Cybill's hand and saluted it, then bowed. "I do not wish to poach on another gentleman's property, my lady. Besides, I fear my wife might object." He looked past her at Kent, whose impatient expression grew disdainful.

"Until later then," she said with a moue dimpling her cheek. Kent practically dragged her behind him after dismissing Alex as if he signified no more than an insect. Obviously the spy did not recognize him as the boy he'd met at Quintin Blackthorne's plantation a decade ago.

Alex was desperate to find his wife, who was flitting from man to man on the ballroom floor like a flame in the breeze; at the same time he was duty bound to follow Kent and Cybill, who might lead him to sir Rupert and who knew what sort of valuable information. There was no time to leave a message, no way to reach Joss as she vanished in the press of dancers.

With an oath of frustration, he turned and slipped behind the marble pillar, trailing after Cybill's lingering perfume.

Joss must have held her breath for hours—at least it seemed an eternity since she'd felt Alex's gaze on her. His expression had appeared startled, disbelieving, then perhaps pleased. She had waited with her heart in her throat, frightened, dizzy, quite desperate for him to come to her—she prayed, to claim her.

But he had not. The uncertain hope of that fragile moment was shattered when Cybill Chamberlain glided up beside him and placed her hand possessively on his arm. As soon as Alex turned toward the beauteous brunette, a crush of gentlemen surrounded Joss, obscuring her view while they clamored for the next dance. When next she could see her husband, he was kissing Cybill's fingers.

The naked pain sliced clean to her soul. So much for Barbara's well-intentioned matchmaking. He believed her to be ridiculous, his gawky crusader, masquerading as a belle. She had embarrassed him. Yet even though Alex found her wanting, it appeared the rest of the men present tonight were all quite smitten. *But I want only Alex, damn him!*

Biting the inside of her cheek until the acrid taste of blood filled her mouth, Joss wrenched her anguished thoughts away from her husband and accepted the Marquess of Clarence's hand as the music resumed. When next she looked over to where Alex stood, he and Cybill Chamberlain had vanished.

The evening passed in a dizzying whirl of laughter and wine and music. It should have been the most exhilarating time of her life. Repeatedly she was pronounced the ton's latest nonpareil. Everyone from the old prune-faced dowager duchess to the young dashingly handsome Duke of Westover assured her it was true.

Outwardly Joss smiled. Inwardly she died. But she endured until the midnight supper. As the ladies and gentlemen queued up to enter the sumptuous Chitchester dining hall, Joss refused numerous requests to escort her. When it became apparent that Alex was not going to return for her, she went in search of her mother-in-law. Pray heaven Barbara would understand her desire to depart. Monty was nowhere to be found, but Octavia stated acidly that it was his wont to desert her in favor of some disgraceful gaming hell on most social occasions.

Seeing how crestfallen Joss was, Barbara made their excuses and had a Chitchester footman send around Monty's carriage. As they rode through the dark, deserted streets, she attempted to console Joss. "I cannot fathom Alex's behavior, but I'm certain he had an excellent reason for it." *He'd best, else I shall flay him alive with a Muskogee skinning knife and make divan cushions from his thick, insensitive hide!*

Alex crouched beside the bow window, hiding behind a boxwood hedge on the grounds of the Mayfair estate to which he had followed Wilbur Kent. The spy, now dressed in buckskins, sat inside, closeted with the Chamberlains. His Majesty's government was paying handsomely to keep the colonel and his lady in high style, Alex thought with disgust. He strained to overhear their conversation as he observed the trio seated around a Pembroke table.

"This is it, Kent. A small fortune, courtesy of the foreign secretary. See you spend it well on your savage allies," Sir Rupert said, handing him a money belt heavy with gold.

Kent stiffened. "Those savages are the key to stopping American advances on the frontier."

The colonel raised his left eyebrow, emphasizing the saber slash that had cleft it in twain. "I shall expect a complete accounting when we rendezvous at Fort Charlotte."

"Really, Rupert, you act as if you do not trust poor Willie," Cybill said, languidly placing her hand on the sleeve of his uniform. Her eyes glittered with sick excitement as she pitted the two hostile men against each other. Alex could almost smell her arousal. The thought that he had come close to bedding her sickened him.

"I shall bring the whole Creek Confederacy in league with Tecumseh by summer's end," Kent boasted.

"See that you do. 'Tis likely his majesty's government

shall be at war with your United States before that."

The colonel stood up, dismissing Kent, who headed for the door, saying, "Until we meet again in Mobile."

Chamberlain nodded brusquely, then turned back to his wife. "I sail on the morning tide. Shall you miss me, pet?" he asked Cybill mockingly.

"A pity I shall be left all alone with you sailing for Mobile and Willie to Charleston. Whatever shall I do to amuse myself?" she asked with a pout.

"I am certain you shall contrive to find male companionship," her husband responded. "Just be certain, whoever he is, that he is useful to our cause."

Alex watched the officer pull on his gloves and adjust his sword, preparing to take his leave of Cybill. He cursed in silent frustration. The two malfeasants were sailing on different ships to stir up more grief on the frontier. What should he do, intercept Sir Rupert? Or Kent? He could not do both.

Hearing Kent summon his carriage, Alex made a snap decision. Relieving Kent of the money with which to purchase arms for the Red Sticks must take precedence over stopping the colonel. Surely locating Chamberlain's ship before morning should not prove difficult. A man-o'-war the size of the *Walsingham* would be difficult to miss. He slipped from the hedges and hid in the dense shadows by the roadside where Kent's carriage would pass.

When it lumbered by, he jumped onto the jack in the rear of the conveyance. He did not see the tall, thin figure who watched him stow away, then followed.

By the time Kent reached his destination near the docks, Alex was battered and filthy, his elegant evening clothes ruined by the ride. He climbed silently from the back of the carriage and slipped down the dark alleyway after Kent, who carried the thick money belt Chamberlain had given him.

Child's play. Alex congratulated himself on his luck,

withdrawing the knife from his boot. As he neared Kent, he reached out and slipped an arm around his quarry's neck. Kent stumbled backward, choking as Alex clubbed him on the head with the heavy handle of the blade. He slumped unconscious in Blackthorne's arms, then dropped to the muddy earth as Alex released him.

Quickly Blackthrone knelt and unfastened the fat purse. He slipped it around his own waist and started rolling Kent toward a pile of broken kegs. Suddenly the shrill whistle of a charley broke the silence. "What's the problem there, gov?" he yelled from the far end of the alley, advancing swiftly, truncheon in hand.

Crouching in the shadows, Alex cursed as his eyes scanned the surrounding doorways and windows for a place to hide. He did not want to be forced into harming some stupid watchman, but he could scarcely allow himself to be taken before the magistrate as a common cutpurse!

Just before he reached an intersecting passageway, a voice whispered, "Hide in that doorway. I'll take care of the charley."

There was no time to argue as the tall regal figure of the Baron of Rushcroft stepped into the moonlight and stood over Kent's unconscious body. "So grateful you happened along, my good fellow. This wretched denizen of the docks attempted to assault and rob me." Monty held up his cloak, which he had just sliced with his own concealed blade.

In a few moments' time, the baron readily convinced the charley that Kent was a robber who'd attacked him as he was en route to a rowdy gambling hell near the wharf. Monty's elegant attire and speech immediately marked him as Quality, while the unconscious Kent, clad in frontiersmen's clothing, was obviously an American. The burly watchman dragged him off to Newgate with few questions asked.

Once they were alone, Alex materialized from the shadows. Leaning on the splintering door frame, he said, "Not that I mean to appear ungrateful, milord, but how the bloody hell did you find me here and why did you lie for me?"

The baron shrugged. "One can scarcely have one's own nephew dancing on air outside Newgate. Quite bad for the family name. Anyway, Babs would roast my balls on a skewer if I didn't look after her only son. When I saw you following the infamous Mrs. Chamberlain I might have assumed it was an assignation but for the fact she had that disagreeable American chap already toadying about her. I felt you might require assistance. It appears my instincts were once again dead-on."

"I'm afraid you've just sent a British agent to Newgate and foiled your government's attempt to incite an Indian war on the Georgia frontier. I was acting on instructions from the American chargé d'affaires."

Monty appeared singularly unconcerned about his brush with treason. "I sold my commission back in eighty-three after the bloody bungling incompetents in Whitehall signed away the richest part of the New World at the Peace of Paris. A fracas such as the late and unlamented war of American rebellion has left me without the faintest stirrings of patriotism, my boy, difficult as that might be for a young idealist such as yourself to comprehend."

"I'm better able to understand than you might think, milord," Alex said with a faint touch of humor. "I'm scarcely any more enamored of my government's policies than you are with yours. My highest loyalty in this is to my father's people."

As they made their way out of the warren of narrow alleyways to the open wharf where his carriage awaited, Monty chuckled. "Still the noble red Indian's champion."

"That was how Jonathan Russell lured me into this imbroglio. Now I'm off to locate a certain British man-o'-war."

"Perhaps it might be useful if I accompanied you."

Alex shook his head. "No. You would be recognized. Best if you return to the Chitchesters and placate Joss and Mama."

"Whatever shall I say? Alex is off rescuing your red in-laws from the royal navy?"

"You may laugh, but we are only a hairsbreadth from a senseless war between Britain and the United States."

"Dear me, Alex, what would you have to do then, shoot me?" the baron said as he signaled his driver to bring up his carriage, which waited on the wharf.

"I sincerely hope not," Alex said with a fond smile. "I owe you a great debt, sir."

For once, Montgomery Caruthers made no light rejoinder. Earlier at the Chitchesters's he had overheard two cabinet ministers discussing the impending declaration of war that they knew was on its way from Washington. "Consider us even, my boy . . . for your uncle Quint. I almost hanged him once—as a spy. Ironic that you should choose to follow in his footsteps. But then again, perhaps not."

Alex reached out and enveloped his uncle in a fierce embrace. "I shall miss you."

Rushcroft returned the hug, then stepped back, still holding his nephew's arms. He cocked his head and said, "Let us hope it will not be as long a war as the last one, Alex."

Sensing that events beyond their control would soon separate them, Alex said with a lump in his throat, "Until we meet again, Uncle Monty."

"Milord, my boy, call me milord," Rushcroft replied as he climbed inside the carriage and waved jauntily.

Chapter Fifteen

His head was splitting. If someone had cleaved it in two with a broadsword, it could not have felt any worse. After spending all night drinking in waterfront taverns, Alex found even his prodigious capacity for liquor had been taxed. And all for naught. After fecklessly looking up and down the docks for the *Walsingham*, he'd begun questioning dock workers and sailors in the waterfront ale houses. A grizzled salt indicated he knew the location of the man-o'-war but would divulge it only after Alex had joined him in toasting every bloody British naval victory since the defeat of the Spanish Armada.

By the time he finally reached the mooring, Chamberlain's ship was sailing down the Thames bound for the gulf.

All he had to show for a perfectly wretched night was Kent's money belt. And no doubt a furiously angry pair of women, he thought grimly as he climbed the side steps of his house. At least he could have some badly needed sleep and a bath to sober himself before facing either of them. After twenty-four hours without sleep, a brush with the night watch and a dozen pints of ale, he was in no condition to think.

But his mind kept returning to the magnificent woman with the tawny hair. It was her fault that he had botched his mission so badly. He had been unable to get her out of his mind all night. She was wearing his mother's rubies, no mistake about it. Perhaps that was why he imagined her to be Joss. But the eyes—those wide, clear blue eyes that had looked right into his soul, they were Joss's eyes. He *knew* they were.

"I'm losing my bloody mind," he muttered as he turned the brass knob to open the door, then tripped on the sash, almost falling into Fitch's arms.

The haughty butler inspected his filthy clothes, then sniffed the fumes of cheap ale disapprovingly before saying, "Good morning, Mr. Blackthorne."

Alex was in no mood for pleasantries. "Have Foxworthy draw me a bath—very hot water."

"Very good, sir," Fitch replied in a tone that indicated exactly how much his employer needed to bathe.

Alex made it across the hall to the door of his bedroom before his mother's voice froze him in his tracks.

"The bath can wait, Fitch. Bring a pot of coffee to the sitting room—very strong, black coffee," she said in a tone of voice Alex had not heard since he was sixteen and she had caught him sneaking Lizzie Clayberry and a jug of whiskey into his bedroom.

He cursed savagely under his breath and turned to face her. The wretched butler was smirking! Making a mental note to fire Fitch at the earliest opportunity, or perhaps even gut the wretch, Alex walked unsteadily down the hall to meet his fate.

Barbara inspected her only son with blazing blue eyes. "Pray, have a seat, Alex. You look as if you need one," she said with mock levity, leading the way into the sitting room and seating herself on one of a pair of easy chairs.

He sank obediently into the other while his mind churned frantically. "Why are you here?" was all he managed to blurt out. *Brilliant, Blackthorne, bloody brilliant.*

"You might better inquire if your wife is still in residence. You do remember your wife . . . Jocelyn, don't you, Alex?" she asked with deadly sweetness.

"Of course. I expected her to be at school by this time. She always is." The moment the words escaped his lips, he wanted to call them back.

Barbara pounced. "How convenient. She arises early to go about her duties before you creep in from your nights of debauchery. Do you expect her not to care?"

"No—yes—er, that is . . . ah, hell, Mama, it's all too complicated for me to explain r.ght now."

"I should think so. You reek of ale and look as if half of Wellington's cavalry has ridden over you. Have your guttersnipe drinking companions turned cutpurse?"

"I haven't slept in nearly two days," he said, anger beginning to smother the muddled remorse he had been battling all night.

"And whose fault is that, pray? You are the one who chose to desert your wife in front of the whole assembly at the Chitchesters and spend the night God knows where. How could you do that to her, Alex?"

The note of genuine distress in her voice cooled his temper as quickly as it had risen. "I did not intend to desert her but . . . was that *her*—I mean, my God, the red dress, the hair . . . it scarcely looked like my Joss."

He looked guilty, confused and for all the world like a six-year-old boy caught out in some grave infraction. She stifled the urge to coddle him, an impulse she was certain every female from seven to seventy had upon confronting a distressed Alexander Blackthorne. "It was she, Alex," she replied sternly.

"But—but, Joss never dressed . . . she never looked . . . like she did last night. I insisted she buy new gowns, have a maid . . ." His voice faded away in bewilderment as Fitch strode into the room with a heavy silver tray. He set it on the tea table between them and poured two cups of richly fragrant coffee. Barbara's he sweetened and added cream to, the other he handed to Alex black.

Barbara dismissed him with thanks, then said, "You have never really known your wife at all, have you, Alex?"

Was this a trick question? In what sense did she use the word "known"?

Not giving him a chance to reply, she went on, "Only a fool or a blind man would not have recognized the potential in Jocelyn. She has a striking face and a beautifully proportioned figure. All she needed was a bit of guidance and a physician's help to see without those horrid spectacles. Did you ever think to take her shopping yourself?" When he shook his head dumbly, then winced in pain, she replied crossly, "I thought not."

As he held his aching head cradled in his hands, his mother continued her scolding. "Lud, as much time and money as you've lavished on light-skirts since you were scarce out of knee britches, I'd think you should have realized what a beauty she could be."

"Joss and I are friends—that is, I've always loved her just as she was . . . rather endearingly . . . disheveled." He cursed and took a hearty swallow of the coffee. Without the usual cream and sugar, it was scalding hot, burning the roof of his mouth. He gasped as it went down his throat, searing at least three layers of membrane.

"Perhaps you've never thought enough about what it is precisely that Jocelyn wants," Barbara suggested.

Alex sighed and stared into the murky depths of his coffee cup. "I've ruined a wonderful friendship with this marriage. Joss isn't happy. I'm not happy. Damn, I never meant to hurt her. How the hell could things have gone so bloody wrong?"

"Why did you leave her at the ball, Alex?" Barbara asked, more gently now.

"It was not what you think, Mama."

She arched one golden eyebrow disbelievingly. "Really? I saw you and *Mrs.* Chamberlain."

"I spent not a moment after that in the woman's company, you have my oath upon it," he replied grimly.

Alex had never lied to her. She knew he was telling the truth. "But then, why—"

"I'm bound by my word not to reveal the reason, but you must believe me when I say the matter is not at all what it seems. I was not out carousing."

Barbara nodded. "Very well then, we shall speak no more about it. But that still leaves the matter of you and Jocelyn and your marriage. You say you love her, yet it sounds as if you feel toward her much as you do toward one of your sisters."

He shook his head again, instantly regretting it. Now the pounding ache was joined by a nausea and dizziness. "No, that's not how I love her . . . but . . . it's not . . . it's just . . ."

"Well, that's certainly clear," Barbara rejoined. "Tell me what's happened, Alex? Is there another woman—one of your Cyprians?"

"No, not a Cyprian! At least I don't think she was. She was a virgin." Bloody hell, he must be even drunker than he'd thought to blurt that out to his mother!

The expression on Barbara's face was shock. "You met an innocent girl and seduced her? After you were wed?"

"I didn't meet her—it was dark—I've never even seen her face. Oh, hell, I was drinking too much that night as well," he said in misery.

"It would appear that a temperance vow would most probably be a salutary way to begin setting your life in order," Barbara replied tartly. "Pray continue."

He combed his fingers through his hair and tried to unscramble his brain. "I came home late one night and was surprised to find her asleep in my bed. When I awakened her . . . well . . . one thing led to another." He dared not look up to see how his mother was taking this. "It was only the next morning that I realized she'd been a virgin. One of my friends must have sent her. I made inquiries everywhere but she vanished without a trace. I have no idea who she was."

Barbara was beginning to have a pretty good idea about his virgin's identity, but she held her peace for the present. *Men are such idiots!* "And you've not been able to forget this lone encounter?" she prompted.

"It doesn't mean I love Joss less," Alex replied at once. "But it's not the same thing as . . . the other," he added lamely.

"And Jocelyn's feelings about . . . the other?" Barbara drawled sweetly, not the least bit embarrassed.

Alex was embarrassed enough for both of them. "We have, that is, Joss has indicated no desire, er, no wish to . . ."

"You waited for *her* to indicate such! Pray, Alex, did you expect her to come scratching on your bedchamber door?" Her tone was contemptuously sarcastic.

Hell, he had all but confessed the nature of his agreement with Joss to his mother—although in recent weeks he had been growing increasingly unclear of what that relationship was himself. He stood up slowly and was rewarded when his head stopped spinning after a mere half dozen revolutions. Cursing Jonathan Russell for the tenth time in the past hour, he said, "I am not going to discuss my relationship with my wife any further, Mama. The matter is private, for Joss and me to work out."

As he stalked from the room, struggling to walk a straight line, Barbara's voice carried after him. "See that you *do* work it out."

*　　*　　*

Alex soaked in a hot tub, then collapsed for a few hours of troubled sleep, which were all too soon interrupted by an urgent message from the charge d'affaires. Feeling utterly out of charity with the whole of the United States government, he sat at the table in his dressing room and tore open the sealed envelope.

"Bloody hell! Foxworthy, bring me a clean shirt and breeches," he instructed the valet, who stood deferentially in the doorway of his dressing room.

A short time later he leaped from Sumac's back in front of Joss's school and strode swiftly inside the gray stone building, making his way toward the sound of children's laughter. He was nearly trampled by a hoard of stampeding urchins when the clang of a bell indicated their dismissal. Seeing Joss gathering up her books, he froze in the doorway, stunned.

She was different—deliciously different. Her hair caught the sun from the window, gleaming a tawny bronze blond. The style was not elaborate, just a few soft curls about her face and the rest tied back with a blue ribbon that matched the dress she wore. The supple cotton revealed the sweet curves of a pair of small high breasts and flowed over softly rounded hips. She was not thin at all, just long-limbed and slender. His mother was a miracle worker—or had he simply been too blind a fool to see what lay beyond the tip of his nose?

Joss sensed his presence and looked up. The same shy, startled expression she'd worn when she saw him last night swept across her face, then vanished, replaced by the pink flush of embarrassment. Her clear blue eyes met his in spite of it. Joss was nothing if not self-possessed.

"Alex, what are you doing here?" She could tell he'd been studying her and fought the urge to smooth her hair back or wrap her arms about her waist protectively. Did he think she was an utter cake, an old tabby dressed like a debutante?

239

"Joss." Every thought fled from his head as he stared into her eyes. "The spectacles . . . they're gone. How can you see?" he finally managed.

"Your mother took me to see a marvelous physician who gave me some drops to put in my eyes. I still cannot see clearly enough to read, but for distance it's really quite liberating. I can observe Willie Balum and Pug Wilson misbehaving in the back of the classroom and stop the worst of their mischief." She was babbling, she realized, as she pulled her eyeglasses from her pocket and placed them on her nose to give her a sense of detachment, but somehow the spell was not broken. He continued to stand staring at her in a most unnerving way. "What do you want, Alex?"

The question finally penetrated and he stepped into the room, closing the door behind him so as not to be overheard by Mrs. Breem.

"First of all, I wish to apologize for my abominable behavior last night," he said, stiffly. "My mother was waiting to ring a peal over me when I returned home this morning." He smiled ruefully then, trying to gauge her reaction. "I know there is no adequate excuse, Joss, but I had good reason for leaving the ball."

"I'm certain you did, Alex. Mrs. Chamberlain is exceedingly beautiful." The moment she said it, she wanted to call back her words. "I sound a perfect shrew and I have no right—"

"Yes, you do have the right. I gave my word to escort you and I broke it—but not because I was pursuing Cybill Chamberlain or any other woman. I was working for the American chargé d'affaires, Joss."

"The chargé d'affaires?" she echoed in amazement. That was the last thing she would have imagined.

"I was a spy of sorts for him," he confessed.

Joss felt a weight lift from her heart. She began to smile.

"I'm not such a patriot that I feel constrained to turn you in, Alex."

"When you hear the news, you might change your mind," he said grimly. "I have just received word that our Congress has declared war, Joss."

"War?" Her voice was a hoarse croak. What she had feared and dreaded for the past two years had come to pass.

"I shall have to leave at once before Mr. Russell delivers the formal documents to Whitehall. It might be difficult to secure permission to sail for America after that."

I shall have to leave. The words tore at her heart. She swallowed and nodded numbly. "You plan for me to remain behind then?"

"I . . . hell, Joss, I wasn't certain what you'd want to do." He began pacing across the floor, running his fingers through his hair nervously. "You're so very English . . . I can't imagine you living anywhere else. I'll provide funds to support you if you choose to stay. It's up to you, Joss." He stopped pacing and stood facing her, waiting.

What should she do? If he wished to be rid of her, this was the perfect opportunity. She tried to read his expression, which seemed wary—or was it confused? Uncertain? This morning before she left for school Barbara had insisted she not give up on Alex. Her mother-in-law had scolded her, in fact, for not having the courage to fight for the man she loved.

Taking a deep breath she said, "As you pointed out, Alex, we are married—even though it isn't a conventional arrangement. What would your mother think if I refused to go home with you? I believe I am resourceful enough to survive America. I shall accompany you, Alex . . . but only if you wish it."

He had not realized that he was holding his breath until she agreed to come with him. He smiled broadly then and reached out to take her hands. "I should have missed your friendship, Joss, if you'd stayed behind."

Friendship. Her heart squeezed. Was that all that would ever be between them? In spite of her pain she returned his smile. "Speaking of friends, what shall you tell Drum? He will be most upset with your leaving."

He looked at her with a surprised expression on his face. "Why ever should that occur to you? I thought you detested Drum."

"Once I did, but . . . let us just say we have come to an understanding. After all, he did save your life."

"We have no time to spare, but I shall try to locate him for a proper farewell after I inform Mama we must leave. There will be precious little time to pack, Joss. Can you be ready to sail by dawn?"

She laughed merrily, suddenly exhilarated by the adventure ahead of her. "La, I suspect I shall have our household ready in half the time it takes Barbara to repack all those trunks she brought from America!"

"You know her well," he said with a chuckle and turned to leave, then paused in the doorway. "I'm very glad you're going with me, Joss." With that he was gone.

As Sumac's hoofbeats echoed down the cobblestone street, Joss went in search of Mrs. Breem to let her know the Mission Society would have to find another teacher.

As Joss had predicted, she supervised the packing of all Alex's and her belongings and had the servants unload them on the deck of the *Muskogee Maiden* two hours before Barbara arrived. Alex had not returned from his search for Drum. The authorities were not yet aware of the state of hostilities between His Majesty's government and the brash young republic across the Atlantic, Captain Broderick informed them, but as soon as Mr. Blackthorne was aboard it would be wise to sail.

"I hope he won't be long," Joss fretted to Barbara. "I have no idea about how he wishes to assign quarters for the trip," she said, indicating the huge pile of chests and crates sitting on the deck of the schooner.

Barbara cocked her head inquisitively. "Assign quarters? Why, that shan't be at all a problem. Come, let us decide right now." She seized Joss's hand and led her toward the stairs below deck.

"But . . . but I can't do that!" Joss said, aghast. They stood inside the small first mate's cabin adjacent to the captain's quarters. "This will serve for Alex. I shall share your cabin."

"Do not be a cake, Jocelyn. That would quite give away the game Alex plays, would it not?" Barbara replied in exasperation.

"Oh!" Joss pressed her fingers to her lips. "Then he has not . . . confessed our situation to you?"

Barbara shook her head, choosing her words with great care. "His exact words were 'Mother, I will not discuss my marriage with you!' You would be a wise wife not to force him to do so."

"But I cannot just . . . just crawl into bed with him."

Barbara arched one eyebrow and studied Joss. "You did so once before with rather felicitous results—or did you not like it?"

Joss blurted out. "Oh, yes! It was divi . . ." She flushed furiously and her mind raced in circles. "It was all an accident . . . there was a fire . . . I was asleep in his bed, in the dark, when he came home . . ."

"Hmm. I've heard the story before—the little blond girl and the bears."

Joss's flush deepened. "Barbara, this is no child's tale."

Her mother-in-law nodded. "I warrant that, darling, not at all suitable for children. Pray continue."

"At first, I thought I was dreaming, but then I awoke. Alex . . . Alex was doing things to me, and I tried . . . to get him to . . . to . . ."

Barbara coached, "Stop?"

Joss nodded, then continued. "But after a bit, I didn't want him to . . . to . . ."

"Stop?" Barbara added helpfully.

Joss nodded. "Even worse than that. I began to ... to ..."

"Respond?"

Joss whispered quietly, as she stared at the floor. "Yes."

"So you are Alex's mysterious virgin. He's combed London looking for you, you know."

"*He* told you?" Joss could not believe it. Still, how else could Barbara have known about that night?

"As a matter of fact, he did confess that much—not altogether willingly, but I had him at a disadvantage. He was quite properly foxed and had not slept in two days."

"Thank God. Then he doesn't know it was I."

"No, and I see no reason to enlighten him yet. Once things take their proper course, he'll figure it out soon enough," Barbara said dryly.

"Their proper course?" Joss echoed dubiously.

"Whatever do you think will occur now that you will be forced to actually share the same living space?"

"How shall I explain my temerity? I am really a coward, you know, when it comes to Alex," Joss confessed.

"Nonsense. You just need a wee bit of encouragement. You must simply point out the obvious—we were fortunate in securing passage on the only Blackthorne sailing vessel currently in London. There is little provision on a cargo ship for passengers, so we must make do with what quarters are available. Besides, he won't want me to know the exact nature of your arrangement, will he now?" Barbara asked manipulatively.

Joss looked exceedingly dubious. "There are two bunks," she said, walking into the small cabin. "I suppose we could work something out."

Barbara smiled and nodded. "Of that, I have no doubt, my darling."

When Alex finally reached the ship, Joss had all their

belongings secured. She sat perched on the edge of the room's lone chair, like a rabbit ready to bolt, clutching a book that she pretended to read.

Alex knocked, then entered. Standing in the cramped quarters he seemed larger than life, bronzed as a great golden lion in the flickering candlelight. He closed the door behind him and stared at Joss with unreadable eyes.

Joss swallowed a lump the size of Eastcheap and said, "I was worried about you. Did you find Drum?"

"No. I searched everywhere but it seems the bloody bounder is off in the country somewhere. I shall have to send him a letter before we sail, bidding farewell." He paused, then said, "My mother informed me about our, er, cramped sleeping arrangements."

"I'm quite certain we shall deal famously once we set a schedule for retiring and arising to preserve each other's modesty," she replied, trying to sound matter-of-fact.

"Oh?" He leaned against the door and crossed his arms over his chest.

"Yes, well, I am by habit an early riser and go to bed accordingly. You have always preferred the nights and arisen late. So—"

"You will be all tucked in with the candles doused when I return each evening," he supplied helpfully. Damn but she looked fetching in spite of the bloody eyeglasses that perched on the end of her nose.

"Unless you would prefer a different arrangement?" she said hesitantly.

Alex blinked, then realized what she meant—or at least, what he *thought* she meant. Doubtless, she wanted to share his mother's cabin . . . but maybe . . . He quickly dismissed the ridiculous idea. "The arrangement suits, Joss," he replied coolly.

"Do you prefer the upper bunk or the lower?" she asked, moistening her lips with the tip of her tongue.

His mouth felt dry as dust. "Lady's choice, Joss, but I'd imagine with a night rail, you'd find the bottom one easier to deal with."

She nodded. "Very well. It's all settled then."

He looked at her for a moment without saying anything, then strode over to the writing box sitting on top of his trunk. "I must dash off something to Drum."

Drum dropped Alex's letter on the small table next to his chair. What absolutely damnable luck! His friend had searched for him in all their usual haunts, but he had been out of the city, forced to visit his father to placate the old man and insure the continuance of his allowance.

The dandy closed his eyes and rubbed his temple. Still and all, perhaps it was for the best. A public good-bye would have quite unmanned him. Alex, Alex . . .

Opening his eyes, he fingered a smaller envelope that had been delivered along with Blackthorne's, then tore it open and extracted the note.

My Dear Drum,

Perhaps you are correct about the females of our species possessing the traits of the spider. I am already becoming devious. I intercepted the footman whom Alex sent to deliver his letter and will add this missive.

Of course, I did not presume to read his sentiments. However, if my husband is as inept as most men in expressing their love for another of their gender, then he has made a most miserable parting with the truest, most loyal friend he has ever had. I cannot chance such a failure when it concerns one to whom both Alex and I owe so much.

Therefore, Drum, should you find your life as unsatisfactory as I would find mine without the nearness of Alex, I shall welcome you to America.

I expect that we will meet again . . . soon.

Yours in friendship,
Joss

Drummond smiled. "My Amazonian friend! What a remarkable creature you are. And what a superlative choice our Alex has made . . . hmmm . . . well, stumbled upon. Nonetheless, what a delightfully ridiculous idea. A Drummond in America!" Alvin Frances Edward Drummond laughed, and the lamp on the little table seemed to burn brighter.

Chapter Sixteen

"Have a care and close your mouth lest a gull fly in," Barbara said merrily to Joss, who stood staring up into the rigging where Alex climbed into the sun and wind.

She turned to her mother-in-law with a startled gasp. "He's going so high I fear he'll fall into the ocean," she said, looking once again at the bronzed half-naked figure moving with sensuous grace and skill.

"La, I'd not worry. Alex first stowed away on a ship bound for the China trade when he was twelve. He was gone for over a year before one of our captains was able to bring him home tanned and toughened as seaman's hardtack."

"He does seem to know what he's about. He told me he'd run off to sea," Joss replied, forcing herself to look away from Alex's mesmerizing figure. The amused yet sympathetic understanding in Barbara's eyes made her cheeks bloom with color. "Am I all so obvious, then?"

"You're his bride. People expect you to look a bit lovesick."

" 'Tis a sadly one-sided lovesickness," Joss replied with a touch of wistfulness in her voice.

"How is the sleeping arrangement working out?"

Joss sighed. "Quite smoothly. We've scarcely seen each other the past two days."

"Not precisely what I had in mind when I proposed it," Barbara said dryly. "Perhaps 'tis time to reschedule things a bit."

Joss, who was once again drawn to observe Alex's descent from the crow's nest, only half heard Barbara's remark. Once he reached the deck and disappeared among a crowd of sailors, she turned back to Barbara. "Reschedule what?" she asked vaguely.

"I have an idea . . ." Barbara replied, taking her aside.

Alex stood at the bow of the *Maiden* watching the western sky fill with brilliant stars. He never tired of the magic of nightfall. "I never realized how much I missed the sea," he murmured to himself as he stared at the dim horizon where the roll of black water and the calm of night sky merged.

In a few weeks he would be home in America. *With an English wife in tow.* How would Joss adapt to living in a country at war with her own? Would she find his Georgia and Muskogee relatives crude, offensive? Since they'd set sail she seemed to avoid him, continuing the estrangement that had begun after they were wed. He had hoped her agreeing to accompany him to America meant that the old camaraderie would return, but it obviously had not.

He was disturbed by the transformation his mother had wrought in Joss as well. Why the devil had a female of such iron-willed and serious-minded determination decided to deck herself out in ruffles and curls? She was disturbing. She was just not . . . Joss. And he missed his old laughing, accident-prone, disheveled companion a great deal.

His disquietude might also stem from sex—or rather the decided lack thereof for the last few months. The cargo ship had taken on several other American passengers eager to return home before actual hostilities commenced. One was a perky little redheaded widow from Philadelphia who had been eyeing him with predatory interest since they sailed. Perhaps he could reach an agreement with her that might please them both, he mused idly, but the idea held no particular appeal.

His ruminations were interrupted by a loud rumbling purr and the flick of a tail as an enormous black cat brushed against his pant leg, then leaped gracefully up onto the railing and looked at him with one glowing emerald eye. The other had been lost in a legendary waterfront contest with a huge rat.

"Tar, you old rascal. I thought Captain Neale would have thrown you overboard for stealing from the cook's larder by now," he said, scratching the grizzled ears. The cat butted his big head against Alex's chest and let out a rasping meow as if to say, "Surely you jest. Neale could never catch me."

"I'm amazed you haven't tangled with Poc yet, but then that might explain your absence since we set sail." The mention of the terrier brought Alex's thoughts once again around to his sleeping schedule in the crowded quarters below. "Well, fellow, it's past time I turned in."

Tar watched him stride across the deck and vanish belowstairs.

The corridor was dimly lit by a low-burning tallow candle flickering on the wall as Alex made his way to the cabin, suppressing a huge yawn. It had been a long time since he'd done seaman's work. Strenuous exercise and fresh salt air combined to make him more than ready to sink into his bunk.

In bed before midnight and all I can do is sleep, he thought with grim amusement as he shed his shirt and boots before quietly lifting the latch to their cabin door. He was always careful not to awaken Joss, who he knew rose at daybreak. As soon as he opened the door a thin shaft of pale light startled him.

Alex froze. His eyes widened as he stared at the vision silhouetted in soft candlelight. She wore a sheer voluminous garment that swathed her from neck to ankle in soft white cotton yet fully revealed the outline of her body—slender but lithe with high breasts, sweetly rounded hips and long, long legs elegantly curved. Her hair was thrown over one shoulder as she plied it with a brush that sent sparks crackling through the curls. The candle glow illuminated soft yet brilliant highlights of bronze and various shades of gold from tawny to pale.

A bolt of pure lust shot through him with startling ferocity, rooting him in the doorway. Poc broke the spell, jumping off the lower bunk, which he had taken to sharing with Joss. He let out a soft yip of welcome as he walked over to sniff Tar's scent on Alex's breeches.

Joss turned with a startled intake of breath. The brush tangled stubbornly in her long, heavy hair as she struggled to pull it free. Although she did not know it, her raised arms all the better outlined the upthrust fullness of her breasts.

"You're up late," he said idiotically, unable to think of any excuse for spying on her so blatantly.

Joss stared at the thick gold hair on Alex's bare chest, longing to sink her fingers into it, remembering the crisp, springy texture from her one night of passion. In the small confines of the cabin she could smell the scent of aroused male calling forth from her a deep feminine response, although she was unaware of her own musky perfume. She felt as if a hard fist had clenched tight inside her belly.

Her breath hitched. He was staring at her and she was practically naked! What if he did not like what he saw? She was too tall, too thin, too lacking in female wiles for this. Barbara had been mistaken. Yet he continued to stare at her as if she were a prime roast of beef and he a starving man.

Gathering her scattered thoughts, she yanked the brush free of her hair, pulling the tawny mantle around her shoulders. She fought the urge to clutch her hands over her intimate parts like a silly virgin and instead stood straight and met his glowing dark eyes. "I am sorry I did not retire at my usual time. I . . . became engrossed in reading." She laid down the brush and picked up a slim volume. "*Lyrical Ballads. I am especially fond of Mr. Coleridge's *Rime of the Ancient Mariner*. It teaches a superb moral lesson, don't you think?"

She was prattling on like a ninny, unable to stop herself from drawing nearer, her extended hand offering him the book.

"I've never been much for moral lessons, Joss," he replied, forcing a grin that was much more like a grimace. He felt as if he'd explode if he did not do one of two things—seize her and ravish her or leave at once.

"I'll peruse Mr. Coleridge while you finish preparing for bed," he replied, grabbing the book and disappearing through the doorway.

When Alex reached topside, the last thing on his mind was reading about a sailor cursed because of an albatross. Hell, he had his own curse to bear. Clutching the book in his hand, he walked to the railing at the bow of the ship and stood staring into the darkness, letting the cool night wind blow against his scorched bare flesh. He struggled with the inner demons of lust that cried out his deep, pulsing need for this woman.

She is your wife. You have a right to her body, they seemed to say. But she was Joss, his friend and companion, a woman of maidenly sensibilities to whom he had given his bond of honor. He could not touch her. What would she think? She offered him a volume of poetry and he returned such civility with naught but crude lust. She would be appalled, angry, disgusted. It would be a betrayal.

Their former closeness was already in jeopardy. He

cursed himself once more for ruining everything with his crack-brained marriage proposal and prepared to spend yet another sleepless night. The redheaded widow in the cabin down the hall never even crossed his mind.

Joss sank onto the bare wood chair, her knees having turned to water after Alex had gone. She was trembling violently, hot yet cold at the same time. Dressed in practically nothing, she had let him look his fill. But he had stood like a somnambulist, his face grim and forbidding. Hardly the sweet impetuous expression of newly discovered love!

And she, always a cake, had further ruined everything by rattling on about poetry! Small wonder he seized the book from her and ran. "He doesn't want me. Barbara's mistaken," she sobbed woefully.

Poc began to whine sympathetically, licking her hands and face as she knelt down and wrapped her arms around him, then buried her face in his wiry fur and cried.

"Hold still. 'Tis difficult enough getting these pins set on a pitching ship without you turning hither and yon," Barbara scolded as she worked on Joss's hairdo. The sky, calm and sunny for the first few days of sailing, had suddenly turned pewter gray, and winds whipped the ocean into a frothy frenzy of high waves. The ship bounced from one crest to another, hitting the bottom between them with sickening thuds. Joss, who had never sailed before, was terrified.

"It is getting a bit rough out there," Barbara said calmly.

"A *bit* rough? That is like saying the Prince Regent is a *bit* fat! I vow every bone in my body will shatter ere we reach terra firma again."

"You'll soon get your sea legs." Barbara finished fastening the last ivory pins in Joss's heavy hair, then stood back to admire her handiwork. "Not bad if you would only contrive not to have your face match the shade of your gown."

"You do not think green becomes me?"

"To wear it, yes, to *be* it, no."

Just then the ship took another deep roll, sending the hairbrush and mirror sliding from the table to the floor. Barbara caught the mirror handily while Joss lunged for the chamber pot.

The storm did not abate for several days. Neither did Joss's indisposition. She lay pale and limp in her bunk while Barbara patiently urged hot broth and cool compresses on her. Utterly humiliated by her weakness, Joss protested that she was best left alone.

"I've never been ill a day in my life before this," she said wretchedly the third morning as Barbara sponged her off and helped her change into a clean nightshift.

" 'Tis not unusual on one's first voyage. I was deathly ill on my first crossing to America, then again when Dev and I returned to London after we were married. He was so patient and tender caring for me . . ." Barbara considered how alike father and son were. Perhaps it would be best if she ceased shooing Alex away and set him to caring for his ill wife.

Joss was too awash in her own misery to see the gleam of yet another plan in her mother-in-law's eyes. When she drifted off to sleep, Barbara went in search of her son to plead exhaustion. Perhaps she would even develop a slight case of mal de mer herself.

Alex set down the tray on the table near Joss's berth and knelt beside her. Her long tawny skein of hair spread across the pillows. She must have worked the plait loose tossing in her sleep. He reached out to touch the wondrous stuff, so thick and soft. His mother was responsible for the marvelous color, but how had Joss concealed so much hair in that awful knot? Why had she swaddled her delicious curves in drab, oversize gowns?

"What were you hiding from, Joss?" he murmured softly. She stirred but did not awaken as his fingertips lightly traced the strong elegant contours of her brow, cheekbones and chin. Perhaps she had not so much been hiding as he and all of his kind had been blind.

Her thick dark lashes lay like lacy fans against her cheeks, concealing those incredibly blue eyes. A pair of spectacles lay within her reach. Odd, now that she no longer was so dependent on them, he did not mind when she wore them. They, like her sharp wit and fierce pride—even her clumsiness—were a part of Joss. He had not yet found a facet of her that failed to charm him.

She moaned restlessly as he studied her face. He was alarmed at her pallor. "Joss, you must eat," he said gently, touching her shoulder to awaken her.

She heard Alex's voice indistinctly, not making out the words, as if he were underwater or far, far away. "Hot, I'm so hot," she murmured, kicking off the covers as she rose to consciousness.

The night rail was prim and high necked yet very sheer. All too clearly he remembered just how sheer. "I, er, think it might be best to keep at least the sheet—you might take a chill," he said, pulling the linen back up.

Joss blinked and struggled to lean up on her elbows, then squinted around the cabin. Where was she? This was not her bedroom. She had not used her drops. Where were those dratted glasses? Then Alex spoke again.

"Careful, Joss. You're weak. Let me help you sit up."

Then it all came rushing back to her—they were aboard ship and she had been wretchedly sick. Barbara had been nursing her. But her mother-in-law was nowhere in sight. It was her husband who sat by the side of her bed, fussing with the bedclothes!

"Alex?" she gasped out, shrinking away from him, clutching the sheet up to her chin in horror. Her hands felt the tangled mass of hair falling over her shoulders. She must look a positive fright! "W-what are you doing here?"

"I've brought you some beef broth and a slice of fresh bread. Cook just cut open the loaf this morning. You'd best enjoy it while you can. In a few more days there will be nothing left but hard biscuits and salted meats."

"Don't speak of food," she wheezed, struggling to control her rebellious stomach. She would *not* be sick in front of him.

"You must try to eat, Joss, to keep up your strength."

"Where's Barbara?"

"A bit under the weather but not as ill as you," he replied with a grin. "She needs some rest so I'm here to nurse you."

"Oh." She digested that. Poor Barbara was probably exhausted after the past few nights sitting up with her. But how could she let Alex see her in such a weak, wretched state? "I'm never ill. I've never had the headache and I don't take cold. This has never happened to me in my life."

"You've never been aboard ship before," he replied reasonably, lifting the lid on the soup tureen.

"I shall contrive never to be again once my feet touch dry land."

He chuckled. "Here, let me feed you a few spoonfuls of broth."

"I can feed myself," she replied ungraciously, reaching for the spoon.

"Your hand is trembling, Joss. You're too weak. Let me take care of you. It's only fair, you know—you took care of me."

"That was different. You were injured."

"And you suffer from mal de mer, which can be quite serious."

"I've long since abandoned the fear of dying. Now my only fear is that I shall live," she said, holding her arms about her cramped middle.

He laughed and slid a spoonful of broth between her lips. "That is my line, I believe, reserved for particularly virulent aftereffects of overindulgence."

"The effects of overindulgence are not an illness, merely a penance," she chided.

"Easy for you to say," he replied dryly, continuing to spoon the broth until she raised her hand, pushing the spoon away.

"I dare not take another sip."

"Then try a few small pieces of dry bread. It's said to help settle the stomach."

She looked dubious but nibbled slowly on several morsels. "That is a bit better. Perhaps—ooh, noo." Abruptly she rolled over to the side of the bed where an empty slop pail sat at the ready as choking heaves wracked her body.

Alex was at her side at once, holding her shoulders and lifting back her hair. When she had lost all the contents of her stomach, he gently laid her back on the bed and wiped her flushed face with a cool, wet cloth. She turned her head into the pillow, awash in a misery of embarrassment, fighting back tears.

"Don't cry, Joss, please," he crooned, stroking her hair away from her face. "You can scarce afford to lose any more moisture," he added, trying to elicit a smile.

A tiny one wobbled on her lips, then vanished on a hiccup. "I am so humiliated for you to see me this way."

"I am your friend, Joss . . . and your husband," he said gently.

She blinked back her tears and managed a meager smile. "I warrant you never imagined a situation such as this when you offered either friendship or marriage."

"No, I suppose I did not," he admitted.

She groped across the surface of the table, almost tipping the water pitcher before seizing upon her glasses, then put them on and looked at Alex, all traces of levity gone. "Do you regret it, Alex?".

He knew what she meant. "At first . . ." He groped for words, combing his fingers through his hair as he sat beside her with his elbows on his knees. "Ah, hell, I—"

His response was suddenly interrupted by a sharp rapping on the cabin door and the first mate's voice calling out, "British man-o'-war sighted, Mr. Blackthorne. Capt'n wants to know what he should do."

Joss would have given much to know what Alex had been going to say, but the spell of the moment was broken. He made hasty apologies and went topside with the mate, leaving her alone to ruminate.

The next twelve hours were a tense and frightening time for all the passengers and seamen as the *Muskogee Maiden* raced ahead of the British ship. Several times the Americans were almost overtaken, but by moonrise it finally became apparent that they had escaped.

When Alex returned to their cabin, he was exhausted and she knew the subject of their marriage was best dropped.

"How are you feeling?" he asked, sinking wearily onto the chair.

"I've been able to hold down a cup of broth that your mother fed me . . . so far. Alex, why did we run from the royal navy? Surely they mean us no harm—this is a civilian cargo ship."

"It's an American ship, Joss, and our countries are at war. They could confiscate the cargo, even impress our men."

"Would they truly do that?" she asked. She had heard rumors about American sailors forcibly dragged onto British ships, but had not believed them to be true.

"I'm afraid so. It's one of the reasons Congress voted for war—although I'll admit not the main one."

"You're worried about how the hostilities will affect your father's people, aren't you?"

"They're my people, too, Joss," he said defensively. "It was because of my Muskogee blood that I became involved with the Chamberlains."

Joss detected a chill in his manner as he rose and said, "I'm going to eat, then try to get some sleep. Would you like something from the galley?"

"No, I dare not eat anything more, thank you. I shall be

asleep when you return," she replied in a subdued voice, not comprehending his abrupt departure. Was he angry with her because she was English and that man-o'-war had tried to capture them? Or was he merely disgusted with her for being a wretchedly poor sailor, not to mention an unsuitable wife to present to his family in Savannah?

Over the next two weeks Joss began to recover, although she vowed she would never make a sailor. Alex remained tense and standoffish. For her part, Joss avoided him as much as possible after the brief interlude when he had nursed her through that humiliating bout of seasickness. After their unsettling confrontation the night she waited up for him, Joss was scrupulously careful to douse the light and slip into bed before he entered the cabin.

As she felt stronger, she ventured abovedeck to take the fresh air, at first relying on Barbara for support. The crew and motley assortment of other American passengers aboard the *Maiden* provided some pastime during the long days of the crossing. Mr. Soulard, a lively New Orleans Creole who served as supercargo on the voyage, had been particularly solicitous during her convalescence. She began to look forward to their breakfast discussions at the captain's table.

After one such diverting morning, Joss strolled around the deck with the expansive Gaspar Soulard. Poc accompanied them, always on the alert for the elusive and annoying black cat he scented nightly on Alex. From high in the crow's nest where he was just completing a watch, Alex observed the pair laughing and talking animatedly.

Ever since his wife had begun to recover from her mal de mer, she had drawn the attention of every man on the vessel, from grizzled old Captain Neale to the fourteen-year-old cabin boy Tom. They followed her about like damned lap dogs. The rough seamen's attention did not bother him half so much as that of the male passengers, especially that damned Frenchman. He scowled as Soulard made some bon mot that sent Joss into peals of laughter. He'd always loved her laugh, rich and hearty, utterly unaffected. Now, as the enchanting sound floated up to him, he gritted his teeth.

Damn the woman, why did she have to change this way? She had made him desire her when he had no intention of leg-shackling himself to her in a conventional marriage—as if she would be anything but horrified if he made physical demands upon her!

When the third mate began to climb the mast to the crow's nest, Alex was glad to relinquish his watch and descend to the deck below. He had seen enough of Joss in her bright yellow gown, laughing and flirting with the damned supercargo. The Creole had bought smuggled French wine in such excess that all of it could not fit in the already overcrowded hold and had to be stored abovedeck, lashed between the mainmast and the mizzen. During the earlier storms the lashings had worked loose.

Soulard should have spent his time securing the expensive wine, not squiring around *his* wife! Intent on expressing those sentiments to the supercargo, he climbed toward the deck. Tar, sunning himself on a coil of rope, spotted Alex and jumped down to meet him.

The big tom crossed the deck just as Joss and Soulard, along with Poc, turned at the bow and headed aft. Sighting his nemesis, the terrier let out a ferocious growl and barreled down the length of the deck toward his quarry. Rather than run, the cat bowed its back, legs splayed, claws flexed. Every hair in his heavy black pelt stood straight out from the top of his ears to the tip of his tail. A low feral yowl split the deckside quiet as Poc tried too late to put on the brakes.

"Poc, no!" Joss cried, dashing after him.

Gaspar Soulard gallantly followed her to lend what assistance he could without getting close enough to the contest to have his new doeskins mussed. Fur and blood were devilish difficult to get out of kerseymere. " 'Ave a care, *ma petite*, that you are not scratched," he said in his heavy French accent, taking her arm to move her back as Poc ran afoul of Tar's first lightning swipe.

With a yip of pain the dog leaped back, nose bloodied. The game was suddenly not fun any longer. Did this imbecile feline have no sense of sport whatsoever? Before Poc could regroup, the tom got in a second raking blow to his muzzle, then turned and began jumping gracefully up the pile of wine crates, as if saying, "Catch me if you can."

Once the business end of Tar was occupied clawing into ropes and wooden slats, Poc was galvanized into hot pursuit. Although far from graceful, he made up in determination what he lacked in speed, scrambling after the cat. As they neared the top of the eight-foot pile of crates, the roughhousing of the two animals began to loosen the already precariously frayed hemp lashing the wooden containers together.

With one scornful glance over his shoulder, Tar leaped effortlessly from the top of the kegs onto the mizzen and climbed to perch atop a yardarm, then looked down as if bored with the whole game. Robbed of his quarry, his nose smarting keenly, Poc clambered onto the top crate with a loud bark, then jumped against the mast in frustration as if to jar the cat from his secure position high above.

Unfortunately it was not Tar that was jarred loose, but rather the crates upon which the dog was jumping. With a loud ripping sound, the whole pile began tumbling helter-skelter, wooden slats splintering and the wine bottles within flying through the air like cannonballs to shatter against the deck.

"Poc!" Joss cried out, trying to reach her pet, who tumbled right along with the cargo, vanishing from sight in the avalanche.

Just as she stepped forward, Alex seized her around the

waist and hauled her back to safety. "He'll either land on his feet or we'll have to dig him out. You can't help him by getting coshed on the head," he yelled over the sound of cracking wood and shattering glass.

"Let me go! What if he's hurt?" She flailed ineffectually at him as he set her behind him, maintaining his hold on her arm.

"When the dust clears, we'll see if he's hurt," Alex replied calmly over the sound of loud cursing in an interesting hybrid of French and American English.

Gaspar Soulard had not been so fast on his feet as Alex had. He stood in the center of the deck, his embroidered silver waistcoat, sky-blue cutaway jacket and cream doeskins drenched in fine French claret. Ruby droplets fell like spring rain from the points of his carefully waxed moustache and soaked into his once snowy starched cravat. He blinked his eyes against the sting of acidic wine and ran one hand through his hair, only to come away with a cut on his palm from a shard of glass caught in his tight dark curls. Stamping one foot, he cursed even more volubly, shaking his head almost in sync with the equally soaked dog, who did likewise as he emerged from the wreckage, none the worse for his ordeal.

Joss smothered a burble of laughter when man and dog let fly another spray of wine upon one another, but Alex held nothing back, laughing uproariously as he cried out, "This may be the first time a man employed by the Blackthorne line drowned in wine rather than saltwater."

Soulard scowled furiously. "Blackthorne Shipping weel lose thousands of dollars on thees wine."

"It was worth it, Gaspar," Alex replied, placing one arm possessively around Joss's shoulders.

From across the deck, Barbara smiled silently. Matters were progressing slowly but in the right direction.

Chapter Seventeen

Joss stood on the deck surveying Savannah. *What did I expect—London?* This was the Americas, new and raw and boisterous. The city was small and mean by comparison to any modern European port, yet there was a look of enterprise about the inhabitants. The bank of the Savannah River was lined with all manner of ships, from sleek massive Indiamen to wallowing coastal trawlers.

This flat, swampy coastal lowland was unlike anything Joss had ever seen or read about. Huge oak trees trailing grayish ribbons of moss stood sentinel in the heavy air. Now that they were several miles inland on the river, the brisk salt breeze of the open ocean was gone. Insects hummed ominously in the sultry noon heat.

She felt light-headed, at once eager to quit the hateful rocking of the ship, yet afraid to set foot on the alien soil. More than anything else she was nervous about meeting the rest of Alex's formidable family. Barbara was English but Devon and their children were entirely American. What if they did not like her?

You're being a cake again, she reminded herself. Barbara had continually assured her of a warm welcome by everyone. If only she and Alex were truly husband and wife, if he loved her, then she would have felt able to cope with any extremity. But their marriage was a sham and she was alone. Terrified.

As if to reassure her, Poc came up and sat beside her, thumping his tail against the deck loudly. She reached down and scratched his chin fondly. "Will you be my guardian in this strange new land?"

"There's nothing to fear, Joss. Georgians may be a little rough mannered by English drawing room standards, but they're friendly," Alex said as he walked up behind her.

"Even if I am English and our countries are at war?" she asked dubiously.

"You married me. I guess that makes you an American now. My father was a Loyalist during the revolution. He fought for the British as a King's Ranger."

"You never mentioned that before," she said, digesting that bit of heartening information.

He shrugged. "It was a long time ago. He's had thirty years to become reconciled. Uncle Quint fought for the rebels. His good offices went a long way toward smoothing Papa's entry into the Savannah business community."

"Then no one held his political beliefs against him?"

"His politics were less of a problem than his Muskogee blood. Some people will never accept that," he said flatly.

"Oh . . . I had thought that here in America . . ."

"That it would be different for a mixed blood than it is in Europe?" he asked bitterly.

Joss had never seen this side of Alex before. If he had ever been bothered by his Indian blood or felt discriminated against because of it, he had not spoken of it. Before she could frame a reply, he caught sight of a familiar face on the dock and waved excitedly, calling out something in a heathenish tongue she assumed was Muskogee.

The rolling plank surface of the deck seemed to evaporate like fog beneath her feet when she saw the virtually naked, copper-skinned savage who returned Alex's greeting. Every inch of his flesh—and there was a good deal of it visible—was covered with hideous blue tatoos. His scalp was shaven except for one long lock of inky hair, which was adorned with shells, beads and feathers. Heavy copper loops pierced his earlobes, stretching them grotesquely.

Dear God, this could not be Devon Blackthorne! Could it?

The Muskogee climbed aboard the ship—and the two men embraced as they continued to jabber in that foreign dialect. Then Alex turned to her with a broad smile wreathing his face. Seeing the way she stood frozen in horror, his own expression quickly shifted to stormy hostility. "Joss, may I present my father's cousin." He uttered some utterly unintelligible name, then translated it as "Pig Sticker."

Joss gathered her scattered wits and made her curtsy, weak with relief that the naked savage was not her father-in-law. But she could see that she had angered Alex with her vaporish reaction to meeting her first full-blooded red Indian. She certainly did not disdain him for being of another race, even though she admitted not feeling at all comfortable seeing so much bare—not to mention disfigured—skin exposed.

"Pig Sticker taught me how to shoot my first bow," Alex said, a warning in his voice.

Joss recovered sufficiently to smile at the austere countenance of Pig Sticker. "I am most pleased to make your acquaintance, Mister, er, Sticker."

He smiled for the first time and the harsh impassivity of his features softened. In perfectly intelligible English, he replied, "My heart is glad Sun Fox takes a mate."

Poc chose that moment to edge his way around her and move in front of the Indian with a sharp bark of excitement, sniffing the red man's unfamiliar scent.

"This is Poc, Pig Sticker, my wife's guardian and a brave little warrior in his own right," Alex said as his companion stretched cut a gnarled hand for the dog to sniff. Apparently it met with Poc's approval, for he gave it a slurpy lick and wagged his tail.

Surprised at the dog's reaction, Joss explained, "He doesn't usually take to strangers easily."

"Like his mistress," Alex muttered beneath his breath as Barbara approached. She gave the Muskogee a broad smile of welcome and he in turn inclined his head regally to her.

"It is good to see you again, old friend. Is Dev in the city?" Her voice held a hint of breathless eagerness.

Pig Sticker nodded. "He speaks with *micco* of Savannah."

Barbara sighed her disappointment. "If he's tied up with the mayor, we'll not see him soon," she said to Joss. "That man can blather on for hours."

"Pig Sticker has learned some disturbing news," Alex said to his mother as they walked down the rickety planking to the riverbank. "It's rumored that Tecumseh is returning to confer with the prophets he left behind in the towns."

"And to stir up more grief among our people, I vow," Barbara said grimly.

Joss listened to their exchange in puzzlement, piecing together that they spoke of some Indian leader from far away who had come to persuade the Muskogee to war against the whites. She noted, too, how Barbara had used the words "our people," identifying herself with the savages. How could a cultivated and charming English lady such as Barbara Blackthorne have allied herself with a group of naked, tattooed men with shaven heads? Did Alex's beloved Grandmother Charity look like Pig Sticker? She shuddered to find out.

Joss's troubling thoughts were interrupted by Barbara's sudden outcry of joy. "Dev!" She broke away from them and ran into the arms of a tall, golden-haired man who swept her into a fierce embrace. Joss stood back, somewhat embarrassed by the ardent kiss Alex's parents exchanged, yet longing for Alex to treat her with that same eager abandon.

They finally broke apart as Alex approached. While the two men embraced each other, Joss studied her father-in-law. Despite the fact that one fourth of his blood was Indian, he looked no more like Pig Sticker than did Alex. The resemblance between father and son was amazing, as if she was seeing in Devon what Alex would look like in thirty years. His thick, dark gold hair was threaded with silver at the temples, his face seamed with fine wrinkles around his remarkable dark eyes, which were the very likeness of his son's.

"So, this is my new daughter-in-law," Devon said as he reached out and took Joss's hand, saluting it with a kiss. "I am very pleased to meet you, Jocelyn."

"And I to meet you, Mr. Blackthorne," she said, instantly liking him.

"Please, call me Dev. Everyone does—or at least everyone who doesn't call me less flattering names," he said, merrily winking at her and Barbara.

"He's an utterly incorrigible rogue," Barbara said, taking his arm.

"As your son, I've had to strive mightily to best your notorious reputation," Alex said to his father.

"Ah, but now you're the same as I am, a married man. Your days of debauchery are over," Dev rejoined as they walked over to where an open carriage awaited them.

"How did you know we were arriving?" Alex asked, neatly sidestepping his father's allusion to wedded bliss.

"Jeb Sewell came in from Tybee after he sighted the *Maiden*. I was obliged to listen to Seth Wainwright's complaints about how our new warehouse will spoil his view of the river, so I sent Pig Sticker as a welcoming party."

At this juncture the cousins exchanged a flurry of words

in Muskogee with Alex joining in now and again. Barbara said to Joss, "They're discussing the situation on the frontier. Please don't feel left out. You know how men are about politics."

As he helped the women into the carriage, Devon apologized to Joss. "I did not intend to be rude. Please forgive me."

"I'm certain you and Alex have much to catch up on since he's been away for nearly two years," Joss replied easily.

Pig Sticker did not join them but bade farewell to his family before turning to Joss and saying, "Welcome to our land, wife of the Sun Fox. We shall meet again."

Were his words an invitation . . . or a threat? She wondered.

While Joss was settling into the Blackthorne's big city house and meeting her new family, another far less pleasant meeting was taking place at a plantation house upriver.

"I've waited in this pestilent wilderness for nearly two days—two days of swatting mosquitoes and perspiring so heavily I've ruined all my clothes," Cybill Chamberlain said furiously, swiping her hand across her damp forehead.

Wilbur Kent ignored her outburst as he brushed the dust from his coattails. He was bone weary after his long ride from Charleston and thirsty as the very devil. Pouring himself a generous tumbler of brandy from the decanter sitting on the sideboard, he took a sip and said, "I came as soon as possible after receiving word you were in Savannah."

"You bungled matters abysmally, getting thrown in prison and losing all that money," she snapped.

"Have you brought more? I'll need it for weapons. The Red Sticks can't fight without guns and ammunition."

"It was no simple matter, I can assure you, but yes, I was able to convince the foreign minister to advance the funds again, although it took considerable prevarication on my part. I could scarce admit that you allowed yourself to be overpowered by a single opponent. Hardly the sort of tale to inspire confidence," she sniffed.

Kent laughed nastily, then downed the rest of his brandy in one gulp and reached for her. "I well know how easily *prevarication* comes to you, don't I, dear lady?" He pulled her roughly against his chest and kissed her.

She endured the crude mauling for several moments, then twisted away with a startling oath. "Rupert would slice you to ribbons for that."

"If your husband were to kill all the men who've swived you, the British Army's ranks would be sadly depleted. Old Boney could walk into London with scarce a shot fired," he replied as he refilled his tumbler.

Cybill observed the vile American lout, making an invidious comparison between his pale, long face and lank tan hair and Alex Blackthorne's chiseled features and golden head. How had she ever borne Kent's touch? One did what one had to for king and country—and one's husband's promotions, she thought grimly. Kent was useful to their cause and for now that was of paramount importance. "When will you be able to report your success to Rupert? He awaits word in Mobile."

"In a month I shall have the entire Creek Nation doing the Dance of the Lakes."

She scoffed snidely. "Just so they step to the beat of a British drummer."

Joss sat on a dainty cushioned chair in front of the oval mirror in her dressing room, brushing her hair before retiring for the night. Poc snored blissfully on a Duncan Phyfe armchair by the fireplace. Devon and Barbara's home was as gracious and charming as were they themselves. The rooms were beautifully furnished with pieces by the finest colonial cabinetmakers. It was a testament to the wealth

Devon and his foster brother Quintin had accumulated for the Blackthorne dynasty.

Her head still swam with all the names she had to put to new faces. There were four of Alex's siblings and their husbands, including six lively children and a new baby, not to mention Quintin and Madelyne and three of their five offspring with attendant grandchildren.

Alex's family was indeed large and boisterous, the very sort of warm, welcoming group to which she had always dreamed of belonging. But they were intimidating, too, so brashly open and informal. Joss was certain that her British sense of decorum had made her appear stiff and reticent. She wanted so desperately to belong, yet felt like an outsider, a fraud entering the family under false pretenses. She was not truly Alex's wife—never had been as far as he was aware. After her wretched indisposition aboard ship, Joss was certain he could never desire her.

As yet they had had no chance to discuss sleeping arrangements. While Alex remained downstairs with his father and uncle Quint discussing the tense political situation, she hurriedly readied herself for bed. His large, masculine bedroom had an oversize bed obviously designed for a tall Blackthorne male. He could sleep in it. She intended to make use of the big leather sofa next to the fireplace. When he came in she would be swaddled demurely in blankets a dozen feet away from him with all the candles doused.

She had observed Alex laughing and playing with his nieces and nephews that afternoon. Small wonder he had so easily charmed the children at her school. He'd certainly had a lifetime of practice, surrounded by little ones. Did he never dream of having children of his own? Or would he one day regret his precipitous arrangement with her and wish for a real marriage?

If only things could go the way Barbara believes they will, she thought wistfully, staring at her reflection in the mirror. Who was the woman in the glass looking back at her? A stranger she scarcely recognized, attractive enough, she supposed, thanks to Barbara, yet obviously not the woman for Alex.

Alex stood in the doorway, transfixed by Joss. His wife, yet not his wife. Elusive. Beautiful. Distant. When had he started to think of her in those terms, she who had been his faithful companion, as comfortable as a pair of old shoes?

His mother had wrought a marvelous physical transformation in her. She sat with that magnificent tawny mane of hair spread over her shoulders, partially concealing the body of an Amazon queen, slim and strong yet generously curved. In spite of the heavy brocade robe she wore, he remembered only too well her body silhouetted by candlelight. But for all the unwelcome lust her appearance evoked, his discomfort with her was much more profound.

She had changed, Joss herself. She was aloof and tense, withdrawn from him. The only member of his family she seemed attuned to was his English mother. Had it been a mistake to bring her to America? In England he'd been the carefree rake, a lovable scoundrel for her crusading Methody soul to reform. But here he was the Sun Fox, a Muskogee mixed blood. God, he could still see the expression of horrified incredulity on her face when she'd first laid eyes on Pig Sticker.

What does that make me—a mongrel to shrink from—or the sort of exotic savage who appeals to women like Cybill Chamberlain?

He did not much care for either alternative, but that was of no immediate consequence. He would be leaving in the morning. Angrily he strode into the room and closed the door.

Joss whirled around, startled from her reverie, clutching her hairbrush to her breasts. "Oh, Alex, I did not expect you so soon. That is—I had planned to be in bed—er, not in bed but—"

"Planning sleeping schedules again, eh, m'dear?" he said

as he slipped off his jacket and began unbuttoning his waistcoat.

"I had thought to take the sofa and leave the bed for you . . . if that is all right."

Just bloody lovely, he wanted to shout. Instead he took a deep breath and said, "The bed is quite large enough for the two of us." What insane impulse had made him blurt out such an untenable idea! He'd meant to chivalrously offer her the bed and take the sofa himself.

"I don't think that would be a wise idea," she equivocated, her mouth gone dry at the prospect of actually sleeping in the same bed with him again. She looked away as he continued to shed clothing, tossing waistcoat, boots and hose, then his cravat and shirt helter-skelter. Soon he'd be as naked as that Pig Sticker person!

"Wise idea?" he echoed. "We're married, Joss. It would be a deal more remarked upon if we did *not* sleep together. Remember, the servants will come in tomorrow to gather up the linens."

"Oh, I had not thought of that," she said in a subdued voice. *Why are you making this so difficult, Alex?*

If he'd heard her silent question he could not have answered it. "It will only be for one night, Joss. I'm leaving at dawn for the Muskogee towns."

Startled by his casual announcement, she forgot her quandary over the sleeping arrangements. He was leaving her alone in this strange new country! "But we've only just arrived—your family—"

"Papa is going with me. Pig Sticker has already started ahead. We have to see if Tecumseh is really returning to Muskogee land."

"Who is this Tecumseh?" she asked, stumbling on the foreign name.

"A great Shawnee leader from far to the north—the land of the Great Lakes. He has dreams of a vast confederacy of Indian tribes stretching from Canada to the gulf. A noble idea, but one which is doomed to fail. The United States government will use the rebellion as an excuse to slaughter Indians and take even more of their land."

"And the British are merely exploiting your people for their own political aims," she ventured, wondering if in spite of what he'd said back in London, he blamed her for being English.

"Your mind is as keen as ever, Joss," he said with grudging admiration. "Uncle Quint has learned from his agent in Virginia that an American traitor is planning to rendezvous with the Red Stick leaders, supplying them with guns. We mean to stop him."

"Will this be dangerous?"

He shrugged. "The Red Sticks—they're Muskogees who favor a war to drive out the whites and mixed bloods who live like whites—their faction has been violent, but my father has considerable influence with the Muskogee leaders. He's been a government-licensed trader among them for thirty years. Many of them will listen to him rather than Tecumseh."

The sleek bronzed muscles in his shoulders rippled as he flexed his arms and stretched. She could not tear her eyes away, much as she knew it was prudent to do so. He was so splendid to look upon.

He glanced over to her as his fingers began to unfasten the top button of his fly. "I would suggest, Joss, to preserve your maidenly modesty that you douse the candle and climb into bed like a good girl, for I intend to sleep at once. I'll be leaving before dawn and it will come all too quickly."

She blushed fiery red, remembering all too well that he slept without a nightshirt. "I shall wrap one of the sheets about me and you may have the other . . . so our, er . . . limbs do not touch," she said, scrambling to rearrange the covers.

Alex chuckled in spite of his frustration. "My ever practical and always resourceful Joss."

* * *

The night was hellishly long for both of them, lying stiffly and silently alongside each other, afraid to move, virtually afraid to breathe, lest the acute and uncomfortable awareness humming between them trigger a reaction neither could control. Joss hugged one edge of the large bed with her slender body. Alex, in spite of his much larger frame, clung to the opposite side.

True to his word, he slipped from between the sheets at the first faint light of false dawn. His keen night vision enabled him to dress quietly and gather the items he needed for his journey. He was just about to open the door to the hallway when Joss's voice whispered, "How long will you be gone, Alex?"

He stopped and turned to her as Poc, awake and watching him, jumped onto the bed with his mistress. "I can't say for certain. There are scores of towns on the streams that catacomb the land from Georgia to the gulf. That's why the whites named us Creeks. Months perhaps."

"Oh, so long," she replied, taken aback. He was distancing himself from her physically now, as well as emotionally. *That's why the whites named* us *Creeks.* He was one of them and she was . . . who? Alex's wife, or a lonely Englishwoman deserted in a foreign land? "I shall miss you, Alex."

Her voice sounded so forlorn, he fought the impulse to go to her and give her a fond brotherly buss upon the forehead as he used to do. Somehow that no longer seemed appropriate. "I shall miss you, too, Joss," he replied in a strained voice.

Then he was gone. She sat, hugging Poc as the tears she'd been holding back for so long began to fall.

By the time Joss came down to breakfast, Barbara had finished reading all the letters that had arrived in her absence and was again perusing the last one that Pig Sticker had brought to her from Coweta, her mother-in-law's village. She looked up at Joss and took in her tear-reddened eyes and listless manner.

Damning her foolish son for his willful blindness, she smiled and gestured to the chair next to hers. "Sit down and let me ring for some breakfast. You look as though you need a good fortifying cup of hot black coffee."

A servant quickly appeared, bearing a large pot of fragrant coffee and two cups. After accepting the coffee and ordering enough food to satisfy the appetite of all the climbing boys in London, Barbara turned her attention back to Joss. "I would venture that you've had no more sleep than have I . . . but with far less pleasant reasons for being deprived of it."

At times her mother-in-law sounded indelicately American. Joss felt her cheeks sting with heat. "Alex showed no more interest in me last night than he did aboard ship or in London. 'Tis quite useless to persist in this folly, Barbara. He does not want me."

"Twaddle," Barbara said with a dismissive wave of her hand. "He wants you quite desperately. Why else do you think he's been such a grumpy old bear since the night we sailed?"

"The thought that he heartily detests being saddled with an accident-prone, seasick wife did cross my mind," Joss replied dejectedly.

"Honestly, you are as blind as he," Barbara exclaimed in aggravation. "But that is of no moment."

"No, it certainly does not matter what I believe, for he is gone and I shall not see him for months."

"You will see him in a few weeks, perhaps less."

Joss set her cup down, sloshing coffee onto the snowy white tablecloth. "What do you mean?" she asked uneasily. Barbara had a gleam in her eye that Joss had learned usually meant mischief.

Barbara rustled the pages of the letter sitting beside her plate. "This is from my mother-in-law."

"Alex's Grandmother Charity?" *The Indian lady.*

"Yes. She is a dear soul. You shall adore her just as I do."

Visions of a female version of Pig Sticker, tattooed and shaved, flashed into Joss's mind, but she reminded herself the woman had been educated by Methodist missionaries. Surely they had taught her to dress modestly! "But . . . I thought she lived with the Muskogee." Already Joss was not liking this.

"She does. In the Lower Creek town of Coweta. Dev and Alex will use it as a base from which to make trips to other key towns up and down the river system."

"So you are saying if we go to Coweta, we will find them?" Live in a Muskogee village deep in the snake-infested wilderness!

"Charity is most eager to meet her only grandson's new wife. She has invited us to come spend the rest of the summer."

Chapter Eighteen

Alex and Devon rode for days, through teaming mosquito-infested woodlands, across steep ridges and down into overgrown brush. All was lush from summer's verdant rain and heat as they forded the hundred small streams and swift-flowing rivers that gave the inhabitants their name—the Oconee, the Ocmulgee, the Flint and the Chattahoochee. Then they struck deep into the territory of the Upper Creeks, the towns held by the Red Sticks between the mighty arms of the Tallapoosa and the Coosa rivers.

Devon smoked with the *miccos* at every town along their route and spoke before their councils, attempting to show them the dangers of casting their lot with the northern tribes, who were already at war against the Americans. All listened politely, for that was their way. Some heeded his plea, others withheld commitment until they could consult with the prophets from the North and the great Tecumseh himself. Most believed that the Shawnee would make a second journey south to sway the Creek Confederacy to his dream.

"We need to have a face-off with Tecumseh," Alex said in frustration after a long night of speeches and feasting in the *idalwa* of Kulumi.

Devon, stripping off his elaborate ceremonial feathered turban and copper jewelry, replied, "That, my son, is becoming painfully obvious. My guess is that he will strike for Sawanogi or go up the Tallapoosa to Kailaidshi."

"His first stop coming south through Tennessee would likely be Black Warrior's town on the Tombigbee," Alex said, spreading out a water-stained map on the hard-packed dirt floor of the summer brush arbor they had been given for sleeping. He pointed to a small *x* far to the north.

Devon grunted. "A hell of a ride, and our mounts are all but played out from the riding we've already done. This land is made for canoe and portages, not horses. We must convince old Timpoochee to lend us a canoe and several warriors to help us portage between the rivers."

The steamy dawn saw them on their way up the Coosa River with two powerful young Muskogees paddling along with them. The long, monotonous journey gave Alex more time to brood about his relationship with Joss. They simply could not continue the way they had been, he thought, remembering the hellish night in bed with her in his parents' house. One more time such as that and he'd fall upon her like a ravening wolf.

Echoing his thoughts, Devon said, "Is the honeymoon not going well, son?"

Alex sighed. "Is it that obvious?"

"I'm afraid so. You looked as if you'd not slept the night before we left." He grinned then and added. "Neither did I, but I suspect the reason was different."

Alex looked at the two Muskogees paddling the canoe. Neither understood English. He could speak freely to Devon. His father waited, leaving the choice open. He could vent his feelings if he wished, or not. Growing up,

Alex had always appreciated Devon Blackthorne's way. Now he felt guilty for his deception.

"Everything is all tangled up inside of me. I don't even know myself what I feel for Joss anymore, Papa. When we wed . . . well, it seemed simple, but now . . ."

"Is it the war? Does she resent coming to live in the camp of the enemy?" Devon asked, hoping this was not the problem, for he liked the Englishwoman, who in some ways reminded him of his wife when she was young.

"No, she chose to come with me to America. Joss cares about people, not politics."

"Perhaps it's just a lovers' spat. Your mother and I fought like owls and crows when we first met. By the time we return to Savannah, she'll have cooled down."

Cooling Joss down was not the problem, Alex wanted to say. Cooling his own lust for her was, but he volunteered nothing, staring out over the gleaming silver ribbon of water, thinking of his wife. . . .

When they finally drew near the Black Warrior village, there was an air of excitement among the people. The powerful Shawnee leader had returned! Dev seldom journeyed so far to the northwest, and the leaders of the Black Warrior town were suspicious of the two mixed bloods whose golden hair proclaimed them more white than red. Yet the laws of hospitality combined with Devon's longstanding position as a fair and honest trader gave him and his son entry to the meeting that night.

They sat in one of the four open-fronted assembly boxes that faced the public square, watching uneasily as the Shawnee prophet Sickaboo and a group of his Red Stick Muskogee followers did the Dance of the Lakes, an eerie, supposedly supernatural demonstration. The dancers, naked and fearfully painted in red and black, began to tremble and moan, howling at the starry night sky like demented creatures. As the frenzy built with the accelerating pace of the drums, they eventually fell to the ground in convulsions, rolling about.

Observing the awestruck and often frightened reaction of the audience, Alex whispered to his father, "Pretty impressive."

"Last year while you were away, Tecumseh predicted the approach of a comet, even an earthquake."

"And they both occurred?" Alex asked, amazed.

Devon nodded. "Exactly when he said. Pretty scary business. He's had enough contact with whites to have learned about the comet but no one predicts earthquakes."

Alex's expression was at once grim and rueful as he asked, not totally in jest, "Are you certain we're on the right side?"

"Not always," Dev replied wearily, "but it is the lesser of two evils, especially considering what I overheard from Bear's Paw. An American working for the British has been moving down the Tallapoosa, arming the Red Sticks with British Brown Bess muskets."

"It's Wilbur Kent." Alex cursed. "I knew I should have slit his gizzard while I had the chance."

"He must have escaped from prison," Dev speculated.

"More likely Cybill Chamberlain somehow secured his release," Alex replied. "We have to stop him, but how?"

Before Dev could reply, the *micco* stood up and walked toward the fire as the last dancers were helped from the square. He began to orate about the famous Shawnee visitor who waited in the shadows between two of the assembly boxes. When the *micco* finished his speech, Tecumseh strode to the center where the fire seemed to lend his fierce, handsome visage a mystic quality. He was a tall man, powerfully built, in the prime of his years, seasoned by war yet filled with youthful vigor.

His ceremonial cape flowed behind him as he walked, wearing only a breechclout and beaded, fringed leggings. On his bare tatooed chest a massive silver gorget gleamed in the firelight, as did his armbands, bracelets and heavy copper ear bobs. His massive head was bare of turban, shaved smooth but for the central comb, *en brosse* in front, in back long and splendidly adorned with feathers, quills and gemstones.

Yet for all his daunting appearance, the man's real power was only realized when he began to speak in a low rich voice that held the assembly mesmerized.

"Your blood has become white. Your tomahawks have no edge. You have buried your bows and arrows with your fathers. Brethren of my mother," he cried, his voice rising, reminding them of the blood ties he shared with the Muskogee people, "brush from your eyelids the sleep of slavery. You must strike vengeance for your country. The time is overdue. The bones of our ancestors bleach on the hills. Is there no son of these brave men to strike the palefaces and quiet these complaining ghosts?"

He went on to outline the long history of broken treaties, the promises that the Americans had made regarding the red man's lands—lands that the white settlers encroached upon and stole. He described the killing of Indian women and children, driving the once great natives of the northern and southern confederacies farther and farther toward the Father of Waters in the West, even beyond. He spoke angrily of the treachery of the Indiana territorial governor William Henry Harrison, who had burned Tecumseh's own town while he was away in the South the preceding year, killing his brother and enslaving all those he could capture. If ever there had been an opportunity for peace, it was forever gone.

"Only the great king across the water will aid us. He brings us food and blankets for our families, guns and bullets for us to fight the Americans. Let us join together in a holy war and build a nation of our peoples that shall stretch from the Great Lakes of the North to the gulf waters of the South!"

When Tecumseh had finished speaking, several of the other leaders rose and addressed the people. Then Devon Blackthorne, the Golden Eagle of Coweta, was allowed to have his say. Alex watched in rapt attention as his father strode deliberately across the square, circling the fire so its flickering light reflected brightly on his elaborate ceremonial garments, a high red silk turban adorned with eagle feathers, a vermilion cloak of rich velvet and shirt and leggings of butter-soft white buckskin painstakingly embroidered with silver quills and crimson and blue beads.

He paused for dramatic effect and his dark eyes swept the four crowded boxes with hypnotic intensity. Then he spoke.

"I will tell you first that all the great Tecumseh has spoken about American treachery is true. How could I deny that the settlers steal our land and that the Father in Washington allows it to happen?" There was a surprised murmuring at this, for the people had expected the mixed-blood trader to disagree.

"Many of you know me. I have lived and worked among you all of my life. I am Wind Clan. And I was once as Tecumseh is now, the English king's man. In the last war between the English and the Americans I fought for the English because they promised that our ancient homelands would be preserved, our women and children would be well fed and safe from harm.

"But that did not happen. Instead the Americans defeated the king's army. And the English climbed into their canoes and returned far across the water from which they had come. They left us alone and at the mercy of the Americans."

Alex sat listening to his father, proud of Devon's spellbinding oratory, yet even more proud of him for sharing such painful memories from the past. He knew it could not be easy for Devon to describe his years as a King's Ranger, to remember his fallen comrades, their lost cause, the cruel backlash that followed on the heels of the British retreat from Georgia in 1781.

Alex looked around the assembly to see if the speech was swaying people to consider the consequences of another alliance with Britain. The Red Sticks in their vermilion and black war paint would never reconsider. The fanatic light of hatred burned in their eyes. But many of the more thoughtful, especially the calmer and wiser older men, might prevail. They remembered the last war. That was all he and his father could hope for in these perilous times.

"Whatever do you mean, you cannot ride a horse?" Barbara asked incredulously. "Jocelyn, this is no time for jest!"

"I do not jest," Joss replied over the lump of terror forming in her throat as she looked up at the equine behemoth standing before her. "The only time I've ever been on a horse was when Alex was holding me."

"Well, that does strike a facer to my plan, doesn't it," Barbara said with a rueful laugh. "We could go by canoe, but it would mean long walks through swampy lands when we have to portage—and between here and Coweta we'd have to portage a great deal. How do you feel about quicksand and snakes?" Barbara asked.

Joss shivered. "I like them even less than horses."

"We're making progress then. Capital. You shall learn to ride en route."

"A baptism by fire, I believe Papa used to call it," Joss said dubiously.

"Do you wish to see Alex before the year's out or not?"

Joss sighed in capitulation and reached for the reins of Sugar Baby. The white gelding shied, sensing her nervousness. Doggedly she held on, letting the groom assist her to mount. The horse carried a regular man's saddle. Shockingly, Barbara insisted they ride in the manner of Muskogee women. Astride, she said, one had a more secure seat in the rough terrain.

The women wore mid-calf-length voluminous skirts of lightweight cotton to enable them to straddle their horses, and knee-high deerskin boots to protect their legs from scratchy brush. Joss felt anything but secure or protected as she looked down at the great distance to the ground. If she had not loved Alex Blackthorne so damnably much, she would never in this lifetime have climbed on a horse again. Ever.

"Once we reach Coweta, I promise you shall believe it worth the ride," Barbara assured Joss, kicking her heels against her sleek chestnut's sides.

Thinking of teetering atop this bouncing behemoth for two hundred miles across swamps filled with snakes, fording swift-flowing rivers and then reaching a cluster of mud huts filled with tattooed, naked red Indians did not sound at all worth the ride to Joss. And she had yet to confess to Barbara that she did not know how to swim.

Poc, however, was eager for the adventure, although it took a bit of cajoling and some very stern admonitions from Joss before he deigned to stay in the wicker hamper lashed to one of the packhorses. Quicksand and snakes, not to mention wild boars and alligators, were as deadly as they were unfamiliar to the London-bred terrier. This was a time when his fearlessness could well be his undoing.

The four youths who accompanied them were mixed bloods who lived white and worked for Devon's trading company. Barbara carried on a lively conversation with them and Joss was drawn into it gradually as her terror at being on horseback abated. Other than being bitten by mosquitoes and sweltering in the intense heat, she made it through the first day without calamity.

Until she tried to dismount that evening. The pain in her derriere, which had been steadily growing, blossomed into a screaming fiery ache that shot down her legs, enveloping her knees and calves, which buckled under her the moment she tried to take a step.

Swallowing a frightful blasphemy, she clung to the cantle of the saddle until she could bring her rubbery legs back under control. Making a mental note to chide Alex for allowing his vocabulary to rub off on her, she let go of the saddle and took one step gingerly, then another toward the merrily crackling campfire that promised some small respite from the carnivorous insects feasting on every exposed inch of her body.

"The soreness will pass in a few days," Barbara said cheerfully. "In the meanwhile, try rubbing this on the regions that pain you." She handed Joss a vial of salve.

Joss opened it and gagged. Her eyes watered at the horrid smell, which was much like a combination of London sewer and offal from hospital surgery. "You cannot expect me to put this on my body," she exclaimed.

Barbara shrugged. "Think of it this way—'twill keep the mosquitoes at bay while it soothes your bottom."

The trip became a routine of weary monotony—other than Joss's narrow brush with drowning when she slid from her horse midstream in the Altamaha River. Lemuel their guide and Poc rescued her. After confessing that she, too, had been unable to swim when she was shipwrecked on the Georgia coast, Barbara undertook teaching Joss whenever they made camp near a suitably safe body of water.

Unfortunately, during the first lesson she sank like a rock, but with more practice, she did manage to master a somewhat clumsy dog paddle. Even her horseback riding skills improved markedly as they neared Coweta. She no longer clutched her gelding's mane so tightly she tore hair out of it, and she could dismount without her knees buckling and her posterior throbbing. She had learned to endure the stink of Barbara's salve.

When they approached the Muskogee town where Alex's family lived, Joss found herself even more tense and uncertain than she had been when meeting the Blackthornes in Savannah. With the notable exception of Pig Sticker, everyone there had hair and wore clothes! The aboriginal inhabitants of these teeming swampy woodlands seemed to prefer neither. After two weeks of cooking over smoky campfires and lying awake on the hard damp earth, waiting fearfully for snakes and bugs to crawl inside her blankets, Joss longed with near religious fervor for a hot bath, a well-cooked meal and a good night's sleep in a house with a real bed. She was certain there would be no such luxuries among the Muskogee.

But when they arrived she was somewhat surprised. The large town on the banks of the Chatahoochee appeared neat and orderly with real houses made of plastered mud built over sturdy wooden frames with heavy thatched roofs. Many of them were two stories high and all looked quite substantial. Surrounding each small cluster of three or four buildings were well-tended agricultural plots. All the houses were situated around a central square that appeared to have four long, low, open edifices for public seating. At one side of the square stood a huge circular building with a high pointed roof; at the opposite side, a playing field stretched between two goalposts, the chunky arena that Alex had described to her.

To Joss's immense relief all the females were decently clad in brightly colored full skirts that fell below the knees and cotton chemises belted at their waists with ropes of beads. Some wore high deerskin boots; others showed bare bronzed legs and were shod in low moccasins. Their hair was plaited, not shorn into scalp locks. Smaller children did run naked, much to her distress, and the men mostly resembled Pig Sticker, although a few wore the rough buckskin clothing common across the American frontier.

It was an alien world to Joss. She looked at Barbara, who was smiling and waving to various women as they rode through large open fields at the edge of the village.

"These are the common fields. The men break the soil in the spring and help the women plant them; then the women and children tend them until harvest," Barbara explained as they rode by high rustling cornstalks and neat rows of bean plants.

"What about the small plots surrounding the houses?" Joss asked.

"They are owned and cultivated by individual families for their personal needs. Muskogee life is communal in most respects, but individuality is also encouraged."

"You truly admire them." Joss hoped the amazement was not evident in her voice.

"La, I thought them utter savages—just as you do now, my dear—when I first came here; but after living among them a few months, I learned to love them and to respect their ways. You will, too. Only give it time."

Barbara was English, born and raised the daughter of a baron. If she could adapt, certainly a woman raised in London's seamy East End could do likewise, Joss reasoned. She squared her shoulders and tried to sit her horse with as much grace as she could muster.

They rode until they neared the central square, then stopped by a cluster of four buildings, all quite substantial looking. A small birdlike woman wearing a coronet of snowy white braids stepped outdoors, her face lighting with joy as Barbara dismounted. In spite of her European hairstyle, Charity Blackthorne wore traditional Muskogee clothing, including the requisite feathered silver ear bobs and beaded belt. She was thin but her swift light step indicated a wiry strength that belied her seventy-five years. Charity was as bronzed as Alex and Devon. Only the pale amber color of her eyes spoke of her English father. Her high cheekbones, straight prominent nose and high forehead bore the Muskogee stamp.

Joss dismounted carefully as Barbara and Charity hugged each other, exclaiming over their mutual joy at being reunited. As their guides led the horses away, Barbara turned to Joss and took her hand, drawing her forward.

"Charity, this is Alex's bride, Jocelyn. Jocelyn, this is your new grandmother."

"Welcome to my home, child," Charity said, reaching up to embrace Joss. "You look tired by the long journey. Please, let's go in out of the heat and have some refreshment while we become acquainted."

Charity Blackthorne's voice had a soft, well-modulated tone to it, and Joss was reminded that the woman had been educated by missionaries. "I am pleased to meet you, Grandmother Charity. Alex has spoken often of you."

Charity's eyes danced merrily. "That young man has always been a rascal—so full of devilment, just like his father and grandfather. I wish Alastair could have lived to see his grandson." A wistful remembrance clouded her eyes for a moment, then vanished as she turned and agilely climbed up a ladder to the second floor of the house.

The ground level was filled with agricultural tools, hunting and trapping paraphernalia and storage bins, but the second story was obviously a living area with several windows letting in the bright afternoon sunlight. The room contained a blend of European and Indian artifacts. A bouquet of summer wildflowers graced a small table of polished oak, which sat in the center, surrounded by caned chairs. Dishes and cups were neatly arranged on it. Sleeping pallets on thick cornhusk mattresses lay neatly around the walls and backrests made of buckskin stretched over pole frames sat between them. The place was clean and functional.

While Barbara and Joss sat down, Charity poured from a china pitcher and handed them each a cup of cool water, which had a slight tang of mint to it. "I suppose you'll wish to know about Dev and Alex first," she said. "At my age I find it best to go straight to the point. After all, I never know how much time I have left," she said, chuckling merrily. "They arrived here several weeks ago, hale and hearty, spent a day resting their horses, then left for the Tallapoosa towns."

"Did they hear any word about Tecumseh's return?" Barbara asked.

"Only rumors brought downriver by several mixed-blood trappers," Charity replied, going on to explain the dangerous situation in the interior towns of the Upper Creeks. She concluded by reassuring Joss and Barbara that their men had sent word they would return within a few weeks to reprovision. After that, Barbara excused herself to go visit a number of her old friends in the village, leaving Charity and Joss to become better acquainted.

Charity asked Joss questions about her earlier life and how she and Alex had met. Joss explained, but did not reveal the circumstances of their marriage. All too soon when Alex returned, she would have to face what was to be done about their future. In the meanwhile it was their problem, no one else's.

Charity listened attentively to the lovely young woman whose nervous demeanor indicated her attempts to conceal her unease in what must be an exceedingly alien environment. "Once Alex returns we will have a great wedding feast to honor the son and daughter-in-law of the Golden Eagle and the Dawn Woman. In the meanwhile, you will have time to learn our ways. I know they must seem strange, even frightening to you," she said gently.

Joss felt a bond with the older woman, whose kindness and keen wit were apparent. "I have wondered . . ." she began uneasily, then faltered.

"Why I chose to return here after being educated by my white father and marrying a white man?" Charity completed Joss's question, smiling. "I loved Alastair dearly but I was not welcome in Savannah. The only people who accepted me unconditionally were here. After my husband died and my son was grown, there was nothing left for me among the whites. The Muskogee had need of me. I could teach our children the skills they require to survive in a world that will one day belong to the Americans.

"My brother also grew up white. Then he was known as Nathaniel McKinny. Now he is Tall Crane and I am Listening Woman among the Muskogee. We have chosen to build a bridge between red and white in this place. My son's wife has also done this. Will you as well?" Her clear amber eyes studied Joss as if looking deep into her soul. It was disquieting yet in no way unfriendly.

"I, too, was a teacher of children who needed help to survive in a hostile world in London. I will try, Grandmother Charity."

Joss rested that afternoon on the surprisingly comfortable mattress in the upstairs quarters of an adjacent house, which Charity had given them. Then she joined Barbara for a tour of the village. When Barbara indicated that it was time to join the women for their daily ablution in the river, Joss was horrified.

"You mean undress and bathe in . . . in front of everyone?" she asked, aghast.

Barbara smiled. "Not everyone, just the other women and very small children. I had a bit of trouble with it at first myself, but one quickly learns to shed modesty when the alternative is to itch and perspire in the heat. Perhaps for the first few days we can go to a secluded spot farther upriver where no one will disturb us."

Joss nodded gratefully and they set out after gathering up drying cloths and clean clothing. Barbara included two pairs of the low-cut beaded leather slippers she called moccasins, but Joss indicated that she could not bare her legs in public no matter how hot and uncomfortable her boots were.

"Just watch that you do not get sweat blisters. Any wound festers in this heat."

Marvelous. Joss was liking life in the wilderness less with each passing day. After a bath and a swim in a secluded inlet of the swift-running river, she felt refreshed.

She applied a cooling salve that Charity had given her to the numerous scratches and insect bites on her body, then dressed and began to brush out her hair. With the harsh American sun beating down on her head daily she no longer needed lemon rinses to keep the tawny bronze highlights in her hair, a small consolation for all her miseries.

Her eyes were irritated from the river water so she did not attempt to put drops in them. Instead she took her spectacles and perched them on her nose, ready to walk back to the village. Barbara had left her moments earlier with the admonition not to wander off while she went to spend time with the other women at the communal bathing pool. Since Poc remained to guard her, Joss was unconcerned.

The pair were following the path toward the village when three youths, around twelve or thirteen years of age, approached her. Poc growled softly, then decided they meant no harm and quieted. Joss was not so certain. "G–good day," she stammered, unable to remember the Muskogee words of greeting Barbara had been teaching her.

The boys were unsmiling, their dark eyes huge in their round bronzed faces. Solemnly they studied her with a thorough curiosity bordering on rudeness. She was uncertain about whether to ask what they wanted or simply to try to walk on and hope they would let her pass. She noted the sharp-looking knives attached to their breechclouts.

An exchange in their language ensued, after which one of the boys stepped forward, extending his hand toward her, an expression of awe on his face. What did he want?

Chapter Nineteen

The youth muttered something in his guttural dialect as he touched her spectacles with his fingertips, then jerked his hand back as if burned. Another exchange of words followed in which it seemed the boys were arguing among themselves. Every so often they would cast a wary glance her way before resuming the debate, which seemed to have something to do with her eyeglasses. She had no way of knowing that the sunlight reflecting off the heavy lenses gave her eyes what appeared to the Muskogees to be magical properties.

Poc watched the youths with his head cocked in curiosity, tail wagging. Apparently, he sensed no animosity. Taking off her spectacles, she offered them to the boy who had touched them. How did one pantomime "looking" to savages who had probably never seen a spyglass?

"These help me to see," she said slowly, hoping they understood a bit of English.

At first the boy jumped back as if the spectacles would bite him, but in a moment curiosity won out over fear and he took them gingerly in both hands. She held her hands up to her face, mimicking putting the eyeglasses on. "Like this. Try it," she urged.

The boy raised them with grave hesitation, squinting through the lenses from a foot away, then slowly brought them closer to his face as the other two watched spellbound. He finally perched the frames on his nose and attached the earpieces, holding out his hands in front of him. Then he blinked and let out a loud squawk of horror.

Because his vision was normal, he could see nothing but distortion and blurring through her lenses. He must have thought he'd been struck blind! As Joss stepped closer to remove the eyeglasses from the panic-stricken lad, a gnarled old man carrying a tall pole adorned with ceremonial paraphernalia came running down the path.

He raised the lance and shook the rattles on it menacingly at her, crying out something in Muskogee. Joss needed no translation to know his actions were decidedly hostile. Neither did Poc, who growled and stepped in front of his mistress as the boy tore the spectacles from his face and thew them to the ground, then took off pell-mell after his friends.

The old man remained behind, shaking the staff at her angrily. She squinted, desperate to retrieve her eyeglasses. Without them she'd never be able to find her way back to the village. Kneeling down, she groped myopically, trying her best to ignore the furious diatribe of the old man, whom Poc was holding at bay with a businesslike growl.

Just as she caught a glint of light reflecting off the lenses and reached out toward it, the old man bent down with amazing speed and dexterity, seizing the prize and scuttling off with it as Joss called out for him to stop.

Poc started to give chase, but upon hearing his mistress's frantic cries, returned to where she sat on the ground. He gave her several slurpy kisses of consolation as she calmed herself. Sighing, she held on to the dog and said, "Well, Poc, you shall just have to find the way back for me. Slowly

293

now, so I don't break my neck in this barbarous wilderness."

While they made their way up the twisting woodland path with branches slapping her face and roots tripping her, Joss vowed to use her drops no matter how irritated her eyes. She would never again be at the mercy of these savages! That was if she lived to find the village, she thought in dismay, imagining every leaf a poisonous spider, every tree root a deadly snake.

By the time she stumbled into Charity's house, the commotion created by the influential Shawnee prophet who had come to live with them this past year still had not died down. Joss did not realize she was connected to his ranting.

"Thank heaven you've returned, Jocelyn," Barbara said. "We were just going to search for you."

"I lost my eyeglasses—no, they were stolen by some strange little man carrying a long staff with rattles on it."

"Turtle Snake," Charity said with distaste. "He's a shaman among the Lake People, a real troublemaker."

"Why would he take your spectacles?" Barbara asked, baffled.

Joss quickly outlined what had transpired. "So, if not for Poc, I'd still be wandering around in the woods."

"Oh, dear. This is going to cause trouble, I fear, just the sort of display Turtle Snake loves to put on," Charity said. "He will tell everyone the white man's magic has placed a curse on the boy's eyesight through those spectacles and it must be cast out before everyone in the *idalwa* is struck blind."

"That's absurd! All he need do is give me back my eyeglasses," Joss replied indignantly.

Barbara patted her arm sympathetically. "I think it wise to let Grandma Charity handle this, Jocelyn."

While waiting for Charity to return, Joss dug out her spare pair of spectacles and as an extra precaution, put drops in her eyes so she could see.

*   *   *

About half the town turned out the following afternoon to watch Turtle Snake cast out the curse in Joss's spectacles, which were sitting atop a huge drum placed in the center of the public square. The performance took several hours and involved a great deal of chanting, incantation and dancing before the cursed object could safely be returned to its owner.

She was torn between acute embarrassment and righteous anger when Turtle Snake brought the eyeglasses, suspended on top of that long decorated pole of his. He poked it in her direction and she snatched the spectacles from it, feeling like a fool with so many people watching her.

"What should I say?" she whispered to Barbara.

"A simple thank-you would suffice," Alex replied, moving through the crowd toward her.

"Alex," she squealed in surprise. He took her arm proprietarily as he exchanged a few words with Turtle Snake and the other religious leaders, then led her back into Charity's house. Devon and Barbara faced each other outside the doorway.

Alex could hear his father saying, "I should have known you'd not remain behind like a sensible, obedient wife." The rueful resignation in Devon's voice did not match Alex's mood. His parents were always overjoyed to see each other. At that moment he was not certain if he wanted to hug Joss or throttle her.

Recovering herself a bit, Joss turned to Alex as he moved into the shadows of the interior. He still had a firm hold on her arm. "When did you return?" was all she could think to say. *Idiot.*

"Not soon enough to prevent you from getting into all sorts of trouble, apparently," he responded, going on the offensive. "I told you to remain in Savannah."

"You did no such thing. You merely assumed that I would," she retorted, stung by his cool greeting. He did not want her to be here. Well, fine. She didn't want to be here either now that it was too late to do anything about the regrettable fact.

"I also assumed you'd have enough sense not to meddle in Muskogee religious taboos."

"I wasn't meddling—that horrid man stole my glasses, preaching some sort of twaddle about their being cursed."

"Only after you let a boy look through them and get frightened half to death."

"I was only trying to be helpful," she said as her anger built. This was so unjust.

"Helpful?" He harrumphed. "And were you being helpful to my uncle when you gave him a lecture on the evil of liquor after observing his morning Black Drink ritual."

Someone must have told Alex. Her cheeks flamed as she recalled the humiliating blunder. Early this morning she and Poc had been taking a leisurely walk about the perimeter of the village, when she had chanced to see a tall, reed-thin man swilling something from a gourd. The fellow had given a loud belch, doubled over and retched. He was still at it when an incensed Joss had reached his side. She had witnessed the scene far too often about the streets in London—poor wretches suffering the effects of over-indulgence.

As the man straightened, wiping his mouth, Joss launched into an impassioned sermon on the evil of strong spirits and drunkenness. She earnestly urged the offender to follow the path of sobriety.

The elderly man had stared at her curiously. He obviously did not understand English. Joss silently cursed her limited Muskogee vocabulary. But she refused to give over this poor benighted creature to the demons of drink. She thought for a moment and then began to pantomime. She swilled from an imaginary cup, staggered about, pretended to vomit, and then collapsed on the ground. She arose, then gazed into the man's eyes, which oddly enough reminded her of Grandmother Charity's. Joss pleaded, "Spirits will kill you! Make you sick!" The man nodded. Joss waited.

"You are absolutely correct, wife of Sun Fox. The white man's rum and gin are a potent poison," the tall man agreed in perfectly precise, unaccented English. "That is why my nephew Golden Eagle refuses to allow any of it into Muskogee lands."

"But—but you just finished drinking whiskey," she sputtered.

The old man smiled gently and explained, "What you just witnessed was a cleansing ritual. The drink is a powerful purgative, and taking a morning draught of it is a common custom among the Muskogee—although I must confess that my nephew and grandnephew seldom embrace this particular custom of their people."

Joss's face burned, "Oh, my . . . you must be Mr. McKinny. . . ."

"Yes, my niece, I am Tall Crane, Charity's brother. I've only recently returned from Cusseta."

Joss blurted out, "Please, sir, forgive my impudence and accept my apology." With that, she had turned and run.

Her unpleasant reverie was broken by Alex's caustic comment.

"You naturally assumed an ignorant savage knew no better than to swill down whiskey until he vomited."

"I admit that I made a foolish mistake. But why are you being so hateful?"

"Why are you *here?* It's obvious you don't want to be."

"I was invited by your grandmother—she wanted to meet me."

Alex sighed in defeat. "And of course my mother leaped at the chance to come and—"

"Have a proper celebration of your wedding," Barbara said as she, Devon and Charity entered the house. Seeing the tense confrontational stance of both Alex and Joss, she continued, "Your father and I were unable to be present at

Shirl Henke

your nuptials in London. The least you can do is to allow us to have a feast in your honor with our family here."

Groaning inwardly, Alex knew he was trapped.

The ceremony was even more elaborate than Turtle Snake's casting out of the curse and much better attended. Everyone in Coweta and many people from surrounding towns came to join in the feasting in honor of Golden Eagle's son and his English wife, who was now being called Magic Eyes.

Alex sat beside Joss at the head of a long low table, dressed in his Muskogee finery. The leaping flames from the big fire in the square bathed his face with glowing bronze highlights and shadows. To Joss, seated on the cool earth beside him, he looked like a savage stranger, not the laughing, charming Alex she knew so well. Or thought she had known.

Now he was dressed in a beaded buckskin jacket, open to the waist and sleeveless. A breechclout and fringed leggings revealed an alarming amount of his dark skin, made even more coppery by the firelight. On his chest a heavy silver gorget gleamed and he wore barbarous-looking armbands over his rippling biceps and heavy silver loops in his ears. His ears had been pierced all this time and she'd never even noticed it! A massive turban decorated with gemstones and feathers covered his head.

The only evidence of his predominantly white blood was the gleam of golden hair on his forearms and chest. He sat talking in that infernal unintelligible language with his uncle and various other of the Indians, occasionally making a comment to his parents or grandmother. To his wife he said almost nothing.

Nor was Joss at all inclined to speak to him, especially when a tall sultry-looking Muskogee woman walked sensuously up to him and sat down. Alex greeted her affectionately and they chatted in her language for several moments, laughing with great familiarity. *They were lovers.*

Joss could sense it at once, remembering Alex's sanitized descriptions of the wild debauchery of his Georgia backwoods days, which had led to his English exile.

The woman was striking, with gleaming ebony hair plaited in two fat braids that were intricately coiled at the sides of her head and decorated with feathers and beads. She wore an emerald green tunic and a short skirt that revealed a shocking amount of her long, shapely legs. A pang sliced through Joss's heart. *She belongs here with him. I do not.*

Charity and Barbara had outfitted Joss in Muskogee finery, too. She wore a bright red skirt of soft cotton, trimmed with tiny shells, and a tunic of deep rich indigo tied about her waist with an elaborate belt of engraved silver. Her moccasins were beaded, and displayed—to her way of thinking—too much of her ankles and calves to be decent, but Barbara had insisted she looked lovely. Since Charity had made them especially for her, she could not refuse to wear them, or the heavy copper and silver jewelry on her arms and at her throat. Her elaborate ear bobs were so heavy she feared they would pull her ears off! In her heart of hearts Joss knew she was not as attractive to Alex as the girl he addressed in English now as Water Lily.

Joss stared down at the strange food on her plate. She'd been living on fresh fruits and nuts and the vegetables grown in Charity's garden. The feast introduced her to a plethora of peculiar things she was loathe to try such as the ash cake on her plate, a pallid-looking conglomerate of pulverized corn shaped into patties and cooked in the ashes of the hearth. A bowl of purified bear fat mixed with honey sat beside them for dipping. Eggs that she knew were not from chickens and various kinds of fish and wild meats were offered her. She ate sparingly of the fish while declining the bear meat, turtle and other exotic game, all the while grateful for the bowls of fresh plums and peaches.

What I would not give for a plain lamb chop, she thought

wistfully, but in truth Water Lily had caused what little appetite she had to depart.

"You've scarcely touched a thing," Alex chided. "Try the sturgeon if you won't eat buffalo or bear," he commanded, offering her a flaky slab of baked fish wrapped in some sort of leaf.

It did smell agreeable but Joss was not inclined to feel that way. "No, thank you. I'm quite content," she replied primly.

He scowled. "You look anything but content, dear wife."

His cold clipped tone made her want to shout and ask what had happened to her merry rogue from those halcyon London days. Instead she stiffened her spine and shifted uncomfortably on the ground as several dancers began to perform for the assembly.

The festivities dragged on interminably with rounds of speeches, and drinks to the health and good fortune of Sun Fox and Magic Eyes. After one long speech regarding Joss's fertility and the hope she would give him many fine sons, Alex had had enough. He would certainly not translate that message for her! Heartily sick of the charade, he did not wish to offend his Muskogee friends or hurt his parents and grandmother. So he did the only thing he could think of to escape.

He picked up Joss and carried her back to Grandma Charity's guesthouse, thinking to deposit her there and slip away to brood in peace. But he had forgotten the custom about wedding nights . . . perhaps because he'd hoped never to have one.

The entire assembly let out congratulatory cheers, then rose to file after him, surrounding the house. He was left with no choice but to climb the ladder with Joss, who had been struggling and protesting ineffectually ever since he'd picked her up. Out of patience, he gave her rump a good hard swat which was received with general laughter from the men.

"Hold still or I'll drop you from the ladder on that hard English head of yours," he gritted out as he climbed to the upper floor. At least they would be away from the crowd, which he devoutly hoped would disperse in short order.

Joss stilled, mortified to be the subject of such public humiliation. When he set her on her feet in front of him she stepped back, rubbing her derriere, which she was certain bore a red imprint from his hand. "My father never in my life spanked me!"

"He bloody well should have. You're acting like a petulant twit!"

"You have no right—"

"I have every right. I'm your husband," he said furiously, looking around their bridal bower, which his mother and grandmother and probably half the women in Coweta had decorated for this special night.

"So you keep reminding me—when it suits you to belittle me or demand my blind, unflinching obedience."

He crossed his arms over his chest and stared at her. "What would you have me demand, Joss . . . ?" The insinuation hung between them as his eyes traveled down her tall, slender body with insulting thoroughness. When they reached her curved calves and incredibly slim, delicate ankles, she blushed and took a step backward.

"This marriage has been a mistake, Alex," she said, tears and anger churning in her belly, thickening her voice.

"This marriage has been no marriage at all," he snapped.

" 'Tis as you proposed it be," she replied.

"And you now propose something else?" His tone was low, lethal. Long months of acute sexual frustration had built into a crescendo of lust when he'd first caught sight of her tall, slender body and wild mane of tawny hair this afternoon. She'd seemed appalled with everyone and everything around her, an English noblewoman looking down her blue-blooded nose at ignorant, superstitious savages . . . at him.

And still he desired her.

"I propose that we end the charade." Her voice sounded unnaturally calm. "We should never have begun it. You don't want me—"

"Bloody hell I don't want you!" he snarled, seizing her wrist and yanking her against his chest before she could utter a sound. Her body fit his so perfectly, her unusual height a complement to his own. Her soft curves seemed to mold themselves to his very bones, to melt into him as if they were two streams flowing into one river.

Joss could feel his heart slamming in his chest—or was it her heart keeping a matching thunderous beat? She could not tell as his mouth came down on hers fiercely, hungrily, as if he were angry and wished to devour her. This was quite unlike the way his first seduction had been with its butterfly-light kisses; no, this was raw, desperate.

Her palms pressed against his chest, feeling the flex of muscle, the crisp abrasion of hair that had been graven on her memory for all eternity. A deep compelling need filled her like a deluge of rainfall, wild and turbulent, destructive. Doing this would only bring her more pain, yet she was powerless to stop herself. She slid her hands up his chest, over his shoulders and around his neck, clinging to him as he repositioned his lips over hers, his tongue plunging deep inside her mouth, ravaging.

Joss let her own tongue twine with his, instinctively trying to gentle it, but instead he opened his mouth wider and sucked it in until she was imitating his actions, tasting of him as he had of her. Would he be shocked? Repelled? She no longer cared. He groaned and pressed her tighter against him, the rocking of his hips urging her on.

He tangled his fists in her hair, pulling out the feathers and beads Barbara had so artfully woven through the long masses. The sharp pressure on her scalp tilted her head back and his mouth at last left hers, trailing harsh wet kisses and bites down her jawline to her exposed throat.

Somehow in this rough encounter he'd lost his headgear and his long straight gold hair fell around his face. He'd not cut it since they left London. Her hands reached up, fingers digging into his scalp as she grabbed fistfuls of it, pulling his head closer against her body, lower, lower, toward the aching crests of her breasts. Her nipples were drawn so tight that they burned; *she* burned for his hands and mouth upon them.

Alex could feel her spine arch, feel the hard peaks of her breasts pressing against his bare chest. The little witch was offering herself to him, damn her! And damn him if he wasn't going to have her, devil take the consequences come morning. He reached up and tore open her tunic, ripping the buttons until the two pale mounds were exposed, glowing in the moonlight.

The deep coral tips seemed to beckon him, tilting upward toward his mouth. Cupping one in his hand, he raised it as his lips skimmed along her collarbone, then down the milky swell of her flesh to suckle. Her low keening cry, her hands pulling his hair, her hips pressing to his, all spoke of her wanting . . . and sharpened his wanting. He feasted on one nipple, then the other until they glistened darkly in the moonlight.

When he raised his head Joss could feel the cool night air on her breasts and cried out again. She clung to him, her knees too weak to hold her up if he should let her go. For an instant she feared he would when he reached down, but instead he unhooked her belt and ripped the remnants of her tunic from her body, tossing it aside. She shivered, but not from cold, as her upper body was bared for his inspection.

When she started to wrap her arms over her breasts he said in a hoarse, guttural voice she scarcely recognized, "God, you are perfection."

He swept her arms away and took the aching globes in his hands. *How perfectly they fit,* he thought as she came

Shirl Henke

again into his embrace. Her hands slid inside the open front
of his shirt, pushing it from his body, pressing her nails
into the tense muscles of his shoulders. She clung to him
desperately as he encircled her waist with one arm and
pressed her to him once more.

Joss could feel the pressure of his erection through his
buckskin loincloth and the layers of her skirts. His pelvis
rocked hers in that ancient and now familiar rhythm as he
took her mouth once more in another voracious kiss while
one hand continued to knead her breast. There was no
breath left in her. Her knees buckled with the surge of desire that washed over her. The heat of him scalded her, his
hands, his mouth, the hard furry wall of his bare chest, but
most of all it came from that part of him yet clothed, straining against her belly. A low piercing ache moved from her
breasts downward, into her belly, pooling in her groin.

Alex felt her hips buck against his hips, exerting even
more pressure on his sex. If he did not sheath it inside her
he would explode! Thinking of nothing but the woman in
his arms, he sank to the fragrant pine planks of the floor.
She came willingly with him. They knelt a dozen feet from
the bridal pallet, which had been decked with flowers and
sweet herbs. Later, there would time for the bed.

"Now," he groaned as he pressed her back onto the floor
and slid his hand beneath the voluminous cotton skirt, moving up her leg until he encountered her very English undergarments, frilly lace and silk. This should have stopped
him, this reminder of who she was, what their agreement
had been . . . but it did not.

She felt his hand glide over the curves of her bare calf,
ruching up her skirt until it bunched around her hips in a
crimson billow. When his hand hesitated an instant at contact with her silk drawers, she feared he would reject her.
Then with a muffled oath he reached high to the tape at
her waist and tore them off her in several vicious yanks,

304

leaving her exposed, feeling her own dampness in the night air.

He reached over her mound of soft, pale brown curls, cupping it with one large, warm palm. Her hips rose against the pressure of his hand, bucking again. His smile was more a fearful grimace of inevitability. This had been bound to happen from the moment he'd married her. The thought crashed over him in sudden revelation. She was his wife. He desired her and she desired him as well—at least for the moment. Alex was unable to think further, for when his fingers probed her petals they came away wet with the sweet musky essence of feminine desire.

His intimate touch was even sharper, sweeter, more intense than she remembered. Joss gasped and cried out his name, writhing in feverish need as the mind-numbing pleasure rushed over her so hard that it hurt. Her young body had been starved for his touch since that first night of initiation into the way of men and women. She wanted him. She needed him. She ached for the union of their flesh with feverish urgency.

Alex tugged at his breechclout with fingers made clumsy by desperation, tearing the soft leather away to free his straining shaft. He covered her body, positioning himself between her legs, guiding himself home with little thought for her virginity. Some small remnant of consciousness broke through the haze of his lust when she flinched as the head of his sex pressed at the edge of her portal.

She is a virgin. Go slow. He bit down on his lip and stopped from plunging in a headlong hard stroke, even though every fiber of his being screamed for him to do it. Instead he took the head of his staff and circled the gates of paradise, reveling in the creamy wetness of her, the slickness that promised the sublime.

Joss remembered the pain, even expected it. She welcomed it, for had it not come the first time he had penetrated her body? Yet afterward it had quickly faded. Surely it would do so again—if he would only join himself with her. *And the twain shall become one flesh.* She arched up in supplication.

He groaned out a guttural oath and gave in, unable to resist driving himself deep within her sweet welcoming heat. The tight fit, the old yet new sensations that he had been deprived of for months smothered him, blotting out everything but the urge to thrust relentlessly inside her. There was no virgin's barrier, no cry of pain or even a stiffening indicating discomfort. Yet none of that registered as he felt her arms around his neck, holding him fast, her lower body rocking up and down with his, her legs opening wide to accommodate him, then closing tightly around his hips to draw him deeper.

This was homecoming, the most perfectly made female body he had ever possessed, made just for him like no other . . . but one. The nagging familiarity of her aroused scent, the tentative yet passionate responses of her tongue, hands, hips—all of it cried out that he had known her before. But at the moment Alex's mind was not functioning. The pleasure shut down all else, building and building. His only thought was to make it last.

Joss felt the powerful thrust of his staff deep within her, filling her, stretching her. Yet magically there was no pain this time, only a boundless, slowly increasing pleasure that was so keen it was almost pain. And with that ecstasy there was a nameless need, a hunger that far transcended any she had ever experienced before in her life. Every stroke of his body in hers, of hers closing around his, brought her one step nearer the brink . . . of what?

She concentrated single-mindedly on that need, just as he seemed to, all else blotted out as his mouth nuzzled her throat, then rose to her lips to claim them in a fierce kiss that mimed the stroking of their lower bodies. Joss dug her nails into his back, instinctively tightening her thighs around his churning hips. She could feel the dampness of perspiration on their bodies. The night air, at first cool, was now hot, redolent with the heavy perfume of desire, the heady scent of their musk, the essence of each blended together as they ascended to the summit of the abyss.

And plunged over it. His mouth muffled her cries when the first rippling waves suddenly swept over her, radiating out in ever-widening circles. She was robbed of breath by the splendor of it, this wondrous, unexpected gift of his body to hers. This was the very essence of life . . . and life giving.

As she quivered in fulfillment her sense of him seemed to intensify. His staff swelled even more, while his whole body stiffened and arched, pressing her hard against the unyielding floor. Trembling, he collapsed on top of her, his hands clenched in the spilled silk of her hair.

Alex's mind was still miles behind his body, even after the orgasm struck him with the force of a cannonball. She had drained him utterly. A sense of exhausted, mindless euphoria swept over him for several moments. He simply reveled in the satiation so long denied his body. How perfect this coupling had been. How perfectly she fit with him. How familiar that fit, that body, those responses were!

He was poleaxed after inhaling her scent once again. Rolling away from her, he heard her faint murmur of protest. She lay open and vulnerable as he sat up and looked down into her dazed face, a furious expression on his own. "You know I searched for you for four months." His voice was cold, deliberate, lethal.

Joss, still awash in the aftermath of her first orgasm, tried to focus on his words. The sense of loss when he withdrew from her left her bereft. For a moment his words did not register any more than did her dishabille. Then the cold, accusatory look in his eyes skewered her and she realized she lay bare-breasted with her skirts ruched above her bare legs, with his seed wet on her thighs.

Struggling to cover herself, she sat up, trying to frame a

Shirl Henke

reply . . . if only she could remember the question! Her hair fell around her shoulders, meager protection for her breasts, yet welcome as she swallowed and forced herself to meet his hostile gaze. He had refastened his breechclout and sat with his clothes neatly back together. She hated him for destroying this moment, for being so angry yet self-possessed at the same time.

His eyes glowed like dark coals from some hellish hearth. "Why did you do it? To make a fool of me?"

"I did not have to *make* you one, Alex Blackthorne. You already managed that quite nicely yourself," she snapped back. At least her wits were returning. And so was a deep painful emptiness in her heart. "You are a heartless philanderer who takes his pleasure selfishly, even despoiling an innocent virgin."

"I could hardly *despoil* my own wife, now, could I?" he asked sarcastically.

"You were drunk," she accused.

"And you were willing. What the hell made you climb into my bed and lie in wait for me? We had an agreement—or at least I believed we did."

"I did *not* lie in wait for you," she denied vehemently. "You were to be away for the weekend and there'd been a fire upstairs, remember? I scarcely planned it." She was not certain if she meant the fire or the seduction.

Neither was he. "You'd been tippling sherry—fair reeked of it." Alex no longer knew what was fueling his anger—her deception, his reaction to his mysterious virgin, or, most alarmingly, the fact that his ardor for his wife had been growing even before that night. He desired a woman who looked down on his Indian blood, a woman who would never make a loving wife for a man like him. Hell, he'd never even wanted a wife in the first place! "Why in blazes did you do such a reckless thing?" was all he could think to ask.

Remembering her two "fortifying" glasses of sherry to

308

give her the courage to sleep in his bed—her own husband's bed—Joss stiffened her spine. How could she answer? She would never reveal her love or her cowardice to this hostile angry man accusing her of wanting to be what she now irrefutably was—his wife.

"It was a regrettable accident on both of our parts, Alex," she finally got out over the lump in her throat. "Just as tonight was. An annulment is no longer an option if you wish to rid yourself of me." *Do you wish me gone, Alex?* She waited, holding her breath, as he studied her with brooding dark eyes.

"Damned if I know what I wish to do, Joss," he replied as he rose to his feet. Looking down at her, he said, "You may have the bridal bed. It's expected. I'll sleep downstairs. No one will know in the morning." With that he turned and climbed down the ladder, leaving her alone in the moonlight.

Chapter Twenty

Joss spent the night lying on the soft fragrant bed strewn with flowers and sweet herbs, the bridal bed she and Alex should have shared. Sleep would not come. She squeezed her eyes closed to keep from crying and muffled the sounds of her sobs in the mattress when she could not. How had they reached such a terrible impasse? She had always believed marrying him and spending her life with a man who was unaware of her as a woman would be the worst fate that could befall her.

But she was wrong. Alex was certainly aware of her as a woman. The wildly passionate, almost furious mating on the floor had made it abundantly clear that he desired her as fiercely as she did him—and that he resented it bitterly. He did not want to want her. After all, had he not persuaded her to wed him just so he would never be encumbered with a real wife?

She had not intended to deceive him that night she slept in his bed. It had been completely innocent, an accident that was every bit as much his fault as her own. If he were not such a randy womanizer he would never have seduced a female unexpectedly found in his bed—in pitch-darkness to boot! The rogue. The cad.

While Joss pitched and tossed above him, Alex paced like a caged tiger, eager to get as far away from his troubling wife as he could, yet unable to leave the house without attracting the attention of revelers who wandered about the surrounding houses. Gossip in a Muskogee town spread every bit as fast as it did in London. He would not shame Joss by seeming to reject her as his wife.

His wife. She had been so since early spring and he'd never even known it. Why had she not told him? Small wonder she'd been so upset that following morning, using the silly excuse about the fire. *An excuse you eagerly seized upon,* his conscience taunted him. He had considered that she could have been his marvelous bedmate but had pushed the thought aside as ridiculous. Had he always desired her, no matter that she had been dowdy and plain, a bluestocking puss with an acerbic wit? Perhaps that explained why he'd been so insistent that she marry him. Perhaps he was simply losing his mind, he thought, ceasing his pacing to press his palms against the door frame of the house and hang his head in perplexity.

At least one issue was resolved. She certainly had not been repelled by the physical intimacies of the marriage bed. Whoever would have believed prim, cool Jocelyn Woodbridge, missionary's daughter and reforming zealot, could be such a passionate creature? Just thinking about their explosive coming together upstairs made him hard again.

He desired her more intensely than he ever had another woman. What did Joss feel in return besides the obvious lust they shared? She certainly did not fit in among the Muskogee, nor had she seemed to do well with his white family in Savannah. Surely Joss was not like Cybill Chamberlain and so many of her ilk, excited by the thrill of the forbidden, beguiled by his mixed blood.

No. If there was one thing he knew of Jocelyn Woodbridge—Blackthorne, he amended—it was that she was not shallow. She, like him, had been caught up in a passion that they could no longer deny.. If they continued living together, he'd soon make her pregnant and they would well and truly be bound together. He would have the responsibilities of a wife and children, the very things he'd sworn to avoid.

Would that be so awful? his inner voice asked. He considered it and realized that there had been a time—most of his life, in fact—when he would never have even conceived such a thought, much less turned it over in his mind. Time. That was the key. He needed time to think, time away from Joss and she from him, so they both could deal with all the roiling emotions jumbled up inside them. And, too, he needed time to get used to the idea of her sneaking into his bed in London and then never telling him that she had done it. She had made a fool out of him and it still rankled. How Monty and Drum would laugh if ever they learned of it! They never would from him—or Joss, or by heaven he *would* throttle her!

With the dawn, Alex slipped from the house and went down to the river for a brisk swim to clear the cobwebs from his mind. Usually there was a large gathering of men at the spot, for all Muskogee bathed each day religiously. But it was barely light and the preceding evening everyone had feasted and danced until quite late. He had the water to himself—until a runner from Talisi approached him with the news that an American king's man had brought many fire guns and shot to the Upper Creek town. He was urging the people to follow Peter McQueen, the Red Stick war leader who had accompanied him.

Alex dressed quickly and went to raise his father. Devon

was awake, sitting with Barbara in their quarters, sipping hot coffee. They made an intimate tableau and for an instant Alex wondered what it might be like if he and Joss settled into such domestic bliss. The idea was swiftly dismissed as they discussed the alarming news.

"This American 'king's man' has to be Wilbur Kent," Alex said.

"Now that we know he's in Talisi, we may be able to stop him," Dev replied. "Tall Crane and Pig Sticker should be able to convince enough others to ride with us."

A hastily convened council decided to send a dozen warriors with Dev and Alex. They were ready to depart within the hour. As Alex swung up on his horse, Barbara approached him after a fond farewell kiss with her husband. "Have you told Jocelyn good-bye?" she called out.

Alex cursed beneath his breath, wheeling the big gelding around. "There is no time, Mama. Tell her I'll return when this is over."

"But she'll worry, Alex. Besides, after last night, don't you wish to give her your love before riding away?" she asked with a knowing look in her eyes.

Damn, she was positively gloating . . . as if . . . as if she'd known the true situation all along. Had Joss confessed *everything*? Surely not. "You may do so for me, Mama," he said stiffly, kicking his horse into a trot and heading for the road as if the hounds of hell pursued him.

Barbara sighed in aggravation. What had gone wrong now?

Although she knew that evasive replies frustrated her mother-in-law, Joss was loathe to explain the argument she and Alex had had the preceding night—even if she understood its cause, which she did not. Nor did she wish to describe the wild intimacies before it.

Feeling decidedly blue deviled, Joss spent the following day in her quarters, where the beautifully decked out bridal bower only served as a reminder of all that was not right between her and her absent husband. She browsed through several of the books Charity had left her, but could concentrate on nothing. Later in the day she decided to go for a walk.

Summoning Poc, without whom she never left the village, she strolled down by the river, admiring the deep lushness of the woods filled with magnificent stands of hickory, oak and walnut trees, as well as a wide variety of colorful wildflowers that she had never seen before. Nature had lavished a great bounty on this raw new land. Wild blackberries glistened, fat in the afternoon sun, and peach trees groaned under the burden of their sweet juicy harvest.

"Now that I'm growing accustomed to it, I must confess I'm learning to appreciate the beauty here," she murmured to Poc as he dashed across the grass after a butterfly, then came trotting back to her side.

"That is a good beginning," a soft voice said, seeming to float out on the warm afternoon breeze. Then Tall Crane materialized from behind a thick stand of arrowwood bushes. He smiled courteously, his bow as courtly as any London gentleman's, if not for the fact he was dressed in buckskins and blankets with roached hair and a tatooed body.

Joss was still embarrassed over her foolish gaffe with him. Yet a part of her continued to feel it had not been unreasonable to admonish a man who gave every appearance of being wretchedly indisposed from overindulgence. Black Drink indeed! The stuff was a vile, hideous emetic concoction, not a religious rite at all, in her opinion.

Nevertheless she returned the old man's smile and greeted him politely as he fell in step beside her. His name fit him well for he was tall and thin, long of limb with a stringy toughness. His face had a great beak of a nose and was lined and creased far more than that of his sister. Poc seemed to like him well enough, thumping his tail in welcome.

"You are becoming accustomed to the place. You will become accustomed to the people as well. In time our ways will not seem so strange or foolish to you."

Her cheeks blazed. It was as if he could read her mind, a disconcerting thought indeed. "Oh, I did not intend to offend you—I'm afraid that my upbringing at times shows the worst of me. My father was a Methodist minister."

"That would explain much," Tall Crane replied gravely with just a faint hint of humor in his voice. "Tell me about your family, Jocelyn."

"There isn't much to tell really. My mother died when I was young and Papa raised me. His mission was to the poor in London's slums." She looked at him questioningly.

He nodded in understanding. "I have read about your great city," he replied.

An enigma, just as his sister was. Educated people who chose to live as aboriginals. But then perhaps their father's white blood was not sufficient for them to gain acceptance into colonial society. Joss remembered the pain in Charity's voice. *I was not welcome in Savannah.* Joss sketched her childhood and her work among the poor, glossing over how she and Alex had met and wed. Tall Crane was an attentive listener, seeming to digest each word thoughtfully.

They walked a bit farther in silence when he said, "You love my nephew and your heart is good."

"Even if I am an English outsider who's afraid of horses, alligators and just about everything else in this new land?"

"Yes, even us . . . although I do not think you are so frightened as you were when you arrived."

"Did I show it so much?" she asked, feeling awful to have insulted Alex's family.

He nodded and the smile softened his austere features even more. "All this is strange to you. Our ways are different, sometimes primitive and superstitious to white eyes." When she started to protest he raised his hand and said, "Remember, I am half white, too, so I have been able to look at each side of my family with the other's eyes."

"Yet you chose to live here and marry a Muskogee woman."

"Yes, unlike my sister. Her husband Alastair Blackthorne was a good man. We each followed our hearts . . . as did Golden Eagle when he chose Dawn Woman. I did not approve of their love when first my nephew brought the Lady Barbara here."

Joss was taken aback by the confession. "But she is greatly beloved by your people now."

He smiled. "Yes. I feared her high birth and Devon's mixed blood would cause them both great pain if they wed, but they proved me wrong and I am glad of it. Here she is the Dawn Woman whose golden goodness is welcome as the sunrise itself. She won her place among us because she loved her husband so greatly that all could see it."

"How can I do that, Tall Crane? I love Alex with all my heart yet I cannot even convince him of it." The words simply tumbled out of their own volition. Joss was taken aback at how easily the old man had insinuated himself into her confidence.

"Golden Eagle was much like his son in that. He fought against loving, thinking he was overreaching, but in the end he accepted what was meant to be."

It seemed to Joss that her position with Alex was quite the reverse—she was the one overreaching for her beautiful golden rogue. "And you believe Alex and I are also . . . meant to be?" Her voice was filled with doubt, yet tinged with hope as well.

"I know it is so here," he said, raising one fist to thump it against his heart. "But you must teach your man this thing."

She waited patiently.

Seeming to change the subject he said, "Charity teaches

the Muskogee children to read, write and cipher so they may deal intelligently with the whites. You did say you were a teacher of the disadvantaged across the great ocean. Here, our people are equally in need . . ."

He let the suggestion trail off. Joss considered, remembering the curious boys to whom she'd given her spectacles and the disastrous aftermath. "Do you suppose all the elders would be happy with me teaching their children?" she asked hesitantly.

"Not all, but then, those who follow Turtle Snake do not bring their children to my sister's school."

He left it up to her. She had been bored and restless since they set sail from England, having nothing useful to do, not fitting in anywhere, feeling more and more alienated from Alex. Tall Crane was offering her an opportunity to find her own way here in Alex's country . . . if she possessed the courage to seize the chance. "Tonight at supper I shall ask Grandmother Charity if I may help her," she said.

Tall Crane nodded. "I said that your heart was good."

Peter McQueen cursed in a mixture of Muskogee and English as he squatted before the crackling campfire deep in the hilly ravines of the Tallapoosa River country. Wilbur Kent stood back in the shadows until the savage with whom McQueen had been conferring left, then sauntered forward. "I take it matters are not going well," he said tightly, swatting at a mosquito that feasted on his neck.

"It be them accursed Blackthornes! Old Devon and his whelp. Half the towns reject the Red Sticks to sit around the fires and talk peace. Old women. Faugh!" He spat into the fire in disgust.

Kent looked down at the filthy half-caste who sat tamping down a pipe filled with a noisome mixture of tobacco and foul-smelling dried weeds. McQueen's blunt stubby hands were callused and grimy with blackened broken nails. His hair was long and hung stiffly, dressed with bear grease, which repelled the mosquitoes that tormented Kent but also unfortunately repelled anyone who stood within twenty feet of McQueen.

"Blackthorne has become much more of a hindrance than I'd believed possible. Even Weatherford is considering his cautions and warnings. We must deal with him and the son," Kent said, stroking his chin thoughtfully as he neared the fire, careful to remain upwind of his companion.

McQueen pulled a wicked-looking tomahawk stained with gore from his belt. "I will kill them."

"That might be more difficult than you imagine," Kent replied, rubbing his head where he still bore a scar given him by Alex Blackthorne in a London back alley. He had deduced who his assailant was only after Cybill had come to secure his release from prison. He would settle matters with the younger Blackthorne another time. Now the critical issue was Golden Eagle.

"My warriors will lie in wait for them when they return to Coweta," McQueen said.

"No. Even if you succeeded, you would only make martyrs of them. I have a better plan."

McQueen exhaled a thick cloud of smoke and squinted his cold black eyes. He knew the American was cunning. "What?"

"His wife is English, a noblewoman. She is currently in Coweta, visiting her Muskogee family."

"Fine yellow hair to decorate my scalp pole," McQueen replied, grinning.

"Not so quickly. We will not kill her, only take her prisoner and fetch her down to Mobile. Then let the Blackthornes follow her scent into an English stronghold . . ."

An unholy light glowed in McQueen's eyes as he nodded in understanding.

"Sun Fox returns. I have heard the runners cry the message. If you hurry"—Panther Woman gestured to a path leading into the woods—"you will be able to greet him privately."

Joss was not disposed to trust Panther Woman, who was not only Turtle Snake's wife but the beauteous Water Lily's mother. "Are not his father and the other warriors with him?" she asked suspiciously.

Panther Woman shook her head, smiling beguilingly. "He has stopped by the river to swim. See, here the others arrive without him now."

Joss could see Devon and his Muskogee warriors surrounded by an excited crowd of people. Alex was not with them. Perhaps this was a golden opportunity. Visions of him alone, naked in the water, left her mouth dry with nervous excitement. She nodded to the older woman. "I thank you, Panther Woman."

Grateful she had put drops in her eyes and did not need spectacles, Joss hurried across the square and around the gathering crowd of laughing, talking people. Poc accompanied her, a safety precaution she no longer felt was really necessary.

The men's communal bathing place was just downriver of the one the women and children used. Her heart hammered in her chest as she smoothed her hair back, hoping it was not too tangled. The damp heat made it curl wildly and the children had pulled on it every opportunity they got, always exclaiming how it shined like bronze.

As she walked, Joss smiled, thinking of how wonderfully rewarding the past couple weeks had been. She was immensely grateful to Tall Crane for suggesting the idea about helping Charity with the children. She was a good teacher and they were wonderful pupils, every bit as bright, inquisitive and full of mischief as those in London. Having something useful to do had kept her worry at bay while Alex was gone. Barbara tried to put on a display of confidence, but Joss knew her mother-in-law was fearful about the men's dangerous mission.

But they were back safely—for now. Would they ride

away again? She did not understand all the complexities of Creek Confederacy politics but she knew the situation was highly volatile. If only her family remained safe. She smiled to herself, realizing that with the passing of weeks what Barbara had assured her of was indeed coming to pass. She was becoming a part of this community.

These people possessed a highly complex society based on adherence to noble principles. It was strange to outsiders and there were still aspects that she did not approve of—such as tribal leaders taking more than one wife. But there were also many Muskogee customs that she felt whites would do well to emulate, such as allowing women control of all property. She only hoped Alex would be proud of the way she was adapting.

Joss heard the rich tone of his voice and the sound of splashing water coming from beyond the elderberry thicket up ahead. Joyously she sped up her pace, the dog with her. But then she heard the sound of a female voice, breathy and laughing as it blended with his in conversation. At once, she reached down to quiet Poc. The dog obeyed, looking at her questioningly.

Alex and the woman spoke in Muskogee. Although she was beginning to acquire some of the basic vocabulary of the language, Joss could not follow their rapid exchange. She stood still for a moment, afraid to peer through the undergrowth and see them.

No wonder Panther Woman had sent her here. The hateful woman wanted her to find out that Alex had taken up where he left off with her daughter. Perhaps she even hoped Water Lily would become his second wife! Being conversant enough in Muskogee custom now to know a husband could not take a second wife without the first's approval, she vowed grimly that such would never happen.

But Alex had always been a womanizer. She'd known it when she wed him. That had been one of the very reasons he'd proposed to her, she thought miserably. He would never reform. Should she leave? Slink off to lick her wounds alone in misery? No! She would not be a coward. Perhaps she had misread the whole situation. The least she could do was give her husband the benefit of the doubt and see what was going on. After giving Poc a low command to stay, she stepped forward and peered out at the water.

Joss regretted her decision. Alex stood waist deep in the stream, as naked as the bronze goddess who faced him—with her hands on his arms. Her breasts were large and heavy with dusky chocolate nipples standing up proudly as she wrapped her arms around his neck, nearly knocking them off balance in the water. His powerful arms encircled her as they splashed, nearly falling backwards.

Joss could not bear the sight another instant. She turned and ran like the coward she'd named herself, tears streaming down her face. The dog raced protectively at her side. Roots tripped her and branches slapped at her as she fled heedlessly through the woods. Alex had always been a rake. Their marriage, even now that it had been consummated, meant nothing to him!

Alex held on to Water Lily to keep them both from going under in the swift current. The cunning little minx seemed to have more hands than a centipede had legs, and she knew how to employ them. He had taught her all too well! But that was when they were younger, running wild with no thoughts of marriage. Still he was reasonably certain that he had been her first lover. They had parted as friends and he did not wish to hurt her.

Neither did he wish to resume their old liaison. He winced, thinking of Joss lying on the floor of their bridal bower with her tawny hair spread like shiny silk and those clear blue eyes staring up at him. She was his wife. He wanted her and no other, frightening as the fact was to him. Water Lily's considerable charms did nothing to rouse the lust of years gone by. He simply felt nothing for her, except regret that he must hurt her feelings.

She had approached him boldly in the water, saying that her mother had assured her he would take her as a second wife now that he had settled down with the first one. She had already proven her fertility by bearing a son to another warrior from the Bear Clan. She would make a fine wife. Then she had launched herself at him before he could protest.

"Careful, Water Lily, lest you drown us both. We're out too far in the current for this horseplay," he said, attempting to unclasp her hands from his neck once he'd regained his balance.

"You are a strong swimmer and so am I. Not like your pale English wife. I will be of great help to her. I can do twice the work she can."

"I am certain you could—but you know that white men do not take more than one wife at a time."

She pouted prettily, trying to draw closer to him again, although he held her at arm's length now. "You are Muskogee—the Sun Fox."

"I am Devon Blackthorne's son and he has chosen to keep only one wife. I honor his custom, Water Lily," he said gently.

Her huge black eyes began to pool with tears. "But she is skinny, pale and weak. She does not know how to please you in bed—or even enjoy your splendid man root."

Remembering that he'd thought precisely those same things about Joss, Alex winced. Joss was far from skinny or weak and although she might despise his Muskogee blood, she'd given ample evidence that she liked his "splendid man root" well enough. "She pleases me, Water Lily. I can have no other," he said simply, guiding her toward the shore. "Please, you must go now. Wed that brave warrior from the Bear Clan and have many more fine sons with him."

"You choose your white blood because your Muskogee blood is thin," she said angrily, breaking away and splashing regally through the shallows to shore, thinking she had delivered the utmost insult to Sun Fox, who was only one-eighth Muskogee.

He watched her go, admiring her lush backside with a sigh of regret. Wasn't this the very sort of thing his marriage to Joss was to allow? He would be disporting with the lusty Water Lily on that mossy bank right now if not for his wife. But he knew he did not desire the angry beauty who stiffly yanked on her clothing and stalked away. He wanted Joss—only Joss, curse him for a fool!

After finishing his ablutions quickly, Alex shaved and dressed in fresh buckskins, then mounted up and rode the short distance into camp. After the way they had parted, he would have a deal of making up to do. He wondered how she had spent the time while he was absent—reading? Perhaps sewing. Keeping to herself, he was certain of that. Her unease with his people still rankled him. They would have to discuss that. Joss was not normally prejudiced or unkind.

By the time he arrived at Charity's house, it was nearly dusk. The family had gathered upstairs in his grandmother's living quarters to share their evening meal and Devon was explaining what he and Alex had accomplished while they were gone. Joss was standing beside Charity. When he climbed up the stairs, everyone crowded around him with happy greetings, but Joss hung back, a cool, unreadable expression on her face. Blast the perverse woman!

How could he just stand there, Joss thought, looking so wonderful that she longed to melt at his feet? He was all charm and smiles on the outside while inside he hid the heart of a born philanderer. His dark eyes swept hungrily over her as he made his way across the crowded floor.

"Hello, Joss. Miss me?" His voice was husky, as intimate as the soft kiss he pressed in her palm after taking her hand.

She swallowed audibly, feeling like a fool. "Hello, Alex." Her voice was frosty and prim and it must be obvious to one and all that she had not missed him at all.

Before he could frame a reply to her cool greeting, Charity said excitedly, "Joss has the most wonderful news for you, Alex." For one startled instant, he thought she was going to say Joss was with child, but then reason reasserted itself. It had only been a bit over two weeks since they lay together. Joss could not know that yet . . . but the possibility did give him pause.

Recovering himself, he took Joss's arm, saying to no one in particular, "I think my wife and I have a deal of catching up to do."

Smiling, Charity said, "I will send some dinner to your quarters later on."

Everyone beamed conspiratorially as the newlyweds left the room. All but Barbara, who sensed the reticence in Joss the instant Alex had touched her. At times she wished to take the two of them and knock their stubborn heads together.

Crickets and other night insects hummed in the thick air and large animals called out from the woods at the water's edge, their shrill cries sending shivers down Joss's back. Perhaps it was not the scream of the panther or the roar of gators that caused the shivering but the presence of the man walking beside her. He no longer touched her, but she still felt his hand as keenly as if he'd branded her skin. How could he come walking in so calmly after . . . after what he'd just done? Why, his hair was still damp from his bath.

"I know we parted in anger, Joss, but I'd hoped you would have had time to calm down."

"I am calm, Alex." Her tone was as leaden as her heart.

"You act cold, but now I know that isn't the real Jocelyn Blackthorne, don't I?"

Her breath hitched in shock. "How could you say such a thing to me after the way you practically fell upon me like a ravening wolf?" she accused.

He laughed mirthlessly, stung by the fact that he had been rough . . . needy . . . desperate. He no longer knew

Joss. Hell, he no longer knew himself. "As I recall it, I had to do damn little forcing—*either* time we made love, my dear. You want me, Joss, you just don't want to admit it."

They stood on the first floor of the house, facing each other in the darkness. A candle cast down flickering light through the planks from the second floor. Someone, probably Charity, had made the bower welcome for them.

Joss studied his face, unable to read his expression in the shadows. "Yes, I do desire you, Alex," she confessed miserably. *And you desire everything in skirts.*

"So, lusting after a savage like me makes you ashamed, does it?" Looking at her standing there, so wretchedly dejected, so *shamed* by her admission, made his heart bleed as if a panther had sunk its claws into it. *The Blackthorne men love too well.* The old family axiom rang in his ears. No, this was not love! He did not understand love, did not want to, only the other . . . old, familiar lust.

Joss was so stunned by his accusation that she could not for a moment frame a reply. All she heard was "ashamed" and "lusting after," the accusation in his voice, the bitter mockery. "Yes, I *am* ashamed of loving a man like you—a man without morals or honor," she lashed back as the tension between them thickened. With a sob she tried to get past him, to run away where the woodland darkness would hide her.

But Alex would not let her go. He seized her arm and turned her to face him, so close in the darkness he could smell the sweetness of her breath, the scent of her. "Let me show you, dear wife, what a man without morals or honor can do. . . ."

Chapter Twenty-one

Joss could feel a fire trembling in her body—or did it come from his? She could not tell as he embraced her. Yet he made no attempt to kiss her or caress her, just stared at her lowered head in the semidarkness as if willing her to look up and meet his harsh, mocking gaze. She could not.

"Afraid, Joss?" he taunted. "I never took you for a coward."

But I was. This very afternoon. "What do you want from me, Alex?" she whispered.

"What I cannot have—perhaps *should* not have," he answered enigmatically. "But I'll settle for this," he said, raising her chin with his hand, curling his fingers around her jaw to position her lips so his mouth could claim them.

She wanted to scream, to rail, kick, bite, cry out against the unfairness of it all . . . and she could not. Instead she opened to his invading tongue, fervently returning the searing kiss he offered, just as he had taught her. Oh, he had schooled her well in passion, well enough to know the tightening deep in her belly, the ache in her breasts, the wetness that betrayed her want to him. All he had to do was look at her. One touch and she was lost.

Alex felt a small kernel of satisfaction at her fierce response to his kiss, although he knew she hated herself for her body's weakness, and this fueled his anger. "I will do things to you . . . make you do them to me, Joss . . . things you never imagined," he murmured against her mouth. When she moaned in protest, he ignored the plea, continuing the kiss.

She felt his hand gliding up the curve of her waist to cup her breast, finding the hard, pebbly nipple with clever fingers, teasing it in maddening circles. She cursed her traitorous body even as she gloried in it. If there were to be nothing else but this fierce sweet passion between them, then she would accept the crumbs of his love . . . or even his lust. For tonight.

Alex broke off the kiss suddenly. He did not wish to lose all control and fall onto the dirt floor in the darkness, coupling with her like an animal. Instead, he took her hand, leading her to the ladder. She followed like a chastened child, obedient under protest. When he placed her hand on one rung of the ladder and waited, she began to climb. He followed her upward into the light.

The candle bathed the room in its soft golden glow. The air was filled with the smell of fresh herbs and the rich, spicy fragrance of beavertree. This time he led her to the big low bed, a mattress lying on the floor, filled with cornhusks and sweet grasses, covered with Charity's clean linens. White petals were strewn across it like random splotches of moonbeams.

Standing beside it he tugged his buckskin shirt over his head and tossed it aside, then kicked off his moccasins and began to unlace his leggings. "Take off your clothes, Joss," he said as he worked.

For an instant she considered disobeying the peremptory command. Only for an instant. His eyes, glowing dark and compelling, held hers as he disrobed. He was so splendid. Bronzed muscles gleamed with a fine dusting of golden hair. Slowly her hands came up to her chest and she began to unfasten her tunic, sliding it from her shoulders, letting it fall to the floor. She wore nothing beneath it but her sheer camisole. The cool night air caressed her skin and she shivered anew.

In a moment he was finished stripping off his clothes. He stood before her completely unconcerned by his nudity. Rampant proof of his lust jutted from the gold bush at his groin, dark red and pulsing with life, hard, thick and long. How could something that huge possibly fit inside her? Yet she knew it did, gloriously so. Her fingers grew clumsy as she struggled with the waistband of her skirt.

He let her tug ineffectually at her skirt for a moment, watching the rapid rise and fall of those high perfect globes barely concealed by the thin white batiste. Her tawny hair caught the light, rippling down her back, bound by a simple leather cord. He ached to bury his face in the gleaming curls and inhale the soft scent of lavender. Instead he reached out and covered her hands with his, moving them away as he deftly flicked the fastenings loose so the heavy skirt dropped to pool at her feet.

She stood clad only in her soft, thin undergarments. He tugged at the drawstring of her chemise until it slipped loose, then smoothed the open neckline down over her shoulders until it caught on her breasts just at the nipples. He rubbed it across them slowly, back and forth, watching with satisfaction as the hard tips puckered even more. "You want my mouth on them, don't you, Joss?"

She bit her lip, desperate to deny it. The slow, seductive brush of soft cotton continued back and forth, back and forth. The heaviness, the ache intensified until she could not bear it. "Yes . . . yes." Her voice caught in her throat.

Slowly he pulled the chemise down past her breasts, letting it gather around the curve of her hips. Then he reached up with both hands and cupped her breasts, raising them like an offering, teasing the rose nipples with his thumbs. "Lie down, Joss."

She obeyed and he followed her onto the pallet. She could fell the velvety richness of the beavertree petals as she sank into the mattress. He knelt at her side and unfastened the tapes of her undergarments, then peeled them and the chemise over her hips. When she was utterly naked, he sat back on his heels for a moment, skimming his hand over her body from her throat downward, over breasts, belly, hip and thigh, the curve of her calf. One moccasin still clung to her foot. He raised her slim ankle, encircling it easily in his big bronzed hand and removed the slipper, tossing it onto the strewn pile of their clothing.

She was pale as cream, lightly dusted with tiny gold freckles where the hot Georgia sun had touched her. "So pale compared to me. Look at us, Joss, milk white and copper bronze. Does it excite you?"

When she gave no answer, just moistened her lips and stared at him in mute entreaty, he stretched out beside her, then pulled her under him, covering her hips possessively with one muscular thigh, bracing himself on his elbows so he could look down into her face.

Joss felt the crisp abrasion of his body hair as he pressed her deeper into the mattress. When at last he lowered his mouth to her breast, she whimpered her pleasure. He cupped, shaped, molded the small mound as he suckled it, then switched his ministrations to the other one, doing the same. Her fingers dug into his scalp, urging him to continue.

His mouth scalded a trail to her navel, circling it languidly with his tongue, feeling the taut concave skin quiver. Then his lips moved lower, brushing the golden brown curls at her mound, and she withdrew her hands abruptly. He heard her gasp of shock and smiled, nuzzling lower until his tongue flicked at the musky wet petals of her femininity.

"No," she whispered helplessly.

"Yes," he rasped in satisfaction. "You have much yet to learn."

Her hands dropped helplessly to her sides, her fingers curling into the sheet, holding on tightly as his mouth brushed and tongue teased, opening her completely to his silken invasion. The pleasure was sudden and sharp, unlike the gradual building she had learned from his more conventional lovemaking. Her hips came up off the mattress as her back arched rigidly. She held herself open to him like some pagan priestess making a sacrifice to a dark god.

He accepted her offering, tasting the rich honey of her hungry body, teasing and lapping delicately in the soft folds, skirting around the tiny swelling bud of her pleasure until he could make her ready. He went slowly, reveling in every soft moan, each restless arch of her hips, all the panting desperation in her breathing.

Such sweet torture. She felt strung as tightly as a Muskogee bowstring drawn back the full length of an arrow, poised to be released, to fly free, heavenward, up, up, until it vanished in the blueness of the sky. Then his tongue touched her *there*, pressing, rolling. Every nerve in her body centered in this one tiny place.

She exploded. Her cry was high, keening, like an animal in great pain—or the greatest pleasure ever experienced. He felt the hard rhythmic spasms and gloried in what he had done. She was his and his alone. He could give or withhold . . . except that he knew he could never again leave her untouched.

As the rush of madness from that intense climax ebbed gradually, he raised himself up with his arms braced on each side of her hips, looking down at the rosy flush staining her belly and breasts, watching it climb to her throat and face. Silently he willed her to look at him and she did at last, her lashes fluttering open and those wide blue eyes staring up into his face.

Joss was robbed of all coherent thought. Never had she imagined such a thing as this was possible. She needed him as she needed air, sunlight, water. No matter his sins or faithlessness, she would love him always. Nothing mattered but that he return to her after he strayed, that he hold her and let her make believe that he really did love her. But she could not make herself say the words.

He broke eye contact and rolled down beside her, running his hands over her flushed breasts, caressing her arms, nibbling kisses, soft and wet, at her throat, slowly rousing her satiated body to want more. When he felt her begin to respond, that sense of heady pleasure in possession swept over him once more. He took pride in her passion, murmuring low, wicked love words to her, his prim little bluestocking, wanting her to rise again to the feverish peak of desire that still burned unquenched in him.

Joss clung to him, letting her hands, her lips, her whole body say what she could not put into words, that she loved him, needed him . . . forgave him. When her hand brushed against the rock hardness of his staff, he let out a guttural oath of need and she became emboldened to circle it, squeezing experimentally. Perhaps she did not need all that much instruction, she thought when he stiffened in her arms and went very still except for his ragged breathing.

Quickly, lest he spill his seed like a green youth, Alex covered her busy little hand with his, holding it motionless for a moment while he gathered his control once again. Then he showed her how to stroke his staff and caress the heavy sac that hung below it. She was the most gifted student he'd ever taught.

When he removed her hands, Joss expected him to enter her as she lay back, but obeyed when he commanded her to roll over and kneel on her hands and knees. Then he moved behind her. When he squeezed her buttocks in his hands, then thrust into her tight wet sheath, the sudden new pleasure of it almost sent her sprawling flat on her belly.

He caressed her breasts as they hung suspended like ripe fruits in the palms of his hands. His lips nuzzled her spine tenderly while his hips pounded a slow savage rhythm against her derriere, filling her deeply, harshly, wonderfully.

He gritted his teeth, waiting for the signs of her crest before he gave in to the hot, urgent desperation of his loins. When he reached between her legs with one hand and pressed the small bud of her desire, she spasmed and he quickly followed her over the abyss to that bliss beyond all else.

When they collapsed, he on her back, sweat soaked and panting in satiation, Joss expected it to be over. But she was wrong. He rolled them over, locking them tightly hip to hip, chest to chest, caressing her and murmuring low, urging her to touch him in ways she never had before until the hard proof of his renewed desire pressed into her belly and her own feminine parts were swollen and eager once more.

Through the night they alternately loved and slept, then awakened to begin the sybaritic rites all over again. He showed her positions that she had never dreamed anatomically possible; he coaxed forth responses she never dreamed her body capable of giving. It was wicked. It was delightful. It was utterly exhausting. Near dawn she finally fell into a deep sleep, curled securely against the protective warmth of his body.

Alex awakened as a pale golden shaft of light crept over the window. Violet and crimson faded to blue and pink as the sun rose. Gently he disengaged himself from his sleeping wife, careful not to awaken her. She was curled on her side with her hair spread across the mattress in a tangled silken skein. He had used her hard last night. Faint dark smudges circled her eyes, and her mouth was bruised and swollen from his kisses. Whisker burns abraded her milky skin. He lifted the sheet from where it lay tangled at the edge of the pallet and covered her with it, then slipped into his clothing and left their bower.

He and Devon had not been able to catch up with Wilbur Kent and the Red Sticks led by McQueen, but they had some success with the *miccos* in several of the larger towns, who agreed to refuse a British alliance. Still, as long as Kent was distributing weapons and riling the Upper Creeks, the Blackthornes had to continue their search for him. It was time for them to gather fresh horses and more supplies and strike out once more. He was grateful for the excuse to leave behind his troubling and unresolved relationship with Joss.

Within an hour, Alex was ready to leave. He and his father had agreed to split up. Eight warriors rode with him, including his uncle, Tall Crane. Another nine would go with Devon, including Pig Sticker. Alex headed to the towns farther northwest on the Coosa River, his father southwest down the Altamaha, where William Weatherford lived. Devon hoped to convince his old friend to abandon his pact with the British. With luck, one or the other of their parties would cross Kent's trail along the way.

As the men in the square discussed last-minute plans and agreed upon a rendezvous site several weeks hence, Peter McQueen observed them from his hiding place in a thicket of possumhaw near the river. A slow smile edged his thin lips. The fools. They would scour the ridges and river valleys, following the false trails Wilbur Kent laid, leaving their own town almost defenseless.

If only he had a few more warriors with him, he might be able to take Coweta by surprise and burn it to the ground, killing the inhabitants before they even realized who was attacking them. But those were not his orders. He was to steal the English wife of Devon Blackthorne and deliver her to a prearranged meeting place, then proceed to an old fort on the Tombigbee held by neutral mixed bloods and Muskogees. From there Kent would proceed via water to deliver her into the hands of the British at Fort Charlotte.

The plan would most effectively neutralize the Blackthorne men for the duration of the conflict. McQueen would rather have killed them, but he knew the chances of destroying both father and son were slight, and the retaliation of the survivor would be swift and terrible. He hunkered down in the underbrush to wait for his chance to steal the golden-haired Englishwoman.

Joss awakened to the sounds of men's voices and the snort of horses. She rolled over, sensing at once that Alex had left her again. When she sat up, her muscles protested in some exceedingly unlikely places. A hot flush stole over her as she recalled their night of incredible excess. Would he think her as wanton as his Muskogee mistress? As seductive as the Cyprians he'd kept back in London?

Once the very idea of Jocelyn Woodbridge, wanton seductress, would have sent her into peals of laughter. Now she was no longer certain it was so absurd. If she could discern nothing else, she had seen that Alex desired her quite desperately. God knows, she seemed to have a natural affinity for passion. He had uncovered a dark and earthy side of her that she would never have dreamed she possessed. He held her prisoner with it.

Her first impulse was to wish she could be free of his magnetic hold over her body. But further consideration led her to admit to herself that she would take all the passion Alex was willing to expend on her and she would return it in full measure. Even if he could not be faithful to her, she would be faithful to him, in spite of the other women. She was his wife. She knew beyond doubt that he would return to her when he tired of the others. In time the pain in her heart would lessen, she assured herself.

Perhaps, she thought, touching her belly reverently, his seed had already taken root. A slow smile curved her lips as visions of a brood of golden-haired little boys and girls danced before her. Lonely spinster no longer, she would be a mother. Perhaps in time, she and the children might even draw him away from his wicked ways. Clinging fast to the cheery thought, she rose and dressed, eager to see what the commotion in the square was all about.

Poc waited for her at the foot of the stairs. She knelt to pat his head, then winced at her sore muscles. "Come on, you could use a bath, too," she said, making a face at his tangled, muddy fur. When they emerged from the house, one of Tall Crane's grandsons was waiting for her.

He nodded shyly until she greeted him in halting Muskogee. Then he brightened considerably and responded in English, "My brother and I go to set snares for rabbits. Could we take the Little Warrior with us?"

Little Warrior was the name the children had given Poc, who loved to accompany them on woodland jaunts. Knowing the youths would be safer with the dog to protect them, she agreed.

Sensing an adventure, Poc barked excitedly and followed the boys, tail wagging.

By the time she approached the square, it was virtually deserted. No one had replied to her call at Charity's other house. Her mother-in-law and father-in-law were early risers, as was Charity. Perhaps the women were already at the school, preparing for the day's lessons. As for the men, she would find out their plans for the day from Barbara, but first she needed to bathe away the musky residue of her night of passion.

She returned to her quarters and gathered up toweling, a change of clothing and the small pack that held her personal articles, including a new lavender soap Alex had indicated he liked on her. As she made her way along the twisting, overgrown path to her secluded bathing cove on the river, she remembered in vivid detail the scandalous and seductive things he had said to her and done to her last night.

Deeply engrossed in such intense memories, she did not notice the Muskogee warrior who materialized out of the underbrush until he blocked her way. Before she could attempt to speak, a hand grabbed her throat from behind while a hard arm slammed around her ribs, crushing the breath from her.

She kicked and flailed, trying to scream for help, but her tormentor's fingers squeezed her vocal chords painfully, cutting off her air supply. The last thing to flash into her mind before she lost consciousness was that the man in front of her had his face painted half vermilion, half black, the way Alex had described the Red Stick warriors in full war paint!

"Have you seen Jocelyn?" Barbara asked Charity an hour or so later at the schoolhouse.

Charity looked up from the primer she was using, a thoughtful expression on her face. "No, I assumed she was sleeping late after Alex left."

"I checked their quarters, then walked down to the river where the women are bathing. No one has seen her, although the pack containing her soap and combs is missing, which would indicate she intended to bathe."

"Perhaps she went somewhere to swim in private," Charity suggested.

Knowing Joss's excessive English modesty, Barbara nodded. "I'll see if she's farther up the river. It isn't like Jocelyn to be gone so long," she murmured worriedly.

Another hour of searching produced not a trace of Joss. By this time Charity had organized the town's youths under leadership of the few remaining elder warriors to begin a systematic search. Around midmorning one of the old men returned carrying a long strip of toweling that he had found on a pathway to the river. He reported there were unmistakable signs of a struggle. Sun Fox's bride had been kidnapped!

*   *   *

Joss did not know how long she had been unconscious, but the land over which her captors rode looked decidedly unfamiliar. She had awakened tied across a horse's back. As soon as the band of Red Sticks realized she was conscious, one forced her to ride sitting up, thereby allowing them to increase their pace.

She was gagged and her wrists bound tightly in front of her with rawhide thongs that chafed painfully. At least they had not killed her or attempted rape. She tried to console herself with that as her mind tumbled frantically over the deadly situation in which she found herself. Why had they taken her? Where were they headed? As they rode across the high rocky spine of a ridge, she cursed her poor sense of direction.

The one benefit of her dire predicament was that she was too terrified of the Red Sticks to remember her fear of horses. Insects assaulted her skin, sweat trickled down her face and soaked her tunic front and back. Her derriere quickly began to ache as it always did when she rode. Then her stomach began to growl and her tongue, parched by the noisome gag, swelled painfully. Each breath she drew took an effort. And she had thought the journey to Coweta with Barbara was arduous!

At least they had allowed her to keep her belongings, which were tied to her mount. The pack was filled with things she feared might appeal to savages—her scented soap, combs and spectacles, even a bottle of belladonna extract, and of course, her father's gold timepiece. She would give over everything else, but fight fiercely to keep her beloved heirloom.

To take her mind off her misery, she surveyed her captors. There were ten men, led by one whose pale eyes indicated he was of mixed blood. All were decked out in frightening Red Stick war regalia.

When they stopped at twilight, she was so exhausted she

sank to the ground in a heap. They ignored her as she managed to pull loose the thong that held her gag in place and spit out the vile-smelling rag. Then she tried to untie her rawhide bonds with her teeth. Useless. They must have known she could not succeed. No help for it, she would have to try to communicate with them. Surely they understood some English. Alex had not explained much about the complexities of Muskogee politics, but he had said that even the most militant and anti-white of the Upper Creeks traded with the Americans.

"Why have you captured me? Where are you taking me?" She waited for a response but received none as the men unpacked some stringy dried meat from a pack and began to chew, talking with their mouths full. They totally ignored her.

Taking a deep breath, she stood up, testing her legs. Her throat hurt when she swallowed and her head was a bit woozy, but she could walk. There was no hope of outrunning them—even if she had any idea in which direction Coweta lay. Her best hope lay in rescue. Perhaps she could make a trail for Alex to follow. Never for an instant did she doubt that he would come after her.

When she walked up to them, the group of Red Sticks ceased talking and stared impassively at her. Their faces were grotesquely distorted by the red and black paint, their eyes watchful and cold. "I'm thirsty. Do you have water?" She pantomimed drinking and the mixed-blood leader raised a battered canteen, sloshing it from side to side. He did not offer it to her.

She reached for it and he held it back, saying something sharply in his own language. Then he took a long pull from it and handed it to one of his companions, who did likewise. She gasped out the Muskogee words for "water" and "drink." One of the savages grunted and allowed her a few swallows. If she had not been so desperate with thirst, she would have thrown it at one of them. Instead she drank the brackish, tinny liquid greedily.

No sooner had she finished the last few drops of the water, than the Red Sticks mounted up again. One of the full bloods scooped her up and shoved her onto her horse. Joss gritted her teeth to keep from crying out at the bone-jarring pain in every part of her body as they rode off in the gathering darkness.

Her hands groped for her pack, which they had tied in front of her legs onto the makeshift saddle. No one seemed to notice as she reached inside. Numb fingers fumbled through the familiar toilet articles until she found the soap. Breaking off a chunk of it, she dropped it onto the road, praying there would be no rain to wash it away before it could be found.

Near dawn they reined in and stopped. Joss came out of her stuporous sleep of exhaustion and looked up. The mixed-blood leader was speaking in serviceable English to a white man dressed in buckskins.

"I have brought her as you said," he stated to the white man.

She looked at the tall, buckskin-clad stranger. He was thin, but had a look of wiry strength that belied his gawky build. He wore his pale tan hair cut a la Brutus, giving her hope that he was an Englishman. When he spoke, his flat nasal drawl quickly disabused her of the notion. "The hair looks too dark. Let me see her face," he said.

Her captor responded, seizing a fistful of her unbound mane and yanking it cruelly down until her neck nearly snapped. Once the American saw her features, he cursed violently.

"You damnable idiot, McQueen! That's not Lady Barbara. I've never seen this chit before in my life!"

"She is yellow haired, a white woman in the Muskogee village. She speaks with an English accent. Who else could she be, Kent?" McQueen asked.

What does this man want with Barbara? What will he do with me? she wondered with rising panic.

"Who else, indeed," the thin American drawled, studying her face and figure, all too well revealed by the torn tunic and ruched up skirts. He eyed her bare legs speculatively and Joss shivered. His pale, cold eyes were more menacing than those of the savages. She said nothing as he rode up beside her. "What is your name, madam?"

Her mind raced. Would it do her any good to pretend to be Barbara's maid, someone of no value? No, they'd probably kill her in a trice. "I am Jocelyn Blackthorne, Alex's wife."

"Ah," Kent said as a slow, nasty smile spread across his face. "I'd heard the young whelp had taken a bride back in London. Fancy that he's brought you to visit his backwoods relatives. Perhaps you will serve as well as your mother-in-law."

"Serve what end?" she asked, struggling to keep her voice level.

Kent's smile vanished. "You will learn the answer to that when we reach Mobile on the gulf."

"Alex, thank heaven you've returned! We didn't know how long it would take the message to reach you," Barbara cried as her son leaped from his winded, lathered mount.

"Tell me what happened," he demanded grimly. As she related the mysterious events surrounding Joss's abduction, a fist of iron seemed to squeeze his heart. Joss was gone, kidnapped by renegades, perhaps hurt or—no, he would not allow himself to even consider that she was dead. He had ridden away and left her, too proud to confess his confused emotions, to reveal his vulnerability to her. Now he knew he loved her beyond reason. And he had never even realized it until he received his mother's frantic note. He had never told her he loved her. But he would tell her every day for the rest of their lives—once he found her.

Barbara studied Alex's haggard face, glistening with a week's growth of whiskers. His eyes were dark circled and his mouth a bloodless slash. If there had ever been the slightest doubt that her son was in love with his wife, it was gone now. Pray God it was not too late for them. If Joss were killed, she feared Alex might never recover.

"Your father hasn't received my message yet, but I expect his return any time. Will you wait for him?" she asked when she had finished her narration.

"No. I'm leaving as soon as I switch horses. Tall Crane and the other warriors should be along a few hours' ride behind me. Tell him and the rest that I couldn't wait for them," he replied as Poc came running toward him, barking frantically.

"The poor animal's been beside himself ever since Reed Grass and Corn Stalk brought him back the night after Joss's abduction," Barbara said. The terrier had searched the village for his mistress, crying piteously, even refusing food.

Alex knelt and stroked the dog's coarse fur. "I wonder if he could track her for me." He stood up and said, "Show me the place where she was abducted."

Within the hour Alex and four other warriors from the village set out with the dog. The men were armed to the teeth and each led a pair of spare mounts, well provisioned. Alex would not return until he found his wife.

The first day the tracking was easy. In their haste to put distance between themselves and Coweta, the kidnappers had not bothered to hide their trail. Pray God the weather held until he could overtake them. At dusk he and his men came upon the place where the Red Sticks had rested and eaten. The signs were unmistakable. Taking heart, he ordered his men to make camp and sleep until moonrise.

When they set out again he had to rely on Poc's sense of smell. The rocky ground of the ridges obscured any trails, but the tenacious little terrier forged ahead with growing excitement. That was when Poc found the chunk of lavender soap.

Dismounting, Alex picked it up and inhaled the familiar fragrance. Tears choked in his throat as he clutched the talisman. "Ah, Joss, always resourceful." They *were* on the right trail. Whether the little dog was detecting the scent of his mistress or that of the mounts of her captors, Alex could not be certain, but with renewed hope he continued following where Poc led.

The men who held his wife were pushing hard to the south, scarcely taking time to eat or sleep. Remembering how Joss felt about horses, he knew she must be terrified as well as exhausted. Those sons of bitches would pay dearly when he caught up to them.

After that the trackers began to find a slow but steady series of markers dropped along the way, more chunks of soap interspersed with teeth from her comb and small strips torn from her clothing.

"We are catching up with them. They cannot be more than a day ahead of us now," Blue Fish said to hearten Alex when a moonless night forced them to stop.

"She's probably so hurt and tired they couldn't drag her any further," Alex said, his voice breaking as images of Joss's slim, pale beauty flooded his mind.

"They have not harmed her," Blue Fish replied. "They wish to keep her safe. To bargain with, I think."

"I thought the same," Alex said hollowly, praying it was true. He would give them anything, do anything, to secure her safe return.

Be strong, Joss. I will find you, my love.

Chapter Twenty-two

Several times they almost lost the trail and were forced to backtrack. Poc would lose the scent when Joss's captors rode their horses up or down the stream to obscure their trail. Then the rescue party would be forced to search up and down the banks until they found the spot where she had exited. Since the swampy lands of the southern Alabama River country were honeycombed with streams, they began to lose time.

Alex grew increasingly desperate. On the fourth day Tall Crane, Pig Sticker and Devon, with a larger party of Coweta warriors, caught up with them.

That night while everyone else lay exhausted in their blankets, Devon and his son huddled before the campfire. Alex stared into the flames as if hypnotized. His face was drawn and covered with heavy beard, his eyes hollow and red-rimmed from smoke and lack of sleep.

"Tall Crane says there's a fort another ten miles or so to the south on the 'Bama. Although neutrals hold it, the kidnappers may have taken her there."

"Once they reach the main channel of the 'Bama, they can take to the water and we'll never catch them," Alex said with rising despair. He held his head in his hands and shuddered.

Knowing what he would have felt if it had been Barbara who was captive, Devon understood his son's bottomless anguish. "If they can take to water, so can we," he said with determination.

"She's terrified of horses. She can't even swim. I should never have brought her to this wild, dangerous country."

"Don't underestimate your wife, son. Your mother taught her to swim and she learned to ride just getting here from Savannah. You were afraid she wouldn't fit in, weren't you?"

Alex's head jerked up. "How did you know?"

Devon smiled sadly. "I was certain your mother couldn't survive out here either. An English noblewoman living in a Muskogee town?" he scoffed to himself. "I tried to send her back repeatedly. But she loved me so much that she wouldn't go. I think Joss is the same way."

As memories of Joss's appalled reaction to Muskogee life flashed through his mind, Alex replied, "Joss isn't like Mama." She certainly could not love him that much . . . could she?

"Oh, I think you're wrong. She's wonderful with the children according to your grandmother."

"The children?" Alex asked, puzzled.

"I assume you didn't have time to discuss much the night you came home," Devon said dryly.

Alex flushed, remembering their argument and the way it had ended . . . in passion.

"She came to your grandmother and asked if she could help with the school. After all, she was a teacher in London."

"She taught in Grandma Charity's school?" Alex asked as his throat tightened.

"Your mother says the children love her. She has a natural way with the little ones."

"She always did," Alex replied quietly. All the while he had brooded about her rejection of his mixed blood, his fears that she scorned the Muskogee . . . she was teaching in the school. *Joss, Joss, I never gave you a chance.*

With the first rays of light, Alex left with Poc, who seemed especially eager to reach the Alabama River, which lay ahead of them. The rest of the men followed behind them to check signs carefully to be certain they were on the right trail.

Alex rode like a man possessed and the dog, now considerably more wise to the dangers rife in swamplands, led the way. The little terrier was tough and tireless. Finally they broke through the dense foliage of scrub pines and hickory and reached the open marshlands of the delta. Alex's gaze swept across the vast flat plains of sedge. In the distance a thick curl of smoke rose ominously against the clear blue of the western horizon. Alex kicked his mount into a gallop as Poc took off racing.

When he reached the charred ruins of the fort, Poc circled the blackened timbers of the stockade, then crawled inside an opening created by the fire. The ashes were still quite warm but neither dog nor man noticed the heat. Poc whimpered piteously as he circled the compound where a number of small cabins had once stood. Now all of them were reduced to blackened piles of logs and stone.

After investigating three of the gutted buildings, the dog nosed inside the door of the last one, which was at the very back of the stockade that faced the river. Guts knotted, Alex shoved the scorched wooden door further open and followed. The interior was completely destroyed except for what looked like the remains of a table and a heavy old sea chest in one corner.

"What is it, Poc? Was she here?" He could not see in the smoky confines. His eyes stung and his lungs burned.

His heart hammered in his chest and a great roaring filled his ears. He'd seen the charred corpses of half a dozen defenders outside, almost unrecognizable but for the heavy metal jewelry and weapons that marked some of them as Muskogee males. Others were clad in the badly burned remains of buckskin shirts and trousers. Mixed bloods. He had seen no women, thank God.

Until now. In the corner of the room two figures lay huddled together, their bodies all but unrecognizable as female. One looked like a ten- to twelve-year-old girl, judging from her size. The other was a grown woman . . . a white woman? The absence of Indian jewelry suggested as much, although the clothing and hair were too badly burned to be certain. She held the child in her arms protectively.

Alex knelt beside Poc, who paced frantically back and forth around the corner where the bodies lay, sniffing the ground. Surely this was not Joss, his wife. Then the glint of something shiny flashed in the dim light streaming in through the door. Poc was already sniffing at it. The dog sat back on his haunches and let out a long, low, bone-chilling howl.

Alex's blood froze. He could scarcely move as the roaring in his ears reached a crescendo of unbearable intensity. He half walked, half crawled to the shiny object. It was gold, melted slightly yet still easily distinguishable. A man's timepiece. The Reverend Elijah Woodbridge's timepiece.

Joss was never without it. Barbara had told him she carried her personal belongings in a leather pouch and that it was missing along with her. From it she had left the trail of soap and combs. She would never have left her father's timepiece behind. Nor would her captors, had they been alive, have tossed away something of such value, he was certain.

He knelt beside the charred bones and laid his hands over them as if to protect them. And he cried. The dog licked

his face and hands, whimpering in despair, trying in vain
to offer comfort.

That was how Devon and the others found them.

In the vain hope that Joss had somehow been taken away
by river, the men spent the next week scouring the low
marshy banks of the Alabama for miles in either direction.
Alex took Poc and walked the course of the river, up and
down, on both sides, but Poc could find not the slightest
trace of Joss.

The fort had indeed been held by mixed bloods who had
tried to remain neutral in the brewing war between the various factions of the Creek Confederacy. Apparently they
had been surprised by a large Red Stick war party, burned
out without any chance to escape, barely able to fight back
before they were massacred. An entire cache of burned canoes was found neatly banked beside the river door of the
stockade, their frames standing like skeletons. Not one
space on the tiny quay was unfilled.

Devon and Tall Crane reached the tragic conclusion that
the woman in the ashes, whom they had buried beside the
young girl, must have been Joss. But Alex refused to believe it, even when his wider and wider ranging searches
yielded nothing. Pig Sticker led the other warriors from
Coweta back to their town while Alex's father and uncle
waited for his grief to spend itself enough so they could
convince him to give up the useless quest.

Finally a messenger located them, sent from Benjamin
Hawkins, another government trader to the Confederacy,
asking that Devon and Tall Crane come at once to his
agency on the Flint River. The Shawnee prophet Sickaboo
had convinced several of the influential Lower Creek *miccos* to join Tecumseh's rebellion and become king's men.
Golden Eagle and Tall Crane were the only men with
enough influence to dissuade the chiefs.

Tall Crane set out at once to respond to Hawkins's summons. Devon went in search of his son. He found Alex that evening seated on a hollow log at a bend in the river, staring out at the swiftly flowing current, watching the sun set across the water. The bloodred ball cast a ruddy glow over his somber, gaunt features. Poc welcomed Devon with nervous whining, seeming to say, "Do something to help him."

"It's late, son. Time to build a fire and make camp for the night," Devon said when Alex continued staring at the river.

"She's gone, Papa. Gone forever. I never told her I loved her. Not once. What a cold-blooded bastard I was. I never deserved a warm, intelligent, good-hearted woman like her."

The raw, anguished words tore at Devon's heart. "I love this land of my birth but it's harsh and cruel at times. I wish there were something I could do to make it easier for you, Alex, but I know there isn't." He placed one hand on his son's shoulders and squeezed the tense muscles, then set to making a fire.

Watching his father perform the familiar task, Alex said at length, "I offered her an arrangement, did you know that?"

Dev nodded. "Your mother explained how things stood between you two . . . at least as much as she understood of it," he said, hoping to encourage his son to speak of his grief.

"We were friends. I convinced myself that a marriage in name only would be of mutual advantage."

"From what I saw, it was a great deal more than that," Dev replied. He had never understood what had set Alex against the institution of marriage, but he would not question, only listen.

Alex shook his head. "It could have been so much more, more than I ever deserved . . . but I . . . Ah, hell, I ruined it," he said, his voice thick with tears that he refused to shed. "I couldn't make up my mind to be a husband, to ask her to . . . to love me—to admit that I loved her."

"Women have a way of sensing those things, son. Joss knew that you loved her."

"If only I could believe that, Papa." He sat staring into the flames of the fire as Devon prepared a simple meal of coffee, bread and cheese.

Offering him a plate, Dev said, "Hawkins has asked for help at the Flint Agency. Sickaboo's stirring up some trouble. I don't know if Kent's behind it or not. Tall Crane went to speak with the *miccos*. I still have to locate Weatherford." He left the rest unspoken, leaving it up to Alex to decide what he would do.

"Right now I don't care about any of it. I'm sorry, Papa. All I want to do is put this hellish war as far behind me as possible."

"What will you do?" Devon asked.

Alex shrugged. "I can't return to London with the war going on. Anyway, it would hold too many memories of Joss. For now I think I'll head back to Savannah."

Devon nodded. "Your Aunt Madelyne's all alone at the Hall while Quint's in Washington conferring about British attacks on coastal shipping. You might spend some time with her," he suggested.

"With four married children living on adjacent plantations, I doubt she's alone much," Alex replied. "I think I'll go to the city house for now. After that . . ." His voice faded as he envisioned the bleak, endless years ahead without Joss. How would he bear it?

Ah, Joss, if only we had it to do over again, I'd not be such a fool.

Neither man paid any attention to Poc, who sat quietly, staring down the river.

Joss sat in the bottom of the canoe clutching her spectacles in one hand while she concentrated with all her strength on not being sick again. Each morning for the past two weeks—about midway through the hellish trek to the fort—she had been unable to hold down anything solid save dry biscuits. She was uncertain whether it was caused by the stress of her captivity or a reaction to the vile diet Kent gave her.

In truth, she was too weary to think straight after the hairsbreadth escape from the burning stockade. Shuddering, she could still smell the acrid scent of smoke and hear the hideous shrieks of war cries blended with the screams of the dying. After she and Kent had parted company with McQueen and his warriors, the American had taken her into the fort. He'd locked her in a cramped, filthy room with two other female captives, then began drinking through the night.

The attack had come just after sunrise. Kent had raced into the room where she lay. In the confusion she had struggled to reach the pack with her father's timepiece, but Kent cursed her and dragged her away. All she had been able to save was the pair of spectacles that were in her pocket. She could still see the woman and her daughter, cowering in their bed as Kent seized hold of her, yelling that their passage south had arrived in the nick of time.

Two white men, dressed in buckskins, had paddled up to the rickety little dock as gunshots flashed and flames leaped higher around the stockade. By the time they boarded the canoe and reached midstream, the fort had been taken. Unaware that the very man who had given them their muskets was in the canoe, the Red Sticks fired at the little craft, killing one of the paddlers. Bullets flew into the river all about them, splashing water into the canoe as Kent and the other man paddled furiously to get out of range.

The days blurred together on the water just as they had on her overland ordeal. All she knew was that Kent was a traitor to his country, in the pay of the British. He and his companion were renegades of some sort. Joss still had no idea what Kent or those who employed him planned to do with her. She was only relieved that he had made no sexual overtures.

Kent and his companion feared her illness was some sort of plague she had contracted from living among the Indians. "If not for my plan, which requires a Blackthorne woman, I'd kill you now and have done," he had snarled at one point when she sat retching near the fire while the other man broke camp.

The surge of nausea passed and Joss looked out across the river plain, ignoring him. The landscape had been subtly changing for the past day. The dense, wild overgrowth of woodlands was giving way to open flat delta lands crossed by a lacework of narrow, twisting channels that Kent referred to as bayous.

Alligators swam silently, looking like sunken logs until a canoe was almost too close to avoid snapping teeth and deadly tails. Tall white cranes stood on stalk-thin legs in the shallows, sunning themselves, while brightly colored small birds sang in the lacy canopy of trees scattered here and there in the exotic landscape.

The body of water they were on had grown sluggish and wide, muddy brown as it emptied into a vast bay. Joss knew Kent was taking her to Mobile, which was on the gulf in Spanish Territory. Then she saw the fort in the distance, a hulking stone monolith of Moorish style architecture. It sat perched on a high embankment at the edge of the bay. Beyond it a small but obviously European-looking settlement stretched inland. The narrow streets and overhung galleries spoke of its Franco-Spanish origins. It looked alien and slightly menacing to Joss.

"Welcome to Mobile, Mistress Blackthorne," Kent said mockingly.

As they neared the fortification, Joss saw the sentries' bright scarlet uniforms. Englishmen! She felt a swift surge of exhilaration as the gates swung open. They climbed to the top of the high fortress wall, then entered a long narrow corridor and walked to a set of double doors guarded by two sentries standing at rigid attention. At Kent's signal, they were admitted to a large conference room.

Several men clustered about a massive, ornately carved oak table, pouring over the maps and papers spread all over its surface. One wore scarlet and the others white. Her heart hammered in her chest as she mentally prepared her speech while Kent was announced.

"I've brought a captive I believe may be useful to you," he said without preamble, raising the end of the rawhide cord binding her so that her raw wrists were jerked roughly.

Joss started to speak but the words froze on her tongue when the English officer turned to face her. Cold yellow eyes swept from her head to her feet and back with mocking contempt. She would never in her life forget that haughty, aristocratic face with its cruelly perfect features marred only by the saber slash across his eyebrow.

Colonel Sir Rupert Chamberlain studied the tall, slim woman standing before him. He smiled chillingly as he walked closer, circling her as if inspecting a blooded horse. He remembered the ghastly eyeglasses but there was a far different aura about her now. She had quickly gathered her wits and stood coolly self-possessed under his gaze in spite of her ragged, filthy clothing and sunburned skin. Odd, he thought, he'd never before noticed that her body was so well molded or that she had such a splendid mane of hair, now bleached tawny gold by the hellish tropical sun.

"Alex Blackthorne's wife," he murmured, almost to himself.

"Sir Rupert," she replied as formally as if they were in a London drawing room. "I'm surprised you remember me." A chill of foreboding washed over her as he dismissed the Spanish officers, leaving them alone with only Kent.

"Oh, I remember that mongrel's peculiar bluestocking bride. You were the talk of the ton, m'dear. Everyone wondered whyever a young rogue such as he saddled himself with a homely Methody miss. Must've been true love, hmm?" When she did not reply, Chamberlain turned to Kent. "I must confess when I received your communication I was intrigued, but it was the Caruthers bitch, not this one, you'd set out to capture."

"McQueen took the wrong Englishwoman, but I decided it really did not matter as long as she's a Blackthorne. As soon as that pair of vipers learns that we have her we can lure them into a trap," Kent said with a cunning smirk.

"No!" Joss cried before she could stop herself. Kent brought her up sharply with a hard yank on her bound hands.

Chamberlain tsked mockingly at him, then said, "Do act civilized, Willie, even if you are a colonial. Untie the lady's hands."

Kent's eyes narrowed with barely leashed anger, but after a moment's hesitation he slipped a blade from his belt and slashed the rawhide cords, freeing her. "How soon can a message be dispatched to the Blackthornes?"

Joss stood flexing her fingers, trying to restore circulation in her hands as Kent waited impatiently for the colonel's reply.

Chamberlain sauntered lazily back to the table and glanced at the maps and the latest communiqués from his superiors in the Bahamas. "It would do little good to worry about trouble from the Blackthornes now. I do not believe I shall send any word that we have her," he drawled. "Perhaps if you had brought the mother-in-law, I would have considered your plan, but now I find another comes to mind."

"Are you mad? This is our perfect opportunity to stop the Blackthornes from holding the Creeks in the American camp," Kent said with incredulous anger. "I risked my life to get her to you and now—"

"And now," Chamberlain turned to Kent and said in his clipped voice of command, "you are dismissed, Mr.

Kent. . . . Oh, yes," he said silkily, "I do believe there is a small matter of payment, your thirty pieces of silver as it were."

Kent accepted the curt dismissal with glowering bad grace, quitting the room in stiff, furious strides.

When they were left alone, Joss asked, "What do you plan to do with me?"

"What indeed," he said, his cold yellow eyes suddenly turning almost orange with fury as he raised his right arm, which he had until now concealed at his side. Joss could not prevent the gasp of revulsion that escaped her lips as he stretched forth the hideously deformed hand. He pulled off the glove from the withered limb, which was grotesquely blackened from damaged circulation and resembled a claw more than a human appendage.

"Well you should cringe, madam. This is what your husband did to me, consigning me to this wretched backwater filled with rabble and redskins. Unimpaired I'd have been on the front lines with Wellington, defeating the Corsican. But I'm nothing if not determined. I practiced with my left hand until I could use it with the same skill as I had my right. A year spent in utter misery, fumbling and failing, struggling and finally succeeding inch by bloody inch! Blackthorne should have killed me when he had the chance."

An icy dread swept her, leaving her faint and nauseated. She remained upright and met his eyes by sheer force of will. "I repeat, sir, what do you plan to do with me?"

"All in good time, Mistress Blackthorne, all in good time," he replied, ringing for a guard. "In the meanwhile, I shall have a maid attend your needs. Consider yourself a guest here at Fort Charlotte." He turned to the guard who had just entered and said, "Give her the room adjacent to mine . . . across from the one my wife is occupying."

At her shocked gasp, he smiled that cold, awful smile once more. As she was led away, she thought of Rupert

Chamberlain touching her with that ghastly clawlike hand and her stomach churned.

The hour was very late when the door to her room swung open, its rusty hinges creaking as Sir Rupert entered. He held the branch of candles high to better illuminate the curtained bed. When he placed his knee on the mattress, Joss awoke with a start. A low scream tore from her throat as she rolled away from him, scrambling to sit up.

"It will do no good. Scream down the whole bloody fort."

"What of your wife? Surely—"

His harsh bark of laughter interrupted her. "That voyeuristic little slut would relish watching us. She does that, you know. Don't look so shocked. Your Methody innocence is really quite appalling. However, I shall enlighten you," he purred, continuing to unfasten his trousers. "There are places in London, very expensive playgrounds for the nobility, where one can obtain gratification that way. Perhaps your Alex frequented such. I know his uncle has done so."

As he spoke the nausea, quite familiar now, began to churn once more in her stomach. She knew the meal they'd fed her earlier was coming up, along with the large tumbler of water she'd drunk before retiring. Just when he reached out and seized a fistful of her hair, yanking her back across the bed, she gave a great shuddering heave and vomited all over his arms and chest.

He released her with an obscene oath and scrambled from the bed, still cursing violently as he tried to brush the noisome mess off his jacket. Oblivious to him, Joss hung her head over the side of the bed while the wracking spasms continued, gradually subsiding into painful dry heaves. She collapsed onto the mattress, utterly spent and miserable as the colonel stormed out, slamming the door behind him.

For the next several weeks, Joss had a reprieve because the colonel was summoned to a meeting with the British high command in the Bahamas. In spite of her status as his personal prisoner, she cajoled the Spanish commandante into allowing her to walk along the terreplein with a soldier for escort. By the end of the week she was permitted to go into the town under guard and browse through the public market. Owing to her far greater proficiency at French, she gleaned much from the predominantly French-speaking inhabitants regarding the comings and goings of trading and naval vessels in the Spanish seaport that was effectively controlled by the British at present.

She formulated her plan, which necessitated waiting for the arrival of a British man-o'-war, the HMS *Runnymede*, three days hence. If only Sir Rupert did not return first, she would have her chance. Not wishing to bring retribution down on her maid Esmeralda, Joss confided nothing to the faithful servant. On market day the following Tuesday, she went to town as customary but carried hidden inside her unopened parasol a heavy iron poker from the fireplace.

After wending her way into the most densely packed area of the market between the fresh fruit vendors and fish sellers, Joss slipped behind a canvas tent that held barrels filled with lobsters. Grateful her morning indisposition had abated, she waited as the guard came searching, calling her name in alarm. When he walked past, she raised the parasol and coshed him squarely on the head, then made her way to the docks posthaste, searching frantically for a small boat to take her out to the *Runnymede*.

She was busily haggling with a fisherman for the use of his boat when a low familiar voice interrupted. "I should advise you, my man, to tend your nets and leave this troublesome Englishwoman to me."

Joss whirled around just as Chamberlain seized her arm, squeezing so hard the parasol tumbled from her numb hand and fell to the ground with a loud clunk. "Let me go. You have no right to hold me prisoner. I am a British subject. Please, Monsieur, you must get word to the captain of the

Runnymede that this man is holding me against my will."

The little fisherman paled and stepped away, almost stumbling backward into his boat to escape.

"It's fortunate indeed I happened to see that bright hair and fair English skin from afar. Wouldn't it have been a pity if you'd set out in that leaky old boat and drowned in the bay?" Chamberlain said.

"Better to drown than suffer your touch," she gritted out, trying to wrench free of his cruel grip. The pain in her arm was excruciating now but she refused to give him the satisfaction of acknowledging it.

"Ah, so your listless spirits are gone. No more blue devils? Dare I hope your indisposition is ended?" he asked, reaching up with his clawlike hand to snatch her eyeglasses from her face and pocket them. "You're quite helpless without them, I warrant, aren't you?"

"Please give them back," she asked levelly.

"Not just yet," he said with a nasty laugh. Then he studied her face and figure and said conversationally, "You look the bloom of health, m'dear."

As they neared the fort, the soldiers at the gate stood at rigid attention when he walked by dragging her with him. Joss was shuffled off under guard to her room, where Esmeralda waited for her with a frightened expression on her face. She clucked over Joss's injured arm and ordered a tub of warm water, then went in search of herbs to make a poultice for the bruised flesh.

Later that afternoon, Chamberlain entered the room without even the courtesy of knocking. Joss sat in one of the chairs near the window staring out at the open water and beyond to Pinto Island. She looked up but said nothing, squinting at his blurry figure with mutiny in her eyes.

"Still defiant, eh? Good. A sure sign you've recovered. I've been making inquiries with all the servants about the state of your health over the past weeks since you, er, joined us. It seems you alternated between bouts of indisposition and hearty appetite. You still sleep a good deal . . . and you've had no menses."

She sucked in her breath, knowing her face must have given away the utter terror she felt rushing over her. "If you harm this child, you'd best do away with me, too, or I swear, as God is my witness, I shall kill you."

"So dramatic—and such un-Christian sentiments coming from a Methody miss. But then I forget that you've given yourself to that American mongrel who's no doubt corrupted your finer English sensibilities."

She felt so helpless without her glasses, hearing his mocking drawl yet barely able to make out his figure moving across the room. *I can't let him hurt Alex's baby!* The thought hammered at her relentlessly yet she could not think of a way to stop him—until he spoke again.

"I've given considerable thought to your, er, delicate condition," he said, standing beside her chair.

When he placed his claw on her bruised arm, she fought the urge to bolt and bit down on her lip, holding her spine stiff, waiting.

"I do not intend to harm you or the child. No, not at all. I've come up with a far better way to revenge myself on that half-caste bastard. I shall raise his child myself. If it's a son I shall teach him to despise the name of Blackthorne. If it's a daughter . . ." He felt her flinch, then continued, "I shall groom her to replace you as my mistress—and make no mistake, m'dear, as soon as you are safely delivered of the red mongrel, you will be my mistress."

Chapter Twenty-three

Barbara scanned the letter worriedly, then sighed and rubbed her eyes, forcing back the tears. Dev, who had waited patiently as she read her friend Madelyne's letter, walked around the table and took her in his arms. "What word of Alex, darling?" He knew it could not be good.

"Madelyne says he's still drinking. He's scarcely left the house since he arrived nearly two months ago, just sends servants out to buy him more liquor. Dev, he's trying to kill himself." She broke down and began to sob, letting out all the pain for Joss's death and her son's inconsolable despair.

"I prayed he'd come out of it if we left him alone as he asked, but . . ." Dev struggled for words.

"We should go to him, Dev. You've talked with the *miccos* of every major town, even the great council. There is little more you can do now."

He nodded, stroking her back as she struggled with her tears. "We'll go to him, beloved. Perhaps I can prevail upon him now to take an interest in helping me stop the men responsible for his wife's death."

By the time they reached Savannah, a chill early winter rain was falling. The skies were leaden and the wind off the Atlantic bit deeply. Devon was reminded of his years as a ranger in the War of the Rebellion, freezing and starving on the British side while Quint did the same with the rebels. And where had all of it gotten them?

Now they were embroiled in yet another senseless war. No one would profit; neither the Americans nor the English, least of all the hapless Muskogee who even now faced a bitter civil war of their own. Did he even have the right to ask for Alex's help? Damned if he knew, but his son needed a reason to start living again. Perhaps this was it.

Alex was closeted in the library when they arrived. Their worried old butler confided, "Mastah Alex done shut hisself away from th' world like a wounded animal whut cain't take no mo'."

Barbara knocked and pleaded for him to unlock the door. He refused. Frightened, she headed for the pantry to search out a master key. Devon took her aside, saying, "I think he's ashamed, afraid to let you see him in a condition with which I am all too familiar—unshaven, unbathed, red-eyed and reeking like a distillery." At her look of alarm, he said, "When I sent you away after Uncle Robert's funeral I went on a two-week drunk. Let me beard the lion in his foul-smelling den. We need to talk man to man."

Tears glistened in her eyes. "He's in such awful pain, Dev. Go easy on him."

He pressed a kiss on her forehead, holding her close for a moment, then whispered, "I will. Give us some time. You retire upstairs and rest from our trip while I make him presentable," he instructed gently as the butler handed him the master key, then walked away shaking his grizzled head sadly.

Dev let himself into the dark interior of the big book-lined room, which doubled as both family reading center and his business office when he worked at home. The place smelled dank and noxious just as he feared, reeking of stale food, mostly unconsumed, and copious bottles of whiskey, mostly consumed.

Alex sat sprawled on a wingback chair beside the hearth, where the fire was long gone out. His eyes looked as lifeless as the cold ashes. He slouched with his long legs stretched out in front of him, dressed in wrinkled stained clothes he'd no doubt slept in for a week or more. Thick gold whiskers bristled on his face, which was haggard as a death mask.

"I forgot about the damned master key," he said, gesturing with an upraised whiskey glass. A half-full decanter sat by the side of the chair, surrounded by several dishes with beef, cheese and vegetables, untouched. A bowl of soup with the lid half off congealed in the chill air. On the other side of his seat lay half a dozen empty whiskey bottles. He looked at them, then rubbed his eyes, saying, "Odd, but I can't even seem to sustain a decent drunk any longer."

"Drink yourself sober. I've done it a time or two," Dev replied, easing into the opposite chair.

"Every time I close my eyes I see her face. Nothing blocks it out, Papa, nothing."

"Only time will make it ease . . . or so conventional wisdom tells us. I don't know if it's true. I can't say I understand your grief, son. I've tried to imagine how I'd feel if it was your mother who'd been killed. . . ." He shuddered. "I'd probably be doing the same thing you are—hell, I know I would."

Alex polished off the rest of the amber liquid in his glass, then set it on the rug and leaned forward in the chair, resting his elbows on his knees, cradling his head in his hands. "I never had any idea that I loved her so much, that she filled every part of my life . . . and I was too big a fool to recognize what was happening. I left her without even saying good-bye—ran like a stubborn, stupid schoolboy too proud to take a chance on telling her the truth."

"Your mother got to know her well, son. She's certain Jocelyn loved you—and that she had hope for your marriage. What happened . . . it had nothing to do with the two of you or what you could have made together. It was a terrible, senseless tragedy caused by men whose greed and ambition care nothing for the cost in human life. We can't let them get away with this, Alex. What if Polyanne or Susan were taken next? Or any of the other innocent women on the frontier? Alex, if you had been the one killed, what do you think Joss would have done?"

Alex sat very still for a moment, staring down at the litter surrounding him. It signified the wreckage of his life. He was a wastrel and a drunkard, good for no one. "Joss was a fighter," he said hoarsely. "She spent her life tilting at windmills and never felt her causes were hopeless. She was teaching the children at Coweta. I imagine she'd have gone back to them and worked even harder—no, I know she would."

"The Red Stick leaders have turned on their own people using British guns. They're laying siege to Lower Creek towns one at a time. Then they'll strike out against the whites. We might make a difference, Alex, if we went to the Lower Towns and convinced them to unite and defeat the Red Sticks first."

The question hung unspoken between them for a moment. Then Alex replied, "I'll go with you, Papa."

The winter of 1813 was soft in Mobile. As Joss's impending delivery drew near, she was alternately thrilled with holding Alex's child in her arms and sick with the realization that both she and the babe would be completely under Rupert Chamberlain's control. Even the colonel himself felt confident enough of his power over her to return her spectacles.

Her health, so long stressed by nausea and fatigue, bloomed in the latter stages of confinement. She had never felt better or stronger in her life. The small kicking being carried under her heart gave her hope. Somehow she would be reunited with her love. Failing all else, she enlisted Esmeralda in her cause. She and the young servant had grown close over the past months. Without the girl's gentle ministrations and fierce loyalty, Joss feared she would have abandoned hope.

"Here is the letter, Esmeralda," she said, handing the maid a sealed envelope. "Only pray God that this one gets through." To date she had attempted to smuggle out half a dozen letters to Alex through various means—bribing Spanish soldiers and local merchants and fishermen. But as yet it appeared none of the couriers involved had truly delivered the missives.

This time Esmeralda was taking a great risk. Her brother-in-law Jacques was bound for New Orleans to purchase a shipment of wine for his employer in Mobile. He was willing to carry her letter to the American city, from whence she hoped it would be delivered to Alex. The risk was great, both for Esmeralda to smuggle it from the fort and for her kinsman to deliver it across the gulf. As an additional enticement for the French Creole to aid them, Joss had included several key bits of intelligence regarding British military plans in the gulf that she was able to glean during her time spent with the colonel and his staff.

Tucking the slender missive inside a hidden pocket in her heavy skirts, Esmeralda smiled at Joss. *"Está bien,"* she said, hugging her mistress.

"You are good—as good and loyal a friend as ever I have known in my life," Joss replied in Spanish, which had grown quite fluent now.

After Esmeralda left, Joss walked outdoors into a small

garden courtyard where she was allowed to take fresh air when weather permitted. Upstairs on a balcony overlooking the grounds, Chamberlain watched her standing in the sunlight, her face upturned to catch the first warm rays in over a week. A breeze off the bay ruffled her heavy mane of hair and pressed her soft loose dress against her body, revealing the fecund outline of her breasts and belly.

"You are salivating, Rupert. Do contrive to contain your perverse lust," Cybill said nastily. "Why, she looks a perfect cow, lumbering and ungainly. I cannot imagine what you can find attractive in that."

He turned to look at the coldly perfect face of his wife. Her voluptuous curves were revealed in a low-cut violet silk gown that accentuated both the color of her eyes and the whiteness of her skin. Not a hair on her perfectly coifed ebony head was out of place. Somehow she even contrived to stay cool and unmussed after sex.

Reaching out he pressed his palm against the flat surface of her stomach. "Can you not imagine what it would be like to carry my child, pet?" he asked, knowing the answer. "A man can find such fertility most appealing . . . even erotic."

"Pah! The brat isn't even yours," she sneered, somewhat surprised at the direction of his thought.

"Are you volunteering to give me a child, Cybill?" he purred.

"Do not even consider it in jest. I've gotten rid of several already—yours . . . and others. I'd not hesitate to do so again if necessary. I shall never shamble about with a swollen belly," she said with loathing.

He shrugged and turned back to watch Joss as she strolled serenely across the grass, stopping to pluck several jonquils and inhale their fragrance. He did not see the expression on Cybill's face as she, too, stared down on the tawny-haired woman below with slitted eyes turned from violet to black with hate.

*   *   *

Tensions simmered and violence erupted along the Georgia frontier in the spring of 1813. Using Coweta as a base, Alex rode with a force known as the Law Menders under William McIntosh, a mixed-blood planter from a prominent white family. Attempting to stop Red Sticks' depredations across the frontier, Alex threw himself into the heat of battle like a man possessed. He risked his life again and again on the front lines, volunteering for the most dangerous reconnaissance, leading wild charges and seeming to court death at every opportunity.

"His grief robs him of judgment," Charity said to Devon when a group of Law Menders rode in and dismounted from their spent horses. Alex had led them into the interior to an Upper Creek town and brought back numerous Red Stick prisoners.

Poc, catching sight of his long absent master, ran to greet him barking a furious welcome. After Joss's disappearance the little terrier had nearly grieved himself to death while Alex was in Savannah. Upon his return to Coweta the dog had attached his fierce devotion to him.

"I had hoped this fight would be his salvation, but it has only given him a better way to die than drinking himself to death," Devon replied grimly. "Thank God the fighting is almost over."

"You have done everything you can to keep our people from joining the Red Sticks."

"We'll salvage what we can. Quint will help us," Dev replied.

"Do not fear. We have survived war. We will survive the peace as well." She turned from her son to welcome Alex, smiling and opening her arms as he strode toward them, Poc at his side. Hugging her grandson fiercely, she noted the tight haggard lines about his eyes and mouth yet did not remonstrate. "You are safely returned. My heart is glad," she said simply.

"Oh, there is mail for you. It arrived while you were gone," Devon said as they walked to Charity's house. "Mostly letters from your mother and sisters, Aunt Madelyne and amazingly, one from London."

Having heard repeated exhortations from the female members of his family to take care of his health and avoid foolish bravery on the battlefield, Alex was little interested in their well-meaning remonstrations, but the missive from London was another matter. *A link to your past life . . . to Joss.* His heart clenched as he forced the thought aside. "The one from London—is it from Uncle Monty?" he asked as they entered the house and climbed the ladder to Charity's quarters. The dog scrambled unaided after them.

"I'm not certain. I've had little opportunity to familiarize myself with my brother-in-law's handwriting," Devon said wryly as he picked up a bundle of letters and handed them to Alex. Oh, yes, and there was one curious one. The writing is so water smudged I was surprised it found its way to you. It must have come a great distance, judging by its condition."

"This one's from Drum," Alex said as he plucked the London letter from the pile, little noting his father's comment about the mysterious travel-stained missive.

Devon smiled at the animation in his son's face as he read his friend's entertaining narration. A bit of the old Alex showed through the grim soulless air that had settled over him the past seven months since Joss's death.

"He bribed a French wine smuggler to get the letter to an American ship," Alex said with a fond chuckle, reading Drum's amusing anecdotes about the ton. The latest gossip, the peccadilloes and foibles of the Quality seemed a million miles from the grim reality on the Georgia frontier. For a brief moment, Alex escaped back to happier days in that faraway place.

Of course Drum did not know of Joss's death. Since the outbreak of hostilities, there had been no way to reach him or their family members and business associates in England. Considering the gravity of the situation on the frontier, neither Alex nor his parents had taken time to think about London. So much had happened since they set sail nearly a year ago.

He set aside his friend's letter with a bittersweet smile. Perhaps he would read it again while he was out in the wilderness sitting beside a lonely campfire. Shuffling through the other correspondence, he paused when he reached the weather-stained letter his father had mentioned. Then he froze. "It can't be . . . What sort of ghoulish trick is this?" he murmured to himself as he clutched the missive in his shaking hand, staring down at it as if he expected it to burst into flames at any moment.

"What's wrong, son?" Devon asked, perplexed.

"It's Joss's handwriting."

"You must be mistaken," Dev replied gently, peering at the blurred writing.

"I'd know her hand anywhere, Papa. When could she have . . . it must have . . ." Any logical explanation for the letter eluded him.

"You'd best open it, Alex," Charity said sensibly.

His hands shook so badly he almost tore the fragile sheets extracting them from the bedraggled envelope. Having no idea what to expect, Devon and Charity stood silently in tense anticipation as Alex began to read.

"It's dated February twentieth, 1813," Alex said in hoarse disbelief. "Joss is . . . Joss is alive!" Trembling he swiftly scanned the lines as his father and grandmother exchanged worried looks.

"What is it?" Devon responded.

"Joss bribed a French voyager to smuggle this letter out. Chamberlain has her. She's been a prisoner in Mobile since last fall . . . and I will shortly be a father," he finished in a stunned, awe-filled voice.

"You had better sit down," Charity said, guiding him to

the chair he had vacated earlier while reading Drum's letter.

He sank weak-kneed onto it, blinking back the tears that obscured his vision. "She's alive," he breathed reverently, his fingers tracing over the familiar signature in her bold yet precise penmanship. *Your loving wife, Joss.*

"It would seem you've been given a second chance, son," Dev said, his own voice none too steady.

Alex crouched behind the trunk of a huge old live oak a few dozen yards from the walls of the old Spanish fortress that guarded Mobile Bay. He and Joss's faithful dog had made the long canoe journey from the Muskogee town alone in spite of his father's and uncle's remonstrances, explaining that a larger party would attract attention. His best hope for rescuing his wife was to slip in and out swiftly and quietly. Alex circled the perimeter of the high stone walls, finding that the best way to gain entry without notice was via a small gate at the back of the fortress. It looked old. Perhaps he could break the lock.

Joss, are you inside? Are you well? All he had been able to think about on the long dangerous trek downriver was seeing her again, hearing her voice, feeling the soft touch of her healing hands. And holding their child in his arms. If her calculations were correct, the babe was due any day now. What would he do if she'd been brought to bed when he found her?

Cross that bridge if you come to it, Blackthorne, he said to himself, steeling his concentration to get into the fort undetected. He had left Poc at the edge of the swamp with a firm command to stay. When the sentry on the terreplein overhead turned his back and paced in the opposite direction, Alex dashed to the wall below, flattening his body to it, then edged along until he reached the gate. To his wary amazement, it swung open with a slight creak when he pushed on it.

Alex froze, hoping no one had heard the sound. The soldier's footfalls did not alter their steady pace. No one cried a warning. Stealthily Alex slipped inside, then eased his way into the shade of a low-growing honey locust to get his bearings. He began a furtive yet methodical search of the fort, beginning with what looked like the officers' quarters. When he heard Cybill's voice angrily berating a servant, he knew he'd found the right place. He went from room to room, but Joss was nowhere to be found. If Chamberlain were before him now, he would flay him alive for taking her. Rupert was gone but Cybill was still here. Surely the colonel would not have sailed off and left his own wife behind. Surely she knew something.

The lady in question sat at her dressing table sipping a cup of chocolate while a subdued maid brushed her long black hair. The mauve satin robe she wore gaped open, revealing the heavy curves of her breasts, which sagged pendulously without the artifice of stays to hold them up. At length she dismissed the maid with instructions to draw her cool bath water.

As soon as the servant closed the door and walked down the hall, Alex slipped from his hiding place on the open balcony and entered the room noiselessly. Cybill remained unaware, reclining against the high back of her chair with a scented cloth pressed to her forehead. He slipped over to the door and slid the lock, then approached her.

"Is that you, Isolde? Pour the water quickly. I am dying of heat and the headache," she said petulantly.

"Make a squeak and you'll have far worse than a headache, m'lady," he said as his hand curved around the milky column of her throat.

She sat up abruptly and the cloth fell from her forehead. Her large violet eyes blinked incredulously at the reflection in the mirror. "Alex," she barely whispered.

"I'll remove my hand," he said, raising the gleaming blade of his knife menacingly, "but if you attempt to sound

369

a warning, you'll learn firsthand how the Muskogee scalp their enemies."

A flush of excitement bloomed in her cheeks and glowed in her eyes as she nodded. He released her, asking, "Where is my wife?"

She smiled slowly with her lips but her eyes were the cold purple of a Russian sunset. "La, I had hoped you came to rescue me from this hellhole."

"Don't play, Cybill," he gritted out, grabbing a fistful of ebony hair and pulling it tight against her scalp. "I know Kent brought her here and she's carrying my child. Do you have any idea how a Muskogee values his woman and his firstborn—*do you?*" He tugged harder and raised the knife, slicing off a large chunk of her hair.

She gasped in outrage but the blade at her throat kept her silent. "You'd do it. You would actually kill me, wouldn't you?" she whispered.

Her terror was mixed with a sick surge of excitement. He could feel her trembling and was revolted by the smell she gave off, fear and musky arousal. "In a heartbeat," he replied. "Do not try my patience further. We savages are reputed to have little of it."

She licked her lips nervously. "I helped her escape." At his look of incredulity she went on, speaking in fast disjointed sentences. "Rupert wanted her—and worse, he wanted the child she carries. That's why he did not rape her. He planned to use the child to enforce her complaisance."

At his snarled oath, she insisted, "No! 'Tis the truth—if the child is a boy, he intended to raise your son to hate the Blackthorne name, and if tis a girl . . . she was to be your wife's replacement in his bed. I could not permit that," she added petulantly.

"When did she leave? How?"

"At dawn with a French voyager I hired to spirit her north to safety."

"If you're lying to me—or if I find harm has come to her . . ." He raised the blade and ran the flat of the cool silvery metal across her cheek. "I can be very, very savage, m'lady. Now, you are going to ring for your maid and cancel that bath. Your headache has of a sudden gotten much worse. You do not wish to be disturbed until further notice. Is the message very clear?"

He released his painful hold on her hair but held the knife ominously close to her face. She nodded and raised the bell. When the maid knocked breathlessly a moment later, he whispered, "Make it convincing."

She did. Afterward, he bound and gagged Cybill, then bundled her in several fluffy comforters and tied the whole securely on top of her large bed. She could sweat and squirm for hours and not make a sound that could be heard outside the room.

Joss crouched in the titi thicket, holding her breath as Wilbur Kent drew near.

"I know you're hiding somewhere nearby. Come out and I shall return you to the fort. That or remain here as alligator bait. The choice is yours," Kent said conversationally as he approached her.

The only truth to his promises was that, left alone without weapons, she would be devoured by the creatures of the swamp. Joss knew he had no intention of returning her to the fort. *Cybill sent him to kill me.* The fact had hit her squarely when LeBeau, her guide, had been killed and she narrowly escaped from the sinking pirogue. She cursed herself for a fool not to have seen where the woman's vitriolic hate would lead.

Having dispatched her guide, Kent had run her to ground like the vicious bloodhound he was. Her arms were growing weary as she held a heavy chunk of log, ready to use it as a cudgel when he drew close to her hiding place. The nagging ache in her lower back intensified. *Just a few yards farther*. He passed by, ducking to get through the edge of the thicket. A bit far out of reach, but her only chance. She stepped out and swung the club with all her strength.

If she had been two or three feet closer she might have knocked him unconscious, but he heard her moving behind him and turned with a fraction of a second to spare, raising his arm to block the blow. The impact jarred all the way up her arms when the log connected with bone. Unfortunately it was not his skull but his forearm. He wrenched the weapon from her grasp with a sharp curse. Fortunately for her he overbalanced in doing so and fell backward.

Joss knew she could not outrun him. Instead she dropped swiftly to her knees, clawing for the log. She did not see the flash of his knife until it was almost too late. Rolling onto her side, she grabbed the log and raised it protectively in front of her as he scrambled closer still clutching the deadly blade. A feral grimace spread his thin lips wide, revealing long white teeth.

"So, you want to wrestle, eh? I always enjoy a bit of sport. No real satisfaction in an easy kill." He locked gazes with her, seeming to take pleasure in her desperate defiance.

He lunged forward, seizing her club with one hand and wrestling it away. Instead of holding tight, Joss released it and grabbed his knife arm with both hands. They went down, rolling on the soft damp moss. She bit and kicked like a demented thing. *I can't let him kill Alex's baby!* Joss twisted as they rolled on the uneven ground, nearing the edge of a sluggishly flowing stream. With strength born of sheer desperation she continued holding on to his knife hand with both of hers as he yanked her to her feet. Kent tried to twist his arm free but slipped in the mud and fell to his right side, pulling Joss with him.

The force of their landing knocked the breath from her. She felt a sharp pain between her breasts and a red haze exploded behind her eyelids for an instant but not before she saw the expression of utter amazement on his face. A low, raw whistling sound followed as she pushed free of him, backing away on all fours.

Her eyeglasses had been knocked off during the fight. Joss groped for them until she found them. The lenses were cracked but allowed her to see the gristly scene before her. The knife was embedded neatly between his ribs high on the left side of his chest. When he had pulled her down on top of him, her weight must have driven the blade directly into his heart. That wheeze had been Wilbur Kent's death rattle.

Joss struggled to her feet. Kent had pursued her by boat. All she need do was backtrack where he had hidden it. After that . . . well, after that she would cross that bridge when she came to it. She trudged through the awful morass toward the sound of rushing water. When she reached the bank where she had left LeBeau's pirogue, she found it half submerged from the shots Kent had fired into it. Through the cracked lenses of her spectacles she could make out the Frenchman's body floating facedown near a large log a dozen yards away.

When the log started to move she screamed in horror. An immense alligator swam lazily across the river. She backed slowly up the embankment, then circled to give the predator a wide berth before beginning her search of the shoreline. Then she saw the canoe shoved carefully up on the muddy bank.

With a cry of relief, she picked up her pace, heading toward it. The dull low backache that had been plaguing her all day suddenly exploded into a sharp agonizing cramp that wrapped around her belly. She sank to her knees, breathless as a gush of water bathed her legs.

The baby was coming and she was alone in a swamp filled with alligators and poisonous snakes!

Cybill huddled on the chair with sweat streaming in rivulets down her face and body. Her hair hung in damp tangles around her bare shoulders as she sat in only her thin silk undergarments. She had spent several hours tied up, smothered in blankets in this accursed heat, before her husband had found her.

Across the room Sir Rupert paced furiously. It was his unexpected early return to which she owed her rescue. She was not inclined to feel in the least grateful. He was far more furious over Joss's escape and Alex's pursuit of her than he was concerned about his wife's brush with death.

"Now let us review this one more time, m'dear," he said tightly. "Jocelyn Blackthorne, great with child, just slipped magically from her room this morning and somehow managed to find a gate negligently left open allowing her to escape the fort. She simply set out to walk back to American territory—all by herself with no outside aid? Then her husband mysteriously learned she was being held here, broke into your room searching for her and forced you at knifepoint to explain her absence?" His voice was low and deadly with fury and disbelief.

Cybill was nauseated from the heat, dehydrated and now frightened by his quiet raging, yet her jealous anger overcame all else. She flung back her fouled hair and stood up, stamping her bare foot imperiously. "I have told you what happened! They are both gone, escaped!"

"How convenient for you," he sneered.

"You really mean how disastrous for you that you've lost your chance to kill Alex and bed his woman," she shot back.

Chamberlain's eyes narrowed in icy anger. "Why is it, pet, that I have the feeling you are not quite telling me everything, hmm?"

"Don't be absurd," she said shrilly as he stalked nearer. "I should think you'd wish to give pursuit."

"Oh, I shall in the fullness of time, I shall. I have a Red Stick scout searching for their trail right now."

The colonel's manner was cold and contained but he was

holding himself on an exceedingly tight leash. His return from New Providence was made posthaste because he had orders to evacuate the British contingent from Mobile. The American general Wilkinson was en route with a large force to take the fortress and hold the bay. The bumbling British high command had decided to retreat.

"You should pursue your quarry, not bedevil me," she snapped. "By now she could have paddled halfway to Georgia!"

He whirled on his heel at her last outburst and lunged at her, seizing her throat with his clawlike deformed hand. "Paddled—did you say paddled? I believe earlier you insisted she had simply walked into the swamp."

Cybill coughed and tried to evade his punishing grip, but he would not relinquish it. Her face turned from furious red to sickly green, guilty terror etched in every line. Abruptly he shoved her back against the chair and leaned over her until their faces were inches apart. He could smell her foul body odor. The stench of sweat was now permeated by the metallic scent of fear. He was well familiar with the smell of fear. Every night before a battle, he walked among his soldiers, reveling in it.

"Now, you are going to tell me precisely what you did. I will find out anyway, you know," he purred as his crippled hand stroked the bruises he'd put on her throat.

Cybill had observed him taunting his victims like this many times before. He played with them like a cat with a crippled bird, but he had never done it to her. And all over a woman he was obsessed with, a gauche, clumsy bluestocking, fat with another man's child! The anger she had struggled to hold in check bubbled over.

"I'll tell you what I've done!" she spat furiously. Tears of sheer rage brightened her eyes as she leaned forward and glared at his arrogant face. "I've spent all of our wedded life furthering your career, pandering to gouty old generals and pompously dull cabinet ministers. I've lived for nearly a year in this hellish backwater town swatting mosquitoes and watching my ankles swell in the heat while you panted after that pregnant sow without touching her!"

"You incited her to escape—you helped her, didn't you?"

"Yes! And what's more I saw to it the job was done to a cow's thumb! She's dead! And so is her brat! Willie was only too happy to follow her into the swamp and see that she ended up alligator food!"

"Kent!" he roared, losing all composure abruptly. "You sent Kent after her?"

"Yes, and you're too late, Rupert. 'Tis done, finished," she shouted back, coming up out of her chair at him with her long nails curved into claws.

He struck her with his good hand, hard across the face as a blind red haze enveloped him. When she fell backward against the chair, he reached down and clamped both hands around her throat, squeezing, squeezing . . . until she ceased her struggles. Her head plopped limply against his wrist and the long tangled black hair fell like a stringy curtain over her face.

With a sniff of distaste he released his hold and stepped back, looking down on the wreckage of what had once been a beautiful woman. "Bitch," he mouthed softly as he turned and left the room without a backward glance. Let that fat, stupid commandant see to burying her. He was going after Jocelyn, Kent and Blackthorne.

Alex paddled slowly, his eyes watching the shoreline with increasing desperation. The sun was sinking low on the horizon and time was running out. Very soon the night would catch them in its immobilizing inky grasp. The dog sat at the front of the canoe, nostrils twitching in the evening breeze for a hint of Joss's scent. Several times over the past hours when they came to a division in the waterway headed north, he had relied on Poc's instinct to choose the right path. He knew it was probably hopeless, but he also knew he'd remain in this bayou until he found her or died here himself.

Suddenly Poc started barking, breaking the low hum of insects and rhythmic croaking of night creatures coming to life. A faint whiff of smoke teased Alex's nostrils. A campfire? His heart suddenly began to pound as the dog's barking intensified frantically.

"Joss!" he cried, paddling toward the aroma of smoke, repeating her name over and over until he was hoarse. "Joss! Joss! Are you here, darling?"

She came up as from a deep well as the wave of pain ebbed, thinking she had heard Alex calling her name. "Wish for something desperately enough and you hallucinate," she said through parched lips. She fumbled for Kent's canteen on the ground beside her, and started to take a sip when the sound echoed across the water once more.

"Joss! Joss! Answer me, please!" Following the cry a dog's sharp bark sounded.

She nearly dropped the precious water. It *was* Alex with Poc! He'd found her! "Alex, here—I'm here," she responded hoarsely, but her strength had been ebbing steadily over the last hours as the contractions grew closer together. She had used up much of her precious reserve of energy building a fire, cleaning the knife and preparing everything as best she could for her child's birth.

Could he hear her? Frantically she repeated the cry and was rewarded by an answer. "Joss? Is it you?" Poc's barking grew louder, more frantic. She struggled to her knees and peered out at the river. Evening mist veiled it in soft shades of gray.

Joss squinted, seeing a dim shape moving toward the bank. Because of the fading light and her cracked lenses she could not determine who it was. Then a small part of the apparition separated itself with a loud splash, jumping into the water. In a moment she could make out the little

377

dog as he scrambled up the muddy bank, spraying water everywhere as he raced across the clearing and leaped into her arms, licking her face with joy.

She held the soaked, muddy terrier, petting him soothingly as her eyes fastened on the tall shadowy figure nimbly leaping onto the bank and beaching the canoe. "Alex? Alex, is it truly you? I've hoped and prayed and dreamed for so many months . . ." Her voice broke as another contraction began to tighten her belly, squeezing off breath.

"Joss," he cried, kneeling beside her and taking her in his arms as she doubled over, panting. "What is it? What's wrong—are you injured?"

Relief flooded her in spite of the building contraction's painful intensity. Her love had found her at last! She shook her head, then gasped, "Nothing . . . wrong . . . baby's coming."

Alex paled as he helped her lie back on the rude pallet she'd made beside the fire. "Nothing is wrong when you're about to . . . you're having the . . . you can't, Joss—not here without help," he sputtered frantically.

As the contraction eased, she took a deep breath and chuckled weakly. "But I'm no longer without help, Alex."

"But I can't . . . you can't . . . we can't—"

"Yes, we can. We have little choice and little time for a male version of the vapors," she said firmly, taking no pity on his typical male mutton-headedness in the face of impending fatherhood.

He looked around the campfire and saw a Baker rifle leaning in the crook of a swamp oak, the knife gleaming on top of a pile of clean rags, the blanket she reclined on. "How did you do all this?"

"The supplies are Kent's. He is dead," she said with surprising calmness. "He followed us."

"Us?"

Quickly she explained that Cybill had tricked her into slipping out of the fort with an old Frenchman as guide.

"She lied to us both. She'd sent Kent to kill us here and leave no trace."

"I take it Kent killed the Frenchman?"

Joss nodded, then described the struggle that ended in Kent's death.

Every few moments she had to pause as a fresh contraction came. She concluded, saying, "So I found this clearing high enough above water to keep the alligators away, brought his supplies from his canoe and built the fire."

He shook his head, grinning in spite of his fears. "You are one hell of a remarkable woman, Jocelyn Blackthorne," he said with admiration. Just then another contraction began. She squeezed his hand and began to pant with it. He blanched, feeling her pain so keenly he gasped.

She waited until it eased, then patted his hand reassuringly. "Never fear, Alex. Everything is going on quite normally. I should have realized what the low backache meant this morning, but I was too excited at the prospect of escape to think of it."

"Are you sure Kent didn't hurt you—the struggle with him—"

"No, I'm certain he did not. After all, it isn't as if I have not assisted at the delivery of dozens of babies at hospital, Alex. The child is full term." She smiled and looked away, faintly embarrassed. "I knew within two weeks precisely when my delivery date must be."

He knew at once what she meant. They had made love only two nights in Coweta, almost exactly a fortnight apart. "You seem to have thought of everything," he said, still frightened for her yet beginning to calm. Poc, as if understanding the need for levelheadedness, had stretched out beside her pallet, quietly observing their exchange. "What must I do? Only explain and I'll do it," Alex said, praying he was not making a false promise.

" 'Tis pretty much up to nature to take its course, but you can be of great assistance just being with me. Hold my hand and talk to me through the contractions. . . ." As if on cue, another one began. *Tell me you love me, Alex.*

Alex swallowed nervously and stroked her forehead with his free hand while she held the other in a death grip. Too rattled to think of the obvious things he should tell her— had been burning to tell her all these hellish months—he instead explained how he had received her letter when everyone was certain she had died at the wilderness fort. Then he described his rush to Mobile, where he had encountered Cybill, about whom he now uttered some choice epithets.

"Did you really swaddle her in bedding and tie her on the mattress?" she asked, chuckling in spite of everything at the image of the cool and haughty noblewoman gagged and sweating in silent fury.

"It was the only way to keep her quiet. I had to make time before she sicced pursuers on me." Joss and Alex were so intent on each other they failed to notice the dog bristling and growling as Alex continued, "Without Poc I would never have found you in this labyrinth of water, Joss. I doubt anyone could have followed my trail."

"Your doubts are quite unfounded, Blackthorne. A pity, after all you've both gone through to be reunited. So touching, father and mother awaiting the birth of their firstborn child," Sir Rupert Chamberlain said conversationally as he stepped into the circle of flickering light. A Red Stick guide shadowed him. Both held cocked weapons. The Indian's musket was trained on Alex's chest. The colonel's .69-caliber Egg dueling pistol was pointed at Joss's stomach. "I wonder, should I kill her now . . . or allow you both to live and watch as I kill your brat first?"

Chapter Twenty-four

Poc growled more menacingly as Chamberlain approached. Alex made a quick motion with his hand, quelling the dog before one of the men shot him. How could he move the fight clear of Joss? She clutched his hand, gasping in horror when Chamberlain made his vile threats. "Your wife told me that you planned to keep my child and raise it to spite me," he said, slowly standing up, placing himself in the line of fire between Joss and the men.

"Ah, dear fellow, that was before you so conveniently placed yourself into my hands to do with as I please. The chap with me is Devil Dancer, a Red Stick who hates marauding colonials. He is your sworn enemy and a most inventive torturer, I'm told," he added with relish.

"No, you can't—" Joss's cry was breathless and desperate, coming through another rising contraction. They were very close together now. It would not be long. She could not let this twisted madman have her baby or her husband! Sensing his mistress's distress, Poc licked her hands, which were now clenched in a death hold on the blanket. If only she could see what was going on more clearly!

When she tried to sit up, Chamberlain looked past Alex at her pale, drawn face. That split second of distraction gave her husband the only opening he might get. With a loud cry of "Now, Poc," he leaped at the colonel, knocking the elegant pistol aside so it discharged harmlessly in the air. The two men went tumbling to the ground at the same instant that Poc, with blurring speed, slammed into the Red Stick's chest, knocking him backward before he could get off a shot. He dropped his weapon as he fell.

Devil Dancer tried to pull his knife from its sheath, but he was dealing with a trained fighting dog whose killing instincts had been honed in dozens of bloody London pits. The Red Stick raised his arm trying to ward off the lethal terrier as Poc went with deadly intent for his jugular.

Alex and Chamberlain rolled across the clearing, coming dangerously close to the edge of the bank before breaking apart. Each man scrambled to his feet and drew a weapon. Alex had only the wicked Muskogee hunting knife that had caused Drum such consternation back in London, but the colonel unsheathed the long gleaming cavalry saber from its scabbard slung across his back.

"Now, you mongrel bastard, 'tis long past time we finished our business, don't you agree?" he asked as Alex circled warily, keeping out of the far greater range of the sword.

"You couldn't best me in a fair contest before. I suppose you're entitled to a second chance since I robbed you of the use of your good right hand," Alex replied, watching the eerie glow of madness in Chamberlain's eyes.

"Yes, a second chance you will regret, you bloody savage. I'm as good now with my left hand as I was with my right—better than good enough to cut you to ribbons," the Englishman snarled as he lashed out, slicing Alex's shirtsleeve.

A narrow weal of blood seeped from it, but Blackthorne

ignored the fiery sting, all too aware of Joss lying behind them, helpless and in pain. If only Poc could do away with the Red Stick scout, he could handle Chamberlain—he *would* handle Chamberlain. Alex called upon every trick of feinting, thrusting and parrying he had learned as a backwoods brawler and every advantage he had learned from wrestling contests with the Muskogee.

Chamberlain's blade was far longer than his, but it was also heavy and clumsy. He could not wield it as effectively as he would have a foil. "Thrash and swing, Chamberlain. You fight like a scullery maid wielding a broom," he scoffed, goading his foe as he got inside and nicked the colonel's crippled arm. In spite of using his left hand quite proficiently, Chamberlain still suffered under the disadvantage of restricted movement in his right arm.

"Scullery maid, indeed," the colonel echoed arrogantly. "Before I finish with you I'm going to hack off both your hands and this is just the weapon with which to do it." As he spoke, Chamberlain's blade flashed, opening an ugly gash on Alex's forearm.

It was not deep enough to disable him or cause him to drop his knife, but the blood loss would be fatal if he did not end the contest soon. Joss's swift heavy breathing indicated that she needed him desperately. He could hear Poc and the Red Stick thrashing and rolling as his attention remained on the colonel's blade.

Poc made a last snarling lunge and tore out half the Red Stick's throat. Blood spurted like a fountain while Devil Dancer gurgled his last, then went still. The dog remained rigid, straddling the body, still growling.

I have to back him toward them, Alex thought, taking the risk of going on the offensive in spite of Chamberlain's longer reach with the sword. The blunt tip of the blade nicked Blackthorne's face, narrowly missing his eye as he gave Chamberlain's crippled arm an arcing slash. Alex dodged the worst of Chamberlain's counterblow but felt the sharp sting on his cheek. Blood oozed from it but he had the satisfaction of seeing Chamberlain's right arm hang at his side, dripping blood and utterly useless. The man's balance would now be severely impaired.

A wild light of panic shone in the colonel's eyes as he said shrilly, "You maimed me as if I were a damned dog in a bear baiting. All I have now is this deformed claw." He backed another step, stumbling as Alex's blade flashed with lightning speed, this time slicing his sword arm.

Just one more step. Poc had quieted now, still standing on Devil Dancer's chest, seeming to understand Alex's plan.

At the last second, Chamberlain sensed the stumbling block behind him. He chanced a look over his shoulder, then whirled with an oath, raising his sword to slash down on Alex's extended knife arm. But Blackthorne was too quick. He slipped inside, and quickly sliced the Englishman's neck, jumping back out of reach.

Chamberlain's sword clattered uselessly to the ground as he lost his balance, falling over the Red Stick's body. Blood gushed from his wound.

"The last time I did it Drum's way. This time I did it mine."

Lying dazed, Chamberlain tried in vain to reclaim his saber but could not. "Then kill me, you bastard! Kill me and be done with it!" he screamed.

"I have," Alex replied grimly.

Sir Rupert Chamberlain's eyes glazed over as he stared at the gushing blood soaking his uniform an even darker shade of red. He fell back and sighed, then was gone.

Alex turned from the two dead men and rushed back to Joss, who was panting without respite now, her breaths coming in and out ragged and low like an animal in terrible pain. As he knelt beside her, frantic with fear, she gasped, "It's coming . . . the baby is . . . coming soon, Alex. You must . . . pull it free . . . when the head pushes out . . . then tie off the cord and cut it. . . . Use Kent's knife. . . . I cleaned it in the fire. . . ."

Terrified, Alex listened as she described, in far more vivid detail than he had ever wished to know, exactly what was going on. His arm was bleeding copiously. As she talked, he tore a wide piece from the hem of her skirt and bound it as best he could. He dared not pass out from blood loss while his wife needed him. Then he washed his hands in water from the canteen and dried them on a piece of clean cloth.

Poc sat patiently at Joss's side offering moral support. Alex wished he and the dog could change places as he knelt beside her spread legs and waited. When the small head began to emerge, his fears and uncertainties were swept away in the miracle of birth. This was their child, created in the wonder of a love he had not even recognized. He felt humbled and proud all at the same time as he gently pulled his newborn daughter from her mother's body and held her in his hands.

"So tiny yet so perfect," he breathed in awe.

Joss smiled, exhausted but enraptured, while he followed her instructions, laying their lustily crying little daughter on her breast and disposing of the afterbirth. "You're as efficient as any London nurse," she said, caressing the wet cap of hair on their baby's head.

"I didn't think I could do it," he confessed.

"You were splendid," she replied.

They stared at each other through the flickering firelight until the baby gave another fretful wail, breaking the spell. "She should be bathed and wrapped in some of that cloth," Joss said, then added, "and then your wounds must be tended." She reached up and touched the bloody gash on his cheek. "I wish I had the materials to stitch it. It will leave a terrible scar to mar your beauty."

He scoffed. "My 'beauty' is the least of our concerns now, Joss." He soaked a cloth with water and gently cleansed his daughter, then swaddled her lovingly and returned her to his wife's arms. "What shall we name her?"

"I had thought Elijah for my father if we had a son, but since we have a daughter I would like to name her for your mother."

"Barbara it shall be. She saw what I was far too blind to see, Joss. Can you ever forgive me for being such a fool?" he asked as he watched her hold the baby to her breast. "I never told you I loved you, Joss. I never even realized it until it was too late. I didn't know how much until I lost you."

"But you never wanted to be married, to have a wife . . . and now you have not only a wife but a child. In time you might grow restless again—feel trapped. I won't hold you with Barbara, Alex."

"I didn't even know I had a child when I realized what I'd lost in you, Joss. I was immature, irresponsible—hell, I was a callow wastrel." He struggled to find the right words. "I had a lot of time when I thought you were dead to consider why I'd made the bargain I did with you, Joss— why I feared a real marriage so much. My parents are so devoted to each other, if one of them were to die, the other would, too—at least that's what I used to believe. That's the way the Blackthorne men fall in love and it frightened me. I didn't want to take that risk . . . until I met you."

"You risked nothing with an ungainly tabby who could never tempt you. I didn't mean to trick you that night in London, honestly I didn't," she added rapidly, before her courage deserted her. "I couldn't sleep upstairs because of the smoke from the fire, you see, so I came down . . . and yours was the only bed . . ."

"Why did you run away in the morning and pretend nothing had happened?" That still rankled him.

"I had no courage to face you. Not then, nor that day in Coweta when I found you and Water Lily disporting in the river." That still rankled her.

"Water Lily?" he echoed, confused. Then seeing the hurt expression on his wife's face, he realized what must have transpired. "You saw us and thought that I . . . that we . . . ?"

Now Joss was the one confused. "You mean to say she didn't . . . you didn't . . . ?"

"Oh, she tried, but I sent her away, Joss. I'd already realized even then that I wanted no woman but my wife."

His lopsided smile melted her heart. "I misjudged you that day. I should have stayed and faced you, but instead I ran. I still feel as if I don't deserve a man like you—charming as the devil, handsome as an angel . . . my wicked darling. Beside you I feel inadequate."

"Inadequate?" he echoed, dumbfounded. "Why, men flock to you like besotted puppies, Joss. I could scarce believe my eyes when I saw you at Chitchester's ball. You were the loveliest woman I'd ever even imagined—but the greatest irony of all is that your beauty didn't really matter," he confessed ruefully. "I loved you for who you were inside. I fell in love with a bright, witty, bold crusader who feared nothing and no one. Your outside appearance never meant a thing once I figured that out, Joss.

"The question, it seems to me, is can you forgive me for misjudging you? I was afraid you were ashamed of my Muskogee blood when you first came to Coweta. My pride was stung and I treated you abominably, thinking your noble English blood was too fine to mix with a half-breed's. When my father told me you'd been teaching the children at Grandma Charity's school, I knew how wrong I'd been and how brave you were to make a place for yourself there just as you had in London."

Joss felt the joy blossom deep in her heart and send its warmth radiating through her whole body. She reached out her arms to him and confessed, "I fell in love with you the first moment we collided on the wharf during that riot. You were as golden and beautiful as an angel—albeit a very wicked angel—and I was lost."

He stroked her face with his hand. "I love you, Joss, and I vow never to be wicked again . . ." A warm teasing light burned in his dark eyes as he added, "Except with you."

"Oh, Alex, I shall hold you to that vow for the rest of our lives," she said softly, reaching out to take his hand and press it to her lips. Her eyelids lowered slowly and her words became slurred with drowsiness. She was exhausted from her ordeal.

"Guard her, Poc," he said quietly. Then he rose and walked across the camp to where the bodies of Kent and Devil Dancer lay in the shadows. One at a time, he dragged them along the edge of the river about a hundred yards and rolled them into the water. Then he returned to stoke up the fire. He would remain vigilant to protect his family. As he sat down to watch over his wife and infant daughter, a deep sense of peace settled over him.

Epilogue

Alex scanned the crowded decks of the schooner while Devon smiled at his son's boyish eagerness. He had been almost like a child awaiting Christmas ever since he had received the rather terse letter some weeks earlier informing him that Alvin Frances Edward Drummond, "casting himself upon the waters of fate," was coming to "the colonies" to visit his friends and inspect "some rustic inn" he had won in a game of chance.

Frustrated by his failure to see Drum among those lining the ship's rail, Alex cursed quietly, "Damn it all to hell! Where is he?"

At that precise moment, through the dockside din sliced a decidedly English voice imperiously issuing orders. "Stop stumbling about, you oafs! If you drop one of those trunks over the side, you had best be able to dive and swim more efficaciously than you walk!"

A Drummond had arrived in America.

The little dandy, flourishing his walking stick like a teamster's whip, drove three hulking seamen down the gangplank before him, each of them bowed under the weight of a monstrous trunk.

"Drum, damn your eyes, man, I never realized how much I missed that elegant sneer of yours!" Alex exclaimed, seizing him in a powerful bear hug.

Drummond's face flushed with pleasure, and not a little from the powerful grasp of his enthusiastic comrade. "Alex, you great lout, put me down! Surely this is no way for one gentleman to great another, even in this wilderness."

Blackthorne set the little dandy back on his feet. Drum examined his friend with a studied casualness, then asked, "I say, old man, how long has it been since we last saw each other? Over two years? I suggest we never wait longer to renew our friendship. I am quite sure that a three-year reunion welcome would quite snap my spine, at the least!" He turned to the tall man beside Alex, the olive-skinned gold-haired man who had to be his friend's sire.

"I'd like you to meet my father, Devon Blackthorne. Papa, this is the Honorable Alvin Frances Edward Drummond."

As Devon extended his hand, the dandy quickly amended, "Drum to my friends, sir."

"Then you must call me Dev, for though we only just met, I count you a cherished friend indeed. I understand that you saved this wastrel's worthless hide several times." Smiling, he nodded toward his son. "My wife and I are forever in your debt."

Drum shook his head. "No, sir . . . Dev. Friends, sir, friends! Let us not speak of debts."

"Yes, Papa, Drum has a violent aversion to debts—to paying them, at least. And that, I warrant, is why we now have the pleasure of his company."

The Englishman fixed his friend with his indolently haughty green gaze. "Alex, that comment was boorish, unkind and—at least regarding my presence on American soil—totally untrue. Remember, I am a man of property now. Heigh-ho, where are my dear Amazon and your lovely mother?"

"Eagerly awaiting us at the city house . . . with a small surprise for you," Alex replied with a grin.

Standing at the bow window of the Blackthorne city house, Joss watched the three men approaching, gesticulating histrionically, and convulsed with laughter.

"Boys," Joss murmured as she smiled. "Just like boys."

"Be forewarned, my darling, they never outgrow it, no matter how old they get," Barbara said as they walked down the stairs to welcome their guest.

At that moment Poc brushed between the two women to assert his rightful role as official greeter of the Blackthorne household. He barked excitedly and Drum returned his greeting.

"Egad, my little flea-bitten friend, I would have thought by now that a crocodile would have eaten you."

"Alligator, Drum, alligator. Crocodiles live in Africa," Joss said with a big smile.

At the sound of her familiar voice, the little dandy looked up, his gaze settling squarely on her. His smile slowly evaporated as he took in the vision before him, dressed in a gown of soft form-fitting russet muslin. Her heavy mass of sun-bleached hair was piled high atop her head in a cascade of ringlets, and she wore . . . no spectacles!

"Jocelyn? Joss, it really is you! Good Lord, gel, you're a beauty! Your eyes, what happened . . . I mean, your spectacles . . . ?"

Joss smiled, "Dear Drum, it is a long story and we have plenty of time, but first there is someone you must meet."

As Joss took a squirming toddler from her nursemaid, Barbara and Drum greeted each other warmly. Then he turned to see the child in her mother's arms. Drum stared, fascinated. Her hair was dark blond, almost the exact shade of Alex's. Her eyes were a pale hazel and her skin just the faintest hue of light olive.

Joss said with the greatest formality, "Alvin Frances Edward Drummond, allow me to present Barbara Drummond Blackthorne, your goddaughter."

He croaked, "I . . . I . . . am . . ."

"A godfather," Barbara finished for him.

"I stood in for you at the christening, but your name is set down in the church records," Dev explained.

"Now, watch," urged Joss. "She's speaking fairly well for her age."

Joss put her finger on her friend's chest and said, "Drum. Drum."

Little Barbara worked her lips, blew a few bubbles and then repeated, "Dum. Dum."

Lady Barbara commented dryly, "So he seems to have been stricken, child. You are right on the mark."

Everyone, including Drum himself, laughed at the quip. They made their way indoors with the little dandy gingerly carrying his new goddaughter as if she were the crown jewels. As the door closed, Drum was heard to remark, "I say, if this inn of mine works out, I may just be persuaded to become a colonial. Properly overseeing the upbringing of one's goddaughter is a serious responsibility indeed."

Author's Note

The idea for *Wicked Angel* had been gestating in my mind for a number of years before I found the time and courage to write in a Regency setting. Knowing the prodigious amount of knowledge possessed by Regency readers, I was frankly intimidated. My associate Carol J. Reynard began surfing the web for Regency bibliographies, assuring me that if she could deal with cyberspace, I could deal with the British Isles between 1811 and 1820. (After all, that's only nine years!)

Alex and Joss's story was a joy to tell, lighthearted and humorous as the protagonists themselves. We are grateful for the numerous people who helped us along the journey from London to Mobile. Any errors in the work are our own.

The public libraries of St. Louis City and County located for me virtually every research book on the extensive "wish list" Carol extracted from the web. Mr. Mark Hayford, computer wizard extraordinaire, not only introduced Carol to the Internet, but guided her in the selection and installation of all new hardware and software.

To fortify our courage before submitting the manuscript, we wanted to have it checked by a true authority on the Regency. I called upon my good friend and best-selling author Anita Mills. She graciously volunteered to read *Wicked Angel* for any egregiously terrible gaffes.

For our research on this side of the Atlantic, Carol and I did some field work in what is now the woodland country of central Alabama and the beautiful old city of Mobile. We wish to express our thanks to the folks at Fort Condé and the Mobile Visitors' Information Center. For the fabulous antique maps of the Creek towns and the American forts of the era, we are indebted to the National Park Service at Horseshoe Bend National Military Park.

My husband Jim once more choreographed the mayhem in which Alex and Joss always seemed to find themselves. Our friend Dr. Carmine V. DelliQuadri, Jr., D. O., not only armed our heroes and villains, but in his capacity as an opthamologist also gave us the solution to Joss's terrible vision problem, extract of belladonna.

For a few liberties with history I beg my reader's indulgence. The Red Stick Rebellion described in the last segment of *Wicked Angel* began in the summer of 1812. Actually, the fighting did not start until late in 1813 and escalated to the final dissolution of the Creek Confederacy after "Old Sharp Knife," Andrew Jackson, forced a highly punitive treaty on the rebels following the Battle of Horseshoe Bend on March 27, 1814.

Many of the minor characters mentioned in the book are actual historical figures, such as Beau Brumell, Lord Byron, William Wilberforce and Lady Holland in London, and William Weatherford, General James Wilkinson and William McIntosh in Mississippi Territory. The great Shawnee Tecumseh's speech is an oral tradition written down later in the nineteenth century by white men. One more literary license concerns the renegade Peter McQueen, who from all accounts did not speak English, and who, of course, did not abduct my fictional heroine.

For those interested in further reading about the fascinating era of the Regency, the War of 1812 and the Red Stick Rebellion, I offer a few of my major sources. For the Regency: *The Prince of Pleasures* by J. B. Priestly, *The Regency Companion* by Sharon Laudermilk and Teresa L. Hamlin, *Our Tempestuous Day* by Carolly Erickson, *Life in Regency England* by R. J. White and *Regency London* by Stella Margetson. For the New World: *The Old Southwest 1795–1830* by Thomas D. Clark and John D. W. Guice, *The Southern Indians and Benjamin Hawkins* by Florette Henri and *McIntosh and Weatherford* by Benjamin W. Griffith, Jr.

For my research on the Muskogee of the Creek Confederacy, I refer our readers to *Love a Rebel, Love a Rogue* (Leisure Books, 1994), which has been reissued several times and is currently in print. It is the story of Devon Blackthorne and Lady Barbara Caruthers. Look for the story of Alex's cousin Beth and a dashing English earl in *Wanton Angel*, to be released later this year. Carol and I hope you laughed and cried with Alex and Joss, their friends and family. We love to hear from our readers. If you enclose a stamped, self-addressed envelope, we will be glad to answer your letter. Happy reading!

Shirl Henke
P.O. Box 72
Adrian, MI 49221

LOVE A REBEL... LOVE A ROGUE

SHIRL HENKE

NIGHT WIND'S WOMAN

SHIRL HENKE

"Theirs will not be an easy path to travel, but they are fated to love." So speaks the Indian medicine woman when Night Wind leads his beautiful Spanish captive into the remote Apache stronghold. Proud and untamable as a lioness, Orlena vows she will never submit to the renegade who nightly teases her body into a frenzy of longing. For though his searing touch promises ecstasy, his heart is filled with hatred. A long-ago betrayal has made this man her enemy, but a bond even stronger than love will make her Night Wind's woman.

___4507-9 $5.99 US/$6.99 CAN

The Mermaid of Penperro
Lisa Cach

Konstanze never imagined that singing could land someone in such trouble. The disrepute of the stage is nothing compared to the danger of playing a seductress of the sea—or the reckless abandon she feels while doing so. She has come to Penperro to escape her past, to find anonymity among the people of Cornwall, and her inhibitions melt away as she does. But the Cornish are less simple than she expected, and the role she is forced to play is harder. For one thing, her siren song lures to her not only the agent of the crown she's been paid to perplex, but the smuggler who hired her. And in his strong arms she finds everything she's been missing. Suddenly, Konstanze sees the true peril of her situation—not that of losing her honor, but her heart.

___52437-6 $5.50 US/$6.50 CAN

Dorchester Publishing Co., Inc.
P.O. Box 6640
Wayne, PA 19087-8640

Alicia's Song
Susan Plunkett

For Alicia James, something is missing. Her childhood romance hadn't ended the way she dreamed, and she is wary of trying again. Still, she finds solace in her sisters and in the fact that her career is inspiring. And together with those sisters, Alicia finds a magic in song that seems almost able to carry away her woes.

In fact, singing carries Alicia away—from her home in modern-day Wyoming to Alaska, a century before her own. There she finds a sexy, dark-haired gentleman with an angelic child just crying out for guidance. And Alicia is everything this pair desperately needs. Suddenly it seems as if life is reaching out and giving Alicia the chance to create a beautiful music she's never been able to make with her sisters—all she needs is the courage to sing her part.

___52434-1 $4.99 US/$5.99 CAN